For Debbie

To himself everyone is immortal; he may know that he is going to die, but he can never know that he is dead.

Samuel Butler

I

GLORIETTA PASS
SANGRE DE CRISTO
MOUNTAINS, NEW MEXICO

12 May

'They're out near the Santa Fe Trail. Shots fired.'

Patrol Officer Lieutenant Enrico Zamora pressed down hard on the gas pedal, the Dodge Charger's V6 engine growling as the patrol cruiser accelerated along the scorched asphalt of Interstate-25 winding into the shimmering desert heat ahead. Broad plains of desiccated thorn scrub swept toward the Pecos Wilderness either side of the highway, while ahead, the jagged peaks of the mountains loomed against the vast blue dome of the sky. The late season was turning the thick ranks of aspens that coated the mountains' flanks a vivid yellow, the forests glowing in the afternoon sunlight as the cruiser plunged between the steep hillsides of the pass.

'Any fatalities?' Zamora asked as he glanced at his partner, his eyes veiled by mirror-lensed sunglasses.

'Not yet.' Sergeant Barker shook his head, one hand resting on the Smith & Wesson .357 pistol in its holster at his side. 'One man is down and another's injured. Park ranger says that they came under attack.'

'Chrissakes,' Zamora muttered, wondering what the hell had happened out there in the lonely mountains.

The call had gone out ten minutes previously for emergency response teams to converge on Glorietta Pass. Eight tourists, tenderfoots down from the Big Apple on what Zamora suspected was some kind of bullshit team-building exercise, had been caught in the crossfire of a gunfight. One of the park rangers had led them out on a horse-riding expedition, in itself a liability, Zamora thought. Most city types didn't know what a horse looked like, let alone how to ride one. He had seen every injury under the sun suffered by twenty-year-old investment bankers who earned more in a day than he earned in a year, yet couldn't lift a saddle onto a horse's back without pulling a muscle

But this was different. He had heard it in the dispatcher's voice, her tones edgy. Shots were being fired. People were being hit.

'Just up here,' Barker said as they turned off the Interstate and roared up a narrow, dusty track that plunged between the walls of a deep gully. Zamora saw his partner still fiddling with his pistol as he ran the other hand over the bald dome of his head.

'Will you quit it with the weapon?' Zamora said as he followed the track. 'I don't want to see another wild bullet let loose, okay?'

Barker put his hands in his lap but his face remained taut like canvas stretched across a frame. Zamora slowed as, ahead amongst the trees, he saw a group of horses tethered to tree trunks. Crouching amongst them were several men, each staring wide-eyed at the approaching cruiser.

Zamora killed the engine and got out, drawing his pistol and hurrying across with Barker in a low run to where a park ranger was waving urgently at him. The ranger looked at Zamora. He was young, and his skin was flushed with a volatile mixture of excitement and fear.

'You guys bring back-up?' he asked.

'Four more cars and an ambulance are on their way,' Zamora replied calmly, glancing at the ranger's pistol. A faint wisp of blue smoke drifting from the barrel told him to expect the worst. 'What's the situation?'

The ranger shook his head in disbelief.

'I ain't got a clue, man,' he said. 'We were makin' our way back down here when all hell broke loose. Some old guy's having himself a shouting match with a tenderfoot up on the pass, then he pulls out some kind of old musket and shoots the tenderfoot at point-blank range.' The ranger gestured over his shoulder to the city slickers behind him. 'Damned if he didn't take a shot at us too. One of the guys here panicked and tried to ride past an' then everything went to hell and the horses bolted. The tenderfoot's still lyin' up there bleedin' out.' The ranger looked apologetic. 'I didn't want to go back up without support.'

Zamora took a deep breath and gestured to the ranger's pistol. 'Did you shoot the old guy?'

The young man glanced at his weapon as though he'd forgotten he even had it.

'Yeah,' he whispered.

'You did the right thing. How far away is he?'

'A hundred yards, give or take.'

'Stay here,' Zamora cautioned him, 'keep an eye on the tourists. Don't let them move.'

The ranger nodded as Zamora checked his weapon again and moved forward, hugging the rocky side of the trail that climbed up between the tree-studded hills either side of the gully. The sun flared off the rocky terrain. Zamora could hear no birdsong as he climbed, no crickets chirping in the scorched undergrowth. Gunshots could do that, scatter or silence wildlife.

'You smell that?'

Barker's voice was a husky whisper, and a moment later Zamora caught the scent of woodsmoke drifting invisibly through the trees. He wiped beads of sweat from his forehead as he edged around a bend in the narrow track, hemmed in by thick ranks of trees glowing in the sunlight.

He froze.

There, lying face down in the center of the track was a black man dressed in a checked shirt and gray slacks, not the kind of attire one would wear when hiking in the hills. Zamora could see a thick pool of blood congealing in the dust around the man's body. A pair of spectacles lay alongside the body where they had fallen.

'He a dead'un?' Barker asked in a whisper.

Zamora squinted, lowering the rim of his hat to shield his eyes, and detected the man's back gently rising and falling.

'He's breathing,' he said, 'but he's also leakin'. We need to get him out of there fast.'

Barker nodded, holding his Smith & Wesson with both hands.

'You want me to do it?'

Zamora looked up at the steep cliff to their side. The faint smell of woodsmoke was stronger now, closer.

'Looks like whoever did the shooting spent the night here,' he whispered. 'Maybe the tourists spooked them or something.'

A soft whinnying caught their attention. Zamora turned to see a horse tethered to a nearby tree, its head hung low. Across its back lay a blanket, and Zamora felt a twinge of concern as he saw the blanket was thick with dried blood.

'The horse?' Barker said.

Zamora shook his head, swallowing thickly.

'That's not the horse's blood,' he said, realizing what he was looking at. 'The ranger got 'im all right. Go up that gully there,' Zamora said, pointing up to his right. 'Get to the high ground in case this lunatic comes back.'

Barker nodded, and they broke cover. Zamora hurried forward, reaching the body and squatting down alongside it. The nearby burgundy spectacles were those of a rich kid, a tenderfoot. He paused for a moment, looking around for any sign of an impending attack, before reaching down and touching the man's neck. A pulse threaded its way weakly beneath his fingertips. He was about to holster his pistol when the man groaned and rolled over. Zamora judged him as no more than thirty years old, clean-shaven and definitely not a native.

'Don't move,' Zamora cautioned, looking at the bloodstain soaking the man's left shoulder. 'What's your name, son?'

'Tyler Willis,' came the dry-throated response. 'Don't shoot him.'

'Don't shoot who?'

'Conley. Hiram Conley. He's . . . he's unwell.'

Zamora squinted up at the heavily forested hills surrounding them.

'You're goddamned right there, son,' he said quietly. 'We need to get you out of here. You know anything about this Conley?'

Tyler Willis swallowed thickly, grimacing with the pain.

'Don't shoot him,' he insisted again. 'He's extremely old.'

Zamora was about to respond when a voice broke the silence of the pass around them.

'Stay still. Identify yourself!'

Zamora flinched and peered up into the woods. The voice bounced and echoed off the walls of the pass, concealing its location. He could see nothing.

'Officer Enrico Zamora, New Mexico State Police,' he called back. 'This man needs a hospital.'

'There ain't no such thing as a state police, and that man ain't no part of the Union!'

Zamora frowned in confusion. 'This man is injured and he needs treatment. I need to take him back down the pass.'

'He ain't goin' nowhere!' the voice yelled. 'I got no beef with you, boy. You turn your back to me an' I'll let you leave, but I got forty dead men up here if'n you try to cross me!'

Forty dead men? Dispatch had only mentioned one man down. Zamora's gaze edged upward as he searched for corpses among the trees, and he saw a flicker of movement.

It took him a moment to register what he was looking at through the dappled sunlight shimmering in pools of light beneath the trees. The man was old, perhaps in his sixties, a thick gray beard draped down across his bare chest. A navy-blue jacket clung to his emaciated frame, the sleeves marked with narrow yellow lines running from shoulder to cuffs. Across his chest was a thick band of dressing stained crimson with blood. The old man was aiming what looked like an antique rifle over the top of a boulder at him. Zamora looked down at Tyler Willis.

'He's killed forty men?'

'No.' Willis shook his head. 'He's got forty cartridges for his musket. "Dead men" is what they used to call their ammunition, back in the Civil War.'

Zamora frowned at the wounded man beside him.

'Why's he using a musket? And how do you know him?'

'It's a long story,' Willis rasped. 'A real long story.'

Zamora looked up to the woods and called back, 'I can't leave this man here.'

'We had an accord, he and I!' the old man cackled. 'But he did betray me! No secessionist is worth a dime o' dollar, goddamned southerners been aggervatin' us for years! What regiment are you with, boy?'

Zamora blinked sweat from his eyes, and saw Barker's silhouette creeping through the trees toward the old man.

'I'm not a soldier. You?'

'New Mexico Militia!' the old man shouted. 'Born and bred to the Union!'

Zamora realized the old man was either insane or delusional. Maybe from alcohol or exposure to the elements, or blood loss from the bullet wound.

'He's ill,' Tyler Willis rasped from beside him. 'He's

already been injured, lost a lot of blood. He could have shot me in the head, but he didn't. He just needs help, he needs a hospital.'

'You're injured!' Zamora shouted up at the old man. 'Come down here, we can treat the wound.'

'Only thing I'm gonna be treatin's your balderdash, boy, now hike out!'

Zamora saw Barker stand up and take aim, and in that instant the old man sensed the threat and whirled the old musket around. Zamora saw Barker rush forward.

'Barker, hold your fire!'

Two gunshots crashed out simultaneously through the canyon and both men vanished in a cloud of oily blue smoke. Barker's ghostly shape shuddered and dropped into the undergrowth. Zamora leapt to his feet, pistol at the ready as he squinted into the swirling cloud of cordite.

An anguished cry burst out as the old man charged out of the forest, the veil of smoke curling around him. A long-barreled musket cradled in his grip was tipped with a wicked bayonet which glinted at Zamora in the sunlight as it rushed toward him. But in that terrible moment, it wasn't the lethal weapon that sent a spasm of terror bolting through Zamora's stomach.

The old man's jacket had been torn off at the left sleeve, and as he burst into the bright sunlight Zamora could see the flesh of the old man's arm, a tangled, sinewy web of exposed muscles and ragged chunks of decaying gray flesh spilling away as he rushed forward. His hands were gnarled and twisted like those of some ancient crone, his knuckles exposed like white bone beneath almost transparent skin. For one terrible instant, Zamora had the impression of being rushed by a man suffering from the terminal stages of leprosy.

'Get back!' Zamora shouted in surprise, raising his pistol.

'You're gonna be singing on the end of my pig-sticker!' the old man screamed, charging the last few paces. The ragged navy-blue uniform, kepi hat and torn pants seemed to have leapt from some hellish Civil War battlefield, filling Zamora's vision with a nightmarish image of decay and rage.

On the ground beside him, Tyler Willis raised a hand. 'Don't kill him! He's too old to die!'

The bayonet flashed in the sunlight before Zamora's eyes as he staggered backwards, taking aim and firing a single shot at the emaciated face charging toward him.

2

MEDICAL INVESTIGATOR FACILITY, ALBUQUERQUE, NEW MEXICO

13 May

'Okay, who's tonight's lucky contestant?'

Medical Investigator Lillian Cruz strode down a corridor toward the morgue with a practiced stride. Tall and proud-looking, Lillian had worked in the morgue for as long as anyone could remember. She was leading the night shift, as she did twice a week. If working the small hours virtually alone in a morgue had ever bothered her, she couldn't recall. In contrast her assistant, Alexis, was new to the facility and looked nervous, her squeaky student voice mildly irritating Lillian as she filled her in on the details of the night's first autopsy.

'White male, approximately sixty years of age, died from a single gunshot wound to the head fired in self-defense by Lieutenant Enrico Zamora, state PD. The trooper reported that the victim seemed to be suffering from some kind of wasting disease.'

Lillian frowned. Probably a drunk who had got himself injured, or some loser strung out on peyote buttons or crack who fancied himself attacking Injuns and heading them off at the pass out Glorietta way. In her many years as a medical investigator, Lillian had seen just about everything.

'When did he die?' Lillian asked as they turned the corner and approached the morgue.

'Yesterday afternoon, time of death called in by the response team as 3.45 p.m. Victim's been on ice since 4.20 that afternoon.'

Ten hours then. Lillian led the way into the morgue to where a steel gurney awaited them, the contents concealed by a blue plastic ziplock bag speckled with smears of fluid. Lillian checked the door was closed behind them before donning gloves, plastic face-shield and tying her surgical gown.

'Okay, let's get started, shall we?' Lillian spoke loudly enough to be heard by the recorder sitting on the worktop nearby. She picked up a clipboard, ready to make notes, as Alexis grabbed a digital camera to document their findings. On cue, Alexis reached forward over the gurney and with a single smooth movement unzipped the plastic bag.

'Jesus!'

Lillian stared at the gurney as Alexis stifled a tight scream, one gloved hand flying to her mouth. Overcoming a momentary revulsion, Lillian took a cautious pace forward and peered into the depths of the plastic bag as Alexis began taking photographs.

The body that lay within seemed as though it had been stripped of its skin, the internal organs were exposed and decayed, the slack jaw only held in place by frayed tendons and muscles that had either contracted into tight bands or fallen off the body altogether to coil like snakes beneath the corpse. The eyeballs had shriveled and sunk deep into their sockets, and what skin remained drooped in leathery tatters from the bones. Tentatively, Lillian reached out and touched a piece of skin. It felt brittle, like a leather rag left too long in the desert sun. Specks of material crumbled beneath her touch to lightly dust the steel surface of the gurney.

'He's mummified,' she murmured.

Alexis shook her head as if to rouse herself from a daze.

'That's not possible. He died yesterday,' she insisted. 'The rangers and the police independently verified his age, and there are photos taken at the scene by state troopers. He's been on ice ever since. He had papers on him too.'

Alexis handed Lillian an evidence form that listed the deceased's name and social security number: Hiram Conley, born Las Cruces, New Mexico, 1940. She then handed her the photographs taken by the troopers. Lillian looked at the images of the elderly man killed at the scene of the crime, and then at the decomposed and desiccated remains before her.

'There's got to be a reason for this. Let's see you make the case.'

Lillian started making notes and drawings of the observations as Alexis led the autopsy.

'Weight at time of death, approximately one hundred forty pounds. Some evidence of malnutrition and exposure prior to desiccation. Victim had applied field dressings to numerous wounds around the area of the chest, right shoulder and left arm consistent with . . . er . . . some kind of gunshot injuries.' Alexis hesitated before continuing. 'Victim is clothed in what appears to be some kind of fancy dress or memorial attire, consistent with Civil War era. Note: attire may provide evidence of cause or location of death.'

Lillian set her clipboard down and took another long, hard look at the body as Alexis carefully undressed the corpse. With the broad-shouldered jacket and baggy pants gone the body looked entirely skeletal, a bone cage from which hung shriveled tissue and muscle, but this was not what shocked Lillian the most. The remaining tatters of skin on the man's chest bore multiple lesions, deep pits of scar tissue peppering the surface.

'You thinking what I'm thinking?' Alexis asked.

'Smallpox.' Lillian nodded, noting the position of the lesions before examining the remains more closely. The body was a silent witness to more scars and lesions than Lillian had seen in her many years working in New Mexico. Barely an inch of his body seemed clear of damage, and even the bones bore testimony to breaks, cut marks and disease.

'This guy looks like he'd lived a hundred lives,' Alexis remarked in wonderment.

'And all of them violent,' Lillian agreed.

'Most of his teeth are missing,' Alexis said, 'and his gums are heavily receded. Could be the mummification, but it could also be scurvy.'

Lillian stood back from the body and shook her head.

'Doesn't explain the mummification,' she answered.

'Smallpox was eradicated in the late 1970s and scurvy disappeared over a century ago.'

Alexis peered into Hiram Conley's sightless eyes and examined the strange blue-gray irises.

'Odd,' she said. 'Looks like extensive cataracts, but the cataract cortex hasn't liquefied. This guy should have been blind as a bat by now.'

Lillian leaned over for a closer look as Alexis shot more photos.

'Long-term ultra-violet radiation exposure,' she identified the cause of the cataracts, 'denaturation of lens protein. But you're right; they should have blinded him by now.'

'And they're an odd color,' Alexis continued, 'blue-gray. It's like the proteins were constantly being repaired, fending off the liquefaction.' Alexis gestured to Hiram Conley's recently removed clothes, now lying nearby in an evidence tray. 'And he was wearing clothes that look a hundred years old.'

Lillian stared blankly at her assistant.

'Where are you going with this? You think this guy walked out of a wormhole to the past or something? This isn't *Star Trek*, Alexis. We need to keep our brains engaged here.'

'I'm not saying anything like that,' Alexis said quickly, reddening. 'You ever heard of that Japanese guy, Hiroo Onoda? He was a soldier during World War Two who was on operations in the Philippine jungles when the war ended. He didn't believe the leaflets dropped on the jungles to inform soldiers of the end of the war, thinking it was propaganda. He only surrendered when his former commanding officer came to get him after he was spotted by a traveler in the region.'

'When was that?'

'1974,' Alexis said. 'He held out for thirty years. My point is, what if this guy's part of some family out in the Pecos who've just kept on going as they were? The Amish have been doing it for long enough. It explains the injuries, the disease, the old-style uniform. Bad water and improper sanitation can cause dysentery and exposure to the elements frequently leads to pneumonia. Typhoid fever, chicken pox, whooping cough, tuberculosis – I bet if you screen for them half will turn up.'

Lillian shook her head.

'It still doesn't explain the mummification, especially not when it's occurred overnight. This isn't somebody who's walked out of an Amish town. The only explanation is that this is absolute desiccation – the body has dried out in a matter of hours.'

Lillian was about to continue when a metallic sound echoed through the morgue, as though someone had dropped a coin into one of the steel sinks and it was rolling round and round toward the plughole. She looked at Alexis, who stared back before glancing down at Hiram Conley's remains. The metallic sound stopped, and then something fell with a sharp crack onto the tiles of the floor. From beneath the gurney rolled a small, dark sphere no bigger than an acorn. Lillian squatted down and picked the object up in her gloved hands.

'That's a musket ball,' Alexis said in surprise. 'It must have dropped out of him and rolled down the blood-drainage chute.'

Lillian turned to Conley's remains, moving slowly across to where the crumpled, emaciated flesh was dropping in clumps from the very bones themselves.

'He's still decaying,' Alexis gasped.

Lillian shook her head slowly. 'He's not decaying,' she said. 'He's aging.'

3

'He's what?'

Lillian moved across to the opposite side of Conley's corpse.

'He's aging,' Lillian repeated. 'It's impossible for biological decay like this to occur so quickly in the absence of an active catalyst.'

Lillian leaned in close and searched through the winding folds of muscle, sinew and bone until she spotted another metallic sphere. The ball was lodged deep in the man's femur, half concealed by a gnarled overgrowth of new bone that had encased it.

'There's another one,' Lillian said. 'Fetch me a specimen bag, and then get some shots of this.'

'Another one?' Alexis uttered in amazement, grabbing the bag and hurrying back to Lillian's side to photograph the wound. 'It would have taken decades for that much bone to have grown back.'

'It's a much older wound,' Lillian confirmed.

Lillian grabbed a pair of forceps and probed deep into

the decaying flesh of Hiram Conley's thigh, gripping the ball and yanking it free from now brittle bones that cracked like splintering twigs. She dropped the ball into the specimen bag, sealed it and handed it to Alexis.

'Get it to the state crime laboratory, right now. We can't test the metal here. Drive it there yourself, no delays, and have them send me the results directly as soon as they've got them. I'll start on toxicology and bio-samples here.'

Alexis stared at the crumbling corpse for a long moment as though she were looking back into the past.

'What's going on, Lillian?' she asked. 'How can this be?'

Lillian snapped her fingers in front of Alexis's face, and the girl blinked and looked at her.

'One thing at a time, okay?' Lillian said. 'Tell nobody about this, until we've figured out what's going on.'

Alexis nodded and hurried out of the morgue. Lillian turned back to the remains before her, shaking her head. She heard Alexis's car start and pull away into the distance, the engine noise jolting Lillian from her thoughts.

'What the hell happened to you?' she whispered to the corpse.

Suddenly, the lights in the morgue went out and plunged her into darkness. A wave of panic fluttered through Lillian as she struggled to maintain her balance in the complete blackness. She cursed the fact that, like all morgues, there were no windows.

It was a hell of a time for the power to go out. She stood for a moment, waiting for the emergency generator to cut in, but nothing happened. Then the door to the morgue slammed violently shut, the crash sending a lance of terror through her.

'Hello?' she called out. At two in the morning she should have been alone in the building.

Nobody responded in the absolute darkness looming around her.

Slowly she backed away from the gurney until she felt the edge of the worktops behind her. She felt her way around the edge, past the sinks and the polished steel scales until she located her handbag, fumbling inside until she found her cell phone. She lifted it out, hitting a button – any button. To her relief, the screen glowed with bright blue light, illuminating the morgue.

A horrific skull-like face lunged toward her from the gloom. She screamed with primal fear as hands grabbed her with vicious force. As the light from her cell phone was smothered so her consciousness slipped away.

4

CICERO, CHICAGO ILLINOIS

14 May

Keep running. *Don't quit.*

Ethan Warner's heart pounded in his chest and his lungs burned as he ran down the sidewalk, dodging past pedestrians who had already leapt clear of the teenager in the gray hoodie dashing past them on West 27th Street.

Ethan focused on the target, lengthening his stride and trying to control his labored breathing. Several weeks of circuit training had improved his fitness, but he was still nowhere near the level he'd been in the Marine Corps and right now the kid ahead of him was running with the added benefit of fear coursing through his blood. *Semper fi*, Ethan chanted to himself over and over again as the kid sprinted across St Louis Avenue with casual disregard for incoming traffic.

A distorted voice sounded in his ear.

'Where you at?'

'Heading west, 27th on South Central,' Ethan wheezed into a Bluetooth earpiece and microphone. 'Where the hell are you?'

'Stand by,' came the affronted response. 'No need to get yourself agitated.'

Stand by, my ass, Ethan thought as he struck out across South Central Park Avenue, an SUV honking its horn at him as he swerved around the front fender, staggered onto the sidewalk again and almost collided with a woman and two children leaving a convenience store.

The kid ahead of him suddenly turned right, dashing into an alley that cut between rows of buildings and stores lining the streets.

'He's off the main, heading north toward West 26th!' Ethan shouted, hurling himself into the alley in pursuit before seeing the kid standing facing him not twenty yards away.

A gunshot shattered the air in the narrow alley, and Ethan hurled himself down onto the asphalt, rolling sideways and slamming into a large trash can.

'He's got a piece!'

'Copy that.'

Ethan peered round the side of the dumpster and saw the kid was running through puddles toward the end of the alleyway, which was half blocked by an unoccupied black jeep. Ethan leapt up, shouting as he ran.

'Don't make me shoot!' he bellowed, hoping to hell that the kid didn't look back and see that Ethan wasn't carrying. 'Lose the piece!'

The kid ducked sideways to dash past the parked jeep. Ethan accelerated and was about to follow him when the jeep's door suddenly opened. A deep, solid thump echoed down the alleyway as the kid hit the door at full speed, staggering backwards and toppling to the ground.

Ethan slowed as he saw his partner, Nicola Lopez, leap from the jeep and stride toward the disorientated kid who staggered to his feet and whirled, striking out at Lopez with the butt of his pistol. Lopez blocked the blow with a fluid movement of her left arm, batting the pistol aside and following immediately with a round-house right that smacked into the kid's jaw. The boy slammed onto his back as Lopez, drawing a black T-baton tonfa, placed one booted foot on his wrist to prevent him from using his gun and jabbed one end of the baton into his throat.

'You have the right to remain silent, else I kick your sorry ass further,' Lopez snarled down at their quarry. 'Anything you say can and will be used against you in a court of law. You have the right to speak to an attorney. If you cannot afford an attorney the state will appoint one to you who will most likely be goddamn useless. Do you understand?'

A weak voice squealed up at her as Ethan approached.

'Who the hell are you?'

Lopez flashed a badge at the kid on the ground, a silver shield with 'Bail Bondsman' emblazoned beneath it.

'You jumped bail, Mickey,' Lopez said as she turned him over, knelt on his back and cuffed him. 'You're going back to jail.'

Ethan glanced at the vehicle from which Lopez had leapt.

'How'd you get into that jeep?'

Lopez flashed him a dazzling smile as she jerked Mickey onto his feet.

'Door was unlocked,' she replied with an innocent shrug.

Ethan shook his head as Lopez guided Mickey 'Knuckles' Ferranto out onto West 26th Street and along the sidewalk to where she had parked their black SUV. He waited until she'd shoe-horned Mickey into the vehicle and shut the door before speaking.

'You broke and entered?' he said in disbelief. 'Jesus, we're supposed to be *finding* criminals, not becoming them.'

'Got the job done,' Lopez replied without remorse. 'I'd left it to you, you'd both be halfway to goddamn Ohio by now.'

'I was getting there,' Ethan said defensively. 'He hotfooted out of the mall the moment he saw me.'

'The job's done,' Lopez said, brushing a strand of black hair out of her eyes. 'Who cares about the small print?'

Ethan blocked her path as she made her way toward the SUV's passenger door.

'The police? The attorney's office? You can't keep doing things this way, Lopez. What the hell happened to going by the book?'

'It got me nowhere in the force.'

'Yeah, and breaking the rules got your partner killed.'

Lightning flickered behind Lopez's dark eyes as they locked onto Ethan's, and he forced himself not to take a step back.

Since they had begun working together, Ethan had found out about what had befallen Nicola Lopez's former partner in the Metropolitan Police Department in Washington DC the previous year, crumbs of information that had slipped out during conversations. Detective Lucas Tyrell, a long-serving officer, had been shot and killed by his own superior in an apartment way down in Anacostia. To say that Lopez had taken the hit badly was something of an understatement. Now, despite their partnership, Ethan often felt as though he were running a poor second best to Tyrell. Lopez seemed unwilling to share directly with him what had happened, as though she hadn't quite moved on yet. Her casual disregard for the law was a direct and, for Ethan, somewhat unsettling manifestation of that.

Ethan had since watched Lopez abandon the moral principles with which she had conducted her work as a detective in favor of bagging the perps by whatever means necessary. Lucas Tyrell had been a liability to the Metro PD, but he'd gotten results, and Lopez was emulating her fallen mentor just as closely as she could.

'Corruption got Lucas killed,' she shot back. 'Justice got him revenge. You gonna get out of my way or do I have to put you on your ass too?'

Reluctantly, Ethan took a step back. Lopez had a reputation as a short fuse, but since losing her partner she seemed to have relinquished whatever remaining grip she had on her temper. The last time he'd seen her lose it was when they hunted down a bail-runner to a shabby roadside diner in Battle Creek, Michigan. Three heavy-weight bikers from the local chapter of the Devil's Disciples had taken a liking to the fugitive and were vaguely amused to see Lopez arrive with her badge, nightstick and bad attitude. It wasn't their deliberate obstruction that had set her off, just their idle dismissal. Two broken noses, a severed knee tendon and one frac-tured collarbone later, fugitive James Watson sheepishly surrendered and was dragged by Lopez over the groaning bodies of his would-be protectors. It had been over before Ethan had even got through the door.

'Just looking out for you,' he said finally, raising his hands and making for the driver's door. 'We're no good to each other if one of us is in jail.'

'You're the one with history,' Lopez remarked as they climbed into the SUV. 'My record's pearly clean.'

'You's a jailbird?' Mickey Ferranto muttered from the back seat, looking at Ethan.

'Can it, Mickey,' Ethan snapped as he started the engine and looked at Lopez. 'I'm a reformed character. *You're* the one on the slippery slope into shameful lawlessness.'

Lopez shook her head and laughed as they pulled out into their lane.

'We set ourselves up to catch bail-jumpers and fugitives. They don't obey the law, we have to bend the rules to pick them up.'

'That how it is?' Ethan asked rhetorically.

'That's how it is.'

'That *really* how it is?' Mickey Ferranto complained.

'Shut up,' Ethan glared over his shoulder. 'My point is that there's plenty of competition out there and we can't afford to get ourselves busted.'

'We can't afford much at all,' Lopez muttered and jabbed her thumb over her shoulder at Ferranto. 'We're not bagging enough of *these* losers to make ends meet.'

'I ain't no loser,' Mickey complained.

'No?' Lopez turned round in her seat to look at him. 'You're a twenty-three-year-old who's just cost his mother a couple of thousand bucks jail bond for nothing more than possession of an illegal substance. You'd turned up in court like you were supposed to, you'd have probably been released because you're not important enough, Mickey; you're a nobody. Only a loser like you could turn a nothing into a jail sentence.'

Mickey avoided her gaze and looked sulkily out of the window as Ethan turned toward Cook County Jail.

'Maybe we should spread out more, cover more area,' Ethan suggested. 'Maybe even link up with some of the other bondsmen out there.'

'Maybe,' Lopez echoed. 'Or maybe we just need to stop scraping around in the dirt for nobodies like Mickey here and pick up something more lucrative.'

Ethan began to answer when a black sedan pulled out in front of the SUV, passing within inches of his front fender. He was about to remonstrate when another identical car pulled alongside him, boxing the SUV in.

'What the hell?' Lopez muttered, instinctively reaching for her pistol before remembering that she was no longer legally allowed to carry one. Her hand rested on her baton instead.

'Government plates,' Ethan said, glancing at the rear of the sedan in front of them as it indicated it was turning off the road.

'You gonna follow?' Lopez asked.

Ethan shrugged, then turned to follow the sedan.

5

The sedans guided them north on Harlem Avenue before turning off the highway into Waldheim Cemetery. Lonely ranks of gravestones spread across several acres of carefully manicured lawns shaded by hundreds of trees. Ethan followed the lead car until it pulled into a secluded spot off Greenburg Road in the northwest corner of the cemetery.

Ethan killed the engine and looked in his mirrors suspiciously.

'What the hell is this shit, man?' Mickey Ferranto whined. 'I want to speak to my attorney.'

Lopez shot him a toxic look.

'See all these gravestones, Mickey? You wanna join them, you just keep talking.'

Ethan climbed out of the SUV and closed the door. Lopez joined him. For a moment, nothing moved. Then two men climbed out of each vehicle, all sporting gray suits, designer shades and earpieces. They moved to guard the SUV, one of them gesturing to the still open doors of the sedan ahead.

'Great disguise, guys,' Ethan said as he moved toward the car. 'We'd never have known.'

The men ignored Ethan, instead standing rigidly to attention as he walked to the sedan and climbed into the rear seat. Lopez joined him from the other side.

'Very cloak and dagger,' Ethan said as they closed the doors. 'Are we off to Tracy Island?'

Douglas Jarvis, an elderly man dressed immaculately in a dark blue suit that contrasted with his neatly parted white hair, turned in the front seat and offered Ethan a grin.

'I see you're back to your usual self, Ethan.' He looked at Lopez. 'Nicola, how's things?'

'Could be busier,' she replied cautiously. 'What's the occasion? And why not call us instead of damn near running us off the road?'

'Security,' Jarvis replied calmly. 'Calls can be monitored, and we want our little accord with you two to remain discreet, remember? The Defense Intelligence Agency has uncovered an anomalous incident that occurred twenty-four hours ago in Santa Fe, New Mexico. The trail's already gone cold and management aren't keen to send agency resources in to investigate.'

'Which is where we come in, right?' Ethan said.

Douglas Jarvis had once been the captain of a United States Marines rifle platoon, a post he had held when Ethan had served as a lieutenant in the Corps. Their friendship, cemented during the invasion of Iraq, had extended to Jarvis's current employment with the Defense Intelligence Agency and to their unusual, discreet accord with Warner/Lopez Inc.

'Command and control won't throw money at this, and the Pentagon's certainly not interested,' Jarvis confirmed. 'It's the perfect case, well worth your time.'

'What's the story?' Lopez asked, curious, despite herself.

Jarvis produced a glossy black file and handed it to her.

'Santa Fe Medical Examiner autopsied the remains of a desert bum by the name of Hiram Conley, found dead after a clash with state troopers. Ten hours after Hiram Conley died his remains were described as mummified. The examiner attempted to extract material from the body and found an intact bullet that fell from the victim's shoulder, and another, older one lodged in his right femur. They got the older bullet to the state crime laboratory for tests.'

'So what's the big deal?' Ethan asked.

Jarvis gestured to the file that Lopez was holding.

'The state laboratory ran tests on the bullet, which was found to be a musket ball, and we picked up jurisdiction of the case after they made inquiries to the FBI at Quantico. Carbon dating, along with estimates of bone regrowth around the ball prior to extraction, confirms that the wound was sustained approximately one hundred forty years ago.'

Ethan stared at Jarvis.

'That's not possible. A hundred forty years?'

'The tests must have been contaminated,' Lopez said, opening the file. 'If the wound had been opened to extract the bullet, anything could have gotten in.'

'The bullet was lodged firmly in the bone,' Jarvis said,

'the medical examiner's pictures show it clearly. And the tests were run three separate times, once by the state laboratory and twice by specialists on my own team at the DIA when we took over the case. All the tests confirmed the age of the wound.'

Ethan forced himself to think clearly.

'We should get in touch with the medical examiner first, find out everything we can about where the body was found. The troopers who shot him need to be questioned too.'

'Already done,' Jarvis said, 'and all parties signed non-disclosure agreements. However, the medical examiner has vanished and we need her found. Fast.'

'What happened?' Lopez asked.

'An attack on the facility at the morgue. The lab assistant got the musket ball out of the lab for tests, but by the time she'd returned the medical examiner had disappeared, as had all of the evidence. The gurney and the surrounding work surfaces had been completely cleaned-out, not even trace evidence remained.'

'A professional job,' Ethan murmured, his interest now piqued.

'We have camera footage but it's grainy, shot from a nearby building. Whoever did the job was smart enough to take out the medical facility's own cameras before they went in. Four men: black jump suits, Halloween-style face masks. Somebody wanted that body real bad,' Jarvis said. 'The DIA has an interest, but there's no way we can send a team down there without the Pentagon signing off on it, and with the budget the way it is they'll shut us down before we can do any good.'

Ethan nodded, glancing out of the sedan's windows at the cemetery outside.

'So what do you think this is? Some kind of freak ghost story?'

Jarvis smiled thinly.

'I'll leave the detective work to you both, but for what it's worth this guy Conley shot his way out of the Pecos wilderness wearing Civil War era Union battle-field dress and speaking in what was described by the troopers as an archaic dialect.' Jarvis glanced at the file. 'Whatever's going on down there it's in the interests of the United States Government to understand it.'

Ethan nodded and looked at Lopez.

'You did say you wanted something decent to go after.'

'New Mexico,' Lopez murmured thoughtfully. 'Closer to home, and there's at least two bail-runners from Illinois thought to be holed up somewhere down there. Multi-tasking. We'll do it.'

Jarvis eyed her for a long moment.

'Good, although I need to know that the DIA can count on you, Lopez, after what happened out at Cedar Lake.'

Ethan glanced at his partner, waiting to see her response. They had agreed to keep her indiscretion on the South Shore between themselves, but clearly Jarvis's reach went further than Ethan had realized. A lot further.

'It was a one-off,' Lopez said, refusing to be cowed. 'Deal's a deal; it went down, went wrong and then went away, okay?'

Jarvis nodded, letting it go. The fact that Lopez,

having taken a low-life drug dealer and bail-runner called Adam McKenzie into custody had then accepted a bribe for releasing him, hadn't bothered Ethan as much as he'd thought it might. Lopez was supporting herself in Chicago as well as sending much of her meager salary back home to her family south of the border in Guanajuato. Her parents were, like so many people in Mexico, crippled by poverty and reliant upon Lopez's generosity to sustain their home. Without it, they would join the legions of beggars groveling on the streets, and at their age they wouldn't last long. Cash was cash and Lopez needed a lot. Ethan hadn't realized just how badly until that day.

She gave him an accusing sideways glance, but he ignored her and looked instead at Jarvis.

'I'm almost afraid to ask, but what support will we have?'

'Limited tactical and law enforcement,' Jarvis replied. 'Local police know that you've got jurisdiction in this case – I can help indirectly, but the DIA will retain deniability in all eventualities. The President won't want investigations like these all over the media if word should get out, and the Pentagon would rather have the conspiracy theorists chasing after your agency than ours.'

'Convenient,' Lopez said as she closed the file. 'Anything else?'

'Conley was involved in an argument with a man named Tyler Willis, who he then shot, starting the whole fracas. I'd start there if I were you.' Jarvis handed Ethan a clear plastic bag which contained a yellowing slip of paper. 'Hiram Conley's social security details, found on him when he died. They check out, but they're identical to those of an alias we think he was using previously, Abner Conley. We didn't have access to records going back that far at the DIA, so you'll have to chase them down in Santa Fe. Whoever this guy really was he used multiple identities, and there's always a reason for that.'

6

COCHITÍ LAKE
NEW MEXICO

15 May

The broad waters of the lake, surrounded by the soaring heights of the Jemez, Ortiz, Sandia and San Pedro mountain ranges, glittered beneath the sun.

Jeb Oppenheimer sat upon the quarterdeck of a vessel that dwarfed the tiny cutters and fishing boats in the nearby quay, the pearlescent white hull of his yacht almost painful to look at in the bright sunlight.

'Cigar.'

His voice was gravelly from decades of smoking a dozen a day of Cuba's finest, but as with everything else in life Jeb Oppenheimer didn't give a shit. Likewise he didn't care that the yacht upon which he sat was far too large for the lake or that there was no exit to the ocean, the lake itself being a mere aberration in the flow of the Santa Fe River. Jeb had bought the vessel and had it transported there so that he could enjoy the water without the cumbersome irritation of lakeside neighbors on the shore.

A white-suited crewman walked out of the shade of the

yacht's interior with an expensive-looking silver box. He opened it for Oppenheimer, who foraged within with a wiry hand laced with purple veins. He waved the crewman away and opened the cigar, lighting it and inhaling the aromatic fumes deeply. As he sat enveloped in a cloud of blue smoke another of his crew appeared.

'Donald Wolfe is here to see you, sir.'

Oppenheimer polluted the air anew with a cloud of pungent smoke and waved impatiently. The servant bowed and turned, gesturing to a man waiting inside the yacht. The man walked out, his ink-black suit stark against the pure-white deck. Oppenheimer turned his head fractionally, acknowledging his guest with a barely perceptible nod and pointing to one of the chairs opposite.

Donald Wolfe was a full colonel who had been attached to the United States Army Medical Research Institute for Infectious Diseases, or USAMRIID. Wolfe sat down, regarding the old man from behind wrap-around sunglasses, the mirrored lenses reflecting the sky above.

'Why do you wear those?' Oppenheimer pointed at them. 'You look like one of those teenage morons who waste their lives surfing and catching diseases from whores.'

Donald Wolfe's smile betrayed no warmth.

'Better to be young and stupid than crumbling with senility.'

Oppenheimer laughed, slapping one spindly leg beneath his white trousers. The effort provoked a sudden spasm of membrane-tearing coughs that caused Wolfe to wince. Oppenheimer brought what was left of his lungs under control, reached for a handkerchief on the table beside him and wiped a glob of mucus from the corner of his mouth.

'If you weren't so useful,' Oppenheimer smiled, 'I'd have you thrown overboard, you insolent pup.'

'Why am I here?' Wolfe asked.

Oppenheimer folded his skeletal hands under his chin.

'The situation has not proceeded as we had expected. We were not able to extract viable biological samples from the remains.'

Wolfe leaned forward, plucking a grape from a nearby bowl. He popped it into his mouth before speaking. 'That doesn't surprise me, given the state they were in. We agreed that you needed to obtain a live specimen, not one with half its face blown off.'

As Oppenheimer chuckled throatily he saw Wolfe brace himself for another hacking broadside of coughs that fortunately did not materialize.

'It may not come as a surprise that they are reluctant to expose themselves, Donald, for fear of what people like us may do to them.'

'So you say. But then of course you would, if this was all just a charade of ghost stories.'

Jeb Oppenheimer's wrinkled features hardened.

'Two months ago you wrote me off as a madman chasing an illusion,' he rattled, jabbing a gnarled finger in Wolfe's direction. 'Now you're sitting on my yacht wondering what the hell happened in Santa Fe.'

'Indeed,' Wolfe nodded, 'and what the hell exactly *did* happen in Santa Fe, Jeb? From what little I can gather, you've committed abduction and theft of state-controlled corpses.'

Oppenheimer squinted out across the rippling waters of the lake.

'Needs must, Donald,' he said quietly. 'SkinGen has invested over eighty million dollars into the search for and the control of the genes that govern human aging. Those genes, once isolated, will be worth over thirty billion dollars to SkinGen over the next ten years, and I don't intend to see either that profit or the investments I have already made compromised by a militia of illiterate *peasants.*'

The last word sent along a spray of spittle. Oppenheimer paused, reaching again for his handkerchief before regarding Wolfe seriously.

'That material, wherever it can be found, is the future, Donald. Most companies are out there gene testing and spending millions, billions even, on research and development, completely oblivious to the fact that the genes controlling longevity have already naturally evolved. We worry now about our economic woes and climate change, about terrorism and Third World nuclear powers, but all of it is bullcrap. All that matters is who survives, how they survive and when the new world order begins.'

Wolfe frowned behind his sunglasses.

'There are rules, Jeb, political as well as legal. Buying up the patents for specific genes could see you up in front of any number of courts. The United States Department of Health and Human Services will block you regardless of my influence if you try to define who gets what from any published research or medication.'

'To hell with the goddamn rules!' Oppenheimer roared, cracking one fist down on the table loudly enough to make Wolfe flinch. 'This is about survival! How long do you think our world can continue to support six billion people? Seven billion people? Nine billion people? We're at our limit now! Oil, gas and coal are running out – why do you think that petrochemical companies are having to drill in the bottom of seabeds? It's because all the cheap stuff has been used, the wells are dry, gone up in smoke! Four fifths of the population live in poverty Donald, and they want to live like *us*. Well, they can't, and they never will because the world cannot support it. The only solution is to reduce the population so that fewer people can live in greater material comfort. It's as simple as that, and I intend to make it happen.'

'If you can acquire the relevant strains,' Wolfe said, 'and if your wonder bacteria actually exist.'

Oppenheimer's leathery face creased into a smile, one ancient line embedded amongst hundreds more.

'Oh, they exist all right. I've spent the past thirty years searching for them, and I've seen enough to know that they do.'

'But I have not,' Wolfe stated simply. 'You're asking me to subvert entire departments of military research and medical health in order to ensure your discovery can be marketed only to the elite, and yet you've provided me with not a single biological example of a human compatible immortalized cell with acceptable telomere length.'

'Patience, Donald,' Jeb murmured. 'The wait will be worth it.'

'The government have their hands on the lab results from Hiram Conley's autopsy, and they're bound to investigate. I'm supposed to be here waiting for a scientific breakthrough not a jail sentence. What we're talking about goes far beyond gene manipulation.'

'My influence will prevent any unnecessary complications.'

Wolfe laughed. 'Even *you* don't have that kind of money.'

Oppenheimer's smile withered, his rheumy old eyes turning hard as steel.

'I have more money than you could dream of, Donald, and don't you ever forget it. If it's money that makes the world go around then I'm turning the fucking crank, you understand?'

Wolfe regarded the old man for a long moment. 'Collateral?'

Oppenheimer's pale lips leaked a dribble of blue smoke. 'What will be, will be.'

Wolfe took off his shades, regarding them for a moment as his eyes adjusted to the bright sunlight flaring off the decks.

'The President is opposed to corporate pharmaceutical control of patented genes. If he or Congress gets wind of this, the whole charade will be for nothing.'

Oppenheimer removed the cigar from his lips and turned it lit end down toward one calloused palm. He held the glowing tip millimeters from his skin and let blue coils of smoke writhe between his digits as he spoke.

'American citizens do not own America. The White House does not own America. The President does not own America. *We* own America. The presidents of the United States live in the White House because people like us finance their damn political parties. That, my friend, is the glory of a free-market capitalist economy – we're not just bigger than government: we *own* it. We pay for them to sit and spout crap to the world about how much better everything will be, even though everybody already knows it'll just stay the same. The United States of America is a business, Donald, just like any other. We decide who does what, when, how and why, and what the President thinks isn't worth a rat's ass.'

Oppenheimer ground the cigar out on the palm of his hand, and with a flick of one hooked finger sent the smoldering remains spinning over the taffrail and into the crystalline water below.

'Thank God for democracy,' Wolfe murmured.

'I will obtain these materials one way or the other, sooner or later, regardless of what anyone may try to do to stop me. You must ensure in any way you can that congressional and military oversight of the pharmaceutical industry is limited and that if we fail to achieve support from the United Nations, we take the necessary steps to achieve our goal alone. I take it that you'll obtain the infected tissue before traveling to New York?'

Wolfe sighed, seemingly weighed down by the gravity of what they were considering.

'Can you ensure secrecy?' he finally asked.

'Officially you will be staying here upon this vessel overnight as my guest,' Oppenheimer replied softly. 'However, I will have one of my private jets fly you north to Alaska immediately and then across to New York afterwards. Nobody need ever know you were there. What of your man at the site?'

'He's a freelance worker, and I will deal with him,' Wolfe said, 'for the greater good. By the time I reach New York every trace of his existence will have disappeared.' Oppenheimer nodded slowly as though accepting the inevitable. Wolfe continued, 'We must keep any deaths to a minimum, at least for now. Later there'll be blood, one way or the other.'

'There always is,' Oppenheimer agreed, 'but at least there'll be profit, and nobody really cares about a handful of hobos in a pissy little backwater like the New Mexico desert. They'll be better off with the revenue generated by SkinGen anyway, it'll bring some light into their miserable lives.'

Wolfe stood, replacing his shades and walking away from the old man. Oppenheimer called after him as he disappeared into the interior of the yacht.

'This is a good thing. It's a brighter future for a county that has nothing to export but illegal immigrants and bird flu! They'll thank us both one day, if there's any of them left.'

7

ALBUQUERQUE INTERNATIONAL SUNPORT NEW MEXICO

Ethan stepped off the United Express Embraer E-170 onto the asphalt of the airport, the sun hot against his skin after the cooler winds of Illinois. Behind him, Lopez shielded her eyes.

'Like being on vacation,' she remarked.

Ethan hoped that Lopez was in a better mood now that their travels had brought them into territory that was more like home, even though Guanajuato was actually six hundred miles south of the border. Lopez had rarely gotten this far south since her family had given up on their dreams of a better life in the United States and returned to their homeland.

A uniformed officer approached them, extending a hand to Ethan.

'Enrico Zamora,' he said. 'You must be Ethan Warner.'

Ethan introduced him to Lopez, and then the lieutenant led them out of the airport to a marked Dodge

Charger, filling them in on the case and his own disappointments as they drove away.

'The whole thing was way out of our league, so we passed everything on to the FBI. That's when this Doug Jarvis guy got involved, and we were all asked to sign non-disclosure agreements. You wanna let me know what the hell that's all about? Most interesting case in twenty years of service and it's snatched away from me; we don't hear a thing about the autopsy and nobody will even tell me who you guys work for.'

'Standard procedure,' Ethan said, looking at the barren wilderness of New Mexico flashing by as they drove. 'Our employers just like to remain discreet. We don't want a media circus out here.'

Zamora shrugged, and ran the fingers of one hand through his hair.

'I understand that, but it tweaks ma curiosity a little. What's so important that you want it kept under wraps?'

'Maybe you could help us with that,' Lopez said from the rear seat. 'We don't have much to go on, that's why we're here. All we have are the social security details of this Hiram Conley and another name, Tyler Willis. What's the story with them both?'

Zamora seemed to shiver despite the warmth, shifting his shoulders as he drove.

'I don't never want to see that man Conley again as long as I live. Came rushing at me out of the woods looking like a living skeleton, all his skin and things hanging in tatters from his arms.'

'Some kind of disease, maybe?' Ethan suggested,

looking at the distant mountains and wondering if some horrible virus lurked somewhere out there in the lonely deserts.

'I'll say.' Zamora nodded. 'Looked like he was falling apart where he stood, but the strange thing was that he ran like a man half his age. I was lucky to shoot him before he got me with that goddamn bayonet of his.'

Lopez raised an eyebrow.

'He charged you with a *bayonet*?'

'Ain't never seen nothin' like it,' Zamora said. 'We had the weapon checked out by the crime lab: the damned thing was an antique. They identified it as a Model 1842 Springfield .69 caliber percussion-lock musket, which was the last of the smooth-bore models made with a thicker barrel. They were rifled sometime after manufacture to take the conically shaped Minie Ball, the same type of bullet found in Hiram Conley, so I was led to believe.'

Ethan glanced back at Lopez before speaking.

'And the weapon isn't a remake, or a copy?'

'Only about six thousand of that specific type were made,' Zamora said, 'and modern copies for re-enactment groups are easily spotted. This was the real deal, no doubt about it, weighed ten pounds and was damn near five feet long.'

'Was it a type used during the Civil War?' Lopez asked.

'Sure was.' Zamora nodded. 'One of the earliest, although the repeatin' rifles followed pretty soon after, so I'm told.'

'Did this guy Conley say anything to you at the scene?'

Ethan asked, looking out across the passing wilderness and imagining what it must have been like for a Union army marching and surviving in such brutal terrain for weeks and months on end.

'Sure he did, but most of it was kind of garbled. He kept talkin' about the Union, and the New Mexico Militia, stuff like that. I had the guys check out the references, and there was a New Mexico Militia working out this way during the Civil War, but that was a hundred and fifty years ago. We put it all down to this guy being a fantasist of some kind.'

'Then how'd he get the uniform and the weapon?' Lopez asked.

'I'm not saying they weren't genuine,' Zamora admitted. 'Only that he must have lived out in the Pecos for years, maybe as part of a commune or something. From what we could gather he had little documentation and no fixed abode, so he's been living rough for years. For all we know there could be others like him out there.'

'What about this other guy, Tyler Willis?' Ethan asked.

Zamora waved a hand in the air as if in desperation and then ran it through the tight coils of his hair.

'Tyler ain't talking; says he was just hiking in the hills when he was confronted by Hiram Conley, who got in his face and started screaming. Given that Conley opened fire on both Willis and the tourists, I'm inclined to believe him, but . . .'

'But you're not sure,' Lopez finished the sentence for him.

'The ranger who was leading the tourists said it was an argument Willis and Conley were having, both of them going at each other. Willis was injured and, as the victim, I can hardly arrest him, but I'm sure there's something he's not telling me. Maybe you guys will have more luck.'

'Where can we find him?' Ethan inquired.

'He was in hospital with a shrapnel wound to the shoulder but he discharged himself this morning, claiming he had to get back to work. Turns out he's a researcher at the laboratories up Los Alamos way, some kind of high-flying scientist or other.'

Ethan had heard of the famous Los Alamos National Laboratories, where some of the most extraordinary discoveries of the last century had been made. The home of the original Manhattan Project, which had culminated in the dawn of the atomic age when the United States had dropped atom bombs on Imperial Japan to bring a close to World War Two, the laboratories concerned themselves now with advanced technologies in all theaters of scientific endeavor.

'You got any idea what this guy Willis is researching?' Ethan asked.

'Beats me.' Zamora chuckled. 'Most of what he told me went straight over my head and right out of the park. But it was something to do with medicine.'

Ethan looked at Lopez.

'We'll start with him,' he said. 'Right now there's not much else to go on.'

'What about Hiram Conley's social security number?' Lopez asked Zamora. 'You guys got a town hall down here or something, some way we could backtrack the records?'

'Town hall would probably have something tucked away some place, and Santa Fe County offices might have records. Trouble is getting anything concrete about this guy. Last I heard he went by several names, and any one of them could be false or real.'

'Tyler Willis is still our best bet for now,' Ethan said. 'We'll start digging through records once we've got a better idea of why Conley was so important.'

Enrico Zamora chuckled as he pulled the cruiser into a parking lot filled with rental vehicles, stopping outside the reception area where an old Mercury Tracer sedan awaited them.

'Well, good luck with that.'

'I'm sure he's not that bad,' Lopez said as she reached for the door.

'He's not bad,' Zamora agreed, 'but he sure ain't on this planet.'

'What do you mean?' Ethan asked.

'He's one of those who's all for crazy talk,' Zamora said quietly. 'Willis said that he was delirious an' all from lack of blood on account of his shoulder wound, but I was with him up there on the pass and he spoke plainly enough to me.'

'What did he say?' Ethan pressed.

Zamora shook his head slowly as if still struggling to understand. Ethan watched him run his hand through his hair again, and wondered if doing so was a nervous reaction of some kind for the officer.

'Just before I shot Conley, Tyler Willis was begging

me not to fire, tellin' me not to shoot the old man.'

'Why?' Lopez asked. 'Surely he'd have wanted Conley dead after what happened.'

'So you'd suppose,' Zamora agreed.

Ethan thought for a moment.

'You said that the ranger who reported the shooting said that Willis and Conley were arguing up on the pass, and then Conley shot Willis at close range.'

'That's what he told me,' Zamora confirmed. 'What of it?'

'If they were arguing, then they can't have been that far apart,' Ethan said. 'Conley couldn't have missed Willis with a rifle, not at such close range.'

'What are you saying?' Zamora asked.

'That Conley purposefully didn't shoot to kill,' Ethan said. 'For whatever reason he didn't want to kill Willis, and that means he either wanted something from him or he wanted to learn something.'

'Willis could have grabbed the rifle and turned it aside before the shot was fired,' Lopez said.

'Maybe,' Zamora replied. 'But that rifle had a four-teen-inch bayonet on it. I wouldn't have risked grabbing it.'

Ethan opened his door, letting hot air puff into the air-conditioned cruiser.

'Thanks for the ride, Enrico. If you remember anything else, you've got our number.'

'Sure,' Zamora said. 'There's one other thing.'

'What's that?'

'The last thing Tyler Willis said to me before I fired at Conley was the darndest thing I ever did hear. He said not to kill Conley because he was too old to die. You make any sense of that?'

Lopez looked at Ethan, who glanced again at the ranger.

'Probably the sun got to him.'

Ethan shut his door before Zamora could answer.

8

BIO–SCIENCE DIVISION LOS ALAMOS NATIONAL LABORATORIES, NEW MEXICO

'Hell of a place,' Lopez said.

Ethan nodded, looking around at the ranks of buildings and the names of the roads as he drove through the complex, which looked like an oversized industrial park. The 502 East Road had led them onto Trinity Drive, named after the famous atomic tests. Ethan had already spotted various signs such as Bikini Road, named after Bikini Atoll where further nuclear tests were made in the 1950s. Run by the Department of Energy and with an annual budget of $2.2 billion, it was one of only two places in the United States where research into classified nuclear programs was performed.

'It's the largest employer in northern New Mexico,' Ethan said as he drove the Mercury into the parking lot outside the Bio-Science Division building. 'Whatever Tyler Willis is up to in here, it almost certainly has something to do with Hiram Conley.'

Lopez nodded, scanning the file that Douglas Jarvis had handed them back in Chicago.

'Tyler Adam Willis, born 1978, Modesto, California. Studied microbiology at the University of California before joining a research team at Los Alamos. Recently published several papers detailing the results of studies into senescence.'

'In English, please,' Ethan said as they parked.

'Another term for aging,' Lopez said. 'Looks like our boy knows his stuff when it comes to cheating death. According to this he's considered one of the brightest talents in the field of cellular senescence.'

Ethan killed the engine and looked up at the imposing building before them.

'You really think that's why he was shot?' Ethan asked her. 'Something to do with his research?'

'Why not? Maybe this isn't just a freaky ghost story and he found some kind of potion that extends lifespans.'

Ethan got out of the car and walked toward the entrance, followed by Lopez. A clean, sparse entrance hall greeted them, occupied by a narrow desk and a bored-looking receptionist. Ethan walked up to her, leaning against the counter and flashing a smile.

'Hi, we're here to see Tyler Willis.'

'Do you have an appointment?' the girl asked, taking in Ethan's rough-edged appearance and apparently liking what she saw.

'We're here on behalf of the Santa Fe Police Department, Lieutenant Enrico Zamora,' Ethan said smoothly. 'Nothing to worry about: Tyler was injured in an incident a couple of days ago and we're just here with some follow-up questions and to make sure he's doing okay.'

The girl smiled again and picked up a phone, dialing

an extension number. When she'd finished speaking and put the phone down, she directed them toward a nearby elevator.

'Second floor, third on the right. Just call me if there's anything else you need.'

'I'll be sure to do that.'

Ethan flashed another grin at the girl and followed Lopez into the elevator. She rounded on him as the door closed.

'You ever been able to talk to a girl without hitting on her?'

Ethan stood with his hands behind his back, watching the numbers change on the digital display above the doors.

'I was just being polite.'

'Polite? You'd leaned any closer to her you'd have been dribbling into her blouse.'

Ethan looked down at Lopez in amusement. 'What's the problem?'

Lopez shrugged. 'It's just not professional, is all.'

'Like breaking into strangers' cars is?'

Lopez rolled her eyes but said nothing as the doors opened and they turned right into a corridor. Rows of pictures adorned the walls, bizarre, kaleidoscopic images of what looked like microscopic bugs and spores and fungi.

'Welcome to geek heaven,' Ethan said as they made for the third door on the right.

Lopez looked up at one of the grotesque images, portraying what looked like a slug with eight legs tucked up close to its head.

'What the hell is that?' she wondered out loud.

Ethan was about to hazard a guess when another voice answered for him.

'*Demodex folliculorum.*'

They turned to see a young black man standing behind them with a cup of coffee in one hand and his other arm in a sling. He smiled from behind fashionable square-lensed spectacles with distinctive burgundy frames as though almost embarrassed, and gestured with his cup to the picture on the wall.

'It's a tiny mite, less than half a millimeter long.'

Ethan glanced at the picture. 'The image is magnified.'

'Yes. The demodicids just look like worms with legs that are tiny stumps.'

'Is it dangerous?' Lopez asked curiously.

'Not at all,' Willis said. 'You've probably got a few hundred of them on you right now. They live in the pores and hair follicles on your face, and often in the roots of your eyelashes. Women get more of them because of the cosmetics they use. Those little critters just love the chemicals.'

Lopez blanched, staring wide-eyed at Willis. Ethan, trying not to smirk, stepped forward.

'We're here on Lieutenant Zamora's behalf.'

Willis's smile faded and his shoulders seemed to sag. He nodded, and gestured ahead to the open door of his office. Ethan led the way inside, followed by Lopez who was tentatively touching her face. Willis closed the door behind them and slumped into a swivel chair behind a small desk, upon which sat a computer and several paper trays. The office had a small window that looked out over a parking lot, the distant green hills tinged with blue in the hazy sunlight beyond.

'I suppose this is about what happened at Glorietta Pass,' Willis said sulkily. 'I've told the police everything I know.'

'Maybe you have,' Ethan said, 'but then again maybe you haven't.'

Willis opened his mouth to protest but Lopez cut across him.

'We don't have time to mess around, Tyler. This man, Hiram Conley, shot you after an argument in which you were every bit as involved as he was. We have a dozen witnesses and all of their statements correlate. You knew this guy and you know why he shot you. Speak up, and this will all be a lot easier.'

Willis's feeble defiance crumbled, but he shook his head. 'It's not that easy. You don't know what's been happening here.'

'Then maybe you should fill us in,' Ethan suggested. 'This isn't about local law enforcement anymore, Tyler. The government is taking an interest in what happened down here, and what you tell us will get back to them. If they think that you're lying . . .'

Ethan let the loaded statement hang in the air between them. Willis digested its meaning, and set his coffee cup down on the desk before him.

'I'm not lying about anything,' he said. 'The government wouldn't have any interest in me at all if it weren't for what Hiram Conley showed me.'

'Go on,' Lopez encouraged.

'What happened to Hiram Conley's corpse?'

'We were hoping you could tell us,' Lopez said, folding her arms and gesturing out of the small office window. 'Theft of state-controlled corpses is a federal offense. If you're charged, you can get used to a view of the outside world just like that one but with bars.'

'I never saw what happened to Conley after the ranger shot him, I swear!' Willis yelped.

'Take an educated guess,' Ethan said, picking up on Lopez's attempts to entrap Willis into revealing whatever it was he was trying to hide.

'It's too dangerous!' Willis snapped.

'Tell us what you safely can,' Ethan suggested, 'at least then we'll be able to see where it might take our investigation.'

Willis sighed and rubbed his forehead.

'It started a few weeks ago, when I was coming to the end of a two-year study into an illness known as Werner syndrome.'

'What's that?' Lopez asked, already scribbling notes.

'It's a very rare disorder characterized by premature aging, more so than any other segmental progeria. The disease is caused by a mutation in a gene that causes excessive telomere attrition.'

'So, people with this disorder die prematurely?' Ethan hazarded.

'They normally develop without symptoms until they reach puberty,' Willis said, 'upon which they age rapidly, often appearing decades older. Other symptoms include loss of and graying of hair, thickening of the skin and cataracts in both eyes.'

'Is it curable?' Lopez asked.

'That's what I was working on,' Willis said. 'A recent study found that mice which were genetically modified to express the genes thought to cause Werner syndrome in humans were restored to normal health and lifespan when vitamin C was put in their drinking water. The work was incomplete but the potential for study was immense. I'd also been studying cellular defense proteins in humans called sirtuins. Drugs that boost these proteins have already been shown to extend the lifespan of mice by about fifteen percent.'

Ethan thought for a moment.

'So how does Hiram Conley tie into all this?'

'I was working on a number of cellular senescence papers,' Willis said, 'trying to understand how Werner syndrome worked and whether it could be reversed in order to slow aging. I'd published a few when Hiram Conley showed up here, real quiet like. He said he had something to show me, and handed me a vial with what he claimed was spinal fluid in it, from a lumbar puncture. It's not every day that somebody wanders into your lab with spinal fluid, so I agreed to culture it to see what emerged. A few days later I looked at the fluid under a microscope and realized that it was filled with microscopic fauna that I recognized.'

'From where?' Lopez asked.

Willis gestured to a small photograph tacked to the wall of his office that appeared to show tiny bacterial cells suspended in solution, imaged with a powerful microscope.

'Back in 1999, scientists working in a cave complex

extracted bacterial samples from sodium-chloride crystals formed from prehistoric sea salt. The microscopic organisms were revived in a laboratory after being in suspended animation within the crystals. They couldn't identify the species and referred to it as strain 2-9-3, or *Bacillus permians*. What was special about it was that the organisms were two hundred fifty million years old.'

Ethan blinked.

'The dinosaurs were still around then.'

'The dinosaurs had only just got *started* back then,' Willis corrected him. '*Bacillus permians* represents the oldest living organism known to man. In May 1995, forty-million-year-old *Bacillus sphaericus* were found in the stomach of a bee encased in amber. They were also in a state of suspended animation and were revived in a laboratory.'

'How did Hiram Conley get these bacteria, and from whom?' Ethan inquired.

'I don't know. He refused to tell me, except to say that the spinal fluid was his own.'

'I don't believe that,' Lopez said. 'You need to tell us everything, Tyler.'

'Do you have any idea what you're getting yourself into?' Willis burst out. 'This is far bigger than any of us. It isn't about Hiram Conley or any of the others.'

Willis stared at them for a moment, and then realized his mistake.

Ethan pushed himself off the wall, his arms folded across his chest.

'What *others*?'

9

ASPEN CENTER FOR
PRIMATE RESEARCH
LOS ALAMOS

'You cover the reception area, I'll get through the back and break down the doors.'

The battered old 1968 Dodge Camper in which Saffron sat smelled of axle grease, mould and unwashed upholstery. The vehicle was a wreck they'd found abandoned in a farmer's yard in Silver City two days before. Colin 'Hugger' Manx, a lanky, curly-haired geek whom she swore had never washed in his life, had managed to get it running after a day of swearing and wrench throwing, and had driven them to Los Alamos that morning. In the back of the camper sat two furtive-looking teenagers, the self-named Ruby Lily, a wisp of a girl with blonde dreadlocks, and an anemic-looking boy who called himself Bobby, all greasy black hair and white skin, his narrow chin flecked with spots.

'What are you going to do?' Manx demanded of her. 'You can't just stroll in there and expect them to let you into the labs.'

Saffron shook her head.

'They'll have a set of doors that contain a mid-pressure area that people have to pass through. They have them so that contaminants from the laboratories can't flow out of the building, like a HazMat facility. We'll use the gun on those.'

Saffron waited for a riposte from her companions, but nobody responded. She looked down into the footwell of the camper, where an unlicensed sawn-off Beretta shotgun and a handful of cartridges lay at her feet. As if suddenly paranoid, she checked the rear-view mirror. She caught a glimpse of her reflection in the cracked mirror. At twenty-nine, she was older than her companions by some years and regarded by them as something of a veteran. Her long blonde hair was tied up in a tight knot behind her head, as it had been for some months now. On the rare occasions when she let it fall it reached almost to her thighs. Her high cheekbones and clear green eyes made her look like a catwalk model who'd survived a particularly heavy night out. To Saffron all she saw were the subtle features that betrayed her grandfather's influence: the firm line of her lips and the sinister glitter of radicalism that flickered like a distant star in her eyes.

'The shift's about to change,' Manx said, his voice an octave higher than before. He gripped the steering wheel more tightly and looked over his shoulder. 'Everybody ready?'

Ruby Lily and Bobby nodded dutifully, each picking up a baseball bat lying beside them. Saffron ignored Colin. He'd only joined them because they'd needed someone to fix the vehicle, and now he was acting as though he'd conceived of the entire plan. Saffron disliked him. Her dislike had become even more intense after she'd gotten so drunk with her friends at the commune that she'd been too tired to fend off his romantic advances when he'd stopped by her tent in the early hours. She'd barely made any attempt to stop him, and had actually fallen asleep before he'd finished. She'd briefly woken to realize that her comatose disinterest had provoked in him a sudden and embarrassingly flaccid manhood that had caused him to flee her tent in a hail of frustrated expletives.

Now, Manx was on a mission to regain his bruised ego.

'You'll go when I tell you,' Saffron murmured to him.

'I only take orders from one person, honey.' Manx grinned, jabbing a finger at his own chest. 'Me.'

'Fine,' Saffron said, pulling the shotgun from the foot-well and offering it to him. 'You'd better lead from the front then.'

Manx's bravado wilted as quickly as his stubby white dick had the previous night. He blanched, his eyes fixed on the gun.

'You brought the damned thing,' he blustered. 'I'm not carrying it for you.'

Saffron lowered the weapon back out of sight.

'Best you do as I say then, understood, Colon?'

Manx avoided her gaze and ignored the giggles from the rear of the van, shrugging and stroking his threadbare goatee beard as he turned back to watch the front of the laboratories on the opposite side of the road.

'Why the hell are we hitting this little place anyway?' he muttered, trying to draw attention away from her insult. 'It's hardly worth the effort.'

'Any place like this is worth the effort,' Saffron

retorted. 'As long as there's a single vivisection operation in the United States, in the world, it's worth it. Would you want to be in there, being tested?'

She turned as a small knot of people exited the main building, and felt a jolt of apprehension twist her stomach.

'This is it,' she said, sliding the shotgun into a slim carry-all and opening her door. 'Ready?'

More furtive glances from Ruby Lily in the rear seat, and Manx swallowed thickly as he gazed at her, but all three of them moved to exit the camper.

'Go, now!' Saffron snapped.

She climbed out of the camper, shouldering the carry-all and striding purposefully to the main road, crossing it before descending the asphalt opposite. The white building in front loomed above her, the expensively manicured gardens and beautifully crafted logo mounted on the walls hiding the horrors she knew lay within, of animals poisoned, murdered and dissected so that the mascara of Hollywood starlets wouldn't smudge so easily. The thought fired her anger as she approached the scientists now ten feet away, their eyes taking in her appearance and that of her companions and the first flicker of panic distorting their features.

One of them, a young man with a thin beard, turned back for the door.

Saffron took the carry-all from her shoulder, letting it fall away to reveal the sawn-off as her features contorted into a mask of rage.

'Move another step and I'll send you home with buckshot in your ass!'

Five pairs of hands shot into the air. A sixth scientist,

a woman with her hair coiled in a bun behind her head, covered her mouth to prevent a scream and promptly collapsed. As her colleagues moved to her aid, Saffron lunged forward, ramming the barrel of the shotgun in their faces.

'Don't move!' she screamed, prodding them backward and looking at a meek man with a narrow nose and quivering jowls. 'You – open the fucking door, now!'

The man stared at her, his face trembling, beads of sweat spilling into his eyes, but he stood his ground and shook his head. Saffron changed her stance, took one pace toward him and flipped the barrel of the shotgun toward her as she spun the stock. The heavy butt of the weapon smashed up into the scientist's jaw with a dull crack and sent him spinning away onto the lawns amid blood-spattered cries.

Saffron didn't give the man's colleagues the chance to respond, shoving the shotgun toward them again.

'The door! Now!'

'Okay!' one of them shouted, turning and walking back to the entrance door and sliding his card through a reader mounted on a panel. He keyed in his access code and the door slid open.

'Back inside, all of you!' Saffron shouted, turning and gesturing for Manx to grab the incapacitated scientists and drag them into the building.

She watched as the pathetic huddle shuffled past her into the building before hurrying after them and closing the door from the inside. She turned to her captives.

'The labs. Take me there, now.'

The scientist who had opened the door smiled grimly, and shook his head.

'You're screwed,' he said with cold delight. 'The cameras will have seen you, and I set my code to lock us in reception here. The police will already be on their way and there's nothing you can do about it.'

Saffron glanced at the door as Manx pushed the button desperately before looking at her and shaking his head.

'We're stuck,' Ruby Lily uttered in despair.

Saffron glared at the scientists and cocked the shotgun.

'Then we've got nothing to lose.'

Colin Manx's jaw dropped and he raised a hand to stop her.

'Saff, no!'

Saffron ignored him and pulled the trigger.

10

'What others?'

Tyler Willis sighed as he realized he had been cornered. He reached up and rubbed his wounded shoulder, shaking his head as he spoke, 'Hiram Conley was one of seven men I've been studying over the past eight weeks.'

Ethan looked at Lopez, who had now begun recording the conversation using a portable device in her pocket. She nodded once at him, and Ethan turned his attention to Willis.

'Tell us everything, from the beginning,' he said. 'If there's some kind of danger in this for you, then the more we know, the better we can protect you.'

Willis stared at Ethan.

'I want your word. You're government, right? I want your word, both of you, that you can protect me if this gets out.'

Ethan was about to speak, but Lopez beat him to it.

'We'll cover your back, Tyler,' she assured him. 'That's why we're here.'

Ethan swallowed, uncertain of how they could possibly guarantee his safety when they had no clear idea of who was threatening him and why.

Willis sighed, and gestured around him at his office.

'This has been my work for the past three years. Along with Werner syndrome, I've been studying the effects and causes of cellular senescence, seeking ways in which to delay the deleterious effects of human aging.'

'Why?' Lopez asked. 'What's the purpose exactly? Everybody dies eventually.'

'Yes, they do,' he agreed. 'But the purpose of my work is to understand how we age and how to try to develop medicines that will ensure that people age comfortably, without the debilitating diseases that afflict the elderly. By studying things like cellular apoptosis – programmed cell death – it's theoretically possible to reverse the process of aging.'

'Surely that can't work,' Ethan said. 'People have to age in order to die, and nothing is immortal.'

Tyler Willis smiled broadly.

'In fact, that's not entirely true. We see aging as a process that takes place across our own lifespans, and we see others age as we do. It's something we're used to, but in nature not every species ages at the same rate, and for some there is no aging process at all.'

Lopez raised an eyebrow.

'You mean that some animals live forever?'

'Perhaps not forever, but for long enough that to a human perspective they would appear immortal,' Willis said. 'The hydrozoan species *Turritopsis nutricula* is able to return from a mature adult to an immature polyp stage and back again, effectively meaning that it is considered biologically immortal and has no maximum lifespan. Colonies of sea anemones have been kept in laboratories for close to a century, can regenerate any body part and show no signs of aging. Some koi fish, a much larger and more complex species, have lived beyond two hundred years.'

'That's not quite the same as a mammal living for that long,' Ethan pointed out.

'But that's my point,' Tyler insisted, 'delayed senescence isn't species specific and can occur in mammals too. In May 2007, a fifty-tonne Bowhead whale caught off the coast of Alaska was found to have the head of an explosive harpoon embedded within its neck blubber. The four-inch arrow-shaped projectile had been manufactured in New Bedford, Massachusetts around 1890, making the whale a minimum of one hundred seventeen years old.'

'A bit like Hiram Conley,' Lopez said. 'He had a Minie musket ball lodged in his right femur. According to analysis the wound was around one hundred forty years old.'

Tyler Willis grasped the edge of his desk.

'You're sure? You actually have evidence of this?'

'It's locked up,' Lopez replied quickly, cursing inwardly at having revealed too much. 'But our source is reliable. The main reason we're here is to find out what the hell's been going on with this Conley and how he could have ended up not just with that wound but with a fresh Minie ball in his shoulder.'

Willis seemed momentarily distracted, whispering to himself.

'I'll be damned, it's true then.' He looked at them. 'Conley had been shot before I met him in the pass, before the ranger arrived. Somebody else shot him with a musket, maybe one of the others.'

'When you were found,' Ethan said, 'you told Patrol Officer Zamora that Hiram Conley was too old to die, that you didn't want him killed. You knew that he was very old then, didn't you?'

Willis seemed to come back to the present. He looked at both Lopez and Ethan as though weighing them up, and then finally nodded.

'I didn't at first,' he said simply.

'What was wrong with him, exactly?' Lopez asked.

Willis sighed heavily.

'It's very difficult to explain,' he said. 'You need to think differently about life and what it is before you can understand what happened to Hiram Conley. What you need to know is that nobody ever dies of old age, ever. What happens to us, and to all other species, is that the ability of our cells to divide without generating errors decreases the more times those cells are forced to divide. The gradual building up of cellular errors eventually results in programmed cell death, apoptosis, which leads to a specific cause of death such as organ failure, cancer and so on. We die as a result of illness brought on by age, but not by age itself.'

'So technically people could live forever?' Lopez asked, 'if their cells could divide without errors.'

'It's possible,' Willis nodded, 'even as crazy as it

sounds. But unfortunately it's not quite as simple as that.
Like everything else, aging is something that has evolved
through natural selection. Most of the earliest forms of
life on our planet were bacterial colonies and such like,
forms which don't necessarily suffer senescence because,
as a colony, they survive for millions of years and
continue the genetic heritage of the colony as a whole.
However, with most forms of life aging has evolved
because the longer something lives, the more likely it is
to encounter a fatal incident, be it predation or an
accident.'

'We die just in case we have an accident?' Lopez
muttered. 'Sounds like a bum deal.'

'Not really,' Willis said. 'Evolution has resulted in a
situation where it has become an advantage to have
higher reproductive strategies at the youngest possible
age, thus reducing the chances of some fatal event
preventing reproduction and making a species extinct.
Natural selection favors those species which can mate
most effectively when they're young and fit, and so the
evolution of species has resulted in forms of life who
mature early and mate young, before then growing old
and passing away. There's a resources issue too – if
nothing ever died, then pretty soon all the planet's
resources would be consumed and nothing more could
live. Each generation of species must thus make way for
the next.'

'So what was your angle on all of this?' Lopez asked.
'You were trying to eradicate age-related disease, but
how?'

'Disease generally comes about when people age,'

Tyler Willis said, 'that much we know. What people don't realize is that human diseases should have been eradicated by natural selection by now via inherited immunity or random mutation. The reason they haven't been is therefore because humans mate young, and for most of our evolution have also *died* young. The presence of extensive age-related disease is a relatively new phenomenon because it's only recently that people have reached their seventies and beyond on a regular basis. This means that natural selection only acts weakly against age-related disease because resilience to it hasn't yet had the chance to evolve within us. My work involved studying how genetic manipulation might serve humanity by acting as a substitute for natural selection and creating specific genes resistant to such diseases, like Huntingdon's or Alzheimer's.'

'Okay,' Lopez said, 'so how would you go about doing that?'

'Well,' Willis replied, 'the main cause of aging in mammals is the degradation of telomeres in the nuclei of cells. Telomeres are like caps at the tips of chromosomes – you can think of them as fuel for the accurate division and replication of cells. As cells divide, telomeres become ever shorter, and eventually they are unable to support further cellular division without a build-up of errors or deleterious mutations, which cause the signs of aging such as muscle loss, degraded skin quality, organ failure and so on. If we can find a way of allowing cells to divide without losing the telomeres and building up those errors, we have a possible means of extending quality of life, if not longevity itself.'

'Doesn't sound so hard,' Ethan said.

'It's hard,' Willis assured him. 'Mainly because the only kind of cells that naturally undergo this transformation into biologically immortal cells are those that cause cancer. The line between the two may be thin, but it's the difference between curing someone and killing them.'

'And you've figured out a way to do this?' Lopez asked.

'There are a number of potential ways,' Willis replied, 'to slow aging in mammals. Cell loss can be repaired via growth factors to stimulate cell division, such as stem cells, or even by simple methods such as exercise or reduced calorie intake. Senescent cells can be removed by activating the immune system against them or via gene therapy. Extracellular materials like amyloid can be eliminated by vaccination, while intracellular junk requires the introduction of new enzymes that can degrade the junk that our own natural enzymes cannot degrade. Mitochondrial mutations can be handled using gene therapy via cell nuclei. For cancer the strategy is to use gene therapy to delete the genes for telomerase and to eliminate telomerase-independent mechanisms of turning normal cells into "immortal" cancer cells. To compensate for the loss of telomerase in stem cells we would introduce new stem cells every decade or so.'

'Has any of this actually been achieved?' Ethan asked.

'The Dana-Faber Cancer Institute managed to reverse the aging process in mice,' Willis said, 'by targeting the chromosomes in cellular nuclei and the telomeres. They manipulated the enzyme that regulates these tips, telomerase, turning it on and off. When they boosted the enzyme, the mice appeared rejuvenated. There was a dramatic reversal in the signs and symptoms of aging: the brains increased in size, cognition improved, coat hair regained a healthy sheen and fertility was restored. It was the equivalent of taking someone from their eightieth year and bringing them back to their forties. They had in effect undergone rejuvenation, had become young again.'

'Holy crap,' Lopez smiled. 'That could be worth a fortune!'

'It was only in mice,' Willis cautioned, 'and there's a lot of work to be done, mostly in figuring out how to make elderly people more comfortable and to remove the specter of age-related disease. That said, there are people looking to make money out of this – the cosmetics industry would be severely compromised if this became a commercial product.'

Ethan frowned.

'How come Hiram Conley was an old man then? If he'd somehow avoided aging, why was he looking about sixty when he was killed?'

Tyler Willis shook his head.

'You're getting it all wrong,' he said. 'Forget about your preconceptions, about some magical fountain of youth from which you drink and become forever young. These things are the stuff of science fiction, and that's the whole point. Science has been searching for a way to modify cells in order to slow or stop aging, but we've been looking in entirely the wrong place.'

'What do you mean?' Lopez asked.

'Hiram Conley was not in possession of some mystical vial or potion,' Willis replied, 'and he wasn't genetically altered by scientists. He was suffering from an infection.'

ASPEN CENTER FOR PRIMATE RESEARCH LOS ALAMOS

The blast of the shotgun rang in Saffron's ears as the Beretta's powerful recoil slammed the butt into her shoulder. A cloud of choking blue smoke filled the reception area and, as the ringing in Saffron's ears subsided, she heard the piercing screech of an alarm and the crunch of glass beneath her feet.

She stepped forward and rammed the still smoldering barrel of the shotgun into the nearest scientist's belly, doubling him over, then grabbed another by the collar.

'The labs. Now!'

Saffron shoved the man headfirst through the remains of the door and into the reception area, the man sprawling onto a carpet sprinkled with shattered glass.

A hand grabbed her shoulder, and she turned to see Colin Manx's pale features stricken with panic.

'What the hell are you doing? You should have shot us *out* of here, not further in!'

Gripped by a rage coursing through her veins like acid, Saffron whipped Manx's grip aside with a swipe of her free hand and grabbed him by the throat.

'You'll leave when I fucking tell you to, Colon, understood?'

Manx, all pretense of bravado vanishing before her wrath, nodded and backed away, the palms of his hands raised defensively toward her. Saffron turned to Ruby Lily and Bobby.

'Ruby, watch out for the cops. Bobby, look for another way out of here just in case we're cornered, okay?' As the two teenagers nodded and dashed away she turned to Manx. 'You, keep watch on this lot and don't let them move. Think you can handle that without crapping your pants?'

Saffron didn't wait for him to respond, reaching down to grab the scientist still sprawled on the carpet beside her.

'Let's go.'

The man reluctantly hauled himself onto his feet as Saffron jabbed the shotgun under his jaw and shoved him forward. Other employees, seeing one of their colleagues covered in blood and with a shotgun shoved under his face, melted out of their way.

'You'll never get away,' the scientist muttered as Saffron prodded him down a corridor toward the rear of the building. 'The police will be here in minutes.'

Saffron nodded.

'I'm counting on it. Now shut up and keep moving.'

The corridor ended in a solid-looking glass door containing an atmospheric chamber sealed off from the rest of the building. The chamber represented the transition between the normal atmospheric pressure of the main building, and the low-pressure environment of the laboratories within, designed specifically to ensure that, in the event of a breach, air would always flow into the laboratories and not out of them. This meant that any toxic chemicals or hazardous viruses within the center's laboratories could not leak into the outside world.

'Inside, Einstein,' Saffron said, opening the chamber and shoving her hostage inside before following him in and sealing the door. 'Do it.'

The scientist jabbed a couple of buttons on a panel and the air around them hissed gently for a few seconds before a small red light on the panel turned green. Saffron pushed the door to the laboratory open, striding in as a handful of scientists looked up from their test tubes and petri dishes and froze. Saffron raised the shotgun in her hand.

'Anybody moves, I'll give them an enema they won't forget!'

Nobody moved.

Saffron turned toward the sound of animals, and her heart wrenched as she saw cages lining one wall of the laboratories, where half a dozen chimpanzees sat watching her with interest. Their cages were small, matted with straw and hopelessly inadequate for either comfort or movement. Two were hooked up to machines nearby, one of which was clearly for some kind of brain-manipulation of mechanical or robotic arms, coils of wiring traveling from computers directly into the animal's brain stem in a complex tangle.

Saffron's throat pinched tight, and tears blurred her vision.

'We'll let them all go, if you want.'

The voice of her captive standing beside her sent a surge of fury through Saffron. She whirled, driving the butt of the Beretta into his face like a sledgehammer. The scientist crashed backwards into a desk, smashing beakers and vials as he went before slamming onto the tiled floor.

Saffron pointed at the nearest person, a thin-looking man in a white lab coat.

'You. Where's the main database?'

He stared at her for a moment. 'The what?'

Saffron stormed across to him, kicking a chair out of her way and pushing the Beretta up under his chin with enough force to drive him backwards over a table, his legs flailing wildly.

'The fucking *database*, the computer records, everything you've done. Where is it?'

The man, terrorized to the point where he could no longer speak, pointed across the room to a large pair of computer terminals. Saffron took in the tall servers with their flashing lights and humming fans, and strode over to them. She reached into her pocket and called over her shoulder to the stricken scientists watching her.

'You've got about sixty seconds to get every one of those animals out of here.'

Saffron didn't look back at them. She listened to a moment of silent disbelief followed by a sudden manic scrambling as they began grabbing cages and rushing them out of the laboratory. She studied the computer servers as she produced from her pocket two dirty-looking devices the size of large pears. MK 2 fused grenades, bought from an antique dealer near Cedar City, Utah, and refurbished to operational standard by a retired US army sergeant of questionable motives out of El Paso, Texas.

Saffron waited until the laboratory behind her fell silent. She looked down at the grenades in her hands, gripping them tightly, and took a deep breath.

'We can't free this one.'

The voice behind her made her whirl around in surprise. A young woman was standing beside the chimpanzee wired to the robotic arms.

'What?' Saffron stammered.

'He's hard-wired right now,' the scientist said. 'We can't just unplug him like a toy.'

Saffron's eyes welled with tears as she shook her head.

'You bastards, you just don't know when to stop, do you.'

The woman stood her ground.

'His name's Eric,' she said simply. 'He's helping us learn how to help disabled people walk again.'

'He's a victim of your Nazi experiments!' Saffron shouted.

The woman closed her eyes for a second before speaking.

'He broke his back in a fall in Phoenix Zoo, Arizona. When we learn how he can control these robot arms, we can fix him too.'

Saffron choked on her tears and pointed at Eric, who watched her with intense curiosity.

'How long?'

'Ten minutes,' the woman said.

Saffron cursed mentally, but could not tear her eyes away from Eric.

'Do it, now!'

Saffron turned as the woman began unplugging Eric from the machines, and she reached into her pocket and produced a slim black portable hard drive. She plugged the drive into the servers and tapped a few keys before dashing out of the laboratory, checking her watch as she ran. She burst into the reception area to see a dozen cages scattered around and a nervous-looking Colin Manx holding court with a fake pistol in his hand pointed at some thirty scientists cowering on the floor in one corner.

'The cops will be here any minute,' he wailed. 'We've got the monkeys, let's get out of here!'

Saffron ignored him, looking at Bobby. 'You find another way out?'

'Nothing,' Bobby said desperately. 'The labs stand along the back wall of the building. Are we going to be arrested?'

Saffron didn't reply. She strode to the glass doors of the reception area, cocking the shotgun. Without a moment's hesitation she blasted the glass clean out of the doors, the tearing report of the gun replaced by the shrieking of the chimpanzees in their cages.

Saffron turned to Colin and Bobby.

'Bobby, get the van. Colin, get the cages out and into the van first, then let these bastards go.' She gestured to the scientists with a jab of her thumb.

'What about you?' Manx asked in surprise.

Saffron scowled at him.

'Just do as you're fucking told and get out of here. I'll worry about me.'

With that, Saffron hurried away down the corridor back to the laboratory, reaching it as the female scientist was gently lifting Eric's limp body from his seat and folding him into her arms. She looked up as Saffron burst back in.

'Why are you doing this?' she demanded. 'We're not hurting these animals, we're helping them.'

'Shut up,' Saffron snapped. 'Get out, now.'

The scientist looked at the grenades in her hands and the computer servers, her face stricken.

'There are almost five years of research on those servers,' she said. 'Everything we've done.'

Saffron turned her back to the scientist and Eric, hissing over her shoulder, 'Get down behind the counter.'

In the glossy black screen of the computer servers, Saffron saw the scientist stare at her for a moment longer.

'You disgust me,' she said, and then ducked out of sight. Saffron stood before the computer servers with a grenade in each hand. She glanced over her shoulder at the seat where Eric had been sitting only moments before. Tears pinched at the corner of her eyes again.

'I'm so sorry,' she whispered softly.

And then she pulled the pins on both grenades before tossing them behind the huge computer servers and diving for cover. The explosives rattled behind them for a second or two, and then the servers vanished amid a blast of vaporized metal.

12

BIO-SCIENCE DIVISION LOS ALAMOS NATIONAL LABORATORIES, LOS ALAMOS

Ethan Warner glanced nervously at Lopez before speaking.

'Hiram Conley was suffering from an infection?'

Tyler Willis nodded, gesturing to one wall of his office where a series of graphs and charts were pinned haphazardly.

'I tracked the course of the infection over six weeks. Never seen anything like it, some kind of telomere mutating bacterium, not a virus. It shared similarities with *Bacillus permians*, but appeared to have evolved differently.'

'Is it transmissible by air?' Lopez asked, touching her face again.

'No,' Willis said firmly, 'this isn't something that's easy to contract. What's fascinating about it is that I was able to extract a genetic profile of the bacterium, and by tracing its mitochondrial signature I was able to ascertain that Hiram Conley had been suffering from this infection for something over one hundred fifty years.'

Ethan thought for a moment.

'So, what is it? Was this guy some kind of zombie or something?'

Willis shook his head.

'No, but that's not the interesting part. The infection was starting to mutate again, and I was trying to find out what was happening when Hiram Conley was shot.'

'How was the mutation affecting him?' Lopez asked.

'That's the really interesting part,' Willis said. 'He was starting to fall apart and—'

Ethan flinched as the deafening sound of an explosion rocked the office around them as though a truck had crashed right outside the walls and smashed its way across the compound.

'Jesus Christ,' Lopez shouted, yanking the office door open. 'What the hell was that?'

Ethan was right behind her, his ears ringing from the explosion.

'Grenades,' he said, recognizing their distinctive sound from his service with the Marine Corps in Iraq and Afghanistan, when the infernal devices had thundered through caves in Tora Bora or were tossed into buildings as his men stormed Taliban strongholds. 'Come on.'

Ethan led the way at a run, unsure of what he would find as they burst out of the administrative building and into the bright sunlight outside. Instantly, Ethan saw the pall of oily black smoke rising from the laboratories opposite. Dozens of scientists in white coats were scattering across the lawns, shouting at each other and pointing uselessly at the destruction behind them.

Ethan looked across the road as he heard a vehicle, and saw a battered old camper pull onto the main road and accelerate away toward the south. Lopez turned toward her car, but Ethan called out to her.

'Get their plate and let them go! There could be casualties here!'

Lopez obeyed without hesitation, squinting at the license plate of the van for a moment before joining Ethan to dash across to the panicked people.

'Was there anybody inside?' Ethan demanded, grabbing the arm of what looked like the most senior of them.

'Two,' the old man said, his features twisted with fury and fear. 'Goddamned activist is still in there with one of my people.'

Ethan didn't wait to hear anything further, turning and plunging through the shattered glass of the entry cubicle and into the foyer. A galaxy of glass crystals twinkled on the blue carpets as he dashed forward toward a narrow corridor filled with a haze of swirling blue smoke. The thick taint of cordite stung his throat and seared his eyes, but he pushed on until he saw a poster warning of hazardous chemical spills. Ethan hesitated, sudden thoughts of infectious diseases and spores floating on the air flashing through his mind.

'It's okay.'

He whirled as Lopez appeared behind him, a simple fabric mask covering her nose and mouth. She handed one to him. 'I checked, no hazardous chemicals.'

Ethan snapped the mask over his face and advanced further down the corridor. Ahead, another cubicle stood with its glass walls shattered by the shockwave of the detonation. Ethan recognized it as a pressure chamber of some kind as he passed through and into the laboratory beyond.

His gaze was quickly drawn to the smoldering remains of what looked like two huge computer mainframes, sparks hissing and spitting from severed power mains and junctions.

'Anybody here?' Ethan shouted, not sure of how else to quickly locate any injured scientists still inside the lab.

'Here!'

The voice was feeble and coming from behind a row of worktops to Ethan's left. He hurried across and saw a young woman in a white coat with what looked like a monkey wrapped in her arms.

Ethan rounded the corner of the workbench. 'Are you okay?'

Before the woman could answer, another woman leapt up from behind the far end of the bench with a sawn-off shotgun.

'Freeze, hero.'

Ethan obeyed, standing silent and looking at the young girl glaring at him from behind the barrel of the shotgun. The girl glanced at Lopez. 'You, Chiquita, on your knees and face the wall.'

Lopez blinked.

'Kiss my ass you little bit—'

'Lopez,' Ethan warned quietly, 'be a good girl and shut up, okay? The gun's pointing at me.' Lopez, scowling, turned her back and knelt facing the wall. Ethan looked at the girl standing not ten feet away. Her belligerence had flickered, momentarily stunned by Lopez's hostility. He edged forward.

'This lady is injured,' he said carefully. 'We need to get her out of here and—'

'The lady is fine and so is the fucking monkey,' the girl hissed. 'Shut up and follow me.'

Ethan shrugged and followed the girl, noting the hard line of her jaw and the thick blonde hair tied up behind her head. She was wearing the cloak of the fearless eco-warrior, but Ethan could see she was gripping the shotgun so tightly her knuckles were white and the barrel of the weapon was trembling.

'Easy,' he said soothingly. 'No need to let this get out of control.'

'Out of control?' she spat. 'Not the sharpest blade in the kitchen, are you?'

'What do you want?'

The girl gestured to the shattered bulk of the computer servers.

'I want you to crawl behind that and look for anything rolling around back there.'

'Such as?' Ethan asked, maneuvering himself alongside the server. The girl kept the shotgun trained on him.

'Things that go bang,' she hissed at him with a humorless smile.

Shit. Ethan guessed that the grenade he had heard had done the damage to the server and that there must be another one that had failed to detonate. Thoughts crashed through his mind. If it was a fused grenade then it had a three-second delay from releasing the pin. Most modern grenades were highly reliable, unless you were unlucky like some Marines who had served in the jungles of Vietnam, where wiry bushes and twigs had pulled the pins from where they hung on the soldiers' belt-kits. The girl watching over him wouldn't likely have access to modern military-grade munitions. That would mean the grenades were probably old, maybe even vintage, black-market devices crudely reactivated using gunpowder and improvised fuses. Unreliable. Volatile. Sensitive to movement.

Ethan knelt down and peered behind the server, flinching as showers of sparks splashed and crackled round him. Through the acrid wisps of blue smoke he saw the grenade lying three feet away from his grasp, faintly illuminated by shafts of light beaming through the wall behind where shrapnel had punched through to the outside world. Prefabricated double-skin aluminum walls, no insulation.

'I can see it,' he coughed to the girl standing watch over him.

'Good,' the girl shot back. Ethan heard her call out to Lopez and the scientist. 'Get out of here, all of you!' Then back to him. 'You, get off your knees and out of there.'

Ethan scrambled to his feet and backed away as the girl jabbed the shotgun at him, prodding him back into the lab as she moved to look down the back of the server. Ethan glanced over his shoulder to see Lopez herding the scientist out of the labs and away down the corridor.

'You're trapped,' he said to the girl. 'The servers are destroyed, so whatever you've come here to do, you've done. Why not put the weapon down while you still can, before the police get here?'

The girl looked at him for a brief moment, as though considering the suggestion, before shaking it off.

'The police are otherwise occupied,' she said tartly, 'and we're done here.'

'Yeah?' Ethan chuckled. 'And what the hell are you going to—'

Ethan whirled as the girl swung the shotgun to point at his head, and in a fraction of a second he knew she was going to pull the trigger. With an instinct born of self-preservation his legs propelled him without conscious thought sideways as he dove for cover behind one of the benches. The shotgun blasted a round over his head and smashed the ceiling above where he'd been standing. Ethan hit the tiled floor hard on his knees and elbows, sprawling as he did so. He squinted through swirling smoke to see the girl take several steps back from the servers and then point the shotgun at the grenade and fire again. A deafening blast ripped through the frame of the servers amid a spray of sparks and clouds of blue smoke from burning relay circuits.

Through the haze and a fine hail of plaster chunks Ethan saw the girl suddenly dash out of sight behind the server, her small frame squeezing through the narrow gap. Ethan scrambled to his feet and rushed to the wall as sparks showered down around him, just in time to see the girl's feet vanish through a ragged hole torn into the building's aluminum skin. He took a deep breath and pushed his way behind the server, heading for the hole, when the barrel of the shotgun appeared suddenly through the gap and a voice hissed at him, 'Don't even think about it, hero.'

Ethan cursed silently to himself as he dragged himself backwards out of the gap and then turned to sprint through the laboratory.

13

'She's gone.'

Lieutenant Enrico Zamora was outside the laboratories as Ethan burst out into the bright sunlight. A small fleet of patrol cars and ambulances, supported by two fire trucks, had arrived to line the edge of the main road, their lights flashing as though a traveling fairground had pulled up in town.

Ethan glanced at the paramedics treating the injured scientists before looking at Zamora.

'She can't have gotten far,' he said. 'She must be in the woods somewhere.'

'You got a description of her?'

Ethan described the girl, and was surprised when Zamora unfolded a picture from his jacket pocket and showed it to him.

'That's her.' Ethan nodded. 'No doubt about it. Who is she?'

'Her name's Saffron,' Zamora replied. 'One of these here anti-vivisectionists who insist on attacking laboratories having anything to do with animal studies.'

'She wasn't alone,' Ethan said. 'You get a trace on the van we saw?'

The officer nodded as he slipped the photograph back into his pocket.

'Found abandoned a few miles from here. Looks like they probably switched vehicles, took those darned apes with them too. We're guessing they'll pick up Saffron somewhere on the ways round.'

Ethan shook his head.

'Doesn't make any sense. They hit the labs to free the monkeys, that I can deal with. But why all the attention on the computer servers?'

Zamora shrugged.

'Who knows what these tree-huggers have got inside their heads, aside from dope and dumb dreams. We left the world in their hands, we'd be living in caves and praying to rocks by th'end of the year.'

'What happened to you guys anyway?' Ethan asked. 'It took almost half an hour for the first patrol cars to get here.'

'False alarm,' Zamora replied. 'Looks like it was done on purpose to divert resources away from Los Alamos.'

Ethan glanced across at the administrative building.

'They knew what they were doing,' he said.

'Any luck with Tyler Willis?' Zamora asked.

'Some,' Ethan said, 'we'll finish questioning him before we leave, see if he knows anything about the people who hit the building here.'

Zamora was about to reply when Lopez joined them.

'That could prove tricky,' she said.

'How come?'

'Because he's taken off,' Lopez said. 'I've checked both buildings twice and nobody's seen him since the blasts. His car's gone too.'

Ethan rubbed his temples before glancing at Zamora.

'Can you get a trace on his vehicle for us?'

'I'll see what I can do,' he replied and hurried away.

'Why would Willis do that?' Ethan wondered out loud. 'He could be in danger, he said it himself.'

'Yeah,' Lopez muttered. 'In danger of losing money. We know what he was doing here, researching something that may help people to double their lifespans. He'd already set himself up in business to profit from the technology, even though he hadn't figured out how it worked yet.'

Ethan rolled the thought around in his mind for a moment.

'You think somebody else wants his work held up?'

'All's fair in love and cut-throat business,' Lopez said. 'These scientists work for the laboratories but they often found companies based on their research, patenting their drugs and genes and things. Willis could have rivals, enemies even, people who know what he's up to and want to get the jump on him. It would explain the need for these activists to hit the computer servers as well as free the animals.'

'Hired help,' Ethan agreed. 'Which means conspiracy, criminal damage, even attempted homicide. We need to find out if Saffron is working for anybody and put the screws into them to see what they sing about.'

'I got some descriptions from the scientists before the

paramedics got to work on them,' Lopez said. 'It's not much, but Zamora reckons he knows at least one of the activists, a Colin Manx. Trouble is they're hard to pin down. According to local police they live rough out in the badlands, never staying in one place for long.'

Ethan surveyed the scene for a moment, thinking hard. Activists like Saffron and Colin Manx were opportunists, ordinary people who rarely had access to major weapons or possessed tactical skills. The likelihood that they had achieved what amounted to a carefully planned strike on a difficult-to-access laboratory told Ethan that, somewhere along the line, there had to be money involved and, more importantly, motive. Freeing monkeys was one thing, but deliberately destroying scientific evidence and endeavor out of sheer spite was another. Ethan had looked into the eyes of Saffron, and whatever he had seen dwelling there did not match her actions. Aggressive? Yes. Desperate? Certainly. Spiteful? Definitely not. She could have killed someone during her attack but had studiously avoided doing so.

'What are you thinking?' Lopez asked curiously.

Ethan turned to her.

'I'll look into Hiram Conley at the town hall and see what I can find. Willis mentioned that there were other people suffering from the same infection as Conley, so I might even find evidence of them there along with Conley's aliases. I want you to start looking for Colin Manx and Tyler Willis. We need to find them before whoever organized this attack gets to them.'

14

BREVIG MISSION
ALASKA

Donald Wolfe looked out of the window of the Beech aircraft as it descended toward a runway that skirted the bleak waters of Lost River Shoal. To the west, vast mountain ranges towered across the horizon, their lofty peaks swathed in snow, while to the east the slate-gray surface of the Bering Sea churned with flecks of white foam.

The aircraft thumped down onto the gravel runway before taxiing to a holding area at the northern end of the field. There was no control tower or terminal, just grim-looking shacks and a small town crouched low against the bitter Arctic winds.

Wolfe opened the door of the aircraft and stepped out. His nose instantly became numb and frost encrusted his eyebrows as he pulled his hood up against the bitter wind. It wasn't snowing, but the ground underfoot was rock-solid permafrost, bitter tundra and clumps of wiry grass that stretched away as far as the eye could see.

'Mister Wolfe?'

A young man approached him from where he had been waiting beside a quad bike. In the distance, Wolfe could see people watching them, native Inuit families who lived in this remotest of outposts far from even the most rudimentary of luxuries like electricity and drive-ins.

'You are?' Wolfe inquired.

'Jason Moore, sir. It's an honor to have you here and—'

'Cut the bullshit,' Wolfe snapped. 'Where is it?'

'The station is out on the tundra,' Moore said quickly. 'We'll have to hurry. The light won't last much longer and you'll need it to fly out again as the runway only has emergency lighting.'

Wolfe nodded as they walked across to the quad bike. Moore started it and Wolfe took his place on the pillion seat. The ride out across the tundra took almost twenty minutes, but it felt like a lifetime. The searing cold bit deep into Wolfe's bones, creeping through his joints to chill the blood in his veins. By the time he'd first glimpsed through the misty air the tents dwarfed by the vast plains, he could no longer feel his hands or feet and his face was aching.

Moore pulled up alongside two large tents that rumbled in the wind blustering across the plains. Wolfe slowly clambered off the bike, his limbs as stiff as wood as he turned full circle, examining the terrain around them. It was brutally cold, and entirely devoid of life. Satisfied, Wolfe followed Moore into the larger of the two tents.

The interior was filled with the hiss and roar of gas fires that billowed clouds of trembling heat. Wolfe gasped, tearing open his thick coat to let the blasts of warm air touch his face and body, wriggling his fingers and toes as they came painfully alive.

Ahead, he could see a clear plastic partition within the tent which was sealed around the edges. Jason Moore was already donning a Level-B HazMat suit and pulling on oversized rubber gloves and boots. Sitting beside him on chairs were another suit and two helmets with sealable neck linings and respirators.

'You'll need these,' Moore said.

'Really?' Wolfe uttered sarcastically, walking across to the suit as he pulled off his jacket. 'My department's hired some real geniuses out here in you guys.'

Jason Moore did not reply. Wolfe pulled on the cumbersome suit, gloves and boots before donning the helmet. Moore then turned to Wolfe and sealed his neck lining before Wolfe did the same for him. As soon as they were both satisfied that their suits were impermeable, Moore spoke through a filter attached to the helmet's perspex view-shield.

'Walk through the site and don't touch anything. The decontamination cubicle is at the far end of the tent. Just stand there and let the showers do their work.'

Wolfe did not acknowledge him, turning instead and pushing through the plastic partition. In front of him was a solid transparent shield door that opened onto a small cubicle. Wolfe slid the door open and stepped inside as Moore followed him and shut the door behind them. They waited, and a moment later a simple vacuum-motor sucked air in from outside and then sealed the outer door shut. A rudimentary low-pressure system was maintained within the interior of the study cubicle to contain contamination, much like the more sophisticated laboratories at USAMRIID.

And if the world had any idea of what was inside, Wolfe reflected, they would have been relieved.

Moore opened the inner door, and Wolfe stepped inside and looked around.

They were standing in a cubicle of two-inch thick perspex ten feet wide, twenty feet long and eight feet high, constructed from simple panels with the joins sealed with thick layers of duct tape. Even the floor was perspex, the tundra crushed flat beneath the weight of the cubicle resting upon it. In the center of the floor an eight foot by two foot panel was missing, exposing an excavation into the permafrost. On one side of the opening was a row of steel tubs filled with recently removed mud and ice. On the other side, a large object partially concealed beneath plastic sheets. Wolfe walked across and looked down into the cavity.

He recognized it instantly as a grave, dug some five feet deep into the ice-encrusted earth. Beside the cavity, lying under a thin plastic sheet nailed into the frozen soil, was an exhumed corpse. The face of a woman stared up at him, her long black hair matted and dirty, her eye sockets sunken and shriveled and her skin leathery. Her jaw hung slackly to expose yellowed teeth.

'How old is the corpse?' Wolfe asked as Moore came to stand alongside him.

'She's confirmed as having died in the year 1918,' Moore said. 'Tissue samples were tested earlier this week, and we even know the person's name. She still has relatives living at Brevig Mission.'

Wolfe nodded.

'And the tissue samples?' he asked. 'Were they viable?'

Jason Moore nodded.

'Perfectly so,' he replied. 'They've been preserved by the permafrost conditions, and I've already tested a small culture of them. They're alive and they'll be perfect for study by your laboratory, sir. I'd like to take this opportunity to thank you for hiring me. The virus, if it ever got out again, could kill millions, perhaps billions. I'm real proud to be a part of preventing that, sir.'

Wolfe did not hear Moore as he stared down at the corpse below them.

'Where are the samples?' Wolfe asked.

'Over there,' Moore said, pointing to a large metal case sealed with warning tapes and a pair of heavy padlocks. 'It's lung tissue from the deceased's body. The casing will maintain the temperature of the tissue for at least forty-eight hours.'

Wolfe nodded and looked around at the tents.

'And you've ensured that this operation has remained discreet?' Wolfe asked. 'There's no chance that anybody could have come here and been infected, or seen this exhumation?'

Moore proudly shook his head.

'No, sir, not a chance. I set up the tents and the cubicles myself, as agreed, to ensure absolute safety. This won't get out until your team have completed their studies and developed the vaccine.' Moore smiled. 'Then we can tell everyone.'

Wolfe nodded, and then turned to face him.

'Not quite everyone, Jason.'

Wolfe's hands had warmed enough for him to reach into his jacket and produce the small pistol nestling in his pocket. He saw Jason Moore's face register neither fear nor surprise but confusion. Wolfe fired twice, the blasts deafening in the confines of the tent. Jason Moore screamed briefly before losing consciousness as the rounds impacted his chest. His arms flailed wildly as his legs crumpled beneath him and he crashed down onto the hard earth at Wolfe's feet.

Wolfe slipped the pistol back into his pocket before shifting his position slightly and shoving Moore's body with his boot so it rolled over the edge of the grave to thump down at the bottom. Wolfe turned, and tipped over two of the metal bins, spilling soil down into the grave to cover Moore's corpse. He clambered down into the cavity and jumped up and down on the soil, felt it give beneath his boots and heard the muffled cracking of breaking bones.

He climbed out of the grave and walked over to the corpse beneath the plastic, pulling the pins from the frozen earth and then with his boot shoving the infected remains back into the grave on top of Moore's inert corpse. He then reached into his other pocket and retrieved a satellite phone, dialing a number from memory. A rattling voice answered.

'What news, Donald?'

'I've acquired the samples,' Wolfe replied. 'You'll have them within twenty-four hours. Rest assured, there will be nobody willing to investigate this site after what's been buried here in the past.'

'Are you sure, Donald?' Jeb Oppenheimer rasped. 'Nobody knows?'

'Nobody,' Wolfe replied. 'My associate here maintained absolute discretion, something he'll be continuing to do for eons to come. What have you gotten from the remains of the man killed in Glorietta Pass?'

'There is much promising research within, but there is also a problem.'

'Which is?'

'We've been maintaining a watching brief on the Los Alamos Laboratories and the Aspen Center in New Mexico. Apparently, there was an explosion at the center earlier today.'

Wolfe stared into the middle distance. 'What kind of explosion?'

'Activists, according to local police sources. Somebody broke in, started shooting at people and then blew up the mainframes within the laboratories. There were no serious injuries and the police investigation is ongoing, but that's not the main problem.'

'Don't tell me,' Wolfe moaned. 'It's something to do with Saffron.'

'It's who the local police are working with on the case,' Oppenheimer said. 'Two investigators who are not state police were seen nosing around the scene, apparently working alongside the police.'

'Do we know who they are exactly?'

'No names yet,' Oppenheimer admitted, 'but they're backed by someone powerful enough for them to be assisted by state troopers. My guess is FBI, at the least.'

Wolfe cursed silently to himself.

'This is exactly what we needed to avoid,' he hissed. 'If you can't keep things under control out there then this whole thing will be for nothing.'

'Calm yourself, Donald. All you need to do is use your military connections to find out who they are and apply pressure where it's needed.'

'Easier said than done,' Wolfe muttered, and then smiled grimly. 'Of course, it'll cost more.'

A throaty chuckle cackled down the line.

'Worry not, Donald, you'll be compensated for your inconvenience. Once you have identified the investigators, I expect them to be eliminated. We wouldn't want your little detour up there to become common knowledge now would we? Who knows who might investigate what you've been up to?'

Wolfe was about to retort when Oppenheimer hung up. He looked down at the frozen grave at his feet for a moment, then turned and grabbed the edge of another of the mud-filled bins. Moments later, the infected corpse had vanished beneath the soil and ice.

15

BUREAU OF VITAL RECORDS
· SANTA FE

15 May, 12.43 p.m.

'This way, Mister Warner.'

Ethan followed a middle-aged, primly dressed clerk from the reception desk through a large door that led to the record hall. Towering ranks of shelves held carefully filed boxes dating back decades, perhaps even centuries. It had taken a call from Doug Jarvis to get Ethan immediate access to the records, much to the chagrin of the clerk. Most public requests for records could take weeks to disseminate, time that Ethan could ill afford to waste.

The building itself was a large modern construction, allied to the births and deaths office further down South St Francis Drive.

'The census runs back to the 1790s,' the clerk informed him, slightly less frosty now. 'Birth and death certificates are much less complete however, owing to the turbulent and transient nature of our citizens over the earliest centuries of arrival here.'

Ethan looked up at the shelves and cabinets as they walked through the silent hall.

'I've got a birth certificate here, which corresponds to a man by the name of Conley, but we're trying to trace the line further back.'

'Births are over there,' the clerk pointed, to where two rows of cabinets stretched wall to wall. 'They're alphabetically arranged.'

Ethan thanked the clerk, and was about to walk across to the shelves when his cell phone rang in his pocket, echoing loudly across the hall. Ethan grabbed it, setting it to 'silent' before answering.

'Warner.'

'It's Zamora,' came the reply, his accent heavy over the line. 'Picked up something interesting for you regarding the attack on the center in Los Alamos.'

'Go for your life.'

'The woman who led the attack, who you chased in the laboratory – Saffron? Turns out that she's the grand-daughter of none other than Jeb Oppenheimer. You ever heard of him?'

'Should I?' Ethan asked as he walked slowly between the towering shelves.

'He's the sole owner and operator of SkinGen, a global pharmaceutical company that's headquartered in Santa Fe. It's one of New Mexico's biggest employers, and this Oppenheimer fella has his fingers into every government pie going, from local right up to the White House some say.'

Ethan stopped walking.

'What's Saffron Oppenheimer's angle on all of that?'

'She's his only living relative and heir to the SkinGen empire, but she wants none of it. Her parents died in a tragic automobile accident over a decade ago, as did Jeb's wife. She's alienated from him, refuses to have any part in the company and has actively denounced all vivisection operations states wide. In short, they're sworn enemies.'

Ethan blinked. He'd heard of SkinGen, if not its owner, and he knew that it was worth billions of dollars. Saffron Oppenheimer's motivation, or confusion, must be almost superhuman.

'Thanks, Enrico, I'll get back to you as soon as we learn anything more.'

Ethan rang off and grabbed a nearby rolling stepladder, pulling it along behind him until he found a section of shelves marked CO. He stood on the step, reaching up and tracing the letters on the shelf edges until he reached CONL. He found a single box, thick with dust and sagging slightly at the edges, beneath another marked CONN. Ethan levered the box carefully out, carried it to a study table and sat down. He opened the box and began sifting through the reams of papers that became increasingly faded and yellowed the deeper he delved.

The truth was he wasn't entirely sure what he was looking for, but beside him on the table was the document given him by Doug Jarvis back in Chicago. The birth certificate for Hiram Conley, born Las Cruces in New Mexico, 1940. Judging by the documents Ethan was pulling from the box, the layout and style of the certificate indeed most closely matched those dated around 1940. The birth details could still have been forged, but what interested Ethan was that, forged or not, it looked every bit as old as it claimed to be.

'So far, so normal,' Ethan murmured to himself, turning his attention to the second name Jarvis had given him, Abner Conley.

According to the paperwork, Hiram had sometimes used the name Abner, with occasional receipts signed as evidence. Ethan couldn't be sure if that meant that Hiram was deliberately using another name or was perhaps suffering from some kind of age-related amnesia or confusion.

A document appeared as he flicked through a dense wad of papers, the name at the top corner catching his eye. Abner Conley. Ethan gently pulled the aged sheaf of paper from the pile and felt a twinge of intrigue as he read: Abner Conley, born Las Cruces, New Mexico: March 9th, 1880.

He stared at the document for a moment longer, and then began shuffling through the ever older and more fragile scraps of paper, some of them so worn that he feared they would crumble beneath his fingertips. Reaching out, he took a pair of fine rubber gloves from a box on the edge of the study table and slipped them on before continuing, until another document, this one ragged at the edges and soft to the touch, caught his eye.

Hiram Conley, born Las Cruces, New Mexico: March 9th, 1807.

'I'll be damned,' he murmured, and set the documents alongside each other.

It was not unusual for sons to be named after their father, and in fact in states like New Mexico it was commonplace. What *was* more unusual was that none of the names gave any clue that they were inherited. Hiram

Conley III or similar would have been more credible. Not to mention the fact that all three of the supposed births occurred on the same date in the records, March 9th, something that Hiram may have done to ease recall when required.

Ethan looked up at the shelves around him, and then down toward the front of the hall where a computer terminal and copier occupied a sturdy table. Ethan made copies of all of the documents before carefully replacing them in the box and putting it back on the shelves. Then, he sat down behind the computer terminal. The server was dedicated to the county clerk's office, and contained digitized images of all records and photographs going back hundreds of years.

Ethan began typing search commands into the computer, scanning through dozens of records, newspaper stories and photographs relating to the name Hiram Conley. Lists flashed up one by one, older and more vague as he searched.

'Come on, damn it,' he muttered to himself. 'Just one, that's all I need.'

After an hour, he had gone back to the 1880s, finding numerous mentions of both Hiram and Abner Conley, but no images. Given the scarcity of cameras at the time he considered that only to be expected. Those that did exist used albumen print photography that produced images from large glass negatives. Fatigue began to pull at his eyes, and his arm ached as he scrolled dutifully down through endless slides and plates, yellowing images of old frontier towns, families in archaic clothes and tall hats standing in front of colonial-style houses. Paintings of notable figures from history such as Abraham Lincoln, or brave women who had served alongside their husbands, fathers or brothers in the Union army during the Civil War popped out at him and were passed by as he diligently continued his search. An ancient newspaper scrap, torn along the bottom edge but photographed for posterity, caught his eye. A group of seven men in Union uniforms stood shoulder to shoulder beside some kind of old wagon, a tall officer in their midst staring down at the camera with cold, hard eyes above a broad moustache.

Ethan froze, staring at the image.

There, third from left, stood a man with a beard and a huge musket, the butt standing on the floor at his feet and the bayonet resting against his shoulder. The face leapt out at Ethan, and he fumbled in his pocket and produced a photograph of Hiram Conley, taken just days before by Enrico Zamora in Glorietta Pass. He held the image up to the screen.

'Goddamn.'

Hiram Conley stared out from the screen at Ethan, a serious expression on his features and a clay-burner pipe jutting from his mouth. Ethan looked at the title of the photograph.

SURVIVORS OF THE BATTLE OF
GLORIETTA PASS, NEW MEXICO
March 1862

Ethan took one more look at the photograph handed him by Doug Jarvis, and then printed out the photograph from the computer terminal and carefully folded all the documents into his pocket, still unable to come to terms with what the evidence was telling him.

With a brief thank you to the clerk, Ethan hurried out of the hall.

16

SKINGEN CORP
SANTA FE

'I can assure you, Mister Oppenheimer, that your investment in my company will represent a guaranteed return of between twelve and fifteen percent in real terms over the next five years.'

Jeb Oppenheimer sat behind a broad glass desk, uncluttered except for a speaker phone and an unobtrusive plasma screen connected to a mini hard-drive and keyboard. The office was carpeted with deep white pile, the walls painted ice white with massive windows looking out over the Petroglyph and the state park beyond.

'Fifteen percent?' Oppenheimer murmured as he caressed the top of his walking cane, the finely polished chrome handle gleaming in the sunlight.

'Guaranteed.'

The earnest young man sitting opposite Oppenheimer was one of a dozen or so potential investment partners who variously groveled, promised or lied their way into his office each week for the chance to buy into the SkinGen fortune. Oppenheimer only allowed them this far as a means to relieve the boredom of signing endless legal documents and firing employees who had failed their targets for the month. Oppenheimer liked targets: they provided leverage, especially when they were kept mostly out of reach of his legions of staff striving desperately to achieve them and their promised bonuses.

'Twenty percent then, if we can achieve it,' the young man said.

Oppenheimer blinked. He was instantly disappointed – the man's will had broken before Oppenheimer had given any indication that he was even interested, let alone willing to barter. Just like all those who had come and gone before him he was spineless, a runt begging for scraps from the feast of Oppenheimer's table, willing to crawl on his knees through the detritus below to nibble on what meager crumbs he might find.

'Twenty percent?' Oppenheimer murmured, to an eager nod from William Hancock.

Hancock's plan was to harness the remarkable data-storage power of Flash-Ram Memory and the abundance of trashed outdated home computers in order to build small, cheap, portable, solar-powered laptop computers for distribution to Third World countries. Built-in advertising for major firms would cover manufacturing and distribution costs, leaving the rest for profit. No batteries, no demand on electrical grids, the computers themselves built from the recycled plastics of their forlorn predecessors now languishing on garbage heaps country-wide. Minimal outlay, Hancock reckoned, something in the order of twenty-five million dollars. Hundreds of thousands, if not millions, of disadvantaged children would benefit across Africa, India, the Malay Archipelago and a thousand other territories both obscure and irrelevant to Oppenheimer.

'And who is paying for these laptops,' Oppenheimer asked wearily, 'upon delivery?'

'The governments of the countries concerned.' Hancock smiled.

Oppenheimer nodded as though he understood.

'I see. Mister Hancock, much as I admire the principal behind your business plan, it behooves me to remark upon the astonishing imbecility that seems to have infected your puny brain.'

William Hancock's smile collapsed. He opened his mouth to protest, but was silenced by Oppenheimer's wrinkly hand.

'Charity is a remarkable thing,' Oppenheimer said slowly, choosing his words. 'It makes ordinary men commit acts of near suicidal economic stupidity as though, having made successes of themselves, they should then hurl themselves off cliffs. Tell me, Mister Hancock, why you wouldn't instead have built more advanced, more expensive computers and sold them here in America for ten times the profit?'

Hancock, his jaw agape, struggled for words.

'But we're both successful people, and we can afford to invest in technologies that can help disadvantaged families from poor countries who need access to—'

'They need clean fucking water!' Oppenheimer exploded, smashing his cane down across the glass table between them with a deafening crack. 'They need food, clothes, medicines and homes! You know what they'll do with your pissy little computers when they get their dirty little hands on them? They'll sell them on the black market to stall traders or slave dealers or witchdoctors or whoever the hell they can, in exchange for a bottle of water and a goddamned chicken nugget!'

Oppenheimer reined himself in, taking a deep breath as he felt his heart fluttering dangerously within the narrow cage of his emaciated chest. His voice rattled when he spoke, dislodged strings of mucus clinging damply to the walls of his throat.

'The only reason for the starving and suffering of the masses in the Third World is the incompetence of their leaders. We are asked day in and day out to give a dollar for little children dying of starvation in Africa, give a dime for the digging of wells in India, give a few bucks to sponsor some fucking baby panda in China. Doesn't it ever cross your tiny little mind that if their own governments spent a little less on blowing the crap out of each other and a little more on charity at home, then we may not have to keep shoring up their pathetic legions?'

William Hancock stood bolt upright from the table, his face flushed with impotent fury.

'Bad things happen,' he said, 'when good people do nothing.'

Oppenheimer, with some strain, pushed on the top of his cane and got to his feet, leveling Hancock with an uncompromising glare.

'Bad things happen when good people act like idiots,' he snapped back, pacing round the desk toward him. 'When governments overtax their citizens while reducing social services and medical care; when bureaucrats waste millions of taxpayers' money on useless initiatives which are then abandoned; when bankers screw up the economy time and time again and then expect ordinary people to foot the bill while they award themselves billions in bonuses and retire on million-dollar pensions; when criminals are pampered in jail by spineless human rights activists while elderly war veterans freeze in their apartment blocks because they can't afford the heating bills. But do you know who the idiots are? Not the governments, not the bureaucrats, the bankers or the criminals. It's people like you, because you're so busy pissing about trying to solve the problems of people in distant lands who'll never actually receive the help you're offering that you've forgotten about your own damned countrymen!'

William Hancock stared at Oppenheimer, no longer able to speak. Oppenheimer jabbed him sharply in the chest with his cane.

'Get out of my office before I take this and shove it up your ass.'

The horrified Hancock turned in stunned silence and walked stiffly out of the office, passing an attractive young blonde woman who had obviously been waiting outside. Oppenheimer watched her with interest as she glided in, closing the door behind her and briefly displaying the backs of her long slender legs that disappeared up into a short white skirt so tight it made her ass look like two peaches wrapped in silk.

'What have you got for me this morning, Claire?' he asked, trying to ease his strained nerves and forcing himself to breathe calmly.

Claire Montgomery, Oppenheimer's personal assistant of the past two months, strode across to the glass desk
and leaned forward. Oppenheimer gazed down her
blouse as she passed him a file, catching a glimpse of the
pendulous breasts dangling within.

'From Donald Wolfe, sir,' Claire said with a smile that
suggested she either hadn't noticed the direction of his
stare or was too professional to mention it. 'He requested
that you look at it immediately, it's extremely
important.'

Oppenheimer dragged his gaze down to the file.

'Sit down, stay a while.' He gestured to the chair
opposite without looking at her. Claire sat down
obediently.

Within moments of opening the file, Oppenheimer
had forgotten Claire's charms and was completely
engrossed.

Donald Wolfe had used his position at USAMRIID
to obtain information on the events surrounding the
Glorietta Pass shooting of three days previously.
Bizarrely, the government had not dispatched a single
official person to investigate either the disappearance of
the body of Hiram Conley from the county morgue,
nor had they officially supported the county sheriff's
investigation into the disappearance of Lillian Cruz.
However, what was intriguing was the two out-of-
towners who had been given the lead in the investigation,
apparently with the blessing of both the state police and
the sheriff's office.

'Who the hell are these two?' Oppenheimer wondered
out loud as he read.

Ethan Warner, a former United States Marine turned bail bondsman and private investigator. Nicola Lopez, formerly a detective with Washington DC's finest, now partnered with Warner. Oppenheimer frowned. Donald Wolfe's contacts had been unable to figure out who Warner and Lopez were working for, but so far had managed to rule out DEA, FBI and even the CIA as interested parties.

Whoever Warner and Lopez were working for, they could be of little consequence if they were hiring two low-life bondsmen to investigate. Warner & Lopez Inc. operated out of Chicago, which meant they were a long way from home. The will to travel meant that they needed the work, which meant they were most likely poor themselves, and Oppenheimer knew the power of hard cash to change allegiances. They could of course refuse, in which case he knew exactly the kind of men who made their own living disposing of people on Oppenheimer's behalf.

An accident would be arranged, quickly and quietly.

He pressed a button on his speakerphone, and the voice of his events coordinator replied efficiently.

'Yes, Mister Oppenheimer?'

'Have my car and driver ready. I wish to leave in the next thirty minutes or so.'

He needed to clear his mind and rid himself of the latent irritation infecting him in William Hancock's wake. His gaze drifted up to Claire sitting expectantly opposite him. She smiled softly, one leg crossed over the other to reveal a perfectly shaped thigh and flawless skin. Nerve endings he hadn't thought about in months tingled evocatively.

Oppenheimer stood up from behind his desk and beckoned to her with one gnarled finger.

'Come here, Claire.'

His assistant got to her feet and walked slowly round the table to him, a flicker of apprehension passing like a shadow across her immaculate features.

'What can I do for you, Mister Oppenheimer?'

He smiled, putting his cane to one side and pressing a button on his table top. Instantly, the windows in the office turned opaque.

'Just like last time, Claire, understood?'

Claire's beautiful face was now furtive and she refused to meet his eye. Oppenheimer took her thick blonde hair in one fist, turning it firmly in his bony digits so that she was forced to look at him. A pair of wide blue eyes stared into his, the same eyes that had glittered excitedly a month ago when he had discreetly offered to double her salary after working for the company for less than five weeks.

'Your pay rise was performance-related, Claire, remember?' he rattled. 'Everyone has to fulfill their commitments if they wish to remain part of SkinGen. Targets, my dear, are everything.'

Oppenheimer released her hair and gripped her shoulders, turning her to face away from him before pushing her forward and bending her over his desk. He reached down and yanked her skirt up, reveling in the sight of her sublime ass while with his free hand he began hurriedly unhitching his pants before it was too late.

He knew that Claire wouldn't last much more than a month or two before she finally quit, but then none of his assistants ever had and the change did him good. This time, she didn't even whimper as he penetrated her.

As he gripped Claire's narrow waist in his gnarled hands, grimacing as he shunted his bony hips vigorously against her prostrate body, he reflected that everybody had their price. Even Warner and Lopez.

17

NEW MEXICO DPS FORENSICS LABORATORIES SANTA FE

'Seriously, the place was wiped clean, not a trace.'

Lopez nodded wearily, mentally scratching another avenue of investigation off her list. She was standing in the foyer of a laboratory that handled all forensic investigations for Santa Fe's law enforcement agencies, and had been responsible for the investigation of the morgue from which Hiram Conley's apparently mummified remains had vanished.

'Any ideas of who might have had a motive for abducting Lillian Cruz?'

The lab technician, an elderly guy by the name of Rodriguez, shook his head.

'I worked with her a few times out Albuquerque way when she ran the morgue there. She was the best, no doubt about it, been working in the department for as long as I can remember. What she couldn't tell you about rates of decay and infestation wasn't worth knowing. Point is, everyone liked her, never heard a bad word said.'

'And she never had any contact with Tyler Willis?'

'*The* Tyler Willis?' Rodriguez repeated. 'No way, that guy is stellar, something to do with genetics out Los Alamos way. I've read a few of his papers. The high priests don't have much time for us guys down in the morgues.'

'Okay,' Lopez conceded finally, 'thanks for your time.'

Lopez walked out of the foyer, pausing on the side-walk and breathing deeply in the warm air. The mountains in the distance, faded as they were in the haze beneath the flawless blue sky, reminded her again of home, as did the occasional road sign in Spanish and the little stores selling Aztec-style trinkets.

She sighed as she cut across a street to where she'd parked. Almost a third of her meager salary went on supporting her increasingly frail parents. She knew that the rest of her family were doing their best, but there was no substitute for American dollars in Guanajuato. Sometimes she'd even thought about . . .

She froze. A man walking down Camino Entrada toward a nearby steakhouse caught her attention. He was sauntering along the sidewalk with his face shielded from both the sun and from observation by a baseball cap pulled low over his eyes. Lewis Delaware III. Twenty-nine. Possession with intent to supply. Released on an eight-thousand-dollar bond signed by his own legal representative, the creep had vanished right after he'd walked from Cook County Jail.

Lopez turned, letting her long black hair fall half across her face in the breeze as she walked across the street, deliberately not walking toward Delaware but veering to one side to avoid attracting attention – forgetting that she was wearing leather boots and a black vest that hugged her breasts above a pair of tight jeans. It was like trying to hide candy from a kid: any guy within a hundred yards couldn't miss her.

Sure enough, Delaware turned his head and glanced across at her, lifting his chin to check her out. A flare of alarm panicked his features as he stopped mid-stride twenty yards away. Lopez covered her dismay at having been spotted with a cheerful smile.

'Morning, Lewis,' she called brightly. 'Don't run or I'll kick your ass.'

Delaware flashed her a nervous grin, whirled and took off down the sidewalk.

Lopez launched herself in pursuit, wishing once again for the comforting feeling of a pistol by her side. Cans of pepper spray and nightsticks were handy, but they weren't so hot against bullets. Lopez watched as Delaware, scrawny and out of shape, ran with a gangly gait past an automobile trader, barreling past a BMW pulling out in front of him. Lopez dodged past the vehicle with a single bound, lithe as an antelope as she bore down on the frantic Delaware, who glanced over his shoulder at her, his eyes wide with panic.

Delaware aimed for an old Lincoln parked at the end of Camino Ortiz, clearly hoping to make a break for it before she caught him. Lopez gave her all and accelerated as she yanked her collapsible baton from her jeans and flicked it open before hurling it at Delaware's legs. The baton span through the air and sliced neatly between his calves, interrupting their passage enough to send the kid sprawling face down onto the hot asphalt in a tangle of limbs, his cap flying from his head. Lopez reached him as he scrambled back to his feet and yanked his fists up defensively in front of his face, glowering at her as he panted for breath.

'I told you not to run, Lewis,' she said.

'I ain't goin' to jail,' he gasped. 'You ain't takin' me.'

'No?'

Lopez reached out with her left hand to grab his left wrist. As Delaware pulled it back and exposed his face, Lopez jabbed a fast right straight into his eye. He yelped, staggered backwards and collapsed to his knees with his face in his hands.

'Jesus Christ!' he cried as Lopez yanked him to his feet, flashing her bondsman badge as curious citizens watched them from the parking lot of a Saab dealership, and cuffed Delaware.

She dragged him, still whimpering, across the street to a narrow alley. Delaware turned, unsteady on his feet, real fear starting to spread like an infection across his face.

'What the hell is this?' he uttered. 'I want to speak to my—'

Lopez strode forward and drove one knee into his groin. A strangled gasp later and the kid was on his knees. She moved around behind him, squatted down and whispered in his ear.

'Listen good, Lewis. I'm going to empty your pockets and anything I find that I don't like, I'm going to borrow, okay?'

Delaware opened his mouth to reply, but only a faint whistling squeaked from his throat.

Lopez emptied his pockets, finding two hundred bucks in cash, a small wrap of what looked like marijuana and two crumpled packs of cigarettes.

'You've got weed,' she hissed. 'Both know what possession means, right, Lewis?'

'Don't tell 'em,' Lewis whined pathetically. 'Please don't tell 'em.'

'Get up,' she ordered, gripping his cuffed wrists and yanking them into his shoulder blades, eliciting another squeal of pain. 'What they don't find you won't miss, understood?'

With more force than was necessary Lopez pushed Delaware back to where she'd parked her car outside a nearby mall. She was in the process of wedging him into the rear seat when she saw Ethan walking toward her. He glanced at Delaware as she booted him aboard the car.

'Busy afternoon?' he asked.

'Productive.' Lopez nodded, shutting the door and handing him Lewis's packets of cigarettes. 'Saw him jaywalking back there, easiest pull we've had in months. How about you?'

Ethan took the cigarettes from her. 'This all he had? Thought he'd be dealing, all the way out here.'

'Nothing on him,' Lopez said calmly with a shrug. 'Doesn't mean that wherever he's been staying is clean.'

'We don't have time to get search warrants,' Ethan said, and handed her the printed copy of the photograph from the town hall. 'Recognize anybody?'

Lopez scanned the image and gasped.

'I'll be damned. Willis was right.'

'You found him yet?'

'No,' Lopez admitted, swiping a strand of hair from out of her eyes and noticing Ethan watching her as she did so. 'Nobody has any leads on either Tyler Willis or Lillian Cruz. Which means we're left with trying to find either Saffron Oppenheimer or Colin Manx, both of whom probably have nothing to do with the disappearances.'

Ethan filled her in on Saffron Oppenheimer's family history, both illustrious and tragic at the same time.

'There's a motive for her hitting laboratories all right,' Ethan said, the hot wind moaning down the street tousling his light brown hair. 'And it may explain her taking such care to hit the computer servers before she left.'

'Industrial espionage?' Lopez murmured. 'You think that she's actually working for Grandpa?'

'It fits if Tyler's work in any way conflicts with SkinGen's,' Ethan said with a shrug. 'Saffron hits labs working in similar fields to slow down their research. Right now, we don't have much else to go on. Local police have searched Tyler Willis's apartment and found nothing out of the ordinary. Enrico suspects that whatever he was working on, the details are being held elsewhere.'

Lopez nodded.

'Which means that somebody else was looking for them, or at least Tyler suspected that they were, and hid his work.' Ethan smiled at her, teasing her along. 'I'm

not Sherlock Holmes,' she said, 'but I guess it does tie
Jeb Oppenheimer to both Saffron and Tyler Willis. Still,
it's a long shot.'

'Not so long that we shouldn't pursue it,' Ethan said.
'Time to go and join the natives.'

Lopez jabbed a thumb at Lewis Delaware.

'We can drop this asshole off along the way.'

Ethan nodded as he walked around to the passenger
door. Lopez waited until he was on the other side of the
car before discreetly tossing the small wrap of marijuana
into a nearby trash can.

18

JEMEZ CANYON RESERVOIR
NEW MEXICO

'What the hell were you thinking?'

Colin Manx's face was taut with rage, his frizzy hair trembling as he glared at Saffron Oppenheimer.

'I *was* thinking,' Saffron said without concern. 'That's the difference between you and me.'

Manx struggled for a response, glancing at the thirty or so people gathered round them and an aged NAPCO GMC Suburban. A mixture of hippies, college drop-outs and petty criminals with nowhere else to go, they represented a small army of individuals who didn't possess the sense to realize that their actions against the state and science would get them nowhere except jail. They stared wide-eyed at Saffron Oppenheimer, and for a moment she thought that they might go down on their knees and prostrate themselves before her. She, alone, had led them to what they considered their greatest ever victory since casting themselves out from society into the Pecos Wilderness.

Saffron Oppenheimer, for her part, despised each and every one of them.

'Is that what you call it?' Manx raged. '*Thinking?* You fired a shotgun, put several scientists in hospital, stole all the animals and then you blew up the computers in the goddamned laboratory.'

'Go, Saffron!' Ruby Lily squealed from nearby. A ripple of delighted chuckles fluttered through the watching groupies as Ruby pointed at Saffron. 'You should have seen her, she was awesome!'

Manx scowled.

'Yeah, awesome enough that we'll likely have the FBI hunting us down now!'

Saffron sighed, examining a small cut on her finger from her escape out of the laboratories.

'If only you were that important, Colon,' she murmured to another round of sniggers from behind them.

'We were supposed to make a statement and free one of the chimps,' Manx snapped, his bluster losing conviction in the face of her disinterest. 'Not blow the place sky-high!'

Saffron shrugged.

'If a job's worth doing . . .'

Manx glared at her while occasionally peering sideways, seeking support from the crowd. Saffron could tell that none was forthcoming as Manx pulled himself up to his full height, building up to something.

'You've gone too far,' he snarled. 'It's time to cut you down to size.'

With a startling howl of what Saffron presumed was rage, Manx lunged toward her. His big, dirty hands shot out to her wrists in an attempt to force her to the ground. Saffron acted without thought or worry, stepping not away from Manx but toward him, turning sideways and ducking down as his hands shot past her face. With a heave of effort she drove her right elbow deep into his stomach just beneath his ribs. The howl was cut short as Manx gagged and a blast of foul air rushed from his mouth. He doubled over, just in time for Saffron's knee to jerk up and smash across the bridge of his nose with a dull crunch like an eggshell crushed beneath her boots. Winded and blinded in less than a second, Manx flipped over and collapsed gasping onto the hot desert sand. Saffron looked down at him.

'Good work, Colon,' she murmured without pity.

The group around her laughed openly now. They were hers without a doubt. Manx struggled to his knees, coughing and spluttering, tears staining his dusty face as he squinted up at her.

'You're insane!' he bleated.

Saffron turned her back to him, walking away toward the camper van. 'And you're pathetic. Get lost.'

Another round of laughs followed. Saffron saw in the windows of the GMC the reflection of Manx staggering to his feet, clutching his face and stomach as he made his unsteady way toward the main road, a quarter of a mile to the south. She waited until he was out of earshot, busying herself with cleaning her shotgun. From behind, she heard the groupies tentatively approaching, and the gentle noises made by the chimpanzees in the back of the GMC as they guzzled from recently refilled water bottles.

Ruby Lily's voice squeaked again.

'Let's free the monkeys!'

A chorus of delighted cheers burst out as Ruby Lily dashed to the rear of the vehicle to open the main doors, where the cages were stacked. She had almost reached them when Saffron took two paces toward her, gripping her wrist in one hand and twisting it sideways. Ruby Lily cried out in alarm as she dropped onto one knee, trying to get away from the pain. Saffron glared down at her.

'Are you a complete idiot?' she demanded.

Ruby Lily looked up at her in confusion as Saffron released her and looked at the rest of the crowd.

'These are Bonobo Chimpanzees from West Africa. They were raised in captivity and have learned to trust humans.' She paused. 'To a point. They have also been experimented on, kept in cages, and watched members of their troop go into operating theaters and never return. Chimpanzees have a muscle density far greater than ours, and are easily capable of tearing a human being to pieces with their bare hands.' She let the point sink in. 'What do you think they'll do if they get out and can run free?'

Saffron waited until they realized that an answer was expected.

'They'll hurt people,' someone said in a voice that sounded thin, as though they'd been up all night smoking dope.

'Well done, Einstein,' Saffron mocked. 'They can also carry diseases that can kill, Ebola Zaire being the most lethal. We have no idea what was being done to them in the laboratories, therefore we don't know what dangers they pose to us. We'll take them to the nearest zoo in the morning and leave them there.'

Dismay soured the faces of everyone in the group, and Saffron slammed the GMC's door shut.

'Okay then,' she said. 'What do *you* think we should do with them?'

Silence enveloped the group and the desert around them. Saffron waited, feeling like a teacher in front of a kindergarten class. She doubted that the thirty of them could muster an IQ of a hundred between them, doped, drugged and mindless as they were.

'Maybe I should put all of you in the van and let the chimps decide?' Saffron snapped. 'Get their water bottles refilled, and then get the van covered with brush and whatever else you can find. It's going to get hotter and they need shade, understood? I'm going to scout the area, make sure it's secure. We don't want the FBI searching for Colon out here, do we?'

With a mixture of chuckles as well as some discontented mumbling, the group dispersed. Saffron turned and aimed for the nearest hill, hiking up through thick brush along a ridge that lined one of a series of gullys descending down into the valley floor behind her, where the Jemez Reservoir glittered. The blue water was formed by the Jemez Canyon Dam, built in 1953 and owned by the US Army Corps of Engineers. It took almost twenty minutes to reach the high point she sought, where the hot desert winds rumbled. She surveyed the surrounding terrain and fished in her pocket for a cell phone, then dialed a number from memory, waiting for the line to connect and watching the windows of distant vehicles flashing silently in the sunlight on the distant I-25.

'Go ahead.'

The rattling, croaking voice filled her with a loathing that she struggled to conceal.

'It's done.'

'Good. Where is Tyler Willis?'

'Your men took him when we hit the labs,' Saffron said. 'You'll have to ask them.'

'Excellent work, Saffron. I'm very proud.'

'I want your word,' Saffron demanded. 'Not a mark on him, understood?'

A moment later, the line went dead.

Saffron shut the phone off and slipped it back into her pocket before gazing out over the cruel beauty of the New Mexico wilderness. She sighed and wondered again if she was doing the right thing. Colin Manx was a weak man, and weak men did the bidding of the strong. All that she could hope for was that she had hit Manx hard enough, both mentally and physically, for him to fulfill his role.

And that she had the strength to do what she had planned for so long.

19

PAN AMERICAN CENTRAL HIGHWAY NEW MEXICO

'We're chasing rainbows here, you know that, don't you?'

Ethan drove with one arm trailing out of the Mercury's open window, letting the desert wind blow in. He preferred it to the cold caress of air con, and while the car was moving it was cool enough to let him get away with it.

'We don't have much else to go on,' he said to Lopez, who was sitting with her long hair rippling in the breeze and her sneakers resting against the dashboard on which a printed image of Saffron Oppenheimer and Colin Manx was taped. 'Without Willis, we don't really know who or what we're after.'

'I doubt we'll find enlightenment out here,' Lopez said. 'Chances of a bunch of drop-outs knowing anything about experiments at Los Alamos is pretty unlikely, doesn't matter who their grandpa is.'

'You got any better ideas?' he asked Lopez. 'The troopers reckoned this was the likely escape route for Saffron Oppenheimer and Colin Manx after they ditched their original vehicle outside Los Alamos, but they don't have the resources to scour the entire desert.'

Lopez laughed, shaking her head.

'What?' Ethan asked, smiling in bemusement.

'The whole of New Mexico's state police don't have the resources to search a million square miles of desert,' she said, 'but you're driving the two of us out here because you think we somehow do. I can't wait to see how you pull this off. Divining rods? Sifting tea leaves?'

Ethan grinned and shrugged.

'You've got to be in the draw to win it. For all you know, one of them will come walking right to us out of this town.'

'Ten bucks says no way,' Lopez said, extending her hand, her eyes dancing with the unfettered joy of a sure bet.

Ethan chuckled and shook her hand as they cruised through the small town of Algodones. They crossed the railway line and passed a small diner, an elementary school and scattered houses that gave way to open scrubland, the railway line now to their left.

'Looks like you're ten bucks down,' Lopez said as they left the town behind. She settled down deeper into her reclined seat and closed her eyes. 'Win some, lose some.'

Ethan didn't reply as he eased off the accelerator, indicated and pulled into the side of the road. He leaned out of his window as the man he'd seen flagging them down staggered over, his face and shaggy hair a dusty mess and blood trickling from a badly broken nose.

'Need a lift, stranger?' Ethan asked with a smile.

'You goin' Santa Fe way soon?' the man asked, his voice thick with pain.

'Sure,' Ethan said.

Lopez opened her eyes, curious now. Ethan said nothing as the back door opened and Colin Manx slumped into the rear seat in a cloud of dust, slamming his door and looking at them.

'Thanks, I really appreciate this.'

Lopez's jaw dropped as Ethan, his face aching from trying not to smile, reached out and pressed a button on the dash, instantly locking all the doors.

'So do we,' he said, turning in his seat to face Manx and showing him his bail bondsman badge. 'We've been looking for you.'

Manx stared in confusion at the badge, then at the image of himself taped to the dashboard.

'I'm not on bail.'

'Nope,' Ethan said, 'but you're wanted by the sheriff's office so we'll be taking you in.'

'Fine by me,' Manx said sulkily, folding his arms. 'What I was coming here for.'

Now, it was Ethan's turn to be surprised.

'You're turning yourself in?' Lopez asked, finally overcoming her disbelief enough to speak.

'Damn right I am!' Manx snapped. 'They're insane, all of them, especially that bitch Saffron. She'll kill somebody before she's done, and I don't want any part of it.'

Ethan eyed Manx. 'You know where she is?'

Manx nodded, jabbing a thumb out the window up in the direction of the nearby hills.

'Up there, a couple of miles north of the reservoir

with about thirty others. They've got the animals with them in an old GMC. God knows what she's going to do next.'

Ethan looked at Lopez.

'They can't go off-road in their truck, it won't take it, and there's only one way up or down.'

'One on the high ground, the other on the road,' Lopez agreed, sweeping her long hair back behind one tiny ear with her hand. 'They'll be forced out on foot.'

Colin Manx looked at them both in alarm.

'What the hell are you two talking about? I want to go to a police station, turn myself in.'

'We need to find Saffron,' Ethan said. 'It's important.'

'I need to make a statement first,' Manx complained. 'I want the police to know I turned evidence for all of this. I don't want to go to jail.'

'You'll be going to jail anyway,' Lopez snapped. 'It's too late for that, but we can tell the police everything.'

'Then tell them now!' Manx shouted and began yanking desperately on the door handle beside him.

'Sorry,' Ethan said, pulling onto the main road and accelerating the Mercury south. 'We need to get to Saffron before the police do.'

Colin Manx quivered with futile rage and thumped the seat beside him.

'You can't do this! This is abduction!'

Lopez reached back and grabbed Manx's throat with an iron grip.

'It'll be goddamned assault if you don't quit whining.'

Lopez shoved Manx back into his seat. He massaged

his throat, tears in his eyes as he shook his head in despair and looked at Ethan's reflection in the rear-view mirror.

'Jesus Christ, has every woman on earth gone insane?'

'No,' Ethan murmured, keeping his eyes on the road. 'This is fairly standard behavior.'

'She'll likely resist arrest,' Lopez said as she pinned her hair back into a ponytail, clearly anticipating a fight, 'and she's tooled up with at least a shotgun. We've got nothing and we don't know the terrain.'

Ethan glanced in the rear-view mirror at Colin Manx's sulking face.

'We've got a guide.'

'Like hell,' Manx spat. 'I'm not going anywhere near that bitch again.'

'Didn't say you had a choice,' Ethan shot back. 'Besides, the more you do to help us the more likely you are to get leniency from a judge and jury. Course, if you go against us . . .'

Ethan let the words hang in the air between them. Manx huffed and puffed, but as they approached a junction where a road led off to the right round the edge of the huge reservoir, Manx pointed gloomily for Ethan to follow it. Tamaya Boulevard wound its way for almost two miles out of the town of Bernalillo before ending at a small campsite on the edge of a large dam. Scrub and thorn bushes peppered the slopes of hills stark against the hard blue sky, the canyon scored by deep and ancient gullys.

'They'll stay close to the reservoir,' Manx muttered. 'The animals need a lot of water in this heat.'

Ethan nodded.

'So will Saffron and anybody with her. It must be at least an hour's walk into Bernalillo.'

Ethan climbed out of the car, peering back down to look at Lopez.

'You hold the road in case they make a break for it in their truck,' he said. 'I'll see if I can't get hold of her or flush them all out.'

'How come you get all the fun jobs?' Lopez complained.

'Because I want to bring her in alive.'

He was about to leave when Manx grabbed his arm.

'Be careful,' Manx urged. 'She knows some kind of kung fu or something.'

Ethan nodded, eager to get Manx's grubby hand off his arm, and set off up the track that led around the edge of the reservoir.

The heat was already intense with only the merest wisps of white cloud drifting above the distant peaks of the mountains. He knew the temperature here could easily break ninety degrees on most days, and summer still had a few more weeks to go. It crossed his mind that he had no water on him, but he consoled himself with the fact that he would find some soon enough, given the obvious tracks left in the desiccated soil beneath his feet.

Ethan had never been an expert tracker, and as an officer in the United States Marines he had left point duties on patrol to those more naturally gifted. However, following a pair of eight-inch-wide tires was a sight easier than tracking footprints through a mangrove swamp, and after only twenty or so minutes an unnatural shape ahead caught his attention. A mound of thick brush loosely concealed the sharp angles of a man-made object, almost certainly the vehicle used by Saffron Oppenheimer. Ethan slowed as he crossed a ridge, crouching down to avoid exposing himself against the horizon to anyone out on his flanks. Old habits die hard, he reflected, as he found himself tapping his waist with his right hand, searching for the long vanished webbing pouch containing his ammunition. Right now he would have felt a great deal better with an M16 cradled in his grip and a rifle platoon behind him.

Ethan huddled against the side of a low ridge of bushes some fifteen yards from the concealed vehicle and peered over the top. Nothing moved, and there wasn't a sound. He gently levered himself up off the ground.

'Don't move.'

The voice was calm, controlled and icily cold.

20

'Get on your feet, slowly, hands in the air.'

Ethan obeyed, turning to see Saffron Oppenheimer standing with the sawn-off Beretta pulled deep into her shoulder, the barrel pointed unwaveringly between his eyes.

'You found me,' Ethan said. 'Saved me a job.'

'I'll do the jokes,' Saffron snapped. 'How did you get here?'

'Car,' Ethan said, aware that Saffron might not know of Lopez's presence and deciding to tell the best kind of lie, one that involved telling as much of the truth as possible. 'I came out here looking for you and found one of your lackeys limping down the road.'

Saffron's eyes narrowed.

'Colin Manx. He okay?'

'He's got a dent in his nose and an even bigger one in his pride, but he'll live.'

Saffron glared at him from over the barrel of the shotgun for a few moments, and Ethan decided to try her patience and see what he got. He lowered his hands.

'Keep them up!' Saffron snarled.

'What for?' Ethan asked, keeping his voice reasonable. 'You're not a killer, Saffron, and you don't want to be.'

'What the hell would you know about it?'

'15th Marine Division, Iraq and Afghanistan,' Ethan said. 'Two tours in each theater. I know what someone looks like when they're trying to kill you, and you're not it.'

Saffron shifted her weight to the opposite foot, glancing down the hill for anyone else backing Ethan up.

'There's nobody else,' Ethan said. 'I dropped Manx off with a patrol car and came out here. He'll be giving a statement by now in Santa Fe.' He looked at the barren hillside around them. 'There's nowhere to run, Saffron. The game's up.'

'I'll decide when the game's up,' Saffron snapped, but the venom in her voice had weakened.

'No, you won't,' Ethan said. 'Once word gets out about the attack, you'll have the entire state police on your ass, maybe even US Marshalls. You're effectively a fugitive with an already high profile. How long do you think you'll last out here before you quit, or somebody else sells you out for a lenient sentence?'

Ethan saw the barrel of the shotgun slowly dropping, not from resignation but from muscular weakness as the weight of the weapon strained Saffron's arms. Saffron saw the direction of his gaze and yanked the barrel up, and as she did so Ethan made his move and lunged forward, one arm outstretched as he tapped the shotgun barrel sideways and up into the air to point over his head.

Saffron leapt backwards to avoid his charge, but Ethan

was already inside the weapon. He shoved the barrel further up as his other hand slammed down across the stock, smashing it out of Saffron's grip as her wrists failed her. Ethan leapt backwards as he twirled the heavy shotgun through his hands to point upside-down at Saffron, his finger finding the trigger.

'We need to talk,' he said.

Saffron's shoulders sank, and she sighed. 'About?'

Ethan opened his mouth to speak, just as he realized that she was feigning. Her left boot whipped up and knocked the shotgun barrel to one side as she plunged inward and drove her right boot into Ethan's belly with ferocious force. He barely got clear of the blow, catching it on his midriff hard enough to drive the air from his lungs. Saffron danced forward in a graceful pirouette as Ethan staggered back and drove one flat palm up toward Ethan's jaw. He whirled the shotgun in his grasp, the butt of the weapon smashing her wrist aside with a loud crack. He heard her cry out but she did not fall back. Instead she rushed closer to stamp one boot painfully onto his right foot as her left elbow snapped round to catch him on his jaw.

Ethan saw the world quiver as he toppled off balance and slammed down hard onto the unforgiving earth. Saffron was on him in an instant, grabbing the shotgun and twisting it sideways before pushing the stock down onto Ethan's throat, leaning all her weight in behind it. His eyes bulged and he gagged as the weapon crushed his windpipe. He pushed back hard, lifting her slightly, and then drove his knee into her side. Saffron lurched off balance as Ethan pushed the shotgun upward and then yanked it sideways between them, hurling her off him. Saffron relinquished her grip and rolled neatly away, reaching to her waist as she did so. Ethan scrambled up onto one knee in time to see a Bowie knife flicker in the bright sunlight. He aimed the shotgun at her.

'Paper, scissors, knife, gun. I win.'

'The gun's empty.' Saffron grinned. 'I'll be off now.'

Shit.

'Running won't help anything, Saffron,' he said, surprised to find himself slightly breathless. She was as fit as she was fast, he'd give her that much.

'Sticking around isn't a great idea either,' she snapped back at him. 'It's been fun.'

Saffron turned her back on him just in time to see Lopez rush up behind her.

'Who were you callin' Chiquita?' Lopez snarled as her tightly bunched right fist cracked across Saffron's jaw.

Ethan winced as Saffron spun a hundred-eighty degrees and hit the dusty hillside flat on her face. Lopez massaged her knuckles and smiled down at him.

'We'll call that little rescue ten bucks, okay?'

'Where's Manx?' Ethan asked.

'Taking a nap,' Lopez uttered. 'I cuffed him to the door, don't worry.'

Ethan crawled to his feet as Saffron dragged herself to her knees, massaging her jaw and glaring at Lopez.

'You'll regret that, you little squirt.'

Lopez's smile vanished as she made a move toward Saffron. Ethan jumped in between them, seriously uncertain of whether he could prevent the two from tearing each other apart.

'Easy,' he said, giving Lopez a cautionary glance before looking at Saffron. 'We're not here to arrest you, we need your help.'

Saffron got to her feet, still glaring at Lopez.

'With what?'

'We need to find a man named Tyler Willis,' Ethan said. 'Know anything about him?'

Ethan instantly knew he'd hit the mark. Saffron's eyes flared at the mention of Willis's name. Not in recognition, he guessed, but more in surprise, as though he shouldn't have known the name at all. She seemed momentarily lost for words and Ethan took advantage of her indecision.

'You're in deep shit, Saffron, no two ways about it. The more you can help us, the better it'll be for you. Whatever the hell's going on here we need to know about it because before long this whole thing is going to be a government issue, you understand what I'm saying?'

Saffron's eyes narrowed.

'Who the hell are you people?'

'It's a long story,' Ethan said, and tossed the shotgun back to her. 'You tell us what we need to know and this might all be smoothed out a lot quicker. There's no other way.'

A voice from behind Ethan said, 'Yes there is.'

He turned to see a young girl, no more than eighteen with blonde dreadlocked hair parted in the center and hanging in schoolgirl's braids on her shoulders. She stood with a small revolver gripped in her tiny hands, pointing it between his eyes. Saffron turned and dashed to the girl's side, grabbing the pistol from her hand.

Ethan was about to pursue her when perhaps thirty or so dusty, scrawny-looking teenagers appeared on the ridge variously carrying bats, bicycle chains and chunks of rock. Lopez was already moving, but Ethan stalled her with a wave of his hand and looked instead at Saffron.

'This solves nothing,' he said. 'The police will track you down no matter where you go. You hit those laboratories, but you weren't there to free the monkeys, were you? You were there to destroy the mainframes. You're working for somebody.'

Saffron smiled coldly, and shook her head. 'You're living in a dream world.'

'Really?' Ethan challenged. 'Then where did you get the money to buy and activate black-market grenades, the camper, your shotgun and that revolver?'

Saffron didn't bat an eyelid, but Ethan saw her bedraggled companions look at her with sudden interest.

'It's not what you know . . .' Saffron said simply, and turned away.

The girl with the dreadlocked hair shot him a venomous glare that looked eerie on someone so young.

'Get out of here. If you follow us, we'll shoot.'

Ethan called after Saffron one last time.

'Where's Tyler Willis? We know you've got something to do with his disappearance.'

Saffron hesitated for a moment, her back to him, and then looked over her shoulder. 'You call off the police and I'll tell you where to find Willis.'

Ethan bit his lip for a moment before speaking.

'They might not listen to me,' he said. 'They'll

question Colin Manx and they'll be searching out here for you by nightfall.'

'Better than nothing,' Saffron snapped. 'You want to find Willis or not?'

Ethan nodded.

'He sometimes stays with friends in Hilary Falls, downtown Santa Fe. You could try there for information, but I'd hurry if I were you. You're not the only people looking for Tyler Willis.'

Before Ethan could say anything more, Saffron and her army disappeared over the hillside.

21

HILARY FALLS
APARTMENT COMPLEX
SANTA FE

2.15 p.m.

Enrico Zamora drove his squad car to a nondescript block of apartments on the corner of West 42nd.

'You sure this is the place?' he asked Ethan, who sat beside him. 'We searched Willis's own apartment, came up clean.'

'Willis hid his research data elsewhere, or so we've been told,' Ethan replied. 'He must have had a reason for doing that, and our best line of inquiry so far is that he was afraid of becoming a victim of industrial espionage. We need to find out what he was working on, and whether he knew who was after his work.'

Zamora shrugged.

'I thought that these scientists always published their work in journals?'

'They do,' Lopez said from the back seat. 'But whatever Tyler Willis had, he obviously felt it was valuable enough to be stolen from him. He clearly went to some lengths to protect it.'

'What about Colin Manx?' Ethan asked. 'Anything from him yet?'

'Detectives are questioning him,' Zamora said. 'He's had nothing much to say except to implicate Saffron Oppenheimer as the ringleader. You believe a word he says, he wasn't even there.'

Ethan remained silent until Zamora had parked the squad car outside the apartment block.

'Who lives here?' he asked as they climbed out.

'Couple of students, friends of Tyler Willis. No records, clean as a whistle. They're up at the laboratories right now but they agreed to the search.'

'Thanks for getting the warrant,' Lopez said to Zamora as they walked into the block's foyer and headed for the elevators. 'We figured it would be easier than just turning up on their doorstep and hoping for the best.'

The elevator doors opened and Ethan watched two men in smart suits walk out. Businessmen, from out of town most likely. One was a towering, barrel-chested man with a drooping Mexican moustache of silvery gray, the other a younger man of perhaps twenty-five. They smiled politely as they stepped out, and Ethan noticed they shared the same strikingly colored eyes, a hazy blue-gray as though they were father and son. Ethan let them out and then walked in, followed by Zamora and Lopez.

The apartment was on the third story. Zamora led the way with a key in his hand lent to him by one of the students. He stopped at the door, slipping the key in and turning it. The door opened, and he moved inside.

Ethan caught the faint odor of unwashed dishes and musty furniture, the hallmark of student digs. The whiff of cigarettes tainted the air in the lounge. Bright sunlight from outside beamed into the lounge, a kitchen off to the left, two bedrooms and a bathroom off to the right. A pile of blankets stacked beside one of the two couches betrayed Willis's presence.

'Must've been staying here for a while,' Ethan surmised.

'There,' Lopez gestured to a pair of laptop computers sitting on a narrow table beneath the window. 'The students would have theirs with them at college, wouldn't they?'

Ethan walked over to the table, looking down at the computers. He opened one, then the other. Both screens had been smashed and liquid, smelling like turpentine, poured into the keyboards, strong enough to dissolve the delicate microchips and hard drives. The smell of stale cigarettes seemed stronger and vaguely familiar as he stared at the computers. He glanced round the lounge and realized he could not see any ashtrays.

'You smell that?' he asked, looking at Lopez.

'Some kind of chemical?' Lopez guessed.

Ethan turned and moved to open one of the windows to let some fresh air in. As he did so, he looked down and saw a black Chevrolet Impala parked on the opposite side of the street. As Ethan opened the window one of the sedan's occupants looked up at the apartment and straight into Ethan's eyes. Even at the distance, Ethan recognized the big man with the silvery moustache in the elevator. They locked gazes for an instant and then the man looked sharply away.

Ethan turned from the window as dread flickered through his mind. Seeing the kitchen door, he dashed across to it. As he burst inside he saw a stove against one wall and heard the rasping hiss of leaking gas coming from somewhere behind it. The acrid stench of some kind of accelerant tainted the air in the kitchen. Ethan looked about desperately but could see nothing. No open bottles, no drenched rags or papers. Just a cat-litter tray in one corner. With the dense gas in the air even the slightest spark could ignite the fuel and the whole apartment would be vaporized. He whirled, shouting out of the kitchen door.

'Get out now, and get back-up!'

He heard Lopez shout something unintelligible and then a loud burst of gunfire ripped through the apartment, three ragged holes bursting through the kitchen wall in puffs of plaster that showered down over him. He ducked instinctively as the shots zipped overhead and smacked into the opposite wall. Ethan crouched down and ran into the lounge, hurling himself flat onto the carpet, praying all the while that none of the bullets would strike a metal surface and let fly the spark that would kill them all.

Another burst of gunfire punched the air and two bullets smashed through the windows of the apartment, webbed cracks splintering the glass in their wake. Ethan's first concern was for Lopez, lying flat on her stomach near a large couch, her black hair sprinkled with fragments of plaster.

'Man down!' she shouted as another crackle of gunfire whipped through the apartment.

Ethan glimpsed the rounds punching through the walls of the apartment from the hall outside. Automatic fire, three-round bursts. M-16s, probably two of them. He saw Zamora lying on his back, gripping his shoulder, blood spilling thickly onto the carpets. Most of the rounds were being fired high, deliberately it seemed, but Zamora had caught one by chance. Ethan realized that whoever was shooting at them wanted to keep their heads down while starting the fire that would kill them. They probably wouldn't even have opened fire if Zamora hadn't gone for the apartment door. They would have let the gas-filled air do its work alone and vaporize the entire room.

In front of him, he saw Zamora roll onto his side and reach down for his pistol.

'Stay down!' Ethan whispered to Lopez, before crawling on his belly across to Zamora.

Two more rounds zipped through the apartment, crossing at an angle above Ethan's head and smacking into the bedroom door in the far corner behind him and he realized that their assailants were retreating down the corridor outside. He crawled the last three feet to Zamora and grabbed his pistol before he could aim it.

'Don't! The apartment's rigged to blow on a spark!' Zamora lowered the pistol. 'You okay?'

'I'll live.' Zamora writhed in pain. 'They're quitting?'

'No,' Ethan said. 'They're running. And I know why. Call for back-up!'

Ethan got to his feet and dragged Zamora up into a sitting position, the trooper sweating profusely as he radioed their position in.

'We've got to get out of here. Can you walk?'

Zamora didn't reply but instead nodded his head, running his remaining good hand through his hair with a trembling motion. Lopez grabbed him under his good arm and gently helped him up.

A burst of automatic fire shattered the windows of the apartment behind them, letting in a billowing breeze from outside.

'Oxygen,' Ethan said urgently. 'Go, get out of here. Quickly.'

He turned and dashed back to the window of the apartment in time to see the black Impala's doors slam shut. Ethan squinted to read the license plate, but the vehicle's tires squealed as it pulled away and shot out of sight down the street.

Ethan whirled and sprinted for the apartment door.

22

DEFENSE INTELLIGENCE AGENCY ANALYSIS CENTER (DIAC), BOLLING AIR FORCE BASE, WASHINGTON DC

Doug Jarvis strode purposefully down a corridor toward a briefing center deep within the DIAC building, dogged by a sense of foreboding. Being summoned by a department head or senior analyst was one thing, but receiving orders to report to the director of the agency was another entirely.

The office of the director of the DIA was not quite hallowed ground but it represented the command of one of the most powerful and secretive agencies in the United States' arsenal. Most everybody had heard of the FBI, the CIA, even the ultra-classified NSA, but the DIA straddled a mysterious line running throughout the Pentagon's many departments. It was responsible for studying and protecting against all potential threats to United States security, and anything that the other agencies knew about, in all theaters, was also reported to the DIA.

Jarvis stopped at the director's door, passing his assistant at her desk who waved him forward with a dutiful smile that did little to improve his mood. He adjusted his tie before knocking discreetly.

'Enter.'

Jarvis walked in to see three-star Lieutenant-General Abraham Mitchell's broad and craggy form hunched, as it usually was, behind a large desk cluttered with documents and photographs. More of a surprise was the man sitting opposite him, a hawkish-looking individual wearing the uniform of a full colonel of the United States Army, replete with a ceremonial silver pistol in a holster at his side.

'Jarvis,' Mitchell said, gesturing to the stranger with one shovel-like hand as Jarvis shut the door to the office. 'This is Colonel Donald Wolfe, research director at USAMRIID. He flew in this morning from Santa Fe.'

Jarvis shook Wolfe's hand, instinctively cautious of the man's aquiline nose and sharp, beady eyes. He had heard of Wolfe by reputation, a high-ranking US Army officer specializing in nuclear, biological and chemical warfare, but he knew nothing of the man personally. They sat down and Jarvis waited for Mitchell to speak.

'Doug, Colonel Wolfe is here regarding a series of events occurring down in New Mexico. You got any operations ongoing down there?'

'I have a small team investigating a disappearance in Santa Fe,' Jarvis answered before turning to Wolfe. 'They're effectively undercover, so I'm surprised that you're here at all, sir.'

'Donald,' Wolfe murmured in a surprisingly soft voice. 'The matter in Santa Fe was considered serious enough for us to find out who exactly was operating in the area.'

'Serious?' Jarvis asked, glancing at Mitchell. 'I didn't realize there was anything of any more concern than an unusual disappearance.'

'It's the nature of who, or what, disappeared that's bothering USAMRIID,' Mitchell rumbled. 'According to USAMRIID there is believed to have been a possibility of some kind of infectious outbreak surrounding the theft of a corpse from a Santa Fe morgue, the same morgue from which the doctor your team is searching for disappeared.'

Jarvis raised a concerned eyebrow.

'There was no mention of any kind of outbreak by local law enforcement,' he said. 'We received information on the case from the FBI, who had been approached by the Santa Fe county sheriff with biological samples from the corpse of a man shot dead the day before by state troopers. There were some anomalies, apparently, with the samples, so I sent two reliable detectives to Santa Fe to follow it up and see what had happened.'

Donald Wolfe spoke slowly, as though he were verbally stalking Jarvis.

'You sent two agents from one of the government's most powerful agencies to pursue the disappearance of a lowly doctor out of Santa Fe?' He smiled in bemusement. 'Shouldn't you guys be chasing terrorists in Helmand Province or something?'

'I didn't say I'd sent *agents*,' Jarvis corrected him. 'I sent two detectives with a proven track record down there. It's not considered a priority case, more of an interesting one.'

'In what way?' Mitchell asked, his big hands folded together on the desk before him.

Jarvis performed a series of rapid mental gymnastics.

'Because it seemed like a planned abduction. Close-circuit cameras captured the kidnapping, involving several men who were masked and were smart enough to disable cameras and phones in the morgue before attacking. Whatever they wanted it must have been important or valuable, and thus worth sending someone down there to investigate.' He turned to Wolfe. 'Which is why I don't understand why you're here. If there was a biological aspect to this case, we'd have passed it on to the National Center for Medical Intelligence at Fort Detrick. But local law enforcement, forensics and the specialists who work in the morgue found no such thing.'

Wolfe shook his head.

'One of the state troopers involved in the shooting reported that the victim appeared to be falling apart, as though he were decaying. The threat is in the corpse itself and any contamination it may have caused on site. I'd have thought that a possible case of leprosy or worse in the middle of New Mexico would have warranted at least alerting us to the event instead of sending two gumshoes down there.'

Jarvis grinned tightly.

'One of them is a former United States Marine who's worked for us before. The other is a former DC detective. Both are highly skilled and reliable. Quite apart from that, the morgue itself was wiped clean, a real professional job. Any infectious agents were removed from the site at that time. Which is why I don't understand why the NCMI wasn't involved if there was a biological case. It's our own medical department, quite capable of handling epidemiological situations: USAMRIID has no place in this investigation.'

'Nor do your investigators,' Wolfe fired back. 'They cannot be relied upon to handle the work competently should they indeed find an infected corpse.'

'Ethan Warner and Nicola Lopez are highly competent,' Jarvis replied without emotion.

Wolfe glanced at Abraham Mitchell, who looked down at his desk and read from a sheet of paper.

'Warner and Lopez,' he rumbled. 'As I understand it, Warner was almost imprisoned last year after fleeing a major fire-fight in Israel and then killing a church minister in Washington DC. Lopez was hunted down by the FBI at the same time. Both escaped only by the intervention of this agency and the President himself.'

Jarvis shifted in his seat.

'Ethan Warner saved the then Senator Isaiah Black's life, sir, as did Nicola Lopez, who was forced into her actions after her own superior officer was arrested for fraud, corruption and the homicide of her partner. He's currently serving life in a New Jersey penitentiary. Warner and Lopez are perfect for this kind of work. They're incorruptible.'

Mitchell shook his head, clearly not convinced.

'As I understand it, both parties are not at all incorruptible. Ethan Warner has a reputation as a live wire and Nicola Lopez has become known for several indiscretions, to which you appear to have turned a blind eye.'

'In addition,' Wolfe said before Jarvis could respond, 'they're not trained in dealing with infectious diseases, whereas doing so is my specialty. It is imperative that this investigation be handed over to USAMRIID, at least until we can figure out whether there's anything to be concerned about. If not, your NCMI and investigators can carry on as they were.'

'And risk letting the case go cold?' Jarvis challenged. 'This is a criminal investigation being conducted with the support of the state police, not an infectious outbreak. Putting it on hold and handing jurisdiction to a military outfit isn't going to solve the abduction case.'

Wolfe was about to retort when Mitchell raised his hands, silencing them.

'Doug, how long is it before your team finds the missing doctor?'

'Days,' Jarvis promised with a conviction he didn't feel. 'They're already chasing several leads.'

Mitchell nodded.

'Then there's no good reason not to let USAMRIID into Santa Fe to work alongside Warner and Lopez.'

Wolfe snorted incredulously.

'This is ridiculous. We could have a major infectious outbreak here, even a biological agent, and you want to leave an ex-soldier and a cop wandering about—'

'*If* it were an infectious agent,' Mitchell interrupted him, 'then we would expect others to have become infected. They have not.'

'Not yet,' Wolfe snapped. 'And what if they do? If we don't keep this contained, both physically and from the media, we could have national panic on our hands.'

'Not if your people work together,' Mitchell pointed out. 'The more people we have on this case, the sooner it can be resolved. There's no need to involve NCMI while Warner and Lopez are already on the scene, if they're as competent as you say they are,' Mitchell said, fielding Jarvis's protesting stare. 'Given the potentially sensitive nature of this case, can your people be trusted to finish this without arousing unwanted interest?'

Cornered by his own defense of Warner and Lopez, Doug Jarvis straightened his tie and lifted his chin.

'Believe me, there are no two better people for the job. Discretion, sir, is Ethan Warner's watchword. You won't even know he's there.'

23

HILARY FALLS
APARTMENT COMPLEX
SANTA FE

'Fire in the hole!'

Ethan Warner sprinted frantically out of the Hilary Falls apartment block to a row of squad cars and a pair of fire trucks, their beacons flashing as a police helicopter thundered overhead. The exchange of gunfire in the center of Santa Fe had attracted every squad car for miles. He just had time to see Lopez and Zamora diving for cover behind the vehicles as the sky seemed to split over his head. Ethan threw himself down and rolled across the asphalt as the third-story apartment exploded, an expanding fireball of oily black smoke and tongues of flame blasting shattered glass to fall like a hailstorm across the lot. He shielded his head with his arms as the shockwave plowed into him, a blast of hot air followed by metallic thumps as chunks of masonry and brickwork slammed into the nearby squad cars.

The blast subsided as flaming fragments of furniture, paper and window frames fluttered down around Ethan. Ethan got to his feet, his ears ringing from the explosion as fire crews dashed past him with hoses, aiming them up at the burning apartment and spraying thick streams of white water into the crackling flames.

'You okay?'

Lopez appeared behind him, her face a mask of concern as she began tapping him down, searching for breaks or abrasions.

'I'm good, just about.'

Zamora walked up to him, holding his injured shoulder.

'Jesus Christ, it's like a war zone down here. You did good, Ethan. What the hell had they done in there? I could smell fuel.'

'Yeah,' Ethan said. 'They probably frayed the gas line behind the stove to start the leak.'

'Where was the accelerant?'

'Cat-litter tray,' Ethan said.

'How do you know?' Lopez asked.

'No cat, and no cat-flap either,' Ethan explained. 'It's an old Boy Scout trick. Litter burns well when it's doused in fuel and doesn't leave much of a trace of anything. Investigators would have assumed that the gas leak caused the blast on its own, not arsonists.'

Lopez looked up at the apartment and the thick smoke billowing from the windows.

'Neat trick,' she said. 'Nasty too.'

'Those guys were heavily armed and they knew how to shoot straight,' Ethan said to her. 'Probably ex-soldiers. Somebody really doesn't want Tyler Willis's little secret getting out. I saw a car pull away with two men in it who seemed very interested in what we were doing.

They were the same guys we saw come out of the elevator, the ones with the weird eyes.'

'I remember them,' Lopez said, turning to Zamora. 'Can we find their vehicle?'

'I'll see what I can do,' Zamora said. 'But if they're as professional as we think they are, it's doubtful we'll catch up to them now.'

Ethan nodded.

'They'll have swapped vehicles, probably be on their way out of the county and there's too much border to track their movements.'

'We need another line of inquiry here,' Lopez said, looking at the smoldering apartment. 'Wherever Willis is, somebody's trying to prevent us from finding him. Why don't we try another tack?'

'Jeb Oppenheimer,' Ethan said.

'Saffron led us here, remember?' Lopez pointed out. 'We've only got her word about her grandfather, and to tell you the truth I don't like her much.'

'No shit?'

'Look,' she said, 'Saffron is an eco-warrior who's already tried to kill you once. She then tips us off about this apartment so she can make a break for it. When we get here we damn near get blown to pieces. You see a picture developing?'

Ethan sighed, looking up at the apartment.

'I just don't see Saffron as a killer,' he said. 'There's more to her than that.'

'Yeah,' Lopez snorted, 'and I'm sure Adolf Hitler's ma reckoned he was just misunderstood.'

Zamora spoke up from beside them.

'There's a lot more to Saffron Oppenheimer than we thought,' he said, gesturing with a jab of his thumb behind them. 'I did a search for her in our database, new gear we've got that's linked to the FBI's records. Turns out that Saffron was up for culpable homicide five years ago during an attack on a laboratory in Utah.'

Ethan winced as Lopez turned to the officer.

'Go on,' she said, folding her arms and raising an eyebrow in Ethan's direction.

'Saffron was part of an activist movement that tried to blow up a vivisection laboratory. The attack went wrong, one of the activists died and all the accomplices were arrested. Turns out the attack destroyed the closed-circuit cameras monitoring the labs, so all the evidence was circumstantial. All the activists blamed each other, the police couldn't bring them to trial and lawyers argued that the dead activist had only himself to blame. As he had been estranged from his family for over a decade, no charges were brought and the case collapsed.'

Ethan shook his head.

'So what's the deal?'

'The laboratory they'd attacked,' Zamora replied, 'belonged to SkinGen Corp, owned and operated by Jeb Oppenheimer.'

Lopez turned to face Ethan, her arms still folded and her eyebrow still raised.

'Shall we?'

Ethan was about to answer her when several white vans with tinted windows pulled up behind the squad cars, their lights adding to the blizzard of beacons. He watched with Lopez and Zamora as a thick-set man clambered out of the lead van, wearing a gray suit that matched his buzz-cut. He had a squat neck that, with his severely cropped hair, made his head look almost square. He slammed the van door shut and strode across to them, the identity tag on his jacket flapping in the hot breeze.

'Butch Cutler,' he announced himself. 'USAMRIID. We're here to take jurisdiction of the site.'

'You are?' Zamora asked. 'We weren't informed of any risk of hazardous material breaches or such like.'

'Nothing's certain yet,' Cutler said, glancing curiously at Ethan and Lopez. 'You must be Ethan Warner.'

'And Nicola Lopez,' Ethan gestured to his partner. 'How did you know?'

'My boss,' Cutler said. 'He's been talking to yours. They've decided it's best you hand over to us until we can figure out what's going on here.'

Ethan said nothing for a moment as Cutler removed his jacket and folded it over his arm. His sleeves were rolled up and Ethan caught a glimpse of a tattoo on his right forearm, the banner of the US Army Rangers and a winged parachute.

'That the real deal there?' Ethan asked, gesturing to the tattoo. 'Or are you just a fantasist?'

Cutler squinted at Ethan without apparent emotion for several seconds.

'75th Rangers, Long Range Surveillance,' he said. 'What's it to you?'

'15th Marines, Recon,' Ethan replied.

In all of Ethan's years, whenever former soldiers met, especially those who had served alongside each other in grueling conflicts, there was an instant camaraderie, a realization that you were near another man who could be relied upon to get the job done, to find solutions and to survive. Ethan looked into Cutler's eyes and saw there a sudden unease. The tattoo was almost certainly genuine enough, as was Cutler's service – he looked all over like a born and bred ranger, but he was watching Ethan now with a wary expression as though he was being faced with a sudden and unexpected threat.

'Why have your guys been sent down here, exactly?' Ethan asked.

Cutler tossed his jacket into the van and walked past Ethan, who turned to give him room. He felt as though they were two predators circling each other before a fight.

'The apartment, so I've been told,' Cutler replied, 'was the current residence of Tyler Willis, a micro-biologist. His work at both Los Alamos and here in Santa Fe brought him into contact with a number of exotic bacteria, any one of which he could have had on his person when this attack occurred.'

Lopez frowned at Cutler.

'He wasn't in the apartment when it went up,' she pointed out.

'But whatever he had on his person may have remained inside,' Cutler replied.

'The apartment's been incinerated,' Ethan said. 'There's not enough left in there to be an infectious hazard. Nothing could survive that.'

Cutler turned to face him.

'Chemolithotrophic bacteria can live fifteen hundred meters underground in solid basalt rock, survive and reproduce on the edge of space and at the North Pole or beside deep-sea ocean vents where the temperature is well over a hundred degrees and the pressure four hundred atmospheres. That a chance you want to take in the middle of a residential area? Unless you've got probable cause for remaining here on site, I suggest you let us take over before anything else blows up in your face.'

Ethan, standing four-square in front of Cutler, knew that the man was trying to intimidate him. Cutler stood at least two inches taller than Ethan and was maybe thirty pounds heavier.

'It's all yours,' Ethan said. 'Although if there's such a worry about hazardous materials shouldn't you all have arrived here with protective gear on, seeing as we're standing about thirty yards downwind from the burning apartment you're so worried about?'

Cutler's right eyelid twitched convulsively for a moment and then he smiled without warmth.

'It's unlikely we'll find airborne pathogens. Tyler Willis was a research scientist, not Saddam Hussein. Now, if you'll excuse us?'

Ethan stepped aside as Cutler led his team past them toward the smoldering apartment block.

'Interesting,' Lopez said. 'They got here real quick.'

'Too quick,' Ethan said, turning to Zamora. 'You got a Center for Disease Control unit down here anywhere?'

'Not that I know of,' he admitted. 'And we didn't call one in.'

Ethan watched Cutler for a few moments, and then turned to Lopez.

'Let's go and meet Jeb Oppenheimer, and see what he has to say for himself.'

24

JAY'S BAR & GRILL
HIGHWAY 85, LA CIENEGA
NEW MEXICO

The warbling of an old Kenny Rogers number strummed through the half-filled bar as Lee Carson swaggered somewhat unsteadily through the entrance and focused on his surroundings. He'd already downed half a dozen tequila shots after work with the guys, and it seemed to have affected him more than usual. Maybe he was losing his touch.

He looked at his reflection in the glass of the front door. His tasseled cowhide jacket, low-brimmed Stetson and leather ranch gloves were a little too much for him in the warm air, but they looked damned good and he knew it. No, he certainly wasn't losing his touch.

He glanced in the mirror that ran behind the bar as he sauntered across to a vacant stool. The reflection showed his chiseled jaw, the wide sideburns he'd been cultivating for a few days and hazy blue-gray eyes staring back at him from beneath curls of jet-black hair as he removed his hat and set it down on the bar.

'Afternoon, mister.'

Carson flashed a perfect white smile at the young girl approaching him from behind the bar. She looked early twenties, a blonde ponytail framing an angelic face above a cleavage barely contained by her tight white vest.

'Well afternoon to *you*, ma'am.' Carson grinned.

'What'll it be?' she asked, leaning on the bar toward him.

'A shot of your finest bourbon, and whatever you're havin', Miss . . .'

'Eloise.' She giggled, clearly enjoying the attention. 'You got it.'

Carson watched her walk away down the bar toward the liquor rack, swinging her hips with more vigor than was strictly necessary. He glanced over his shoulder at the restaurant. Barely a dozen people, mostly eating at tables and booths. Perfect. He'd have the full and undivided attention of Eloise both now and during the later that he already knew would come.

Lee Carson was, by consensus, a very handsome man. He'd been blessed with genes from his parents that had given him a near classic-cowboy look, rugged and tough, a look that he'd only too happily cultivated by working as a ranch hand doing physical jobs that maintained his impressive physique. His shoulders were broad, his legs long, his chest that of five men, his belly flat and his waist slim. He looked at himself in the mirror again and couldn't help but smile. He looked damn fine, for a man of one hundred sixty-eight years.

'Straight bourbon,' Eloise said, setting his tumbler down in front of him on the bar. 'Mine's a Coke.'

'To y'health,' Carson said, raising his glass and clinking it against hers.

He knew she was watching as he tilted his head back and downed the shot in one, closing his eyes as the bourbon seared the back of his throat and then sank warmly to the pit of his stomach. He exhaled the fumes noisily and set the glass down again.

'Damned if I didn't need that,' he said.

'Hard day at the ranch?' Eloise inquired, leaning further forward on the bar and providing him with a vertiginous view of her creamy breasts.

'Up an' down all day,' Carson replied. 'I've done got me all beat out.'

Eloise chuckled.

'I guess that means that you're tired,' she said. 'Shame. Guy like you needs to keep your strength up.'

'For what?' Carson smiled.

'You never know.' Eloise shrugged. 'Just got to be ready for anything.'

Carson leaned a little closer to her.

'Y'mean I might be up an' down all night too?'

Eloise threw a hand to her mouth and giggled as her eyes opened wide.

'Damn you, mister, you don't know nothing about manners.'

'What's them?' Carson asked. 'And it's Lee, Lee Carson.'

Eloise extended her hand over the bar, and he shook it gently.

'Pleasure to meet you, Lee Carson.' She held on to his hand for a moment longer than was necessary. 'Will you be staying a while?'

Carson nodded. 'Just as long as you're here, ma'am.'

'You'll be needing another drink then.'

Carson watched as Eloise made her jaunty way back down the bar, and then he slipped out of his tasseled jacket, hanging it carefully on one of the bar hooks beside him. Carson had, he knew with absolute confidence, slept with more women than any other man in the history of the human species. He possessed something of an unfair advantage of course, in the fact that he hadn't aged a day since his twenty-seventh year. He thought for a moment. One hundred and forty-one years ago. Damn, it got harder with each passing decade to keep track of time and the things he'd seen over those years, those decades. He shook his head, smiling to himself again. The rest of them, damned fools, had lived their lives in seclusion, had chosen not to take advantage of what God, if He existed, had given them: a gift, a blessing. Or maybe just some damned fine luck. Lee Carson had grabbed that gift with both hands and made full use of it.

He had no need to work. Over time many of his belongings had become antiques, earning him cash whenever he needed it. His home of the last twenty or so years, a simple farmhouse out on the very edge of Santa Fe, had no outstanding mortgage. Carson simply traded up from time to time as the market favored him, and occasionally used his contacts to arrange the purchase of a property under an assumed name, the paperwork leaving the property to him in a 'will'. As long as he left about fifty years between each will, nobody was around to remember the last one. He worked only to stay fit, occupied and healthy, and to avoid any awkward questions from the IRS or nosey locals.

He watched from the corner of his eye as Eloise poured his drink, and saw her surreptitiously looking at him from time to time. The expressions, the body language, the tone of voice: Carson had studied young women for over a century, and knew a sure thing when he saw it.

Tonight was going to be a good night.

Lee Carson once again thanked whatever lucky star he'd passed under all those many years ago and reached down, pulling off his gloves.

A lance of shock pierced the very depths of his stomach and he let out a loud yelp of alarm. As he yanked off the glove, thick chunks of skin spilled from within to sprinkle the surface of the bar. Carson gagged as he looked down at his hand, the stench of decaying flesh acrid in his nose. His skin was crumpled like canvas, pallid gray in color and sagging from the bones he could see within, like white poles propping up a limp tent.

'Jesus!'

Carson stood abruptly, as though doing so could get him further away from his own disintegrating hand. He stared at it in alarm as Eloise returned, her face tight with concern as she looked at his hand.

'What's wrong?'

Carson slapped his good hand over the other and shot her an embarrassed look.

'I . . . er . . . I've gotta go, ma'am. Real sorry, an emergency.'

Eloise looked crestfallen.

'You'll come back, right?'

Carson barely heard her as he grabbed his hat, gloves and jacket and rushed out of the bar into the cool evening air. He stood outside for a moment, taking in long deep breaths to steady himself.

'Be cool, Lee,' he whispered, and looked down at his hand again.

The gnarled, bony fingers were like those of an old crone, reminding him of his grandmother from a century and a half before. The muscles within his fingers had wasted and the tendons sagged uselessly. He tentatively wriggled his fingers and felt a dull ache throb through the joints as though he were . . .

Old.

A fresh wave of panic swept through him as he realized he was suddenly running out of the one thing he thought he'd never have to worry about again.

Time.

25

MANDARIN ORIENTAL HOTEL, MANHATTAN NEW YORK CITY

'Ladies and gentlemen, I'd like to thank you for coming here tonight and for giving me this opportunity to address you directly.'

Donald Wolfe stood before a small lectern overlooking an array of dining tables in the Mandarin Ballroom, each delicately arranged with wine glasses, champagne bottles on ice, dinner plates and elaborately illuminated bouquets of flowers. Along an entire wall, tall windows looked out across the glittering nightscape of the Manhattan skyline. Each table was occupied by smartly dressed men and women, each of whom was potentially worth millions or billions of dollars, depending on which pharmaceutical company they happened to own. Yet none of them was important, at least not to Wolfe. The focus of his gaze rested instead on the small handful of Bilderberg Committee members who were worth *trillions* of dollars, sitting unobtrusively at tables far from the stage.

Wolfe's vision of the future was shared by such men: streets devoid of the wearisome crowds and their gluttony for material wealth. The parasite would soon be eliminated, the infection cured, and what would be left of humanity would proceed onward into a brighter future.

The thought provoked in Wolfe a sense of well-being that was further amplified by the knowledge that his efforts at the annual Bilderberg Conference, a three-day event that had taken place a month before, had come to fruition. It had been a close-run thing, but his determination and dedication had paid off, and he knew his revelations had been laid before the Bilderberg steering committee and discussed at length by its members as a matter of global importance. Their decision, which he was sure would be aligned with his plans, would change the face of humanity forever.

Few people knew of the existence, let alone the importance, of the Bilderberg Group.

Members of the Bilderberg, the Trilateral Commission and the Council on Foreign Relations had been charged by global corporations with the post-war takeover of the democratic process. The measures implemented by this group provided general control of the world economy through indirect political means. The meetings were held annually and attended by most prime ministers and presidents in the developed world. It was not a conspiracy, for attendee lists were available to the public. But its meetings were screened from the public domain and the prying eyes of the media for one simple reason: so that every attendee could speak their mind without fear of public reprimand. No journalist was ever invited to attend the Bilderberg meetings. If any leaks occurred, the journalists responsible were discouraged from reporting them. The group took its name from the location of the first meeting – the Bilderberg Hotel in Oosterbeek, Holland, in May 1954. The concept of Bilderberg was not new. Groups such as Bohemian Grove, established in 1872 by San Franciscans, had played a significant role in shaping post-war politics in the US. The Ditchley Park Foundation had been established in 1953 in Britain with a similar aim.

Bilderberg was originally conceived by Joseph H. Retinger and Prince Bernhard of the Netherlands. Prince Bernhard, at the time, was an important figure in the oil industry and held a major position in Royal Dutch Petroleum. There were usually some one hundred fifteen participants in each annual meeting. Eighty were from Western Europe and the remainder from North America. From this mixture, about one-third came from government and politics, with the remaining two-thirds from industry, finance, education and communications.

The Americans were heavily influenced by the Rockefeller family – owners of Standard Oil – competitors of Bernhard's Royal Dutch Petroleum. Bilderberg business always reflected the concerns of the oil industry in its meetings which centered almost entirely on two unnerving facts: one, that oil was rapidly running out; and two, that the population of the planet and its demands for fuel were still increasing at a trimetric rate. Soon, it would all be over and humanity would come to an end. The search for alternatives was pointless as everything from hydrogen cells to the virtually useless wind turbines required abundant supplies of rare metals which were hoarded by China; materials such as europium, lanthanum, neodymium and countless others. It was now no longer about how to save humanity: it was about who would survive the coming catastrophe.

Donald Wolfe cleared his throat. If this speech went down well, then his next, to world leaders at the United Nations, would herald nothing less than a new epoch in human history.

'The United States Army Medical Research Institute of Infectious Diseases,' he began, 'is the army's main institution and facility for infectious-disease research that may have defensive applications against biological warfare. At the present time, the development and procurement of medical countermeasures for pandemic influenza and other emerging infectious diseases is our chief concern, especially in these difficult times of cultural upheaval, ideological wars fought in the name of opposing religions and ever-increasing population density. Any one of them, at any time, could be the cause of agents that could potentially kill millions of people.' Wolfe smiled. 'So we're handy to know.'

A ripple of polite humor swept across the tables, white smiles above black tuxedos and ball gowns, a couple of the suited magnates raised champagne glasses to Wolfe. He should have despised them for making their fortunes by selling drugs at the highest prices to the Western world while withholding them from those who needed them most, the poor of the developing world, but he couldn't, for he had become wealthy outside his military service on the back of the vast chemical wonderland that was Big Pharma. Hell, it wasn't their fault that some countries couldn't afford medicines: if those country's governments had spent more on their own people than on buying weapons then there wouldn't be such a divide between the healthy West and the sickly East. It was a point of view Wolfe had made on a few occasions when traveling overseas as a representative of his department, and the reason why the higher office he'd sought had eluded him. Washington didn't like straight talkers and people who 'tell it like it is', as a senator had once told him. It risked giving ordinary citizens the illusion that they actually had some kind of influence in government, and that was the last thing that the ruling classes wanted.

'But right now there's a problem, and it's one I know you're already familiar with. Our ability to create new drugs to treat those in need is rapidly declining. In the fields of medicine, biotechnology and pharmacology, drug discovery is the process by which drugs are discovered or designed, and productivity has collapsed over the past twenty years. In the past most drugs have been discovered either by identifying the active ingredient from traditional remedies or by serendipitous *discovery*. A new approach has been to understand how disease and infection are controlled at the molecular and physiological level and to target specific entities based on this knowledge.'

The process of drug discovery involved the identification of candidates, synthesis, characterization, screening and assays for therapeutic efficacy. Once a compound had shown its value in these tests, it began the process of being developed prior to clinical trials. And it was that which was slowing down the arrival of new drugs to the market.

'Despite our advances in technology and understanding of biological systems, drug discovery is still a long, expensive, difficult and inefficient process with low rates of new therapeutic discovery. Currently, the research and development cost of each new molecular entity is approximately 1.8 billion US dollars, a financial burden too great for us to bear. Information on the human genome has been hailed as promising to virtually eliminate the bottleneck in therapeutic targets that has been one limiting factor on the rate of therapeutic discovery. However, data indicates that this is not so and that the genome cannot be relied upon to cure all ills. In short, ladies and gentlemen, it's time for change.'

Wolfe regarded them for a long moment before speaking again.

'We need to focus new drug development to a changed home market. There are now simply too many people with too many physiological variations causing too many mutations in infectious and contagious diseases for our ability to control and treat those conditions, regardless of cost, time or availability. Sooner or later, one of those diseases is going to become a pandemic, with the loss of millions, perhaps even billions of people. In the fourteenth century in Europe, the plague known as the Black Death eliminated some sixty percent of the population, who were suffering from compromised immunity due to chronic malnutrition, a predicament common still in the developing world. It is not the science that is at fault, it is the fact that there are simply too many human beings populating our planet acting as petri dishes for and carriers of exotic infectious diseases. If we do not act now, their carrying of the next great pandemic could spill over into our own countries and threaten humanity's very existence.'

To Wolfe's surprise, there was a sudden burst of rapturous applause that thundered round the stage. Wolfe raised a hand before speaking again as the furore died down.

'There will be some, particularly our friends in the media, who will no doubt vilify my comments as ignorant of the needs of millions of people around the world who have complained for many decades about their lack of access to desperately needed drugs. However, sometimes science reaches a point where the volume of demands placed upon it can no longer be met by even its most talented and determined servants. The truth is, ladies and gentlemen, that we need a reduction in population to improve almost every single facet of our modern lives. There is no silver bullet. There is no miracle cure. And there is no light at the end of the tunnel if we continue on our current path of excess consumption and bloated ignorance of the limits of our planet and our own human ingenuity in solving not just our own problems but those of our fellow man. We have outgrown our beds, and now we are forced to lie in them.'

More applause clattered around the room, and Wolfe turned to wave to the wings of the stage. Instantly, three young girls hurried out, running to his side and clinging to him with shy gazes. They were joined by Wolfe's wife, who stood alongside him at the lectern as he spoke.

'Our global population is impossible to maintain in the face of a world beset by a growing specter of so-called "peak" phenomena, the point at which consumption totally overwhelms resources. We have peak oil, peak water, peak phosphorus, peak grain and peak fish already threatening civilization at large. I say to you all now, to the watching media and the people who will see this on the news, not as the Director of Operations at USAMRIID but as a husband, a father and a human being: for all of our sakes we must reduce our numbers in order to conserve the very resources upon which we depend, before our success as a society becomes our downfall as a species.'

Donald Wolfe, resplendent in his tuxedo and neatly parted hair, replaced the microphone on the lectern and stepped politely off the stage as wave after wave of applause followed him. The diners were all on their feet and clapping far harder than was necessary, as though each and every clap accounted for the millions of dollars that had flowed into their accounts over the decades. Voices accompanied the slaps on his back as he weaved between the tables.

'About goddamn time.'

'Took the words right out of my mouth, Donald.'

'Good work, Wolfe, you'll save our lives with that.'

Wolfe worked his way through the tables, to where one of the discreet men he had been watching stood to greet him and gestured toward the exit.

'We need to talk, Donald,' the man said. 'Please, this way.'

26

SKINGEN CORP
SANTA FE

7.12 p.m.

Darkness. Disorientation. Confusion.

Tyler Willis was lying on something that felt hard and cold. His hands and feet tingled uncomfortably where thick leather straps had cut off the circulation, fastening him down so firmly that he could not move an inch. He could hear movement, the opening and closing of a door and a strange rasping sound, but his vision was obscured by a black cloth covering his head.

The cloth was whipped aside, bright light stinging his eyes. Willis blinked and saw that he was lying on his back on a mortuary slab. Above him, Jeb Oppenheimer looked down into his eyes. The old man's breath wheezed softly, carrying with it the mingled vapors of cigar smoke and peppermint.

'Welcome,' Oppenheimer said.

'Where am I?' Willis asked.

'Somewhere entirely secure,' Oppenheimer replied. 'Trust me, Tyler, it's just you, me and our observer.'

The old man gestured to one side with a nod, and

Willis turned his head to see a middle-aged woman handcuffed to a table a couple of yards away.

'Tyler Willis,' he said, 'I'd like you to meet Lillian Cruz.'

'What the hell is this?' Willis said.

The old man tossed the black cloth down across Willis's legs, and he felt it touch his bare skin. He strained to look down and saw that he was entirely naked. Oppenheimer reached out, and removed Willis's spectacles, slipping them into his pocket before studying him with mild interest.

'The human body is a remarkable feat of nature,' he said. 'The result of eight million years of evolution. It's strange, don't you think, that our scientists spend years researching the origins of life on our planet when we carry the answers within our own cells? Bacteria were some of the first forms of life to emerge on Earth, but they did not make way for more advanced forms of life. Instead they joined us, are a part of the fabric of our existence.' He leaned toward Willis. 'Did you know, Tyler, that there are more bacteria living inside you than there are cells that make up your body?'

'Let me go,' Willis said.

Oppenheimer smiled as though pitying him.

'I'd love to, Tyler, I really would. But alas, despite your prodigious talents, if I leave you to continue on your path the whole population of our planet will pay the price.'

Willis swallowed thickly, shaking his head.

'You can't keep it for yourself. Sooner or later it will be found by others, no matter what you do to me or to anyone else.'

'What the hell are you talking about?' Lillian Cruz demanded.

Oppenheimer smiled but ignored her, tutting to himself and shaking his head as he reached out to an unseen tray nearby and pulled on a pair of thin surgical gloves. Willis felt his bowels convulse with fear.

'The unworthy, unwashed masses can only learn of what we've strived to achieve, Tyler, if they are alive to do so. Soon they will not be. Those of us who remain will not care, because we will be the sole remaining tenants of this wonderful world of ours.'

Willis felt his entire body begin to tremble uncontrollably as Oppenheimer lifted from the unseen tray a brand new surgical scalpel, gently sliding the glinting blade from its plastic sheath and examining the tip intently.

'Hey!' Lillian shouted.

'One of the sharpest tools of the modern surgeon,' Oppenheimer murmured to himself. 'Of course, it's been some time since I dissected a human cadaver, and they were so dull, so lifeless. Most had been in storage for weeks or months, pale, somehow false. So much more interesting to perform the procedure while the subject is still . . . vibrant.'

He looked down, and Willis felt his bowels loosen as his thighs trembled and his ankles rattled loudly against the mortuary slab.

'You don't have to do this,' Willis said in short, sharp jerks.

'Of course I don't,' Oppenheimer agreed. 'But I want answers, and I want Lillian here to know that there is nothing I will not do to achieve my aims and that she would be sensible to comply with my demands. So, tell me, where did Hiram Conley contract his infection and how can I get there?'

'I don't know,' Willis said, hot tears running freely down his cheeks. 'He came to me with the samples, but wouldn't say where he'd gotten them.'

Oppenheimer looked down at Willis for a long moment and then wagged a crooked finger at him.

'Now that's not helping either of us, is it, Tyler? One more time: where did Hiram Conley obtain his infection?'

Lillian strained against her handcuffs.

'Let him go, for God's sake!'

Willis sucked in a deep breath.

'He didn't tell me anything! For God's sake, I swear it's the truth. If I knew I would tell you!'

Oppenheimer leaned over Willis's chest and rested the blade on his sternum. Willis felt a tiny prick of pain against his skin.

'Well, Tyler, we'll soon find out.'

The pain suddenly spread like fire as Willis felt the blade plunge hilt-deep into his flesh. Oppenheimer drew it down toward the navel in a searing line of agony, thick blood spilling across Willis's dark skin as the sound of his own screams filled the room. The terrible pain reached his groin and then changed as the blade was pulled from his flesh with a sucking sound that sent a bolt of nausea churning through his stomach. He felt his blood trickling warmly down his flanks as Oppenheimer's wrinkled features looked down at him as though studying a dissected insect.

'Did that pinch?' Oppenheimer asked.

'I'll do what you want!' Lillian shouted, yanking on the handcuffs as she tried to reach Oppenheimer. 'Just let him alone!'

Willis, his eyes blurred with tears of pain and helplessness, spat his answer in a frothing dribble.

'Go to hell, you evil bastard!'

Irritation sparked across Oppenheimer's face as he turned and jabbed the scalpel toward Willis's groin. The scientist was sucking in air to scream again when a soft digital beep echoed through the room. Oppenheimer turned, looking at a flashing light on the wall as a female voice spoke through an intercom.

'Two detectives are on their way to see you, Mister Oppenheimer.'

Oppenheimer hurried across to the panel and pressed a button.

'Who are they?' he growled.

'An Ethan Warner and Nicola Lopez, sir.'

Oppenheimer started to reply, and as he pressed the button Willis opened his mouth and screamed as loudly as he could.

'Help me! For God's sake, call the police . . . !'

Oppenheimer shut off the intercom and walked across to Willis and slapped a thick adhesive patch across his mouth. Willis watched helplessly as Oppenheimer walked back to the intercom and pressed the button.

'I will be there momentarily. Have my security team on standby.'

Oppenheimer walked back to where Willis lay bleeding, and tapped his chest with the scalpel.

'I shall return, my friend,' he said coldly. 'Have a long

hard think about what you're going to tell me. A wrong answer will lose you a perfectly serviceable kidney, understood?'

Willis screamed beneath the tape, sweating profusely as Oppenheimer turned for the door of the laboratory and looked for the first time at Lillian Cruz. He walked across to her, the bloodied scalpel in his hand, and she reared up and away from him.

'You're sick,' she gasped.

Oppenheimer set the scalpel down and unlocked the cuff from one of her wrists before yanking her across to the mortuary slab and cuffing her to that instead. He looked down at Willis.

'Patch him up,' Oppenheimer snapped. 'I don't want him losing consciousness until I'm fully satisfied he knows nothing.' He looked down at Willis. 'Don't forget now, Tyler. Kidney, or no kidney. It's your call.'

27

MANDARIN ORIENTAL HOTEL, MANHATTAN NEW YORK CITY

Donald Wolfe left his family in the dining hall and followed his companion to the executive suite. His attendance at the Bilderberg Conference the previous month had been his first, when he had delivered a speech to the other attendees on the dangers of future pandemics. It was there he had been approached regarding the search for solutions to what the men had called the 'human' problem, and he had realized how high the stakes were for humanity. He was considering those stakes when they reached one of the rooms, and he was led inside. Four men, all immaculately dressed, waited in the suite as Wolfe closed the door.

'Gentlemen,' he said simply.

They never used names. It wasn't impossible for journalists or even foreign intelligence operatives to bug rooms in the Mandarin, although it was highly unlikely as they would never have known that men of such power were present at all, so secretly did they move through the halls of governments. The four men before him could have passed the average citizen in the street and they would never have known that they were within inches of the most powerful men on earth. One was an elderly oil tycoon who liked to hide behind another individual who was the public face of his company. Another was an equally aged property magnate whose line of work required no public presence whatsoever. The remaining two younger men were both heirs to fossil-fuel fortunes forged before and after World War Two, who had taken the helm of their fathers' companies with ruthless efficiency. All four were worth more than the GDP of a small European country and infinitely more influential.

'What news?' Wolfe asked, his throat tight and dry.

The eldest of the four regarded him for a moment before speaking in a soft, cultured voice.

'The steering committee has considered your suggestions. We agree that the imminent presence of a global catastrophe due to overpopulation, a lack of physical and energy resources and the growing threat of global pandemics is a clear and present danger. However, we disagree that a radical reduction of select elements of the human population is necessarily the correct course of action.'

Wolfe felt a chill plunge down his spine.

'What more practical solution do you envisage?' he asked, struggling to remain calm.

'We don't,' said the shortest of the men. 'There is no alternative.'

Wolfe frowned uncertainly. 'Then what's the problem?'

'Simply,' said another of the men, 'that in your plan the culling of a major proportion of the inhabitants of developing countries is required to affect a solution. Our problem, Donald, is that you're eradicating the *wrong* people. The populations of the Western world are far greater consumers than those of the East. Removing a population like our own, that of the United States, will have a profoundly better resolution for global resources than removing the entire population of India, for instance. We consume more, therefore by your own logic it is we who should be removed.'

Wolfe stared at the men in disbelief.

'The whole point of this is to conserve the better prepared populations for the future!'

'Is it?' the eldest man asked. 'In your proposal it was to save the planet from certain doom.'

Wolfe cursed himself mentally, put off guard by the unexpected hostility.

'It is,' he replied. 'But eradicating ourselves isn't exactly what I had in mind.'

'Eradicating?' asked the last of the men, a young man with hawkish good looks. 'I thought this was about a humane global call for a *reduction* in population.'

'Yes,' Wolfe replied, 'combined with the proposed arrest of aging in selected individuals. The longer that you live anonymously at the head of the Bilderberg Committee, the longer that your objectives and desires can remain in place. We, right now, have the power to take control of the globe and control human destiny for decades, perhaps centuries to come.'

'We?' said the eldest again. 'I take it that by *we* you mean us, yourself and Jeb Oppenheimer?'

Wolfe hesitated for a long moment before replying.

'I said nothing of Jeb Oppenheimer.'

The four men exchanged glances for a moment before the youngest of them spoke again.

'I presume that your men have not yet isolated the source of this supposed *elixir* that you claim to have found?'

'They are working on it as we speak,' Wolfe assured him. 'I have a team in place, and as soon as Oppenheimer locates a viable sample I will acquire it from him and bring it to you.'

Another moment of silence followed before the eldest man spoke.

'You believe that it is imminent, that a pandemic will strike the East within our lifetimes?'

Wolfe nodded, relieved to be on surer ground.

'It is inevitable. The HN-51 virus showed us that the influenza strain has already made the leap between animals and humans on numerous occasions, each time with a new mutation more virulent than the last. Global inoculation is not possible, especially given the locales in which the strain exists and mutates. With the populations in Africa, India and the Malay Archipelago growing at a terrific rate it can only be a matter of time before another, truly lethal, treatment-resistant pandemic spreads to all corners of the globe.'

The four men exchanged glances; it was clear they understood the threat and the choice they were being forced to make: reduce the population of the East to prevent a pandemic, or wait for the disease to spread and see the populations of all countries fall.

'It's eugenics,' one of them said. 'Whatever way we look at it, we're taking away natural selection and playing god with millions of lives, perhaps billions.'

'Perhaps we are,' Wolfe countered, 'but what else can we do? We know it's coming, we know it's going to happen. What would you prefer, given the choice? A controlled, orderly reduction of the population? Or a brutal disease ravaging every continent and killing indiscriminately?'

'Again,' said another, 'why the East? We have our own treatment-resistant illnesses, like MRSA. It too could mutate and we have as many mega-cities as the East, places where such diseases could spread and become epidemic, even pandemic. Mexico City is just across the border and is the largest city in the world.'

'It's simply a question of the odds,' Wolfe replied, staying calm. 'Virulent influenza strains have appeared in the East most often, rarely from South America. We don't know why, but that's just the way it is. It's also preferable from an economic point of view.'

The men nodded slowly, well aware of the manufacturing powerhouses of India and China swiftly rising to threaten the dominance of the United States. Reducing the populations of such countries beneath the veneer of disease elimination could serve greater purposes for those with vested interests in maintaining the balance of economic power.

There were a final few moments of silence, and then the eldest man spoke with a tone of absolute finality.

'There can be no witnesses of any kind,' he said. 'Everybody who is involved in this must be removed from play for the greater good of all mankind. If word ever gets out it will be the end of us all, immortal or not.'

'There will be no leaks,' Wolfe insisted. 'The net's already closing around those involved, and soon we'll have them in total isolation.'

'Where?'

'The New Mexico desert,' Wolfe said. 'There, far from civilization, they can be removed from the equation. Nobody will ever know.'

The eldest man folded his hands before him as he spoke.

'Acquire the samples you claim will render us immune to aging. Prove they work, and we will in turn set in motion the required laws to reduce global population. It will take time, but it will come to pass.'

'Are you sure that you can turn the United Nations?' Wolfe pressed him. 'They will oppose any such enforced population control at every turn, as will the Vatican.'

'The United Nations will have little influence over our plans,' the eldest man said. 'European population growth has been negligible for some time and is even in negative figures in some countries. It is in the developing world where the issue is strongest. China enforced a one-child policy for decades with our help. Others will follow suit or suffer the consequences of trade embargoes: we will use the economic markets to force their hand. As for the Vatican, people care less about its opinion by the year and are leaving the Church in their millions anyway. The Pope's view on this is irrelevant because the

Vatican's only success in its long and miserable existence is to prove that it knows nothing about the nature of either gods or people.'

Donald Wolfe nodded.

'And if an infection breaks before these plans can be implemented?'

The four men glanced at each other again before the eldest spoke. 'Then we must endeavor to keep it beyond our shores,' he said, 'and we can tell the United Nations that we warned them of the danger.'

'I'll get things in motion immediately,' Wolfe said.

'This conversation never occurred,' the eldest man said to him. 'And if your role here should be compromised, we expect that you will remove yourself from existence entirely before our own involvement can be exposed. Do you understand what I am telling you?'

Wolfe baulked, but nodded once without thinking.

'Say it,' the old man insisted. 'Tell me that you understand what I'm telling you.'

'You're telling me that you want me to commit suicide if I am exposed?'

The man nodded once.

'That's exactly what I'm telling you, Donald. You've said it yourself: this is an extremely sensitive issue with immense repercussions. We do not intend to be on the receiving end of any investigation and we cannot trust you alone to shield us from scrutiny. Therefore, you will remove yourself from the equation.'

The four men moved to the door of the suite. The old man turned and looked over his shoulder at Wolfe.

'If you refuse or are unable to commit the act, Donald,

then rest assured we will arrange for somebody to do it for you.'

Wolfe swallowed thickly and watched as the men filed silently from his suite to disappear once more into absolute anonymity.

28

SKINGEN CORP
SANTA FE

7.28 p.m.

'This guy has more money than God.'

Lopez was sitting beside Ethan in the passenger seat of the Mercury, the screen of her handheld showing an Internet page detailing SkinGen Corp.

'Major pharmaceutical chiefs often do,' Ethan said as he pulled into the heavily manned gates of the company's headquarters and showed his identification to the guardsmen.

Lopez scanned down through the Internet entry as they waited for access to the site.

'True, but this one's special,' she said. 'SkinGen's annual turnover is measured in billions, and Jeb Oppenheimer has a reputation for extreme corporate ruthlessness. Says here that he once bought an entire company and then shut it down, in revenge for a deal several years previously that had gone against him. Almost three hundred people lost their jobs overnight, and the shut-down cost Oppenheimer fifteen million dollars.'

'Let me guess,' Ethan said as the barriers lifted to allow them through. 'He took the hit happily.'

'By then fifteen million dollars was small change to him. He owns yachts worth five times that, which he doesn't visit for years. Properties in Manhattan, London, Paris, Sydney and Rome, none of them worth less than ten million, and also a fleet of private jets on permanent stand-by in each of those countries.' Lopez shook her head. 'Seriously, how many private jets can one person need?'

'I'd have just one for business and one for pleasure,' Ethan said. 'No sense in being greedy. What's his line of work exactly?'

Lopez scrolled through a few pages before reading slowly.

'SkinGen's current research involves the manipulation of cellular transdifferentiation in mammalian species.'

'Thought so.'

'Sure,' Lopez smiled. 'Something to do with aging, but most of the research has been done behind closed doors under great secrecy. For whatever reason, the government is either unable or uninterested in monitoring whatever old Jeb's up to in his labs.'

Ethan parked the car in front of the colossal building with ranks of glossy-black windows set into aluminum. The whole place was as perfectly arranged as an operating theater, and seemed completely silent as they climbed out of the car, as though everything was artificial and devoid of life.

'Sterile,' Lopez remarked in the hot silence.

Ethan led the way into a vast yet virtually empty air-conditioned lobby, where an immaculately dressed woman sat stranded behind an elaborately sculptured desk of metal and glass, dwarfed by the empty space around her.

'Ethan Warner to see Jeb Oppenheimer,' he said cheerfully and with a bright smile. 'We called ahead . . .

The receptionist did not return the smile, simply looked down at what he presumed was a concealed computer screen and tapped a few keys.

'You didn't book an appointment,' she intoned robotically.

'We're here on behalf of the Santa Fe Police Department,' Lopez cut in. 'Either inconvenience Mister Oppenheimer right now or we'll come back with warrants and tear this place apart.'

The receptionist stared at Lopez in surprise, then picked up a telephone and dialed an extension number. After a brief conversation, she set the telephone down.

'Mister Oppenheimer is waiting for you,' she said without looking up from her screen. 'Top floor, end of the corridor. You can't miss it.'

'Too kind,' Ethan replied, turning for a bank of elevators about a quarter of a mile away across the lobby.

Lopez walked alongside him, smirking. 'Losing your touch, eh?'

'I don't think this guy's staff are human,' Ethan said as they reached the elevators. 'She was probably just plugged into the mains.'

Lopez said nothing as they rode up to the top floor and walked down a long corridor to where another attractive girl sat behind a desk, a blonde this time. Ethan watched as she put down the telephone she was holding and smiled awkwardly, as though someone had surgically attached the grin to her face.

'Mister Oppenheimer will see you now.'

Something about the way she said the name, and how she immediately looked away from him having done so, struck an uncomfortable chord with Ethan as he opened the door to the office and walked inside.

The office was spartan; broad windows to Ethan's right letting in the sunset through opaque glass, thick carpet underfoot and a long glass-topped desk ahead. Behind the desk sat Jeb Oppenheimer, engrossed in something on a monitor. Ethan closed the door behind Lopez, and they walked together to stand before him.

'Sit down,' Oppenheimer said without looking at them.

Ethan exchanged a glance with Lopez before taking a seat before the old man. He realized almost immediately that Oppenheimer's seat was positioned on a raised platform, so that no matter how tall his guests the old man would still be able to look down at them. A white lab coat was draped over the back of his chair.

Oppenheimer had a face like a large roasted walnut that had been smashed flat with a shovel. Deep, wide gullies and canyons wrinkled his face so heavily that it was hard to figure out where his features actually began. Feeble strands of silvery-gray hair were smeared thinly across a scalp sprinkled with liver spots, and the light from the windows shone on his thin skin and rheumy eyes with their blotchy sclera.

'Thank you for seeing us,' Lopez said.

Oppenheimer finished whatever he was doing on his monitor, before turning to regard her with a cold expression.

'I don't have much time,' he said. 'Say your piece and then leave.'

Ethan instantly changed attitude, matching Oppenheimer's tone in a manner he'd learned when interrogating Al-Qaeda members in Iraq. Sound like them, and they'll be more inclined to speak.

'Saffron Oppenheimer. Tell us about her.'

Oppenheimer's eyes swiveled to probe into Ethan's.

'Since when do you tell *me* what to do?'

'Since now,' Ethan replied coolly. 'We have questions regarding several incidents involving laboratories in the Santa Fe area. You can either answer our questions or we can return with warrants to search this entire premises. Your call.'

The eyes narrowed, brimming with a mixture of fury and bemusement.

'Search for what?'

'Whatever we decide is of interest,' Ethan replied, maintaining an uncompromising expression. 'I have experienced first-hand that your granddaughter has a nasty habit of shooting first and asking questions later, so believe me I don't care how much resistance you might think you can put up. Sooner or later you'll tell us anything we need to know, understood?'

Jeb Oppenheimer shuddered. One hand grabbed an ivory cane leaning against the desk beside him and he slammed it down across the glass surface between them with a crack like a gunshot.

'Goddamn your hide, boy!' He leaned forward across the table, and peered deep into Ethan's unflinching gaze. 'You've got balls, and I like that!'

Ethan managed to remain impassive, and Oppenheimer leaned back and slapped his thigh in apparent satisfaction.

'You know how many spineless, effeminate faggots I get coming in here each day groveling for money?' he asked rhetorically. 'At least half a dozen. No more than two a year could I give a damn about, creeps the lot of them.'

'You're all heart,' Lopez muttered.

The old man grinned, peering at her.

'And I suspected that you might be a little spitfire too. Tell me, what would you like to know about my dear little granddaughter?'

'She's one fatality away from becoming a home-grown terrorist,' Ethan said. 'She hit the Aspen Center and blew up their computer servers, not to mention stealing about a dozen primates. State police are on her case as we speak.'

'Doesn't surprise me,' Oppenheimer said, resting his hands on top of his cane. 'She's been in and out of trouble since she got out of diapers, and this isn't the first time she's been involved in violence. She was in court just a few years ago.'

'So we heard,' Ethan nodded. 'Makes me wonder who's been looking out for her all her life. Or not.'

Oppenheimer held Ethan's gaze for a moment before levering himself out of his chair, walking slowly out from behind his desk and sitting on its edge.

'Saffron's parents died in an automobile accident when she was eight years old,' Oppenheimer said, looking at his cane as he spoke. 'My wife and daughter died with them.'

'I'm sorry to hear that,' Lopez said.

'Life,' Oppenheimer murmured, as though lost in his memories, 'has a well-evolved capacity for biting us in the ass no matter how hard we try to avoid it. My advice, Miss Lopez, is to take everything you can from it, give as little as possible back and enjoy the ride, because there's not a goddamn thing waiting for us when it's over.'

Ethan raised an eyebrow. 'It's your optimism I admire.'

'Optimism is for dreamers and losers,' Oppenheimer said. 'Realism is all that matters. Yet a man can't so much as call a spade a spade these days without being dragged through a court for causing offense. *Offense!* How can someone be offended by truth, especially if they're as stupid as so many people are?'

'That's a sweeping statement if ever I've heard one,' Lopez said.

'Indeed it is,' Oppenheimer said, 'but no less true for it. Do you know how SkinGen began? My father, Jeremy Oppenheimer, marketed a cosmetic skin cream in the 1920s for women, which he claimed would reduce wrinkles. Called it Everyoung. When most face creams contained lead, mercury and ethanol that wouldn't so much smooth wrinkles as burn them off your face, his marketing genius was that the cream was basically dyed Vaseline. It sold out across the country, made him a multi-millionaire.' Oppenheimer smiled. 'Every face cream out there today is exactly the same, just rebranded and remarketed and resold to a gullible and stupid population of self-obsessed women who spend billions on the same crap that SkinGen and others supply them year after year with new labels. You could call that a con, but then what about bottled water? An entire industry built on something that nobody in the developed world actually needs – it's no better than tap water, which we have in abundance anyway. Or vitamin pills? Money for nothing, all of them, billions of dollars spent by people on things they already have.'

'Saffron,' Ethan said, pushing the old man back on topic. 'She opposes your work.'

'She *hates* it,' Oppenheimer confirmed, 'and wants none of her inheritance. Good riddance to her, the ungrateful little bitch. If she could only get over herself and realize that the real science we do here is the future, she could have a proper life instead of living in a flea-ridden shack in the Pecos with a bunch of slack-jawed tree-hugging losers who'd be afraid of soap if they knew what it was.'

'We heard that Saffron has an entitlement to SkinGen,' Lopez said.

Oppenheimer looked at her with an expression of absolute disgust.

'Entitlement? I'll say. My wife and I agreed her inheritance when she was five years old, but the damned fool turned down everything when she turned eighteen.' He sighed deeply. 'As she is now my only remaining relative, she is the only heiress to SkinGen.'

29

'She'll inherit the entire company?' Ethan asked, wide-eyed.

'Every last goddamned dime,' Oppenheimer muttered as though even he couldn't believe it. 'She's said that if she is given even a single dollar she'll donate it to *charity*.' Oppenheimer spat the last word out as though it tasted unpleasant. 'When SkinGen became financially success-ful I created an irrevocable living trust that can be terminated only if the trustees and the beneficiaries consent to the termination.'

'For tax reasons,' Ethan said, quickly catching on. 'You spread the income amongst the beneficiaries.'

'A trust does not have to pay income tax on benefici-aries' income.' Oppenheimer nodded. 'I distributed trust income to as many beneficiaries as possible within my family, and in proportions that took best advantage of their personal marginal tax rates. The beneficiaries then pay the tax on distributions made to them. Simple and effective.'

'Except that Saffron's now the only remaining benefi-
ciary,' Lopez said. 'I don't suppose you know why
Saffron has become so opposed to SkinGen?'

Oppenheimer shrugged, looking at his cane again.

'Saffron is one of those college drop-outs who think
that we can run the world on wind farms, cow dung and
happy songs. Left to her and her ilk, the world would
collapse into colonies of dope-smoking hippies dancing
round trees at midnight and wiping pig shit into their
faces in an effort to cure the endemic syphilis they'd no
doubt generate. Civilization would regress to medieval
times within a generation.'

'Sounds a little harsh,' Ethan said. 'Most of them just
want to see the back of fossil fuels.'

'Pah!' Oppenheimer bellowed. 'Of course they do!
We all do. You know anybody who likes paying half of
their salary just to travel to and from work, or heat their
homes? But these idiots think that we can plug cars into
wall sockets and the problem will disappear. That's
why realism is the only way forward. Go outside to
your car, put it in neutral but don't start the engine.
Then push it all the way home. If you're fifty miles
from home, it'll take you about a week, if you're lucky.
Start the engine and it'll take you an hour. That's how
much energy is in just one gallon of petroleum. Assholes
like Saffron think they'll get the same efficiency out of
hydrogen cells.'

Lopez frowned.

'There's still homes that need heating, stuff like that.
It can all be found in different ways.'

'Such as?' Oppenheimer crowed. 'Wind farms are

useless, a complete waste of time. They generate power so unpredictably that almost nothing can be used efficiently. Twenty thousand of them can't even come close to a single power station, and even the greens don't like them because they spoil the pretty countryside and might hurt birds, who they apparently think don't know how to fly around obstacles. Makes you wonder why forests aren't full of dead birds that have collided with trees. Nuclear power could save us, but the same people who won't let us burn coal also won't let us use nuclear because it might, possibly be dangerous if something bad happened, leaving us with the square root of fuck all to power our homes.'

Ethan couldn't help but grin at the old man's propensity to rant. He instantly wondered whether he was grinning because it amused him or because the old man was right.

'So, oh wise one, what is your answer to our global predicament?'

Oppenheimer sat back down on the edge of the desk, a wide grin creasing his lips.

'Get rid of most of us, and let those who remain live in comfort and security.'

'Genocide!' Lopez gasped. 'Are you kidding?'

Oppenheimer shook his head slowly.

'I expected more of you, Miss Lopez. Not genocide. Why waste the bullets? Natural wastage is the key to reducing the population of the planet to more manageable levels. Imagine, no more over-consumption of the world's resources. No more overcrowding. Reduced spread of disease and antibiotic resistance, improved land yield, reduced conflict, increased living standards. Without it, the human race is doomed and a global disease pandemic almost inevitable. There are no flaws, none whatsoever.'

'Except the little matter of removing a few billion people,' Ethan pointed out.

'Did you know that approximately one hundred fifty thousand people die each day on our planet?' Oppenheimer said. 'That's about fifty-five million per year, and two hundred seventy-five million people over five years. Put simply, if no births occurred on our planet for five years, the equivalent of the entire population of the United States would vanish from our world.'

Lopez shook her head.

'No wonder Saffron checked out,' she said quietly. 'You're not talking about genocide, you're talking about eugenics.'

'Eugenics was abandoned decades ago,' Ethan said. 'You'd be up in court today if you openly supported such measures.'

'Would I?' Oppenheimer challenged him. 'In fact, eugenics is alive and well in our modern society. It never went away.'

'That's ridiculous,' Lopez snorted.

'Marie Stopes,' Oppenheimer replied, 'was one of the leading proponents of eugenics. Her abortion clinics were deliberately established in poor neighborhoods in order to prevent the so-called *undesirables* from breeding through unwanted pregnancies. Today they're upheld as a model of progressive support for the vulnerable, but eugenics was the driving force behind them. Marie Stopes called for undesirable men to be sterilized by surgery and women by X-rays to prevent them from weakening the human stock.' Oppenheimer studied the tip of his ivory cane as he went on. 'The American Eugenics Society only changed its name in 1972, to the Society for the Study of Social Biology. Britain's Eugenics Society waited even longer before becoming the Galton Institute.'

Ethan shook his head.

'It doesn't make any difference. The human right to decide always comes above any philosophical or theological demands on society. It's not up to us, it's up to the mother.'

'Agreed,' Oppenheimer said, 'but in many countries parents breed children in order to send them out to work. The more children they have, the more they can earn, but at a price: they have more mouths to feed. There are only so many jobs available, so such countries end up with endemic unemployment, crime and poverty. These people, Mister Warner, don't know how to help themselves.'

'They're not retarded,' Lopez muttered. 'They don't have a choice.'

'But they do!' Oppenheimer insisted. 'In the West our populations have stabilized. In fact, they're aging because we don't have as many children as we used to, a direct result of sensible family planning and abortion facilities for those who require them. Our populations are sustainable. But those in the developing world are growing at a trimetric rate and they all want to live like Americans, with large houses, pools, plasma televisions and five meals a day.' Oppenheimer looked at her seriously. 'Our planet cannot support them, no matter how advanced our technologies become. Something has to be done.'

'You're wasting your time,' Ethan said. 'A man who needs children in order to earn enough to eat doesn't care about anything you might have to say about it.'

'Which is why,' Oppenheimer said, 'we must endeavor to make the decision for them. It isn't pretty, politically correct or even necessarily possible, but we must try because if we do not, within sixty years we'll no longer have a choice. Society will collapse, either through lack of resources or the conflicts resulting from them. Do you know what the greatest likely cause of war is in this day and age?'

Ethan shook his head.

'Water,' Oppenheimer said. 'Wars over water are already being fought in the Middle East at a local level, but they're spreading fast. Before long, the tribes fighting for water will be nations fighting for control of rivers and aquifers, the first of the resource wars I've been predicting for decades.'

Ethan began to get a picture in his mind of Jeb Oppenheimer, a man whose basic observations were astute but whose mind had been twisted into that of the fundamentalist.

'What's all that got to do with Tyler Willis?' Ethan asked.

The abrupt change of subject seemed to catch Oppenheimer off guard. Ethan noted the rheumy eyes wobble as the old man sought a way past the question.

'Tyler Willis? He was a biochemist of some kind, researching aging.'

'Was?' Ethan repeated. The change of tack had unsettled Oppenheimer's train of thought, and he could almost see the old man cursing himself before he spoke.

'He used to work at the Los Alamos Laboratories,' Oppenheimer said finally. 'I'm not aware of his current research or location.'

'He's had several papers published in the major journals recently,' Lopez said. 'I'm surprised you haven't seen them.'

Ethan noticed that Oppenheimer's stance had not changed for several moments, as though he were a granite statue rooted to the spot. A classic sign, he recognized, of someone entirely caught up in their own desperate thought processes.

'I don't have time to read all of the journals,' the old man snapped, and then shifted his position as though suddenly aware of his rapture. 'There are literally thousands published every day.'

'Willis worked for a rival laboratory to yours,' Ethan said, not giving the old man time to think. 'Strange that Saffron would hit its vivisection laboratories instead of attacking your operations.'

'She learned her goddamn lesson the last time she tried to attack my operation,' Oppenheimer shot back with a scowl. 'One of her grubby little friends got himself killed. He was dead by the time they got him to Santa Fe.'

'And you have no idea of the whereabouts of Tyler

Willis now, or of a medical examiner by the name of Lillian Cruz?'

Oppenheimer peered at Ethan.

'Who the goddamn hell is she?'

'New Mexico ME,' Lopez said. 'Vanished two days ago, along with the remains of a man named Hiram Conley.'

'What the hell would I want to abduct a morgue attendant and a corpse for?'

'Who said they were abducted?' Ethan asked, raising an eyebrow.

Oppenheimer's leathery skin rippled with frustration, his hand wobbling on top of his cane as his temper frayed.

'What do you two actually want?'

Ethan, enjoying the old man's discomfort, shrugged.

'The truth, which we'll get before long one way or the other. I think you're a successful man with powerful friends who believes he can do anything he likes. I'm here to tell you that's not the case.'

Oppenheimer leaned forward and glared down at Ethan.

'Now you listen to me, you sniveling little shit. I can have you out of this office in ten seconds and out of the goddamn county in thirty. You don't come in here talking down to me! You come in here on your goddamn knees and beg for my assistance and cooperation!'

He jabbed the cane in Ethan's direction. As he did so, Ethan noticed the edges of his shirt cuffs were lightly splattered with bloodstains. He looked at the lab coat draped over the back of Oppenheimer's chair. A pair of fashionable-looking spectacles were poking out from one pocket, black-rimmed with burgundy frames. He knew immediately where he had last seen a pair of spectacles like them: at Los Alamos, worn by Tyler Willis.

Ethan leapt out of his chair, grabbed the cane halfway down and spun it in his grasp before thrusting it up under Oppenheimer's chin. The old man pivoted awkwardly backwards and sideways, slamming down onto the glass desk with his own cane pinning him down.

Ethan leaned in close. 'Where's Willis?'

He saw a flash of fear in the old man's eyes and then a flame of outrage. Oppenheimer let go of the cane, reaching out and fumbling for an alarm button concealed out of sight under the desk. Ethan grabbed the frail wrist easily and held it like a vice.

'I can snap you like a twig,' Ethan said. 'Where's Willis?'

'I'll have you for this, Warner,' Oppenheimer growled, spittle flecking his dry lips. 'Government or not, I'll have you gutted from bow to stern.'

'Not before I have the entire Santa Fe police department tearing through this building,' Ethan said, pressing down on the cane and causing Oppenheimer's labored breathing to lodge painfully through his throat. 'Where's Willis?'

Oppenheimer began shuddering, his chest heaving as a cough erupted from his ruined lungs. Ethan leaned back as strings of mucus splattered from the old man's mouth to drool in loops from his cheek. Oppenheimer rolled away off his desk, collapsing beside it and coughing uncontrollably.

'Take it easy, Ethan,' Lopez said in alarm. 'Jesus Christ, and you say *I'm* reckless.'

'Willis is here, those are his glasses,' Ethan said, pointing at the spectacles in Oppenheimer's lab coat before glancing at the opaque windows to check that nobody could see in. 'Come on.'

30

Ethan dashed out of Oppenheimer's office, and strode to where the secretary was still sitting behind her desk. Ethan leaned on the desk.

'Tyler Willis, about twenty-eight years old, five nine, black. Have you seen him?'

The secretary stared with wide blue eyes at Ethan and reared back in her chair.

'No, I haven't seen him.'

Lopez pushed Ethan aside.

'Jesus, give her a break,' she said before looking at the girl. 'What's your name?'

'Claire,' the girl said, one hand on her chest as though her heart was about to burst out.

'Okay, Claire. Your boss has bloodstains on his shirt and Tyler Willis has been missing for several hours. We think that Oppenheimer may have done something to him. This is a criminal investigation and if a crime is discovered, every single employee in this company will be implicated. Do you understand?'

Ethan watched as the girl nodded slowly, her gaze steady now.

'Do you know where Tyler Willis is?' Lopez repeated.

'No,' Claire said, and cast a glance at Oppenheimer's office door. 'But when I buzzed Mister Oppenheimer to inform him of your arrival, I heard someone screaming in the background.'

Ethan stared at her.

'Where was he?'

Claire's face blanched with fear.

'If Mister Oppenheimer finds out that I've said anything, he might do to me what he's been doing to—'

'No, he won't,' Lopez said firmly, 'because he can't now that we've been here and seen you alive and well. Go and help him when we're gone, he'll never know. Where was he when you heard the screaming?'

Claire took a breath and pointed down the hall.

'The quarantine labs, two floors down, third on the right.'

Ethan didn't wait for Lopez, launching himself down the hall.

Jeb Oppenheimer gagged as a thick soup of mucus lodged in his throat, his face aching as he coughed, his lungs burning for air. He struggled onto his side on the thick carpet, his stomach heaving as his vision began to sparkle with stars of light. He was about to pass out when a pair of glossy black heels appeared before him. He swiveled his gaze upward to see Claire standing over him, her legs apart and one hand on her hip as she held in her other hand a small plastic chamber with three twelve-inch rubber tubes hanging from it.

Oppenheimer clawed with one hand for the device, but Claire lifted it out of his reach.

'Double my salary,' she said. 'And if it's sex you want, get some other poor bitch to do it, understood?'

Oppenheimer's eyes widened with rage and he shook his head.

Claire squatted down beside him, the tubes still out of reach, and considered him for a moment.

'Do you realize how hard it is for a girl to get ahead these days?' she asked conversationally as Oppenheimer's terminal breaths gargled somewhere deep in his esophagus. 'It's as if we're just pawns in rich men's games. Tell me, Jeb: how much is your life worth?' Claire's gaze turned stony and cold. 'How much is it really worth?'

Oppenheimer's vision began to darken and his heartbeat pulsed weakly through his skull as he finally nodded frantically. Claire knelt down beside him and shoved one of the tubes into his cold, bony hand. Oppenheimer grabbed it and shoved it as far down his throat as he could. Claire took a second tube, put it in her mouth and sucked hard.

A thick green sludge poured from Oppenheimer's throat into the tube. The old man dropped the tube and sucked in an immense whistling breath as Claire stood up, the mess now contained in the chamber between the tubes. Oppenheimer lay for a moment before slowly struggling to his feet.

'Where . . . did . . . they go?' he whispered to her.

'Quarantine,' she said, then raised the plastic tubes and

chamber to his face. 'Back-date my salary from when I started, or I'll sell out quicker than you did when I sucked this shit from your lungs, understood?'

Oppenheimer glared at her, but he nodded before hitting the concealed button on his desk.

'Security to quarantine, arrest and detain Ethan Warner and Nicola Lopez immediately.'

Ethan rushed down the stairwell, leaping four steps at a time, with Lopez just managing to keep pace behind him. He came to the bottom and barged through a set of double doors into a corridor, just in time to see two large, suited men running side by side toward him, their combined shoulders almost as wide as the corridor itself.

A fist flashed into Ethan's vision. He let his own momentum keep him moving toward the fist as he nipped sideways, a thick arm shooting past his face. He folded his own arm over it as the big security guard stumbled past him, and drove one knee deep into the man's belly. The guard folded over at the waist with a grunt of pain and sprawled onto the ground beside him. Ethan released his grip as the second guard whipped a nightstick from his belt and flicked it open, stepping over his fallen comrade and lunging at Ethan with the point of the nightstick while reaching out for his throat with his other hand.

Ethan dropped instinctively and pivoted on his right foot, coming up under the nightstick and driving his fist into the guard's groin. To his surprise the guard was quick, jerking himself away from the blow that glanced across his thigh and whipping the nightstick down toward Ethan's head. Ethan raised an arm to block it, only to see Lopez catch the man's wrist in one hand and whip her elbow into his eye like a slugger sending a ball out of the park.

The guard staggered backward and away from her as Ethan leapt to his feet, fists up and ready. Lopez pulled her baton from beneath her jacket, prowling forward as Ethan covered her, forcing the guard back toward the door he was protecting.

'You're not under arrest yet,' Ethan said, 'but you try to stop us getting into the laboratory and you will be, understood?'

The guard wavered but stood his ground, switching his gaze nervously between them. He was a big man but he was cornered, outnumbered and uncertain of his chances. Any bravado he might have harbored had deserted him in a hurry. Quite suddenly, he turned and dashed through the laboratory door. Ethan lunged after him, slamming into the door as it closed and a heavy locking mechanism slipped into place on the other side.

Ethan turned and strode toward the fallen guard, seeing keys hanging from his belt, but before he could reach for them the double doors at the far end of the corridor opened and a dozen more security guards blundered through.

'Stay where you are!'

Ethan backed off, watching as they moved to block his access to the laboratory. Lopez held her baton close by her thigh, ready to lash out at anyone who dared touch her. Behind them, standing silently, was Jeb

Oppenheimer. He looked at them for a long moment, then raised one hand and wagged a crooked finger at them.

'Now, that wasn't very nice, was it?' he asked.

'Let Willis go,' Ethan hissed. 'You'll only make it worse for yourself if we report back that he's being held here.'

Oppenheimer's features creased into a soulless grin.

'Who says that you're leaving?' he asked. 'Ever?'

Ethan was about to open his mouth to reply when half of the security guards rushed him at once, smashing into him like a freight train and driving him to the ground. He heard Lopez cry out as she too was overpowered. Within moments, they were dragged to their feet with their arms yanked up around their shoulder blades.

Jeb Oppenheimer walked slowly toward Ethan, leaning on his cane with each stride.

'It would appear we have three subjects for dissection this evening,' he murmured in delight.

'State police will be in here within minutes,' Ethan snapped. 'You'll be in jail by nightfall.'

'For what?' Oppenheimer asked, looking deep into Ethan's eyes. 'Where is your evidence? And there's no reason for the county sheriff to obtain search warrants, no matter how much you cry foul. Corporate privilege, my unfortunate young friend.'

Ethan was about to speak when a disembodied, digital voice interrupted them.

'Mister Oppenheimer?'

Ethan recognized the voice of the old man's secretary,

Claire. Oppenheimer made his way to a panel on the wall and pressed a button.

'What is it?'

'The state police are here looking for Warner and Lopez. What should I say to them?'

'Tell them we're down here!' Ethan shouted. 'Tell them Tyler Willis is here!'

Oppenheimer smiled at Ethan. No reply came from the intercom.

'Money, Mister Warner, provides far greater loyalty than morals.' Oppenheimer's smile disappeared as he considered his dilemma, and then he keyed the microphone again. 'Tell them that Warner and Lopez are just leaving.'

Ethan felt a wave of relief as Oppenheimer stepped away from the speaker and approached him, glowering with fury.

'Rest assured, Mister Warner, that by the time this is all over I will enjoy watching you die.'

'If so, I'll be sure to take you with me,' Ethan growled.

The guards pushed and shoved Ethan and Lopez out of the corridor, maintaining their grip on them as they rode the elevator back down to the foyer. The robotic receptionist didn't even glance up as they were manhandled out of the glass doors, where a pair of squad cars and two USAMRIID vehicles were parked.

Ethan saw Enrico Zamora, his arm in a sling, standing beside one of the squad cars, and called out to him, 'Tyler Willis is inside. We need a warrant right away.'

Zamora offered Ethan an apologetic look, as Butch

Cutler approached Ethan with disdain etched on his face.

'You're to leave this property immediately and not return. You're also to report to your commander at the Defense Intelligence Agency immediately before returning to Illinois right away.'

Ethan stared at Cutler in disbelief.

'There's a man inside this building being held against his will. He needs our help to—'

'There's also a burning apartment in Santa Fe, forensics teams on site examining bullets and a wounded officer standing right behind me. I don't know who the goddamn hell you think you are, Warner, but your time here is done. If you're not out of this county by sundown I'll have you both arrested and locked down, is that understood?'

Tyler Willis lay on the gurney, shivering from the cold and the loss of blood that now lay in thick congealing pools beneath him. The conversation outside of the door had ended, and he realized that Ethan Warner had failed. Beside him, Lillian Cruz stood with tape over her mouth and the heavy-set guard watching over them both.

Jeb Oppenheimer walked back into the lab, closing the door behind him and putting on his gloves. The old man walked across to Willis and picked up the scalpel once more, looking down and without hesitation pressing the sharp blade across Willis's flank. A white-hot lance of pain surged through his body and he gagged in agony. Oppenheimer ripped the tape from his mouth, and through his tears and terror Willis spluttered, 'I swear to you, I don't know anything. I don't know where Hiram Conley got that infection.'

Oppenheimer's face filled his vision as he glared down at him.

'So then, how about that kidney?'

31

GOLDEN
NEW MEXICO

8.37 p.m.

The late-summer sun was sinking behind the mountains to the west, casting long black tiger-stripe shadows against the glowing desert as Lee Carson rode slowly down the main street of the town, a pair of tumbleweeds rustling as they rolled across the dusty earth, vanishing past the old merchandise store. His horse whinnied softly beneath him and he patted her flanks with a gloved hand, trying to forget the horrific image of what lay within it.

The store was made of bricks, but the long landing and porch were clapperboard, the paint faded beneath the wrath of a thousand suns. Rows of sagging buildings lined the streets, the low sunlight beaming through their long-abandoned interiors, while the crumbling ruins of the old San Francisco church and cemetery basked in lonely shadows nearby. Most people would never have dreamed of coming here at nightfall, but for Lee Carson it was one of the few places where he felt at home.

A ghost town.

Golden had been abandoned for at least a hundred

years, its postal service discontinued in 1928. A town constructed far out into the wilderness like many others, its church had been built in the 1830s, but the demise of pioneers and gold rushes had seen the town eventually abandoned to the desert. There were others: La Bajada, Glorietta, San Pedro, Dolores. Carson remembered them all, not as they were now but as thriving towns built around mines and cattle stations, or along the routes of the great western railway lines that crossed the endless wilderness. Now, most of the roofs of the mud-brick buildings were sagging or had caved in completely, leaving skeletal timber frames exposed to the harsh elements. A few faded signs still adorned the awnings of shops, advertising ironmongery, farriers, even a jewelry boutique, distant memories of a once thriving community.

A hot wind moaned down the street, carrying with it the spectral sounds of horses, people and carts, whispers of the past haunting Carson's ears. He turned in his saddle, looking over his shoulder into the deepening shadows behind him. Nothing moved but for a spiraling dust devil whipping up a vortex of sand.

Carson stopped his horse in the center of the street, listening to the ancient town's soft noises, creaking timbers and rustling grass. He closed his eyes.

'State your business!'

Carson's heart bounced against the inside of his chest as he whirled around in his saddle, drawing a pistol from a holster beneath his jacket and aiming the weapon behind him.

An older man leaned back against the wall of the abandoned merchandise shop, lighting a pipe that flared orange in the shadows and illuminated his wide-brimmed Stetson and tasseled hide jacket. Blue smoke smoldered from the pipe as he extinguished the match, peering out at Carson from beneath the rim of his hat.

'We need to talk,' Carson said, lowering his pistol.

'We ain't got nothin' to say, boy,' came the reply, casual and without interest. 'You'll be on y'way now.'

The man turned, his boots striking the clapperboards the only sound echoing through the town's long shadows. Carson cursed beneath his breath, turning his horse and cantering across the street to cut the man off.

'I'd say we've got plenty to be discussin',' Carson snapped, yanking the horse up at the end of the shop's landing.

The man looked up at him curiously, still sucking on his pipe.

'You lost that right, Carson,' he said, a thick moustache rising and falling with each word. ''Bout ninety-five years ago, if ma memory serves me, when you decided to spend your days bedding high-falutin' women and your nights drinking Pop Skull from cheap bottles.'

Carson vaulted out of his saddle, tying the horse to the nearest awning pillar with a loose flourish of the reins before walking up to the man and standing directly in front of him.

'As opposed to what? Foraging for scraps of hardtack out in the desert for ninety years gone by? That what you calling horse sense now, Ellison?'

Ellison Thorne stood to his full height, a good two inches above Carson's, and Carson fought the urge not to take a pace back. Carson was young and strong of build,

clean of features as they used to say, but Ellison Thorne was
a legend amongst men, barrel-chested and well over six
feet tall. It was once said that during a fire-fight with the
Confederates out Fort Union way, a stray musket ball had
started a fire near a barrel of powder on the siege lines.
Most men had run away from the impending explosion.
Ellison Thorne had run toward it, picking up the hundred-
pound barrel and hurling it across the lines toward the
enemy. Twenty yards, they said it had flown.

'You turned your back on us,' Ellison boomed, 'right
after you joined the Jesse Evans Gang.'

Carson sighed. 'Jesus, Ellison, that was a hundred
thirty years o'more ago. Can't you let it lie?'

Ellison Thorne had fallen in with cattle farmer John
Tunstall during the Lincoln County War of 1878, a
bitter county-wide dispute over the control of the
monopoly on the dry-goods trade. Thorne, along with
his comrades from the Civil War, had served in the
deputized posse of the Lincoln County Regulators
alongside Doc Scurlock, Charlie Bowdre and Henry
McCarty, aka William H. Bonney, aka Billy the Kid.
Together, they'd killed a number of Evans Gang gunfight-
ers, including Buckshot Roberts, at the gunfight of
Blazer's Mills. Carson, resenting Thorne, had gone across
to the regulators' arch enemies under Jesse Evans and
Lawrence Murphy. The battles between the gangs had
gone down into Wild West legend, although Billy the
Kid had been pinned for far more killings than he'd been
responsible for, and had never led the regulators. Ever
since, Carson had ridden alone, rarely meeting Ellison
Thorne.

'I got somethin' that'll interest you now, Ellison,' Carson insisted, 'whether you like it or not.'

Ellison Thorne loomed over him, the glow from his pipe demonically illuminating his drooping moustache and craggy features.

'What could you possibly have that would interest me, boy?'

Carson stood his ground and ripped off his gloves, holding his hands up.

Ellison Thorne looked at those ruined hands for a long few seconds, reaching up slowly for his pipe and puffing thoughtfully before nodding once.

'Interesting.'

Carson stared at him for a moment.

'That's all you can goddamn say? *Interesting?* Jesus Christ, my hands are falling off and you're more interested in your pipe than . . .'

Ellison Thorne stood back a pace and slipped off his jacket. Carson's voice trailed off like the summer winds into the night as he stared. Thorne's shirtsleeves were rolled up to his elbows, and in the golden half-light of the sunset his thick forearms were a tangled, sinewy web of desiccated muscle and sagging gray skin.

'Gotten your fill?' Thorne rumbled at him.

Carson nodded blankly as the big man slipped his jacket back on and watched him for a few long seconds.

'What do we do?' Carson asked in dismay. 'This ain't happened afore now.'

Ellison Thorne took his pipe from beneath his moustache and examined its contents as he spoke.

'I haven't heard from the others yet,' he said ominously. 'What were you plannin' on?'

Carson blinked, and shook his head.

'I ain't got no plan,' he admitted helplessly. 'Old man Conley was trying to get help from some guy up Santa Fe way, afore he got shot. He opined that we might find a cure for this affliction.'

Ellison Thorne nodded.

'He was a Jonah who went out on his own hook, mixin' too much with the natives when we needed to keep this amongst ourselves. It ain't what we agreed.'

'We weren't *dying* when we agreed to anything,' Carson protested. 'Besides, I didn't agree anyways. Why'd I want to be stuck out here on my own, away from civilization? We got nobody out here to help us!'

Ellison Thorne nodded thoughtfully and drew again on his pipe.

'We'll meet the day after tomorrow, usual place and time. It'll give us the cover we need to blend in.'

Carson shook his head.

'Another meeting. All that jawing hasn't fixed us up one bit, Ellison. We need something done about this! How well do you think we'll goddamn blend in if we've got bits falling off us all the time?'

Ellison Thorne pushed past Carson with his shoulder and strode slowly out into the darkness.

'Getting yourself into a conniption fit ain't gonna help anyone. The day after tomorrow, Lee. Don't be dawdling.'

'We're dying,' Carson said sadly.

Ellison Thorne slowed and turned to look at him over his shoulder.

'Only temporarily,' he rumbled. 'There are bigger things than just us to consider, Lee. You should have paid heed to that before you started living in the cities, drinking and whoring. Hankerin' after a quick fix now's a lost cause. Stay out of sight until we meet.'

With that, Ellison Thorne walked out into the night to where Carson could see a horse tethered in a dense thicket of bushes no more than fifty yards away. How he hadn't seen it on the way in he didn't know, but then he had long since lost all the survival skills required out here in the lonely deserts. Ellison Thorne and his men had instead remained here for the past hundred forty years.

For the first time in a century and a half, Lee Carson felt lonely and afraid.

32

SKINGEN CORP
SANTA FE

11.14 p.m.

The laboratory was a windowless cell but the clock on the wall told Lillian it was night and she had been working for almost six hours straight under the silent gaze of a SkinGen security guard. She hadn't eaten or drunk a thing and the guard had even escorted her to the latrine.

Tyler Willis lay nearby on the mortuary slab, groaning and shivering occasionally. To her relief, Jeb Oppenheimer had refrained from slicing the poor guy's kidneys straight out of his body, deciding instead to leave the threat unfinished in order to force Lillian into working further on Hiram Conley's remains.

Lillian had been happy to see him leave; she would obey his parting command to find out once and for all what had infected Hiram Conley's body before he finally died. But she was also certain that Oppenheimer had absolutely no intention of letting either her or Willis leave the building alive. They had witnessed too much. Lillian had to escape.

She turned, putting down the scalpel with which she

had been dissecting Conley's crumbling corpse, and looked at the guard.

'That's it,' she said finally. 'I can't go on without something to eat and drink.'

The guard glared at her but remained silent.

'What?' Lillian asked. 'Too many words at once for you to understand? Food. Drink. How's that?'

The guard took two paces across the room and grabbed her throat with one chunky hand, shoving her backwards into the worktops and straining her arm against the handcuff still pinning her to Conley's mortuary slab.

'You stay until you're finished.'

'I can't work properly,' Lillian shot back, refusing to be intimidated, 'if I'm exhausted, hungry and thirsty. I'll make mistakes, miss evidence. You want your boss to find out that you half-starved me and then I screwed up?'

The guard held her for a moment longer, the handful of cells in his brain churning laboriously as he considered her point of view, and then he dropped his grip on her and turned for the door without another word. Lillian watched as he unlocked the doors and left the laboratory, locking the doors behind him.

Lillian waited until he was out of earshot and then looked at Willis.

'Tyler? Wake up!'

Willis groaned, his head lolling to one side as he tried to focus on her. Lillian waved a hand in front of his face.

'Tyler, I need your help.'

Willis licked his parched lips, struggling to remain conscious.

'Water,' he said. 'I need water. And my stomach hurts.'

'The guard's on his way back here with something to drink,' she said. 'I can give you more morphine, but you've lost too much blood to give it intravenously – it might kill you.'

She turned to face his body, his chest and stomach now sealed by a neat row of stitches that she'd administered as soon as Oppenheimer had left. The old man's cuts had not been deep, and none of Willis's internal organs had been damaged as far as she could tell. But he'd lost a hell of a lot of blood, and the old bastard hadn't even given Lillian a saline drip to replace Tyler's lost fluids.

God only knew what Oppenheimer would do to him when he returned. Lillian closed her eyes, and made a swift decision.

Using a syringe, she extracted morphine from the small vial she'd been supplied with, and glanced up briefly at the camera staring unblinkingly down at her from one corner of the laboratory. She turned to shield Willis's body from view, tapped the needle, and then slipped it gently into Willis's femoral artery.

Slowly she saw him relax, his breathing calm and the sweat dry from his forehead. Using her scalpel, she began easing off some of the dressings now brittle with blackened, congealed blood, replacing them as she went. She dabbed at the skin under the dressings with a soft, cool cloth.

'That's good,' he whispered.

'Tell me what happened,' Lillian said. 'Tell me why he's doing this to you. To us.'

Willis swallowed thickly and shook his head.

'I can't, it's too dangerous.'

'Dangerous?' Lillian retaliated in a harsh whisper. 'Do you honestly think we're getting out of here alive? We're already screwed, so the least you can damned well do is explain to me why the hell I'm stuck in here with you!'

Willis sighed.

'Hiram Conley came to me a few weeks ago,' he said, lifting one hand to massage his temples, 'with a sample of halobacteria that he said came from a hidden cave somewhere in New Mexico. He refused to tell me where, only that I should check the bacteria out and then he'd visit me again, said that I'd understand. I did what he said and put the bacteria in solution. Damn me, if they didn't revive. When we checked the age of the samples they came in at two hundred fifty million years old.'

'Bacillus permians.' Lillian nodded, glancing at the close-circuit camera and keeping her voice down. 'I read about it in the papers, the oldest revived species ever discovered.'

'Conley met me again a week or two later, and told me he was infected with the bacteria,' Willis went on. 'He told me he was a hundred ninety years old.'

'He was, give or take a few years,' Lillian confirmed. 'I've run every test on him since Oppenheimer brought me here.'

Willis smiled despite his discomfort.

'I didn't believe him at first,' he said, 'but pretty soon I realized he was telling the truth, not least because he was dying and was searching for a cure.'

'The decay?' Lillian asked. 'On his arms?'

'Yeah, it was like he was coming apart at the seams. Some kind of cellular breakdown.'

'So, you were working with him to try and reverse that?'

Willis sighed again, his eyes closing as Lillian continued replacing the bandages on his stomach.

'Partly,' he said. 'I'd been approached recently by Jeb Oppenheimer, not long after I'd published the papers on *Bacillus permians*. He wanted to hire me as a specialist, offered to treble my salary. I said no; I knew I was onto something big and wanted to keep it to myself. But when Hiram Conley came on the scene, I decided that if I could figure out what was keeping him from aging, I could sell it to SkinGen for far more than just a fat salary.'

Lillian stopped working, looking down at Willis.

'You sold out,' she said finally.

Willis nodded.

'I'm not proud of it, but I was looking at retiring at thirty-five years of age. Who wouldn't have taken the chance? Sure, I could have stuck with it and figured it out myself, but I thought: what the hell? Let Oppenheimer sort it out, and I'll buy myself a condo in the Bahamas and spend the rest of my life sipping cocktails on a yacht somewhere.'

'What happened?' she asked him.

'I offered to take Hiram Conley's blood to Oppenheimer, who could then use it for tests, but Jeb wanted Hiram Conley to come in himself. I met Conley out in Glorietta Pass, and was trying to convince him it was a good idea when he suddenly pulled his gun and shot me.'

Lillian frowned.

'So how come Oppenheimer's got you here now? Surely he could have just left you alone once he'd grabbed Conley's corpse from my morgue.'

'Because I didn't tell him about the cellular degradation,' Willis said. 'He only figured that out once he'd taken a look at the corpse and realized that his people at SkinGen didn't have the skills necessary to manufacture or engineer a genetic copy of the infection. Even the blood samples I'd taken from Conley had degraded. I'd pitched the whole thing to him as good as I could to get the most money, and he was stuck with a corpse that he couldn't use. I guess Oppenheimer wanted revenge, and for me to figure it out along with you.'

Lillian nodded.

'And then he kills us both,' she said. 'Are there other people chasing this?'

'Some,' Willis admitted. 'Very wealthy people, who had also read my published papers and were interested in investing in my work. I don't have any names, but I did some research and know that they were part of something called the Bilderberg Group. You ever heard of them?'

Lillian shook her head.

'Wealthy individuals like Oppenheimer?' she asked. 'Pharmaceutical companies?'

'No,' Willis shook his head, '*way* bigger than that.' He looked up at her. 'And two detectives, government people or so they said. Ethan Warner and Nicola Lopez. They seemed solid, but I got jumped by Oppenheimer's goons before I could tell them much.'

'I think they were the ones looking for us here,' Lillian confirmed, recalling the earlier altercation outside the laboratory.

'You figured anything out yet?' Willis asked her.

Lillian glanced across at Hiram Conley's remains.

'Nothing adds up,' she admitted. 'What little blood I managed to extract shows signs of anemia, but there was nothing to explain the mummification of the remains, especially not overnight.'

Willis nodded, his voice sounding dreamlike, as though he were struggling to connect his thought processes.

'The anemia could be due to a mineral deficiency,' he said. 'I noticed it in Hiram's blood pathology before he died. The mummification is almost certainly calcification.'

Lillian blinked in surprise. Calcification was a conserv-ative-transformative phenomenon by which a corpse could appear petrified when the skeleton rapidly absorbed calcium salts in the presence of bacterial decomposition of internal organs.

'You think that the bacteria inside him affected his calcium levels in some way?'

Willis shrugged lazily, his eyelids half closed.

'Seems likely to me,' he murmured. 'If he was host-ing a bacterial infection as I assume he was, then the bacteria must have themselves consumed resources. That's how they live inside us symbiotically, consuming and replenishing. Maybe Hiram's death starved them of whatever they needed, and his apparent mummification was the result?'

Lillian nodded, glancing again at the corpse.

'Maybe you're right,' she whispered, and then looked down at Willis.

His eyes were closed, and as she watched his breathing slowed gently until his chest stopped moving. Lillian stared at his serene features for a long moment, and then moved away from his body.

The door to the laboratory opened and the guard walked back in carrying a tray of food. Lillian looked across at him and wiped a tear from her eye.

'You're too late,' she said softly. 'Oppenheimer must have cut him deeper than he realized.'

The guard took one look at Willis's inert body, dropped the tray and dashed away.

33

SANTA FE

11.36 p.m.

'What the hell's going on?'

Ethan stood in a hotel room on the city's south side, looking at the twinkling lights outside his window as he listened to Doug Jarvis on the other end of the line back in Washington DC.

'Your man Oppenheimer has friends in high places, Ethan. A guy turned up yesterday in the offices here from USAMRIID, some big-shot who's rated the situation down in Santa Fe as a potential toxic hazard. They're trying to get jurisdiction of the case and have pushed the DIA and our own medical outfit, NCMI, out of the way.'

'That's crap,' Ethan insisted. 'If this was a disease it would have spread by now. The apartment block Tyler Willis lived in is home to hundreds of people.'

'It's not just that, Ethan,' Doug said. 'The high and mighty here at the DIA aren't best pleased with your investigation down there. They need someone who can work under the radar, not start gunfights and blow up apartment blocks.'

'We didn't do the shooting or the blowing up of anything, Doug. Whoever hit that building was either trying to take Willis out, take us out or destroy evidence. Maybe all three. Fact is, they did a damned good job. We've got nothing much left to go on without Willis, and Saffron Oppenheimer's little gang will be almost impossible to find out in the Pecos.'

Ethan waited for a long moment until he heard Doug sigh on the other end of the line.

'There's not much that I can do this end except keep my boss out of the loop and hope you two can come up with something before USAMRIID really start putting the heat on. You sure you haven't got anything else there?'

Ethan looked down at the bed where a photograph lay on the sheet. He picked it up, looking at the faded image of the group of Civil War soldiers.

'Maybe,' he said. 'Lieutenant Zamora's off duty and is meeting us here shortly. He's got some kind of information for us that he couldn't share while USAMRIID were on site at SkinGen. Listen, Doug, can you have a dig around for me, see why it is they're coming down hard on us? They have no real connection professionally with SkinGen Corp, except maybe to monitor their work as part of their remit. Jeb Oppenheimer was talking about plans for population control and eugenics. He seems to think that money can buy him anything at all, and why the hell else would USAMRIID personnel be visiting him down here in Santa Fe?'

'I'm already on it,' Jarvis replied. 'SkinGen doesn't do work into infectious diseases, especially not for the military. According to SkinGen's spokesperson, Donald Wolfe stayed overnight on Jeb Oppenheimer's yacht before flying direct to DC this morning on a SkinGen jet and then on to Manhattan afterward, or so he told Director Mitchell.'

'So?' Ethan asked.

'So I started wondering why someone at USAMRIID would be hanging around Jeb Oppenheimer, flying aboard his jets and such like instead of taking a military transport. I sneaked a peak at the flight plans filed by the pilots of the SkinGen jet. Turns out that it took off fifteen hours earlier than he's saying. Wherever the hell he went it wasn't direct to DC. Seems like Wolfe's used his authority to conceal the aircraft's true flight path. Whatever the hell this guy's up to, he's hiding it from both the DIA and USAMRIID. I might be able to twist a few arms at the National Security Agency and get some surveillance, see where he's really been.'

'At least it'll be something we can work with,' Ethan said. 'Let me know.'

He hung up, looked at the photograph again and then out the window across the city to where the Sangre de Cristo mountains loomed in the lonely darkness beyond.

New Mexico was a huge state largely filled with desert and nothing much else. To survive out in the wilderness men would need specific skills to be able to live off the land with minimal support. He thought back to his days in the Marine Corps with the 15th Expeditionary Unit, and the skills they'd employed.

On November 25, 2001, the 15th MEU Special Operations Command launched an amphibious assault over four hundred miles into Afghanistan, with Ethan's own platoon attached to a Marine Recon patrol. Landing at an airbase southwest of Kandahar, they had established Camp Rhino, America's first forward operating base and conventional ground presence in Afghanistan. Deploying again in 2003, Ethan's platoon, again supporting Marine Recons, crossed the border into southern Iraq and secured the ports of Umm Qasr and Az Zubayr in order to destroy Iraqi resistance and enable follow-on humanitarian assistance to begin.

Ethan had, with his men, learned several important lessons during the initial infiltration into Afghanistan that had helped them upon arrival in Iraq. Chiefly, that the desert might be extremely hot during the day but it becomes extremely cold during the night. Water, though scarce on the surface, was available at depth beneath the dunes and wadis, if you knew where to look for the telltale signs of old river courses betraying the presence of rare downpours and the subterranean aquifers they fed. The ports secured in Iraq had revealed another useful quirk of desert life: the presence of coastal water produces morning mist as the sun rises, which can be captured in suspended plastic bags as moisture, providing limited additional water to troops in time of dire need. But the most important lesson of all, above anything else, was local knowledge. Befriending native Bedouin tribes, trackers and guides had taught Ethan more about desert survival in three months than he'd learned with the Corps in three years.

He looked out into the darkness. A small group of seven men could conceivably live indefinitely off the land without betraying even the slightest hint of their presence. They would only be forced into urban areas to buy medicines. Obtaining food, water and shelter would not require assistance, especially if they did not age.

But an old man, one like Hiram Conley, might tire of such a lifestyle. Ethan remembered what Tyler Willis had said: whatever had kept them alive for so long had not made them younger, it had only halted cellular senescence. They had become frozen at whatever age they were when they encountered whatever it was that had given them the gift of immortality. That meant that Hiram Conley had been around sixty years old ever since the Civil War, which for his era was virtually geriatric. He may have been suffering from various age-related ailments already, and thus cursed with having to endure them forever. Ethan figured that a century and a half of chronic arthritis would be enough to make anyone throw in the towel, immortal or not.

A knock at the door broke his reverie, and he opened it to see Lopez standing with Zamora in the corridor outside.

'Thanks for coming over,' Ethan said to Zamora as he bid them inside, noticing that the officer had removed the sling from his arm.

'No problem,' Zamora replied, 'although I can only speak to you now in an unofficial capacity. Something's going on at town hall and it stinks.'

'They've shut you down?' Ethan asked, closing the door.

'USAMRIID's taken over,' Lopez said as she sat on the edge of the bed. 'Butch Cutler's got a small army of guys crawling over what's left of Tyler Willis's apartment, searching for traces of chemicals.'

Ethan frowned.

'It doesn't make any sense. If we're assuming that for some reason Jeb Oppenheimer or someone within SkinGen decided to blow up the apartment, then why would USAMRIID be in there looking for chemicals? Forensics would be able to detect any kind of explosives or accelerants used in the attack.'

'Maybe SkinGen didn't make the hit,' Lopez suggested.

'What do you mean?'

Zamora took out a photograph, a black-and-white mugshot. A strikingly handsome man stared at the camera, a height chart on the wall behind him.

'You're looking at a man named Lee Carson,' Zamora said, 'arrested for drunk and disorderly outside a bootlegger's called Old Wayne's in Albuquerque. Yesterday, a call came in from Jay's Bar and Grill in La Cienega, south of Santa Fe. A girl who works there reported a man who came in by the name of Lee Carson, whose hand appeared to be suffering from some kind of wasting disease. I recognized it as the same affliction being suffered by Hiram Conley when I encountered him out Glorietta way.'

Ethan felt a pulse of excitement.

'He's one of the others that Willis mentioned? Can we be sure?'

'The girl described Lee Carson as about twenty-five years of age,' Zamora said, and then gestured to the mugshot. 'That was taken in 1929. Old Wayne's was shut down during the great Depression, long before World War Two.'

Ethan stared at the photograph again.

'Well, I'll be damned,' he said finally.

Turning, he picked up the old photograph of the seven soldiers standing beside the cart in 1862, and scanned their faces. Within seconds he saw what he was looking for, and handed the photograph to Lopez.

'Second from right, the one with the hat on,' he said.

Lopez stared at the picture, and Ethan saw her jaw drop.

'He's there,' she said in a whisper. 'This photograph is over a hundred fifty years old.'

Ethan looked at Zamora.

'These people, survivors, whatever they are, must be in contact with each other. They must be experiencing some kind of reaction. Tyler Willis said they were suffering from a bacterial infection. If we assume that they were all infected at the same time, then they'll all be showing these kinds of afflictions. Maybe that's why Hiram Conley came out of hiding: he knew he was dying and needed help. It's the only reason these people would reveal their secret.'

Zamora caught on to where Ethan was going.

'They'll rally together and try to find a solution,' he said. 'They'll seek out medication, a cure.'

'The question is where?' Ethan pondered out loud.

Zamora was about to answer when his cell phone rang. He pulled it out of his pocket, answered, and his face fell as he listened. Slowly, he lowered the phone to his side and looked at Ethan.

'They've found Tyler Willis's body.'

34

LOS ALAMOS
NEW MEXICO

11.58 p.m.

Ethan rode in the passenger seat of Zamora's patrol car as they drove up to the police cordon. Two ambulances and a pair of squad cars were parked, their strobe lights flashing in the night and reflecting off trees and bushes lining the side of a lonely track. Behind them, the main road ran north past the Los Alamos National Laboratory, not more than two hundred yards away, where Ethan had first met both Tyler Willis and Saffron Oppenheimer.

'Keep your heads down,' Zamora said. 'Let's not upset anyone.'

'Are USAMRIID on site already?' Ethan asked in amazement, spotting a large vehicle bearing the department's distinctive badges parked further down the track.

'They were already in Santa Fe,' Zamora said, winding down his window as a police officer approached them on foot. 'Wouldn't have taken them long to get here.'

The officer recognized Zamora and waved them through. They parked before getting out and walking toward the scene of the crime.

'Not far from the research center,' Lopez said uneasily. 'You think that maybe we were wrong and Saffron Oppenheimer got her hands on Willis?'

Ethan shook his head.

'No, but maybe that's what the perpetrators would like us to think.'

They had almost reached the cordon when Butch Cutler saw them coming, turning from looking at what was obviously a body lying in the dirt to stride toward them, one hand pointing at Ethan.

'I'm not surprised you've turned up,' he snapped. 'Trouble seems to follow you.'

Ethan ducked under the cordon along with Lopez and Zamora.

'Think you'll find it's the other way round,' he said, not letting Cutler intimidate him. 'When was he discovered?'

Cutler glanced over his shoulder.

'Two hours ago by a local resident out walking her dog. The mutt found the body, she called the police.'

'What happened to him?' Lopez asked.

Cutler turned his fearsome gaze in her direction.

'Looks like a mugging or similar,' he replied. 'He's been beaten up and stabbed, no cash or belongings on him.'

'You got any idea who might have done this?' Zamora asked, rubbing his temples.

Butch Cutler nodded slowly. 'Some.'

'Jeb Oppenheimer,' Ethan said to Cutler, trying to control the surge of fury now coursing through his veins. 'We were in the SkinGen building when Tyler Willis was there and you had us pulled out.'

'You had no damned right to be there,' Cutler shot back, jabbing a finger into Ethan's chest.

Ethan reacted without conscious thought, swatting Cutler's hand aside and whipping his left palm up toward the USAMRIID chief's jaw. Cutler spun aside from the blow and was about to counter when Lopez leapt between them.

'Cut it out!'

Ethan stood, fists clenched, looking over the top of Lopez's head at Cutler.

'Sooner or later, this screw-up is going to bring you down,' he hissed.

Cutler smiled coldly.

'Just as your deft handiwork is getting you thrown out of the county?'

'This is getting us nowhere,' Zamora said, trying to ease the situation. 'Can we see the body?'

Cutler scowled, but reluctantly gestured for them to pass through. Ethan walked past him, Lopez deliberately keeping herself between them as they moved toward the body lying on the soil nearby.

Willis lay on his back, his shirt stained with blood from what looked like an incision in his chest. His eyes were closed and his features seemed peaceful, but his eyes were heavily bruised from what appeared to be blunt-force trauma, his left temple a bloody mess and one of his teeth missing.

'We know he was at SkinGen,' Lopez said. 'One of Oppenheimer's men could have done this to him. The cut's too clinical, too clean to be a stab wound.'

Ethan looked at the remains for a few moments and then across at Cutler, his rage now withered.

'Have forensics been called?'

'On their way,' Cutler said.

'This was done purposefully,' Ethan said, gesturing to Willis's corpse. 'Somebody wanted to send a message that anybody doing research into aging could end up like this.'

Butch Cutler winced.

'Only if you're assuming SkinGen's involvement, which we're not right now. This has no bearing on Jeb Oppenheimer whatsoever.'

'This man was in his hands when he died,' Ethan insisted.

'So you allege,' Cutler said, and turned to face him. 'But what is an absolute fact is that the last people known for sure to have seen Tyler Willis alive is the pair of you.'

Ethan frowned.

'We interviewed him,' he said. 'Then Saffron Oppenheimer and her band of merry men tried to blow up the Aspen Center. We've been working with Officer Zamora here ever since.'

Cutler shook his head.

'Taking a blade to a corpse wouldn't take long,' he growled. 'What's to say you didn't do it, if circumstantial evidence is enough for you to accuse SkinGen of corporate homicide?'

Zamora raised a placating hand toward Cutler.

'That's pushing it, Chief. There's no motive.'

'There's *always* a motive,' Cutler replied, still glaring at Ethan. 'Or a reason to cover your tracks. Warner here could have committed the crime in that apartment, then had it blown to pieces. Would have destroyed any biological evidence. You said it yourselves: it would have taken someone with professional knowledge, an outdoorsman or a soldier, to have incinerated that apartment with so little evidence as to the cause.'

'You're forgetting,' Lopez snapped, 'that it was Ethan who realized *how* it was done. Pretty damned stupid to commit a perfect crime and then reveal to investigating officers how you've done it.'

'Or cunning enough to throw the investigators entirely off your scent,' Cutler mused out loud before looking directly at her. 'As for motive, money's always a big draw for two-bit bounty hunters looking for their next quick buck.'

Ethan was about to reply when Lopez suddenly whipped round and cracked Cutler high across his cheek. The USAMRIID chief's head flicked to one side as he grabbed his face instinctively before lunging for Lopez, one thick hand shooting out to close around her neck.

Ethan leapt in and slammed his elbow down through Cutler's arm, breaking his hold on Lopez. Ethan twisted at the waist and swung his forearm across Cutler's face, batting him backward a couple of paces.

'You touch her again,' Ethan snarled, 'you'll wind up sucking your dinners through a straw.'

'That's enough,' Zamora shouted, stepping between them. 'Cutler, you've got jurisdiction here. Either start acting your age or I'll have you forcibly removed from the scene. Warner, Lopez, with me, now!'

Ethan, realizing that he was in danger of completely losing it, turned and walked away with Zamora. The lieutenant ducked under the cordon and turned to face him.

'Okay, Tyson, listen up. You pull any other stunts like that, I'll arrest you my goddamned self.'

'We're wasting our time,' Ethan said. 'Whatever's really going on here, we're never going to find it with Cutler blocking our every move. We need to find the men in that photograph and get them to tell us why this is all happening.'

Zamora glanced back at Tyler Willis's corpse.

'My guess is that Cutler's right and money has a role in all of this. You don't abduct somebody unless you're trying to find something out, and whatever Willis knew was obviously worth a lot to someone. Enough to kill him.'

'The photograph,' Lopez said. 'The faces were the same then as they are now. Somebody, somewhere, must be able to recognize them.'

'Yeah,' Zamora said. 'But if we put up images and these guys are around, they'll high tail it out of town the moment they see one.'

Ethan thought back to serving with the Marines in the deserts and mountains of Iraq and Afghanistan.

'They'd have some kind of escape plan, or maybe even permanently base themselves in the desert. You can live in the wild almost indefinitely, if you know what you're doing. But they must have a contact of some kind in the city, someone they trust, who could do paperwork, arrange medication and such like.'

'And they'd have to meet somewhere that they can move freely,' Lopez said to Zamora, warming to the idea. 'You said that Hiram Conley talked with an archaic accent. If these guys haven't all spent much time within modern towns and cities, they might stand out by the way they talk.'

Zamora stood still for a moment and then suddenly he gasped and stared at Ethan.

'Damn my eyes! Why didn't I think of it before?!'

'Think of what?' Ethan asked. 'Tell us quickly. Can we find them before we're thrown out of the county?'

Zamora chuckled to himself and gestured to the old photographs in Lopez's hands.

'I've got a better idea. I'll tell the chief of police that you've already left,' Zamora said, and looked at Lopez. 'You need to go shopping first thing in the morning. By the time we're done, they'll never know you're still here.'

'How?' Lopez asked.

'You'll hide in plain sight,' he said. 'I know exactly where to find those men. Every single one of them.'

35

SANTA FE PLAZA
SANTA FE

16 May, 8.46 a.m.

Saffron Oppenheimer stood unobtrusively beside a small shop selling trinkets on Lincoln Avenue, a grubby baseball cap pulled down low to shield her eyes. She watched the cars flowing lazily through the morning heat flaring off the asphalt, windows down and stereos blaring. Rush hour. Across the street was the plaza, filled with trees and dominated by a large petroglyph, the city's national historic landmark. The plaza was ringed by structures in the Pueblo, Spanish and Territorial styles, tourists and locals alike bustling past adobe shops with cameras and day sacks on their backs. She kept a particular eye open for squad cars amidst the traffic, ready to take flight at a moment's notice. The rush hour would ease her escape, letting her outmaneuver the cops and dash into the warren of Santa Fe's alleys before heading south on the Old Santa Fe trail. Most all cops were either out of shape or downright overweight, having spent their careers sitting in vehicles gorging themselves on donuts, and she had no doubts about her ability to outpace them.

The only man that concerned her was the mysterious Ethan Warner. His tenacity had presented the only real threat she'd encountered so far, apart from the overbearing presence of her grandfather.

The thought of Jeb Oppenheimer coincided almost perfectly with the sight of a nondescript silver Lexus rolling down Main Street. The giveaway was the tinted windows and the unique license plates that betrayed the vehicle as belonging to SkinGen. As the car slid into the sidewalk next to her, a door opened smoothly. The vehicle didn't stop rolling as Saffron reached out, resting one hand on the roof as she slipped into the vehicle and closed the door.

Three men were sitting inside the vehicle. Two were up front, wearing identical gray suits and emotionless expressions. Bodyguards, one driving and the other watching her in the rear-view mirror. The third man sat beside her in his customary white suit.

'You're late,' she said, wrinkling her nose in distaste at the overbearing smell of the polished leather seats and upholstery.

Jeb Oppenheimer didn't look at her as he replied. 'Traffic,' he said, looking out of the tinted windows. 'Too many automatons, robotically going to work for people they've never even met.'

'Without people like them,' Saffron sneered, 'your company would be impotent.'

Jeb turned to examine her, his piercing gaze appraising and distrustful at the same time.

'Without my company they would be jobless,' he countered. 'The chicken and the egg, my dear, and this time the egg that is SkinGen wins.'

Saffron smiled without warmth. 'Pity it's rotten inside.'

'Do you have the data?' Jeb snapped.

Saffron shrugged, not looking at him but instead watching the streets pass by outside as the Lexus slowly circled the plaza. Jeb tutted and shook his head, a throaty laugh tumbling breathlessly from between his thin lips.

'Not this charade again, surely? You have a role to fulfill, my dear, no matter how much it offends you. We all have to meet our targets.'

Saffron finally looked at her grandfather, mastering the revulsion she felt welling up inside.

'There's more to life than your damned targets.'

Jeb leaned close to her in his seat.

'Not for you,' he whispered. 'Now pay your dues, before I change my mind.'

Saffron strained against the overwhelming urge to punch the old bastard as hard as she could, pummel him right here and now in the back seat of his disgustingly luxurious car. An image of his ruined, bloodied and bleating face flickered darkly through her mind and she saw him smiling at her.

'Yes, do it, little Saffy,' he rattled. 'Please do it, and then spend the next sixty years rotting in a high-security cell. It would, I can tell you, make life so much easier for your poor old grandpa.'

Saffron caught a sickening waft of peppermints and decay on his breath, and felt her stomach heave. She reached into her pocket and retrieved a small hard drive, tossing it into Jeb's lap with more force than was necessary. The old man coughed in alarm at the impact, but he still managed to get one hand on the drive.

'There, that wasn't so bad now, was it?'

'Go to hell,' Saffron snarled. 'What did you do to Tyler Willis?'

Jeb Oppenheimer handed the hard drive across to one of his bodyguards, who pocketed it without looking at Saffron. The old man leaned back in his seat, examining the tip of his cane.

'Mister Willis suffered an unfortunate incident,' he replied, 'a fatal one.'

Saffron stared at the creature sitting beside her, an inhumane and emotionless shell that had once harbored her grandfather.

'That's bullshit and you know it. You're a murderer.'

Oppenheimer glanced out of the Lexus and gestured to the masses passing by outside.

'One person's death is irrelevant in the greater scheme of things. You see all these people, Saffy? They're out there in their hundreds, thousands and millions. In just a few generations they'll be gone and all of society's problems will disappear along with them.'

Saffron's eyes narrowed as she struggled to comprehend what her grandfather was talking about.

'That will never happen,' she said. 'No matter how you go about it somebody, somewhere will stop you, even if it costs them their own life.'

'I don't doubt it,' Oppenheimer growled, 'and your pathetic little friend Willis would no doubt have been one of them. Suffice to say, my dear granddaughter, that I had nothing to do with his untimely passing – it was actually unexpected, indeed infuriating. However, soon his plight and that of millions will be an irrelevance.'

'You talk like you're doing the world a favor,' Saffron muttered, nausea twisting inside her throat. 'All you're doing is trying to deny people the right to have children, to have their fair share of the world's resources, so you can take everything for yourself. You're not protecting humanity, you're sacrificing it for your little army of elitist businessmen and politicians.'

'The needs of the powerful few outweigh the needs of the powerless many,' Oppenheimer murmured. 'You will learn that truth one day, my dear, most probably the hard way.'

'More bullshit,' Saffron uttered in disgust. 'You're basing everything that you're doing on myths. The entire population of planet Earth could live comfortably in large houses in the state of Texas alone. We live on just one-twentieth of a percent of the world's available land mass. Half the world's population has a fertility rate below replacement level: Europe, Japan, Vietnam, Thailand, Australia, Canada, Sri Lanka, Turkey, Algeria, Kazakhstan, Tunisia – the list goes on. Even in religious countries like Iran and Brazil, birth rates are falling despite the ranting of mullahs or priests.'

'Population alone is not the concern,' Oppenheimer replied, gesturing to the shopping malls outside, 'it is consumption.'

'Then perhaps you should sell off your private jets, your luxury houses and this vehicle,' Saffron pointed out tartly. 'The world's richest half-billion people, about seven percent of the global population, are responsible for half of the world's carbon dioxide emissions. But the poorest fifty percent of the population are responsible for just seven percent of emissions. Kind of ironic, don't you think?'

Oppenheimer ignored her but Saffron kept going.

'The carbon emissions of just one American today are equivalent to those of about thirty Pakistanis, forty Nigerians or two hundred fifty Ethiopians. It's *us* that should leave the planet because of consumption, not others.'

Oppenheimer continued to ignore her, and Saffron shook her head slowly before gesturing for him to command the vehicle pulled into the sidewalk on East San Francisco Street. As the car slowed she looked at her grandfather.

'They tried this before,' she said, 'years ago. Called it eugenics. Nowadays people don't even talk about it, it was such a sick idea. It was like slave labor and theocracy: they didn't work because they were inhumane and those who championed them were outcast and reviled.' She recalled a line she'd heard once at school. 'Those who fail to learn the lessons of history are forced to relive them.'

Oppenheimer gurgled a laugh that sounded like a clogged drain.

'I'm doing this for all of the right reasons, my dear, using evolution to control a species that has lost its ability to regulate itself. We're nothing more than a parasite infecting a diminishing world. Somebody has to bring about a cull . . .' He smiled. 'As humanely as possible, of course.'

The car stopped and Saffron grabbed the door handle, but she hesitated and turned to look at Jeb.

'Economic Darwinism failed too,' she said. 'The survival of the fittest attitude to corporate business ended up being rejected.'

'It's worked well enough for me.' Jeb smirked at her.

'And for a few very fortunate, very wealthy others,' Saffron acknowledged. 'But the problem was that natural evolution is neither predatory nor altruistic – it is in balance. When it was used in a predatory manner, with small numbers of self-serving members seeking power to control and eliminate those less capable, the gene pool became so small that all that remained was a tiny number of elitists all willing to cut the throats of their competitors in order to survive, because they all believed themselves to be the best.'

Saffron opened her door and stepped out, leaning back in to look at her grandfather.

'In the end only one remained, the strongest of them all, but as that individual was now entirely alone they were worth nothing and collapsed and died, having eradicated their purpose for existing: power over their peers.' She smiled at him, genuinely this time. 'I don't doubt for a moment that you'll suffer the same fate, *dear* Grandpa.'

Saffron closed the door behind her, moving swiftly across the street toward the plaza. She strode past the monument, pulling her baseball cap down and vanishing between the trees. As she walked, she could see the silver Lexus moving around the square as it flowed in with the traffic heading toward Albuquerque.

Suddenly the vehicle slowed, and Saffron watched as

it pulled into the sidewalk once more alongside a diminutive woman with long black hair. Saffron instantly
recognized the woman and watched in amazement as
the Lexus door opened and she got in.

36

Nicola Lopez heard the heavy Lexus roll up alongside her as she walked toward a Five & Dime, searching for the garments Enrico Zamora had sent her to buy, and then the weighty clunk of the door as it opened while the vehicle was still moving. Instinctively, she rested one hand on the baton under her light jacket and glanced over her shoulder into the vehicle's gloomy interior.

'Miss Lopez? A moment of your time, if I may?'

Lopez recognized the gravelly tones of Jeb Oppenheimer and glanced furtively around her at the street. 'I won't keep you long,' came the voice from the interior.

Lopez released her hand on the baton, letting it fall past the pocket of her jacket. She felt the hard cylindrical surface of a pepper-spray can within, and felt emboldened. She turned and climbed into the vehicle.

Oppenheimer offered her an appraising grin as she closed the door and checked out the two bodyguards in the front.

'I feared for a moment that you would not have the mettle to get in,' Oppenheimer said.

Lopez shot him a dirty look.

'Given your habit of abducting people, it should hardly have come as a shock.'

'Baseless accusations,' Oppenheimer intoned. 'Besides, if I'd wanted to abduct you I'd hardly have done so on a crowded street, would I? This was, I assure you, a fortuitous opportunity and I just happened by. Had I been under any real suspicion of such a crime would I not have been arrested by now?'

'We know you've got USAMRIID in your pocket,' Lopez muttered. 'Playing innocent isn't going to win you any laurels.'

'Nor will playing guilty,' Oppenheimer said, his friendly expression hardening in an instant. 'This is not a game, Miss Lopez, it's a serious business and there are many people who would gladly see my company fail.'

Lopez looked around her at the flashy vehicle, the hired hands and Oppenheimer, then rested her hand on her baton again.

'You're one of the richest men alive,' she spat with contempt. 'Loose change to you is a lifetime's salary to most people. Don't insult me again or I'll shove that cane of yours somewhere you'll remember for the rest of your days.'

Both of the guards, who had been staring straight ahead with blank expressions, now turned their heads in unison and focused on Lopez. She met their gazes steadily.

'Laurel and Hardy here won't stop me either,' she added.

Oppenheimer chuckled, a noise that to Lopez sounded like any normal person drawing their terminal breath. The old man waved his bodyguards down, patting the air before him with one skeletal hand.

'Calm yourself, Nicola, you're in no danger here.'

'It's Ms Lopez to you,' she said hotly. 'And I'm sure you made the same promise to Tyler Willis.'

Oppenheimer shifted position in his seat, resting his hands on his cane and leveling a serious gaze at her.

'We have a mutual purpose here, Ms Lopez. Yours is to discover what happened to Hiram Conley. So is mine. Everything else is irrelevant, mere distractions obscuring a much greater goal.'

'Which is?' Lopez asked.

'The very thing which Hiram Conley possessed,' Oppenheimer said. 'A mutation, caused by bacteria, that causes human cellular senescence to cease entirely, rendering the infected individual biologically immortal.'

Lopez took a moment to digest what she'd heard.

'That's why Hiram Conley hadn't aged in a hundred fifty years or more,' she said, deciding not to mention the possible presence of others likewise afflicted, 'a biological infection. But it was your men who took the remains from the morgue, along with Lillian Cruz. Your men who destroyed Tyler Willis's apartment.'

Oppenheimer shook his head.

'My men have done no such thing,' he snapped. 'They went nowhere near that apartment.'

Lopez lost her momentum for a moment as she looked into Oppenheimer's rheumy gray eyes and realized that he was almost certainly telling the truth.

'Then who did?' she asked.

'Rival companies, most probably,' Oppenheimer said. 'You don't think that I'm the only one in this race, do you? There are literally dozens of major corporations out there who would gladly arrange an *accident* for me in order to capitalize on the years of research we've achieved at SkinGen. Why the hell do you think I travel with bodyguards in a bullet-proof vehicle?'

Lopez shook her head.

'Not everyone on the planet thinks like you, Oppenheimer,' she said. 'Some people are decent enough to work things out on their own, not steal them.'

'Quaint,' Oppenheimer observed with a smile that reminded Lopez of a basking alligator. 'The assumption that other people are of good intent is what most often gets one killed.'

Lopez glanced out of the tinted window at the early-morning shoppers strolling past.

'You're boring me, Jeb,' she said. 'What's your point?'

'That we each have something that the other needs,' Oppenheimer said smoothly. 'I want to know where the bacteria that infected Hiram Conley can be found.'

Lopez slowly turned in her seat to face the old man.

'We don't know. All we're interested in right now is finding Lillian Cruz.'

'Really?' Oppenheimer muttered. 'Let me put it to you this way, Ms Lopez. You and your partner, Ethan Warner, are right now achieving absolutely nothing. You're down here working for the government because they daren't get their hands dirty themselves, being paid next to nothing to investigate an anomaly that could potentially make all of us wealthy beyond our wildest dreams. Finding out what has happened to Lillian Cruz is an irrelevance compared to that.'

Lopez peered at Oppenheimer.

'Attempting to bribe a law-enforcement officer is punishable by—'

'You're not a law-enforcement officer, in case you've forgotten,' Oppenheimer cut across her. 'You're a two-bit bail-bond bounty hunter on a lousy salary with mouths to feed south of the border and not enough left over to buy a third-hand car.'

'How the hell would you know—'

'I make it my business to know *everything*,' Oppenheimer interrupted. 'You think that I'm doing all of this for profit but you're wrong. I'm doing what the politicians and governments of this world haven't got the guts to do: finding a way to stop humanity from turning our world into a desolate wasteland.'

'You're such a hero,' Lopez uttered.

'So would you be, if you would only listen to what I have to say. All I need is that one bacterium, a tiny, insignificant life form that could change our lives. That single bacterium is worth more than all of the jewels and fuels on the face of our planet. If you find where it lives, there is nothing that I would not pay to obtain it.'

Lopez raised an eyebrow.

'If I found it, I'd have an auction.'

'If you auctioned it, two things would happen,' Oppenheimer said. 'Firstly, nobody would believe you if you tried to tell the world what you possessed and your auction would fail, because it would take too long to verify your claims to all but a handful of the world's top pharmaceutical companies with knowledge and expertise in senescence. Secondly, those companies would pay handsomely to arrange a particularly nasty accident for you before obtaining the bacterium for themselves, or at the very least preventing anyone else from obtaining it.'

Lopez thought for a moment.

'Tyler's apartment.'

Oppenheimer nodded. 'I genuinely had nothing to do with it, but somebody who knows what's happening here decided to prevent anyone else from grabbing any materials that Tyler Willis may have left behind. This is a situation, Miss Lopez, in which you either help me to obtain those samples or you walk away with nothing.'

Lopez looked out of the windows of the vehicle for a long moment, at the passers-by variously struggling to control children, shopping bags or pets. Hundreds of them, millions, all working their forty hours a week, struggling to pay the bills, being hit with ever more taxes that were then frittered away by the incompetence of successive governments. There were, it seemed, just a handful of very wealthy people for every few million ordinary citizens, and Lopez was more than tired of struggling on a daily basis just to stand still.

She looked at Oppenheimer.

'And if I agreed? What would you want me to do?'

Oppenheimer looked at one of his bodyguards, who silently produced a small black box no larger than a cigarette packet. Oppenheimer took it, and showed it to her.

'This is a full service GPS tracker,' he said, handing her the glossy black device. 'With this, I can track your movements with its pre-installed and activated SIM card.'

Lopez nodded, familiar with such surveillance devices. Usually attached to cars, they could be used together with the Google Earth service in order to monitor the device's movement in real time. A GPS assist function via a network was used to boost sensitivity in the event of the GPS signal being temporarily lost. It was accurate to within fifteen meters. No antennas, entirely self-contained and barely three inches long. Perfect.

'You need do nothing more than carry it on your person at all times,' Oppenheimer said. 'If you or your partner, or anyone you have contact with, should locate the source of the bacteria, you place this marker there and call me. That's all there is to it.'

'There's no way I can trust you,' Lopez countered. 'You once bought an entire company just to shut it down in revenge for a deal gone bad.'

'It was I who was wronged,' Oppenheimer muttered, 'but in a show of good will, perhaps I could transfer some funds for you this afternoon, call it an appetizer? How does fifty thousand dollars sound?'

Lopez's stomach flipped but she forced her face to remain impassive.

'I won't do it for less than two hundred fifty thousand for starters,' she said. 'Wire transfer, for services rendered, all taxes paid. You do the paperwork and send copies to me. I don't want the IRS climbing up my ass after this is all over.'

Oppenheimer forced a tight grin across his features. 'You'll do it then?'

Lopez looked at the tracker in her hand as conflicting thoughts flashed through her mind: Ethan; her penniless family back home; her pathetic apartment in Chicago; the endless search for money to make ends meet. She looked at the hordes of people outside the car, and made her decision.

37

SEDILLO PARK
SOCORRO, NEW MEXICO

16 May, 12.30 p.m.

'Are you sure about this?'

Ethan clambered out of Enrico Zamora's personal vehicle, an old Lincoln Town car, his new jacket and kepi pants feeling alien and awkward. Lopez got out of the other side, looking equally uncomfortable in her new attire, her hair tied up and concealed beneath her cap.

Zamora looked at them both as he handed them a fake Springfield rifle each.

'You both look damned fine, if I say so myself. You'll pass unnoticed here, at least until the show wraps up.'

Ethan looked down at the markings on his uniform. 'Private? You couldn't have found anything with rank?'

'All greenhorns have to be privates at these events,' Zamora explained. 'Just the way it is.'

Ethan looked over the roof of the car to where Sedillo Park was spread before them, a large open space lined with dense thickets of trees. Around the edge were large tents and marquees, various flags flying above their entrances in the hot wind. None of them were emblazoned with banners or adverts in the usual manner. Nearby were old wagons, carts and horses, and on the warm air he could smell the fumes of a hundred camp fires.

A single, broad banner arced over the park entrance, emblazoned with bright red, white and blue text.

SOCORRO ANNUAL CIVIL WAR
RE-ENACTMENT
The Battle of Valverde

Ethan could see hundreds of people mingling around the fires and the horses, rank upon rank of fully uniformed Confederate and Union soldiers, all drinking coffees or Cokes and chatting amiably.

'You *really* think they'll use this as a place to meet up?' Lopez asked Zamora as they began walking into the park. 'They can't be held that often.'

Zamora nodded.

'Just a few every year. Santa Fe's come earlier, in February and March, to coincide with the anniversary of the actual battles. Out here near Arizona the re-enactment groups from south of the border team up with Socorro groups for larger displays. Hiram Conley was heavily involved in many of the re-enactments and was considered an expert.'

'I'll bet,' Ethan replied as they strolled into the park between two large wagons and onto the field proper.

Ethan reckoned that he could see maybe two thousand soldiers, roughly split between Confederates in their smart gray uniforms and the Union troops in dark blue. Enrico gestured to the massed ranks, the bayonets of their rifles glittering in the hot sunlight.

'Back in the day when these battles were fought, the men wouldn't have worn such identical uniforms. They'd have been all beaten up and modified, not to mention the fact that Valverde was fought in the winter so they'd have been huddled up in greatcoats if they were lucky enough to own them.'

Ethan nodded, surveying the scene.

'Hiram Conley and his comrades were Union soldiers. Most likely they'll stick with what they know and be among those troops.'

'Could take a while to find them,' Lopez said, looking at her copy of the old photograph and Lee Carson's mugshot. 'Half of these enthusiasts have grown long moustaches and beards to look more authentic.'

Ethan thought for a moment.

'Let's focus on Lee Carson,' he said. 'He's the one we know has a good reason to find help – his hands are falling off. If we're lucky, where we find him we'll find the rest of them.'

Ethan watched as Lopez and Zamora, armed with their photographs, struck out for the Union lines while he headed for the furthest flank of the army. Since arriving, he had noticed the ranks of speakers lining the edges of Sedillo Park, from which issued the voice of a commentator that rose and fell with flukes in the wind. It had crossed Ethan's mind that they could just put out a call for Lee Carson to come in: he had, after all, been known to live amongst ordinary people during his very long life. The problem was, he might now live under a pseudonym. Any call-out for the wrong name would alert him instantly.

Ethan approached the Union lines and decided on a different tack. He slipped his cell phone out of his pocket as an idea hit him, and dialed Lopez's number. She answered on the first ring.

'Look for men wearing gloves of any kind,' Ethan said. 'If Carson's here, he'll have to keep his hands out of sight.'

'Good call, will do.'

Lopez rang off, and Ethan was about to pocket his cell phone when a voice thundered out across the field.

'You there! Have you absquatulated your senses?! What the blazes do you think you're doing?'

Ethan stopped dead in his tracks as a portly man bearing the uniform of an officer sitting astride a magnificent golden-coated palomino with a white mane vaulted down from his saddle and strode up to him. The officer wore a silvery moustache as long as a canoe, bright blue eyes wide as dinner plates and skin flushed with apparent outrage. He jabbed a thin black cane at Ethan's cell phone, various medals and tasseled ribbons on his shoulders vibrating with the sudden movement. Ethan lowered the cell phone.

'I'm making a phone call.'

'A phone call?!' the officer thundered in disbelief. 'This is 1862, God damn your hide, man!'

The ranks of troops amassed behind the officer had fallen silent, watching the exchange with interest. Ethan blinked.

'No, it's not.'

The officer seemed to rise another inch in height, eyes widening even further as he sucked in more air to shout with.

'You dare defy your commanding officer?' he bellowed. 'By Satan's breath, I'll have you in irons by sundown, you insolent little tick!'

'You really take everything this seriously?' Ethan asked, holding his own temper in check.

'This is the army, boy, not a weekend away!' the officer boomed. 'Where's your bivouac? Where's your commanding officer?' He raised his cane as though to swat it at Ethan.

Ethan took a single step forward to put himself right in the officer's face and then reached down, grabbing the man's balls and twisting hard. The officer went up on his toes as a strained whistling sound squeaked from his lips. Ethan spoke quietly but with force.

'Ethan Warner, Lieutenant, 15th Expeditionary Unit, United States Marine Corps, Iraq, Afghanistan. I'm here on business and I'm the real thing, buddy, not a jumped-up fantasist like you. You either shut up and get lost or I'll kick your ass clean off this field in front of two thousand people, understood?'

The officer deflated like a burst balloon as panic flickered behind his eyes. He squealed in taut agreement. Ethan twisted his grip a little harder while he reached into his pocket and pulled out Lee Carson's mugshot.

'Recognize this face?'

The man's blue eyes swiveled to look down at the picture. He nodded briskly as beads of sweat on his forehead twinkled in the sunlight.

'Light infantry guy,' he squeaked, 'halfway down the ranks, behind the artillery.'

Ethan nodded slowly. 'Now, good officers lead by example, not by force. I don't expect to see you raising that pathetic little stick of yours to anybody else, understood?'

Another jerking nod, the man's breaths now coming short and sharp.

'Well done,' Ethan said, and released his grip.

The officer gasped, resting his hands on his knees as he fought for breath and wiped tears from the corners of his eyes.

Ethan turned, making his way through the lines of soldiers now staring at him and whispering as he headed toward where he could see the ugly muzzles of artillery pieces poking from the ranks. All of them were finely polished, gleaming in the hot sunlight. He searched for gloved hands, looking at the soldiers cradling their long-barreled muskets and rifles. One of them, an old man with a drooping gray moustache and beard, wore leather gloves but was far too aged to be Carson. Ethan was about to move on when the old man turned and jogged down the line of infantry.

Ethan froze. The old man was tall, his shoulders broad and rangy and his step far too spritely for his apparent age. Ethan began following him as he turned off the front line of troops and headed toward the rear of the formations. Ethan moved parallel to him before reaching the back of the ranks to intercept the old man as he emerged. He called out to him as he tried to duck into a nearby tent.

'Carson!'

The old man's head whipped round, a pair of strange blue-gray eyes locking onto Ethan's in surprise. Ethan dashed forward a couple of steps to prevent him from fleeing, raising one placatory hand.

'We need to talk,' he said quickly.

Carson stared at him for a moment, then his rifle twirled violently in his grasp as the butt flashed up toward Ethan's face. Ethan leapt sideways as the weapon whipped past his eyes, stepping in toward Carson in an attempt to wrestle him to the ground. Carson jerked back and brought the butt of the rifle smashing back down toward Ethan's face. Ethan caught the butt in his hands, absorbing the force of the blow as he slipped one foot behind Carson's ankle and then hurled his body weight forward. Carson reeled off balance and staggered backwards, losing his grip on the rifle as he tripped over the tent's guy lines to thump down onto the grass. He was about to scramble away and make a run for it when Ethan spoke.

'I'm not here to arrest you,' he said quickly. 'I know who you are and I know what's happening to you.'

Carson squinted up at Ethan.

'The hell would you know about it?'

Ethan gestured to the nearby tent with the rifle, just as Lopez and Zamora arrived from the other end of the lines to block Carson's escape.

38

The interior walls of the tent rippled in the breeze as Ethan ducked inside, following Carson with Lopez behind. Zamora discreetly stood guard outside to keep any prying eyes away.

Lee Carson sat down on a crude wooden bench inside the tent, Ethan taking a seat opposite alongside Lopez.

'You wanna tell me who you're workin' for?' Carson asked him. 'I ain't agreein' to no tests.'

'We're not working for a pharmaceutical company,' Ethan said. 'We're just here to find out what the hell's been going on. People have gone missing over this and we need to find them.'

'Missing?' Carson echoed with a frown. 'What do you mean, *missing*?'

'A medical examiner named Lillian Cruz,' Lopez replied, 'was abducted after an autopsy conducted on the remains of a man named Hiram Conley. We believe you were familiar with him.'

Lee Carson sighed and reached up to take off his fake beard.

'Yeah, he was an old acquaintance of mine.'

'Very old,' Ethan said and leveled Carson with a serious gaze. 'How old are you, Lee?'

Carson looked right back at Ethan as he removed his kepi hat and ruffled his hair with one gloved hand.

'Last I can recall, I'm about a hundred seventy-two,' he replied. He kept his gaze on Lopez and Ethan for a moment before suddenly chuckling and shaking his head. 'Don't seem right nor real, does it now? Gettin' on two centuries and I can still rustle with the best of 'em.'

Ethan grinned, but the smile faded as he looked at Carson's gloves.

'Not for much longer though,' he observed. 'Your hands, something's wrong with them.'

Carson's own smile shriveled.

'Yeah, I'll say,' he murmured. 'Looks like our lil' ol' gift ain't all it's cracked up to be.'

'Where are the rest of you?' Lopez asked. 'We need to find them.'

'They'll be here someplace,' Carson said. 'But I ain't seen any of them yet, which bothers me. They should've been here afore now.'

Ethan glanced over his shoulder to see Zamora still guarding the tent's entrance. He turned back to Carson.

'We need you to tell us how this all happened,' he said. 'We know that you need help, all of you. But if we don't know how you came to be like this, there's not much we can do for you.'

'Except run your tests an' all,' Carson said. 'Use us like lab rats.'

'We work for the government,' Lopez said.

'Sub-contracted and independent. They only hear what we report back, and right now we're not going to be sending you to any laboratories. We've seen what they might do.'

Carson looked at Lopez for a moment and then smiled.

'You sure look cute in that there uniform an' all, ma'am.'

Ethan saw Lopez raise an eyebrow at Carson as he felt an unexpected lance of irritation.

'Cut the small talk, Carson,' he said. 'This is serious. We need to know how this all started.'

Carson didn't lose his perfect smile as he glanced in Ethan's direction.

'Now don't be gettin' all jealous on me, mister,' he said. 'I was just remarkin' on how beautiful the lady is.'

From the corner of his eye Ethan saw Lopez's features melt into a bright smile.

'We don't have much time,' he said to Carson, and pulled from his pocket the old photograph of the men standing around the old cart. 'Try starting from here.'

Carson looked at the photograph and his smile turned wistful.

'I'll be damned,' he whispered almost reverentially. 'Valverde, 1862. I ain't seen a picture like that for many a year now.'

'It was taken around the time of the battle,' Lopez said. 'Was it before or after you became infected?'

Carson looked at her, his features suddenly taut.

'What do you mean *infected*? You sayin' I've contracted some kind of sickness?'

'Yes,' Ethan said. 'A bacterial infection. We're not sure yet, but the more you can tell us the more likely we'll be able to help.'

Carson nodded.

'That would kind o' make sense,' he said thoughtfully, looking again at the photograph. 'That was taken a few days after the Battle of Glorietta Pass, after we were cut off from our main force at Fort Craig when the Confederates began their retreat toward Arizona.'

Ethan nodded encouragingly.

'Okay, tell us how it went down.'

Carson, one hand resting on his thigh and leaning on the other with his elbow, gestured to the re-enactment preparations outside.

'We were based at Fort Craig originally, down in Confederate Arizona, when the rebels marched up to try an' take the fort out of our hands. Turned out that their commander, a man named Sibley, reckoned our walls were too heavy to be breached by assault so he turned north and went on by with his men over the Rio Grande to the ford at Valverde. We, that is myself and a small company of the New Mexico Militia under Lieutenant Ellison Thorne, were sent out to reconnoiter the enemy and try to find a weakness after a planned attack on the rebels using mules loaded with explosives backfired, literally. The mules came back home and blew up inside our own goddamned lines.'

'And they were still heading north at that point?' Lopez asked.

'To a degree,' Carson said. 'But they got themselves caught up with Union forces guarding the ford, who we then began supportin'. Afore you know it, there's a battle in full swing as the batteries opened up on each other.'

'And you guys went into battle?' Ethan guessed.

'We surely did,' Carson nodded, 'but the rebels had organized themselves right tight, and they broke our lines and forced us into a retreat toward the fort. We lost five hundred men that day and our commanding officer, Edward Canby, lost a lot of respect, though he earned it back in the days and years to come.'

'So you're back at the fort,' Lopez said. 'Besieged?'

'No,' Carson replied. 'We hit the rebels as hard as they hit us. They went north, looking to raid Santa Fe for supplies. We were sent to follow, and where possible harass them. We were in the field for almost a month when our two armies came up against each other in late March at a place called Glorietta Pass.'

Ethan dimly recalled details from his school days and military-service lectures. 'The Gettysburg of the West,' he said. 'A Union victory, that pushed the rebels south back to Arizona and Texas.'

'That was the one.' Carson nodded. 'Trouble was, when the battle was won, myself and six other soldiers were still positioned a half-mile south of the Confederate forces. When they began their retreat we were forced to flee afore them. There wasn't much quarter given to captured enemy troops, especially those from the victor's ranks, and we none of us were willing to chance moving out and round the enemy's flanks. We couldn't be sure of avoiding their pickets, so we pushed hard for the Rio Grande.'

'What happened?' Lopez asked.

For a brief moment, as Carson spoke, Ethan listened to the sounds of marching troops outside the tent and felt as though he had been transported a hundred fifty years into the past.

'We didn't make it,' Carson replied. 'Secondary Confederate forces, snipers and wagon trains were trying to link up with the retreating main force and cut us off afore we could cross the river. We kept runnin' south, barely keeping ahead of them. In the end we were tuckered out and were on the verge of surrendering when we came across some caves down near the border. We decided to take our chances and went in just as deep as we could go.'

Ethan leaned forward eagerly.

'Where were they?'

Carson sighed, glancing at the entrance to the tent.

'Thing is,' he said quietly, 'if'n I tell you, it's as likely I'll be killed.'

Ethan gestured to Carson's gloved hands.

'If you don't tell us you'll die anyway,' he pointed out. 'There's nothing left for you to lose, Lee.'

Carson looked at his hands and shook his head briefly before speaking.

'The caves were near a place you've probably heard of. It's called Carlsbad.'

Ethan and Lopez exchanged a glance of surprise.

'Carlsbad Caverns?' he echoed. 'Everyone's heard of them. How come we don't already have tens of thousands of people wandering around who are a couple of hundred years old?'

Carson smiled mischievously.

'Because they've never set foot in the caves that we hid in,' he said. 'We were there for three days living off the water inside and the mosses growing there. Most people don't go that far into the caves or stay there for as long because it's so hard to get in. But the real reason is that the exact location of the caves is kept secret from the public.'

Ethan raised an eyebrow.

'By whom?'

'Park rangers and such like, I guess,' Carson said. 'We haven't been back since 1986 when they found the entrance. Poor old Hiram Conley went looking for Tyler Willis to find a cure for all o' this.'

'Why didn't the rest of your comrades help him?' Lopez asked.

'Because they're living in the past,' Carson muttered. 'They've all seen their families die of old age, seen their loved ones become a part of history. They ain't so much revelin' in their immortality as enduring it.'

Ethan considered for a moment what Lee Carson had said. The fact was, he'd never even thought about how it might feel to live forever. Everyone else would grow old and die, but an immortal man would live on, abandoned time and time again by those he loved until he might well become the loneliest individual ever to have lived. He might even crave the solace of death itself. Ethan had certainly felt that way just a few years' previously, when Joanna Defoe had vanished without trace from his life somewhere within the dark and dangerous alleys of the Gaza Strip.

'And none of them have thought to break the cycle?' Lopez asked. 'Just go ahead and search for help like Hiram did?'

'Old man Ellison won't let them,' Carson replied. 'He reckons it to be safer to stay out in the Pecos than mix with people.'

'More than that,' Ethan said. 'Hiram Conley was already wounded when he met Tyler Willis at Glorietta Pass. A fresh musket ball got pulled from his shoulder, before the body was abducted from the morgue.'

Carson stared at him for a long moment.

'You're sayin' he was shot by one of his own? One of us?'

Ethan shrugged.

'Can't imagine who else would have done it. You could be in danger by being here, Lee. We need to get you someplace safe before you're found.'

'Is there any way we can identify the others?' Lopez asked Carson. 'Anything about them that makes them stand out, that they can't conceal?'

Carson raised a gloved hand and pointed to his own eyes.

'We all have these eyes,' he said. 'They're cataracts, but they don't solidify so they can't be removed. All of us suffer from them.'

'You need to contact the others for us,' Ethan said, 'and bring them here so we can speak to them.'

Carson glanced around nervously and was about to speak when a deafening blast of gunfire crashed through the tent as though a thousand artillery pieces had opened up at once.

39

Ethan flinched and instantly hit the ground, rolling as the blast roared in his ears. He glimpsed Lopez disappearing in the opposite direction and he saw, through the flaps of the tent, the ranks of soldiers outside, their artillery pieces spewing flame and gray smoke.

Lee Carson leapt past Ethan and smashed Zamora out of the way as he bolted out of the tent.

'Carson, wait!'

Ethan leapt to his feet and rushed outside in pursuit. A thick bank of rolling cordite smoke drifted across the ranks of the soldiers now marching away from them across the open field, Carson having vanished amongst them.

'What the hell happened?' Zamora demanded, getting back onto to his feet.

'He bolted,' Ethan said. 'Get out there and find him!'

Lopez joined Ethan, surveying the wide, deep ranks of men now marching across the fields as another deafening artillery volley rang out.

'We'll never find him in that!'

Ethan saw a small number of soldiers falling onto the grass, emulating men killed in the advance.

'He could end up dead if his comrades are here and they've seen him talking to us,' Ethan said. 'Take the right flank, I'll take the left. Try to get to the front lines and pick him out before he passes!'

Ethan broke into a run, dashing past men twisting and falling as imaginary musket balls plowed through their flesh. If the bullets were fantasy, the thick clouds of choking smoke were not. Ethan's eyes began to stream as the dense and swirling fog hung on the heavy air, ranks of soldiers marching stoically through to the sound of rolling drums.

As he sprinted around the Union army's left flank, he saw ranks of Confederate troops closing head-on, shrouded in their own clouds of smoke and with hundreds of bayonets glittering in the sunlight. He cursed, realizing that when the advance became a general charge and melee their chances of finding Lee Carson in the confusion would be drastically reduced. He turned right as he reached the front rank, jogging down the line and peering through the dense lines of troops. Men glanced at him as he moved past, expressions of surprise on their faces as he ran directly in front of their muskets.

'To the front, fire!' The bellowed command of an officer rang out, and Ethan instinctively ducked as the front rank's muskets whipped up and a blast of smoke and noise billowed over his head. In quick order, the second and third ranks let fly with their musket volleys

and then the commanding officer, still astride his magnificent palomino, raised his saber high in the air.

'General charge!'

There was just enough time for Ethan to utter a curse
and then, with a thousand war cries, the Union army
broke ranks and charged, bursting from the clouds of
smoke and thundering across the field. He dodged left
and right as they rushed at him from out of the gloomy
fog, as at the same time the rebel troops opposite broke
their line and charged in response.

Ethan turned and ran with the Union forces, looking
left and right for Lee Carson through the confusion and
noise. His eyes lit upon a man perhaps twenty yards
away, running with his rifle held in gloved hands. Ethan
changed course, smashing sideways through the ranks of
charging soldiers, stumbling over and around them to a
volley of irritated shouts and curses.

He saw the gloved man glance in the direction of the
shouts, saw Carson's features flare with recognition.
Ethan shouted out above the noise, 'Carson, stand still!
It's too dangerous!'

Carson ignored him and accelerated into a sprint.
Ethan raced after him when suddenly a huge figure
loomed up on his right, his rifle raised high so that the
butt was aiming at Ethan's head. The weapon smashed
down toward him as he caught a glimpse of a drooping
gray moustache and furious eyes sheened with a misty
glaze. Ethan recognized the man he'd seen leaving the
elevators at the Hilary Falls apartments. He dodged right,
under the man's charge and the wildly swinging rifle as
he drove his shoulder into the man's chest. The man's

bulk slammed hard into Ethan's shoulder, spinning him aside as the big soldier charged through. Ethan whirled and slammed down onto the grass, rolling and covering his head as Union troops dashed past or jumped over his body. He struggled to his feet and saw the big man vanish into a dense tangle of screaming bodies as the two armies smashed together in the center of the field. The sound of clattering bayonets and clashing swords rang out, a flickering sea of metal flashing across the field amidst roiling blue and gray uniforms.

Ethan sprinted after the big man, cursing his heavy jacket and pants as he shoved his way through writhing bodies and drifting whorls of smoke, searching for Carson once more. He could see the distant figures of the crowd watching from the edge of the field, and knew that if Carson made a break for it he would be seen almost immediately. He had to stay with his army until they broke off the battle.

A Confederate soldier appeared in front of Ethan, raising his musket and shooting a wiry-looking man in a Union uniform. The Union soldier made a show of clasping his stomach in agony, then toppled onto the grass, his rifle falling by his side. Ethan whirled as someone rushed at him, and he saw a short, podgy man in Confederate dress with a flushed face take aim and fire his musket directly at Ethan's chest. A cloud of smoke billowed into Ethan's face, his eyes watering and a sudden terror rippling through his belly at the sight of a weapon discharged at him from point-blank range. He stood rooted to the spot, his hands instinctively flying to his chest to search for injuries.

The smoke cleared and the Confederate soldier stared at Ethan in outrage.

'Hey, you're dead! That's cheating!'

Ethan took one stride forward, grabbed the rifle's stock and yanked the man holding it toward him, as he punched his other fist straight into the rotund soldier's face. The soldier squealed, grabbed his nose and rolled away onto the grass as Ethan tossed the rifle at him and squinted through the rolling smoke.

A large man, the same soldier who had barged past him, got down onto one knee amid the endlessly running and screaming soldiers and lifted his rifle, taking careful aim. Ethan realized that he was aiming into his own troops and suddenly spotted Carson in amongst the mayhem.

'Carson, get down!'

Lee Carson turned, looking straight at Ethan for a split second before the man with the rifle fired. Ethan saw the bullet hit Carson in the chest. Carson flew backwards from the impact and toppled over two men engaged in a bayonet battle behind him. Ethan sprinted forward as the big man ran past Carson's body, lying among hundreds of others on the grass. Ethan slid down beside Carson and saw thick blood matting his shirt. Carson's eyes were infected now with fear, as though he were once again a twenty-year-old kid. He grabbed Ethan's shirt and gritted his teeth.

'I'm done bad, ain't I?' he gasped with a conviction Ethan couldn't deny.

'You're going to be fine,' Ethan assured him. 'Hang in there.' But Carson's face had turned a pale and sickly white, his gaze drifting as he lost focus on Ethan. 'Stay with me, Lee!'

Carson focused briefly, still gripping Ethan's shirt, his voice a ragged whisper. 'Saffron Oppenheimer,' he rasped. 'Let . . . you . . . kill . . . her.'

Ethan held Carson in his arms and struggled to hear his words over the chaos of the battle around them.

'What? What about Saffron?'

Carson's reply was an inaudible rasp as his grip on Ethan's shirt weakened and he sank back onto the grass. Ethan saw that the blood staining Carson's shirt was no longer flowing, and he realized that the man's heart had given out.

The cries of battle turned to a sudden flurry of gasps and exclamations that filtered through the soldiers around Ethan as they realized that Carson was not acting.

'He's been shot!' a trooper shouted. 'Somebody's got a real gun!'

Panic erupted around Ethan as men began shouting and running from the field. Ethan lurched to his feet and sprinted in pursuit of the large man who had shot Carson. The realization that somebody had actually been killed raced through the ranks almost as fast as Ethan was running, and the soldiers began breaking away from each other, dashing for the safety of their tents.

Ethan saw the officer on the big palomino, swinging his sword at men around him as though swatting flies. As he swished the weapon at a nearby Confederate soldier, Ethan grabbed his wrist and with a yank and a twist hauled the officer out of his saddle to land with a thump on the grass in a tangle of limbs. Ethan grabbed the saddle and hauled himself up to survey the chaotic battlefield, taking the reins and turning the horse full circle.

The big man stood out like a sore thumb among the hundreds of troops, standing head and shoulders above them as he dashed for the edge of the field.

Ethan kicked the horse's flanks, hanging on as the animal dug in and accelerated across the field as though possessed. Ethan bellowed at bewildered re-enactors to get out of the way as the palomino thundered toward them. He saw Lopez and Zamora appearing from the hordes, their faces flushed with exhaustion and surprise as Ethan rode up to them and hauled the horse to a halt.

'Call for police and an ambulance,' Ethan said to Zamora. 'Carson's been shot.'

'Where's the shooter?' Zamora asked, pulling out his radio.

Ethan pointed across the field.

'That way, a real big guy.' He reached down to Lopez. 'Coming along?'

Lopez took two paces, grabbed Ethan's proffered hand and swung herself up into the saddle behind him.

'Who the hell are you now?' she asked over his shoulder. 'The Lone Ranger?'

Ethan didn't answer, driving the stallion forward again. The horse thundered across the field through veils of cordite smoke as Ethan pulled the reins to avoid trampling oblivious re-enactors lying in the grass clasping their various imagined wounds. Ahead, he saw the big man duck under a rope partition separating the spectators from the battle, and flee through the crowd toward the exits.

'Can you jump that?' Lopez shouted above the thundering hooves and wind.

'I'm not worried about the fence,' Ethan replied. 'I'm worried about the crowd.'

Ahead, lines of excited faces clapped and nudged each other, pointing at the palomino with its Union rider galloping toward them. Ethan swung his arm at them, trying to get them to move. Several parents and children started waving back at him.

'Get out of the goddamned way!'

Faces started falling as the spectators became dimly aware that the horse bearing down upon them wasn't showing any signs of slowing down. Suddenly there was a parting of the crowd as people stumbled over each other to get out of the way. Ethan lifted the horse up, the stallion clawing the air as it hurled itself over the partition and landed safely on the other side, angry spectators bellowing at Ethan as they galloped past.

'A touch more realistic than they would have liked,' Lopez shouted.

Ethan concentrated on guiding the horse as they reached the edge of the fields, where the big man was running toward a beaten-up old Crown Victoria parked by the sidewalk. Ethan saw him clamber in and the car pulled away.

'Hang on!' he shouted, and yanked the reins to the left.

The stallion responded eagerly as it followed the car, the thunder of hooves on grass giving way to the clatter of iron on asphalt as they burst out onto California Street between lanes of traffic.

40

'Great move, Zorro!' Lopez shouted over Ethan's shoulder as a pair of SUVs swerved to avoid them and clashed fenders with a whine of rending metal. 'What the hell are you going to do now, head 'em off at the pass?'

Ethan's attention was focused entirely on the road ahead, where the Crown Vic was struggling to pass a slow-moving line of traffic filtering its way past Sedillo Park and north toward the intersection with Interstate 25.

'We've got to stop them escaping. That man's got Carson's murder weapon!'

Lopez gripped him tightly around the waist as he wove the stallion between the lines of traffic, car horns wailing and people cursing as vehicles swerved to avoid the unexpected horse galloping past them. Lopez shouted something back at him just as he saw the face of the big soldier leaning out of his window, his rifle tucked into his shoulder.

Ethan yanked the reins to one side, the palomino jerking out of the shooter's view as the rifle crackled and spat a thick funnel of gray smoke. He felt the shockwave as the musket ball smacked through the air inches from his ear, and beneath him the horse flinched.

A large red truck swerved alongside them, and Ethan glimpsed a pair of panicked eyes beneath a baseball cap as the truck veered off to one side to avoid a collision. Ethan let the stallion pick its own course past, the truck missing them by inches as its driver fought for control of his vehicle.

'Jesus, we need cover!' Lopez shouted.

Ethan guided the stallion between the two lanes of traffic, accelerating again in the flow just two cars behind the Crown Vic. He glanced at the dense traffic and made a decision.

'Can you ride?' Ethan shouted to Lopez above the wind and the sound of the vehicles honking their horns and incredulous drivers shouting insults.

'Sure, I rode ponies back in Guanajuato! Why?'

Ethan hauled the stallion out of the line of traffic and alongside the car in front of them, a navy-blue Taurus driven by a nervous-looking soccer-mom with two kids in the back. He grabbed the reins in one hand, tossing them over his shoulder as he hefted his right boot up onto the saddle and launched himself at the Taurus. For a brief, vertiginous moment it felt as though he were hovering in the void between the palomino and the car and then he thumped down onto the roof of the Taurus.

Lopez shouted something at him and he glanced to see her untangling the reins with a look of disbelief on her face. He turned to face forward, realizing that the terrified soccer-mom beneath him was already slowing down. Ethan lunged forward into the wind buffeting his shirt, strode down onto the bonnet of the Taurus and launched himself at a run into the back of a battered old pick-up in front. The weary suspension on the truck sagged as he landed hard on the metal surface, and he saw the driver look back over his shoulder and shout as Ethan dashed forward and leapt up and over the cab.

'What in the name of God d'you think you're doing?'

Ethan scrambled onto the bonnet of the pick-up and with a single stride launched himself through the air before slamming down onto the rear of the Crown Vic even as the big man was struggling to get his reloaded rifle out the window again. Ethan jumped forward and landed flat on the roof of the car. He grabbed the rifle's stock with one hand as it appeared out of the window, twisting it up toward him and then pulling with all his might to keep the weapon pinned upright, the fingers of his other hand grasping the opposite edge of the roof. He saw the soldier stare at him in shock, and got his first good look at the face. Broad and craggy, with blue-gray eyes sheened with that curious glaze. He recognized the man instantly, not just from the elevators at Hilary Falls. The photograph. The big man in the center. The leader.

Ellison Thorne.

Ethan instinctively ducked as an overhead road sign flashed past, emblazoned with directions for the I-25 south for Las Cruces.

Thorne tugged at the rifle and yanked Ethan toward him. Ethan kept his grip, desperately trying to stay on the roof. Thorne was immensely strong, but his awkward angle, half out of his window, prevented him from pulling on Ethan with all his weight. He stopped trying and instead glared at Ethan, the wind tugging at his thick gray hair and long moustache.

'You're walkin' a road that leads to your doom, boy,' he rumbled, his voice so deep it sounded as though he were under water.

'So are you,' Ethan shouted above the wind. 'You're being hunted. You can't hide forever.'

Ellison Thorne's moustache curled across his face in the wind as he smiled grimly up at Ethan.

'Yes, we can.'

Ellison Thorne suddenly ducked out of sight. Ethan was about to try to yank the rifle out of the car when it jinked hard left and before he could respond, he felt something smash the door of the sedan open. Ethan's precarious grip on the roof was wrenched painfully free and he flew sideways, one hand still clasping the rifle stock as he was propelled off the roof into mid air. In a moment which would be seared into his brain for life, Ethan plummeted beside the car and saw Ellison Thorne sitting sideways in the passenger seat, having turned to open the door and then booted it open with one almighty kick. Then the desert slammed into Ethan's back with enough force to drive the air from his lungs. As he slid across the loose dust at the side of the road he had a brief sight of the Crown Vic turning hard right onto the I-25 and accelerating south toward the endless scorched deserts vanishing into a milky blue-white horizon.

And then everything went black.

★ ★ ★

And then everything went a perfect, flawless blue.

Ethan squinted as the light seared his retina, heard sounds reaching his ears again, voices and the sound of car doors slamming. Then a horse clattering to a halt nearby. The palomino appeared above him against the hard blue sky and looked down at him with an almost quizzical expression.

'You just don't know when to quit, do you?'

Ethan blinked and then saw Lopez peering around the palomino's head from the saddle. He tried to lift his head, a deep ache throbbing throughout his body. Lopez jumped down and helped him up into a sitting position and searched with her hands beneath his thick hair.

'Well, you haven't damaged your head, leastways not any more than it already was. You were lucky you hit the dust and not the asphalt, and you missed that street-light by inches.'

People were gathering around now, staring down at Ethan and the big rifle he still held in his hands, which were now bloodied where his knuckles and knees had scraped across the stony ground. He tentatively moved his legs and then his arms, wriggling his fingers and toes.

'Any sign of Zamora?' he asked Lopez.

'The police aren't here yet,' she replied. 'They're probably busy sorting everyone out back in town. Carson got shot, remember, and you just rode a horse straight through a crowd then down the goddamned highway. First thing they'll probably do when they get here is arrest us both.'

With an effort, Ethan struggled to his feet. Lopez slipped the heavy uniform jacket from his shoulders and turned it in her hands. The thick fabric was torn where Ethan had landed on his back, but it had protected him from injury. She showed it to him.

'You realize that luck does run out, eventually,' she said.

Ethan nodded, looking up as a squad car pulled up nearby with lights ablaze and sirens wailing. Ethan limped toward them with the rifle in his hands, relieved to see Zamora climbing out of the car.

'They went south in a silver Crown Vic,' Ethan called out, and gave Zamora the registration number before handing him the rifle.

'This the murder weapon?' Zamora asked.

'Yeah.'

Zamora turned and tossed the rifle into the back of the squad car.

'Hey, that's evidence,' Ethan protested, pointing at the rifle and then wincing as pain bolted up his arm.

'Yes it is,' Zamora agreed. 'It has fingerprints on it and we'll have them analyzed, but as evidence for homicide it's useless. You're thinking about ballistics, aren't you?'

'The barrel's rifled,' Ethan said. 'It may have a distinctive effect on the ball, if you've recovered it from Carson's body.'

'USAMRIID has Carson's body,' Zamora said. 'They're on the scene already, arrived within a few minutes of the shooting. What you're forgetting is that these weapons all have rifling, and that means it's not enough to prove that this weapon fired the ball that killed Carson. More than that, the ball isn't fired like a modern weapon – it doesn't have an imprint like a modern bullet so it can't be connected to any one rifle.'

'I know,' Ethan said. 'But having the weapon is better than not having it. The fingerprints are evidence enough.'

Zamora sighed, rubbing his temples with one hand before gesturing them to join him in his squad car. Ethan sat in aching silence and watched as Zamora recovered the palomino and had it transported back to Sedillo Park before he drove back in silence. They arrived to see ranks of re-enactors filing en masse from the field which, in its center, now had a police cordon.

Butch Cutler was there already, directing his staff with bellowed commands. He turned as Ethan limped across to the cordon, Zamora and Lopez either side of him. Cutler looked at Ethan's bedraggled, bruised and bloodied form, and smiled.

'You look like shit, Warner, but I'm pleased to say it's the last time I'll have to see you at all because if I do, I'll arrest you on sight.'

'We're leaving,' Ethan said without emotion. 'We captured the murder weapon, it's in Officer Zamora's patrol car.'

Cutler raised an eyebrow in surprise.

'What of the perpetrators?'

'Escaped,' Zamora replied. 'We've got their license plate out, one of the patrols will find them soon enough.'

'Not if they go into the deserts,' Ethan said.

'Either way,' Cutler growled, 'it's none of your business now, Warner. Once again you've brought chaos to New Mexico and now you've outstayed your welcome. Get off this field, get cleaned up and then get the hell out of here or I'll have you in a cell by sundown.'

Ethan said nothing as he turned his back and walked away, trying not to limp.

'How the hell did they get here so damned fast?' he asked out loud.

Lopez walked alongside him. 'They're up to something. Question is, what are we going to do about it?'

'We'll do what Cutler wants, and stay out of Santa Fe,' Ethan replied. 'Tell Zamora to let us know when his men find that car. We'll go pick up some equipment, and start taking the fight to the enemy.'

41

SKINGEN CORP
SANTA FE

2.53 p.m.

'What news, Donald?'

Jeb Oppenheimer sat behind his desk, the windows around his office opaque once again and his monitor showing an image of Donald Wolfe at the USAMRIID headquarters at Fort Detrick, Maryland.

'We've got a USAMRIID team working in Santa Fe and Socorro counties, trying to keep up with everything that's going on down there. So far we haven't recovered any useful material from the apartments or from any of the crime scenes.'

Oppenheimer leaned forward on the table keenly.

'What about the body, the one found at Sedillo Park?'

Wolfe smiled.

'Perfectly preserved – we had the corpse on ice within an hour of death. So far the level of decay is minimal. However, the acceleration is irreversible once death has occurred. Sooner or later the remains will also be useless to us.'

Oppenheimer leaned back in his chair and sighed with relief, still unable to believe that he had finally obtained what he had searched for for so many decades.

'How could they have known about this man before us?' he demanded. 'Lee Carson? I've been searching for these people, chasing legends and stories for thirty years or more, then Ethan Warner and Nicola Lopez stroll down here and identify one of them within two days.'

Wolfe shook his head, his hands raised in a gesture of helplessness.

'I don't know, but it must have had something to do with Tyler Willis. We know that Hiram Conley was talking to him. He could have identified the survivors to Willis, who then told Warner and Lopez.'

Oppenheimer shook his head slowly.

'No, Willis was too afraid of what I would do to him to have held anything back. They must be coming out of hiding for some reason. Willis didn't know where Conley and Carson had gained their longevity, but he did say it must have been bacterial.'

'If you hadn't damned well killed Willis we could have asked,' Wolfe murmured.

'It was an accident,' Oppenheimer replied. 'I had no intention of killing him. Tyler Willis was one of the finest researchers into the field of senescence, far too valuable to simply eradicate.'

'So what do we do now?' Wolfe asked.

'I need to have a chat with Warner and Lopez, how shall I say, more *discreetly* this time.'

'That could be a problem. According to reports, Warner and Lopez have gone off the radar.'

'What do you mean?'

'They've left Santa Fe and Socorro county. My men on the ground don't know where they are right now.'

Oppenheimer struggled to comprehend what Wolfe was saying.

'Then goddamned find them again!'

'It's not that easy,' Wolfe countered. 'New Mexico is huge. If they've gone out into the wilderness it could take an entire army to locate them. Warner is a former Marine. If he wanted to, he could hide out there for years and we wouldn't find him.'

Oppenheimer closed his eyes, sitting back in his chair and forcing himself to think clearly. It had for years been a major problem in his quest that the individuals he sought were almost certainly spending large amounts of time living out in the Pecos wilderness, or under pseudonyms in small towns scattered all over the state. Tracking them down was almost impossible as they moved regularly to avoid detection, and they seemed to always have some kind of support from within the towns – people who supplied them with medicines or money or clothes. Oppenheimer had never identified these mysterious benefactors any more than he had the extremely aged men he sought.

'We'll have to go after them,' he said finally. 'If they make contact then this whole thing will be for nothing.'

'Perhaps not,' Wolfe said, 'depending on how we play it.'

'How so?'

Wolfe's expression hardened as he spoke.

'It would appear that whatever afflicts these men, it isn't permanent.'

Oppenheimer's heart seemed to skip a beat in his chest.

'What do you mean?'

'Lee Carson's hands and lower forearms were decaying *before* he was shot,' Wolfe replied. 'It may be that this condition of theirs was starting to recede and that they were looking for help. It would explain why Hiram Conley came out of hiding and approached Tyler Willis in the first place.' Wolfe took a breath. 'They may be dying.'

Oppenheimer shook his head vigorously.

'No, that's not possible. You know for yourself now, it's true. These men are some two hundred years old and haven't aged since they encountered whatever it was that caused this.'

Wolfe leaned back in his chair, seemingly unperturbed by the revelations.

'I doubt, Jeb, that your clientele would appreciate discovering that their elixir of youth would only extend their lives by a few decades.'

Oppenheimer cracked his cane down on his desk, pointing a finger at Wolfe's image on the screen.

'It makes no difference. What nature provides we can improve. Once we know how the bacteria work we can make the necessary genetic alterations to enhance performance. By the time my clients realize that they're vulnerable we'll have had another fifty, sixty or seventy years to research improvements.'

Wolfe grinned coldly.

'But the price, Jeb,' he said. 'It will suffer.'

Oppenheimer felt his throat constrict. His voice gurgled as he struggled to control himself.

'You worry about ensuring that what happens in New Mexico stays in New Mexico. Let me worry about who's paying for what. Right now we're selling a concept that alongside global population control will enhance the quality of the human race a hundredfold in just a few decades, and the glory of it all is that we'll still be around to see it.'

Wolfe examined his fingertips as he spoke.

'And if any one of those clients were to see the state of Lee Carson's arms in the meantime?' he suggested offhandedly.

Oppenheimer growled his reply.

'I take it that your silence on this matter is required once more.'

'As you like to say,' Wolfe replied, 'everybody can be bought. And my price just doubled.'

Oppenheimer ground his teeth.

'So be it.'

Wolfe's demeanor instantly changed. He held the cards now, and Jeb knew it. For as long as Wolfe was the only security against Oppenheimer's exposure, he could call the shots.

'Good. I'll see what can be done this end to ensure Lee Carson's body remains in our possession. In the meantime, I suggest that you carry out your search as quickly as possible.'

'What's the rush?' Oppenheimer asked. 'They've been out there for decades and they're not going anywhere.'

'No,' Wolfe smiled, 'but Lee Carson was reputedly killed by one of his friends, a man who fled the scene with several accomplices. That suggests discord within their ranks. Their vehicle was found abandoned in the wilderness seventy miles south of Socorro. If Carson was killed by his own companions – the men that you seek – how long before they wind up taking themselves out altogether?'

Oppenheimer grimaced. 'I don't possess an army to conduct the search.'

'No,' Wolfe conceded, 'but I have connections with ex-soldiers, people willing to work without asking questions. I will send a hundred of them down to New Mexico under the guise of a civilian survival-training course. They will be at your disposal from when they arrive, and I will ensure they are equipped to deal with your *little* problem.'

With that, Wolfe disconnected their video link. Oppenheimer sat in impotent silence for a moment, cursing Wolfe's apparent stupidity. A hundred men might take a decade, even a century, to find two fugitives in the desert. But of course, Oppenheimer had an advantage that he would not share with Wolfe, one that would ensure that once the bacteria were in his hands, Wolfe could go sing for his payment.

Oppenheimer tapped a few keys on his computer, accessing Google Earth and zooming in to New Mexico, then typed in an Internet Protocol address. Moments later, a tiny flashing dot appeared deep in the desert, and Oppenheimer smiled.

'Hello, Ms Lopez.'

USAMRIID
FORT DETRICK
MARYLAND

2.58 p.m.

Donald Wolfe stared at the now blank screen of his monitor for a long moment, thinking about what Jeb Oppenheimer had said, before he looked up at the pockmarked face of the soldier standing before him. Red Hoffman had a round, pale face and fiery ginger hair that gave him his name, and his eyes were like narrow slits pinched between his puffy features. He stood to attention wearing all-black combat fatigues festooned with radios, pouches and a pistol holster.

'Gather your men,' Wolfe ordered. 'They'll be tasked with a search and destroy training mission concerning some potentially lethal carcinogens being carried by suspected terrorists.'

Hoffman nodded, saluting smartly.

'Can we expect resistance from the targets?' he asked with military efficiency.

'From one of them at least.' Wolfe nodded. 'Ethan Warner. The rest are nothing that should concern you. I feel certain that with odds of one hundred to eight in your favor, victory should be assured.'

Hoffman smiled, saluted again, then marched out of Wolfe's office.

42

GLENCOE
NEW MEXICO

5.20 p.m.

'You sure about this?'

Lopez's voice sounded tiny in the immense silence of the wilderness surrounding them. Ethan stared out across the barren landscape and took a mouthful of water from his bottle before pushing it back into his webbing. His limbs and joints still ached after his earlier unplanned flight from Ellison Thorne's car, but not enough to hold him back.

'Only way to get to the bottom of this is to find these people and figure out what the hell's happening to them.'

Lopez was wearing a rucksack like Ethan's, a military-issue Bergen containing a bedroll, sleeping bag, supplies and a webbing belt with water bottle, ration packs and medical kit, all picked up in Albuquerque on the journey south. The load weighed almost as much as she did, a burden she would never have carried as a detective in DC's Metropolitan Police Force.

Since boldly handing in her badge and founding Warner/Lopez Inc. with Ethan, Lopez had come to realize that working for herself was not all it was cracked up to be. A steady, predictable salary in the force had been replaced with an endless succession of good months and bad months, traveling expenses and now hiking through ninety-degree heat in a desert. To top it all, they were not armed.

'Maybe,' she said, taking a drink from her own water bottle as they walked across open ground toward a vast mountain range ahead. 'But we're blind here, Ethan, following a hunch that could lead us further from the truth, not toward it.'

Ethan shook his head, jabbing a thumb over his shoulder toward the small town of Glencoe now far behind them on trail Fs443, beyond the rolling hills trembling in the heat haze.

'Ellison Thorne and his men abandoned their car a mile outside of Glencoe on this track. That means they were heading south, and they've obviously decided to do so on foot. There must be a reason for that and it can't just be about getting away from SkinGen and Jeb Oppenheimer, or anyone else for that matter. These guys are good at staying out of sight: they've done it well enough for the last hundred forty years. They must be heading in this direction for a good reason.'

Lopez looked about her in disbelief.

'Well, they couldn't have picked a worse place to go. There's nothing out here but shrubs, dust and scorpions for a hundred miles.'

Ethan smiled.

'You'd be surprised what you can find out here to survive on, if you know where to look.'

'Thanks, oh Great White Hunter,' Lopez said. 'I assume that all you ex-Marines can mix up gravel, flowers and a chunk of horse crap to make a bomb or something.'

'Something like that.'

Lopez shrugged, looking down at her feet as she walked. 'You think we're doing the right thing?'

'Sure we are,' Ethan replied. 'We'll catch them up in no time.'

'I didn't mean that,' Lopez said. 'I mean everything, bail-bonds, the DIA, the whole nine yards?'

Ethan slowed in his walk, scanning the horizon thoughtfully as he did so.

'You getting cold feet?'

'Just thinking, that's all. We're not making much out of the bonds we're tracking down – too much competition. It's getting hard to make ends meet, and now we're out here sweating ourselves to death for the DIA with no guarantee we can earn our fee.'

Ethan stopped walking and looked at her.

'Without the DIA we'd only have bonds and bounty hunting. Things would be a lot worse then.' He sighed. 'I know things are tight for you right now, but you've only got to ask.'

Lopez looked away from him toward the lonely mountains in the distance.

'I got it covered,' she lied.

'That's what you always say,' Ethan pointed out. 'If you've got it covered, then why are we having this conversation?'

Lopez started walking again. 'I'm just worried about tomorrow is all.'

'Would you have asked Lucas for help?'

Lopez stopped in mid-stride, her head flicking round with a swirl of long black hair and her dark eyes glaring at Ethan.

'The hell's that supposed to mean?'

'That maybe you'd rather be back in the force. Maybe this venture of ours isn't enough for you, and you need the stability you had before.'

Lopez stared at him for a long time as though unsure of what to say.

'What about you?' she retorted. 'The only reason you got into all of this was because you were looking for Joanna.' Truth was, Ethan had rarely spoken of his fiancée to Lopez, and whenever it had come up he had avoided the issue. 'We've both got our reasons for being here, even if they aren't what we'd want them to be.'

'I got cleaned up,' Ethan replied, not taking offense. 'People change. Fact is I'm not the one who's been breaking the law for a quick buck.'

'It's for my family,' Lopez shot back, 'who are poor and who I see maybe once a year, if that. Yours are wealthy, living in the same goddamned city and yet you haven't spoken to them in years.'

'That's different.'

'Sure it is. But I'm not the one questioning your loyalty.'

A silence descended upon them as they walked, Lopez feeling somewhat disappointed but unsure why. Maybe she'd been alone for too many years, self-reliant, self-sufficient and yet lonely all the same. Next to the late Lucas Tyrell, Ethan was the closest thing to a real friend that she'd had since arriving in America twenty years before. The realization tempered her mood slightly.

'So, when do you think you can pick up their trail?' she asked.

Ethan scanned the horizon, checked the angle of the sun and finally looked at his watch with a smile that told her their argument was over, for now at least.

'Well, best guess would be about five minutes ago.'

'My ass.'

Ethan pointed at the dusty earth beneath their feet, just to the right of where Lopez was walking.

'They're smart guys, wearing flat-bottom boots to minimize impressions and they're weaving between bushes to avoid snapping off twigs. But they were in a hurry to get away from the Interstate after the shooting, so they've had to move fast. You can see the occasional scuff here and there, definitely human, not running but walking real fast.'

Lopez squinted at the dusty, stony earth, unable to see a thing.

'Can you tell what color pants they were wearing?'

'They're heading directly south,' Ethan said, ignoring her. 'And are unlikely to be trying to throw us off the scent. They won't be expecting the police to follow them out here, even with dogs. They left nothing of any use behind at the scene to track them from. I'm hoping they'll keep running until they get right away from inhabited areas, and that's where we'll catch them up.'

'Supposin' you're right,' she said cautiously. 'What do we do then?'

Ethan blinked the sweat out of his eyes, and shrugged.

'Before Lee Carson died, he mentioned Saffron Oppenheimer's name. She's obviously got something to do with all of this.'

'What did he say about her, exactly?' Lopez asked.

'It was weird,' Ethan replied. 'He said "Let you kill her". I don't know what he meant.'

Lopez said nothing, and together they hiked out further into the wilderness, the sun rising high into the burning blue sky above them and beating relentlessly down on the parched barren land.

It had been some years since Ethan had pushed out over rough terrain, carrying weight on his back, in pursuit of the unknown. In Iraq and Afghanistan, his platoon had found itself under fire from Taliban soldiers intent on driving American forces from their lands or dying in the process. Now they had only the wilderness itself to fear, but Ethan felt strangely certain that they were not alone as they trekked further away from civilization. He looked up at the hills around him, peppered with thorn scrub and bushes, perfect places for their quarry to hide out with a rifle and check their tail. Tactically, he and Lopez were sitting ducks following the trail in the depths of the valley, but Ethan guessed that Ellison Thorne and his mysterious companions would be trying to put distance between themselves and law enforcement before placing sentries.

They walked for another three long, hot hours, resting every now and then in what shade they could find, rationing their water and consulting the map Ethan had brought with him to ensure they were not drifting off course or too far from water. The sun was starting to sink toward the horizon, filling the valleys with deep shadows, when Ethan paused to kneel over a patch of dirt between the bushes. Lopez stood beside him, looking down at the same nondescript area.

'What? You think one of them had a crap here?'

Ethan looked over his shoulder at her in bemusement.

'No, but they've split up somewhere behind us. I can only see one track right now, not the three we had before.'

Lopez squatted down alongside him, glancing around her nervously.

'These guys have got rifles, Ethan, and all we've got is matches,' she said. 'You think they're trying to ambush us?'

Ethan looked at her, and then moved closer, their faces only inches apart as he spoke.

'Don't move a muscle.'

43

Lopez's dark almond eyes were fixed on Ethan's as he turned slowly to face her, and although she did not move he saw a flicker of amusement twinkle behind her eyes.

'Are you hitting on me?' she whispered.

Ethan leaned in even closer to her. 'Getting excited?'

Lopez looked at him furtively for a moment.

'Not just yet.'

Ethan's hand shot down to her right foot and snatched something that flashed past her face in a writing mass. She saw his hand gripping the neck of a colorfully banded coral snake that had been coiling itself across her boot.

'Jesus!'

Lopez leapt backwards and landed on her ass as Ethan tossed the snake away into the bushes. He made sure the snake was gone before looking at her.

'Sorry, had to do something subtle else you'd have freaked.'

'Christ, Ethan, you think?' she said as she got back to her feet. 'That damned near scared me half to death.'

'The hitting on you or the snake?'

She looked at him, and managed a brief smile. 'Both.'

'Come on,' he said, 'we need to find out where we are.'

Lopez squatted back down beside him and pulled out their map from one of her webbing pouches. In the fading light the map was not easy to read, but Ethan did not use his flashlight.

'We're here, southeast of these hills,' Ethan said. The map showed where a series of long dried-out streams had joined another, larger flow where they now were, which then split once again ahead of them. 'They're probably following a track each, all still heading roughly southeast.'

Lopez traced a finger along the map.

'Dammit, Ethan, there's nothing out here at all until Artesia, and that's seventy miles away. We're going to be a long way from any supply line.'

Ethan nodded, looking up toward the horizon. New Mexico was divided into life zones: lower Sonoran, upper Sonoran, transition, Canadian, Hudsonian, and arctic-alpine. Each contained its own vegetation and terrain, with shrubs and grasses giving way to piñon, juniper woodland, sagebrush and chaparral then ponderosa pine and oaks mixed with conifers, aspen and spruce forests on the higher ground. And their quarry could be hiding out in any one of those varied terrains.

'We'll have to move quickly,' Ethan agreed. 'As you just found out, we're not the only living things out here.'

Ethan had already spotted pronghorn antelope and ring tails. He knew that black bears roamed the higher ground too, formidable creatures not averse to attacking humans if hungry or provoked. Tarantulas, coral snakes and rattlers infested the deserts wherever one traveled, and could end a life in a flash of fangs.

Ethan scanned the map directly south of their position.

'There's the town of Hope, but that's almost as far. The rest of it's just wilderness.' He squinted up at the sun now setting behind the seemingly lifeless hills and valleys. 'They must have another vehicle stashed out here, or horses perhaps.'

Lopez nodded.

'Or they're really hard core, and intend to stay on foot and take their time getting to wherever they're going.'

Ethan was about to reply when something caught his eye, a flicker of movement up on one of the valleys, stark against the bright orange sky. He didn't move, slowly folding the map and slipping it into his webbing pouch while looking at the ridge above with a fixed gaze. Lopez sensed his sudden tension.

'You got something?' she whispered, as motionless now as he was.

'Something just sky-lined itself up there to the right of us,' he whispered. He was about to write it off as an animal or bird of some kind when it moved again, the unmistakable shape of a human head bobbing as it hurried down the hillside.

'There's another one,' Lopez said, nodding across to their left.

Ethan felt a sudden chill as he realized they were in the floor of the valley with the surrounding heights occupied by people unknown.

'They're trying to ambush us,' he said finally. 'Must have spotted us a while back when the sun was still high enough to illuminate the valley floor.'

'What are we going to do about it?' Lopez intoned, looking nervously up at the hills and betraying her city-girl roots. 'We're exposed here.'

Ethan reached slowly around and slid his Bergen off, setting it down beside a bush.

'There's nothing to worry about,' he said. 'If they were competent enough to launch an ambush, they wouldn't have revealed themselves so easily. We'll go and have a look.'

An instant later, the deafening report of a gunshot thundered down the pass, echoing off the hills around them as they hurled themselves face down onto the ground.

44

SANTA FE

9.22 p.m.

Butch Cutler strode into his hotel room, tossed his key-card onto the bed and gratefully dragged his shoulder holster off. Since he'd been assigned to USAMRIID after leaving the Rangers he'd always felt somewhat uncomfortable carrying a weapon around in public. Not that he was afraid to use it — just that somehow being armed while surrounded by civilians just didn't float his boat. He laid the weapon down on the bed and yanked off his tie before loosening his shirt and looking at himself in the mirror next to the bed. He looked older now, gray-haired and maybe a little haggard. Once upon a time he'd felt invincible, a soldier in one of the finest combat regiments on earth. Now he just felt weary, a hired hand in powerful men's games.

Butch poured himself a well-earned drink, and was about to slump into an easy chair when a knock sounded at his door. Without really thinking about it, Cutler was on his feet with his gun in his hand, moving silently across to stand to one side of the door with his back to the wall.

Never peer through the peep-hole – block the light, and an assassin has only to shoot straight through the door.

'Who is it?'

The voice that replied sounded feeble and strained.

'I'm here on behalf of Colonel Donald Wolfe. My name is Jeb Oppenheimer.'

Cutler frowned uncertainly.

'He too busy to pick up the phone himself?'

'He's not aware that I'm here,' came the reply. 'I was hoping that perhaps we could speak privately?'

Cutler thought for a moment, then turned and unlocked the door before snapping it open and pointing his pistol into the wrinkled face of an old man a foot shorter than he was. In an instant, Cutler caught sight of four heavy-set men standing guard nearby.

'Don't worry about them,' Oppenheimer said, gesturing at them with his cane. 'They're here to protect me, not to attack you. Can we speak inside?'

Cutler turned aside as Oppenheimer limped his way into the hotel room, his entourage of four guards following him. Two moved to stand outside Cutler's room, while the remaining two followed the old man inside and closed the door behind them.

'My apologies,' Oppenheimer said, 'for the intrusion. There's no need for your gun – I wished merely to know how the USAMRIID investigation is proceeding.'

Cutler, his pistol still in his hand, strode across the room and picked up his drink. He cast a glance at the two heavies guarding Oppenheimer, and felt reassured. Both were exuding all the menace of cartoon characters, standing with straight backs and their hands clasped before them, trying to look tough but failing. Both were young but neither looked military, more like nightclub bouncers than close-protection specialists. More to the point, standing as they were in the manner of Mafioso henchmen meant that, if they were armed, they wouldn't reach their weapons in time to stop Cutler putting a bullet in both their brains. As he had learned long ago, bravado was no match for already having your weapon in your hand.

'You could have called to find that out,' Cutler said to Oppenheimer, not putting his gun down. 'What do you want?'

Oppenheimer leaned on his cane.

'Your help, Mister Cutler. You are leading the investigation at USAMRIID for Colonel Wolfe, and I believe that I may be able to assist you.'

'That won't be necessary,' Cutler said, taking a long sip of his drink. 'We have the situation under control.'

Oppenheimer raised an eyebrow.

'Is that so?' he asked rhetorically. 'And what about Ethan Warner and Nicola Lopez?'

'What about them?'

'They are hindering your investigation, are they not?'

Cutler chuckled, and drained his glass before speaking.

'By now Warner and Lopez will have left the state,' he said. 'They're not a problem.'

Oppenheimer shrugged.

'If only that were true. However, I have it on good authority that they were last seen traveling out into the desert somewhere south of Glencoe.'

Cutler stared at the old man for a long moment.

'And how would you know that?'

'Because I make it my business to know,' Oppenheimer snapped. 'And right now, what I know could help us both achieve our aims.'

'Which are?' Cutler asked, remaining impassive.

'The acquiring of certain . . .' Oppenheimer delicately selected a word, '*tissues* that are required for SkinGen to produce a new drug. Tyler Willis, before his unfortunate death, was working on just such a drug.'

'Anything that we find will be delivered directly to Colonel Wolfe at Fort Detrick,' Cutler replied.

Oppenheimer grinned.

'But if some were to be inadvertently lost,' he suggested, 'or left behind?'

Cutler eyed the old man for a long beat of his heart before replying.

'Such things have happened before, occasionally.'

'Of course they have,' Oppenheimer agreed. 'Human error, environmental issues, sheer bad luck. Of course, you will enjoy a considerable amount of financial good fortune should such an occurrence take place.'

Cutler set his glass down, his pistol still in his hand.

'And where might these tissues you refer to be found?' he asked.

Oppenheimer gestured vaguely about in the air.

'They might well be located by Warner and Lopez in the near future,' he suggested. 'Perhaps if you were there you could ensure that viable specimens are passed on to SkinGen instead of USAMRIID.'

'Viable how?' Cutler asked.

Oppenheimer's grin turned cold as he leaned forward on his cane.

'Alive, Mister Cutler. Just one of them, alive.'

Cutler stood immobile for what felt like several minutes, the beating of his heart thumping in his ears.

'Who?'

'Let Warner and Lopez guide you,' Oppenheimer suggested, 'you'll know well enough when you find them. I'll compensate you fully once you've returned them to—'

'Five hundred thousand dollars,' Cutler interrupted, '*all* in advance, wired to my account by tomorrow morning, or this conversation is over.'

Oppenheimer ground his teeth in his jaw, his gaze turning icy, but he nodded once.

'As you wish.'

Oppenheimer produced a card and handed it to Cutler. The card bore the details of a SkinGen subsidiary bank account, as though Oppenheimer were used to bribing people and had made cards specifically for that purpose.

'Call your bank,' Oppenheimer said, 'and clear the transfer with them. One call, Mister Cutler, along with a single live human being, and your work will be done.'

Oppenheimer turned without another word, one of his guards opened the door for him and he left the hotel room. Cutler watched the door close behind them, and stood alone in silence for several moments, looking down at the card in his hand.

The he turned, and picked up his cell phone.

45

NEAR GLENCOE

Ethan hurled himself to one side as a bullet cracked the air beside him, bursting through the fabric of his Bergen. Lopez leapt for cover behind a dense thicket of bushes to her left as the bullet ricocheted off the stony ground and zipped past her.

'I thought you said not to worry!' Lopez shouted.

Ethan rolled sideways into cover, squinting up at the hillside as bits of dust and grit stung his eyes. The sky was darkening swiftly, the glow of the sunset giving way to the deep blue of evening. He remained silent and still. Against the sky he could see occasional movement, furtive and sporadic. For a moment he couldn't believe that their attackers could have launched such a perfect ambush and yet expose themselves so easily at the same time, and then he suddenly understood.

Another shot cracked out, and Ethan spotted a tiny burst of muzzle flame just before it smacked into the earth a few feet behind where he lay. The shot was at least a hundred yards closer than the figures milling about on the hillside.

'They circled back on themselves,' Ethan whispered to Lopez, cursing his complacency for thinking that professional soldiers, no matter how old, would have failed to cover their retreat. 'They're clearing their tail.'

Lopez's voice whispered back to him.

'That'll teach you to respect your elders.' Ethan shot her a disapproving glance, which she ignored. 'There's too many of them.'

'I don't think they're all on the same team,' Ethan whispered back, looking across to where his Bergen had fallen when the bullet had struck it. 'We'd better move before they fall back.'

Ethan belly-crawled across to his Bergen, fumbling inside for a moment until his hand rested on something cold and hard. He pulled the weapon out, checking its mechanism in the darkness before looking up at the hillside.

'Is that a pistol?' Lopez asked in amazement.

The Beretta M9 9mm had been the standard issue sidearm of the Marine Corps in Ethan's day, and he had liked the weapon despite concerns about its stopping power. Compact, light and easy to use, Ethan kept one for what he liked to call 'special occasions'.

'These aren't boy scouts we're following,' Ethan whispered. 'I thought it best to come prepared.'

Lopez didn't argue, although he could sense a certain tension in the air between them as he started up the hillside, dodging from cover to cover. He knew that she was pissed at him both for not telling her that he'd been carrying and because she would be wanting a piece too.

Another shot burst out, a flash of muzzle flame perhaps sixty yards ahead and twenty higher, illuminating a dense patch of bushes. The shot zipped over Ethan's head with no more than six inches to spare, the supersonic shockwave thudding through his eardrums.

'Jesus,' Lopez whispered, 'another one like that and we're going back down.'

Which is what they wanted, Ethan knew. It was the practice of all troops in the Marine Corps, especially special-forces units like recon, that when faced with an attack by a numerically superior force you did the last thing they expected you to do. You advanced, and turned a firepower disadvantage into psychological warfare.

Ethan dropped onto one knee to aim at the spot where the last muzzle flash had appeared and fired two quick shots into the darkness. *Two.* Instantly he sprang up, running full tilt for twenty paces straight up the hillside before dropping down and firing another two shots into the same area. *Four.*

Behind him, he heard Lopez laboring up the hillside in pursuit.

Another rifle shot, from further away this time. The shot went over Ethan's head, higher than the last. He immediately aimed and fired two more shots directly at where the muzzle flash had briefly lit the edge of the hillside. *Six. Nine rounds remaining.* He leapt up and dashed ten yards forward and a few yards down the hill, dropping down onto one knee again and aiming at the edge of the hillside. Lopez reached his position and sank down onto her knees, breathing heavily.

'The hell you doing?'

Ethan didn't look at her, keeping his eyes fixed on the gloomy hills ahead.

'Trying to make them think there's more than two of us.'

Lopez was about to speak when suddenly three rifle shots rattled out across the valley, one after the other. Bullets zipped past them, rustling through the bushes or snapping over their heads. Ethan flinched, throwing himself forward and flat onto the earth as Lopez did the same alongside him.

'Great,' she whispered as the reports echoed away down the valley behind them. 'Now they're all shooting at us.'

Ethan got up and fired two more shots, one each at two of the enemy positions, and then began advancing toward them in a low crouched run. *Eight.* He dropped down and let fly two more shots, hoping against hope that the enemy would have fallen back in retreat. *Ten.*

Two more answering shots crackled across the valley, close enough to leave a ringing in his ears, and Ethan saw a larger spurt of flame and a puff of blue smoke less than thirty yards away. A second, from lower down, was forty yards distant and right on target as the shot split the air above their heads. Ethan realized he had a problem: the enemy was now advancing on him.

'They're coming back at us,' Lopez whispered. 'We need to fall back.'

Ethan shook his head. If they gave ground now they'd end up in a running retreat, and with night now fallen it would be doubly hard to track their quarry. Despite the risk, it was better to remain within range and know where they were.

'We need the high ground,' he replied. 'Otherwise they could flank us and pin us down here.'

The rifles cracked again, the muzzle flash now close enough to illuminate the ground around Ethan. A bullet smacked into the ground five feet from where he and Lopez lay flat against the earth. Ethan rolled sideways, bringing his pistol up and firing back. *Twelve.*

'Goddammit, we need to get out of here!' Lopez snapped.

Ethan looked about desperately in the darkness as a series of rustling noises through the bushes both above and below them betrayed the presence of an enemy-flanking maneuver. Ethan clambered up onto one knee, firing three shots at the nearest shapes moving through the shadows. *Fifteen.* He reached down to the webbing pouch at his waist, closest to his right hand, grabbing a second magazine. As he yanked it free of the pouch a shout rang out over the hillside.

'He's out of rounds! Pig-stick him!'

A burst of noise from the bushes to his right startled Ethan, and he turned to see a figure leap out of the undergrowth and sprint down toward them with a cry of fury. Ethan glimpsed a dark blue coat with yellow arm-stripes, a kepi hat, khaki pants and a bearded face, the man's mouth agape as the flash of a metal bayonet raced toward Ethan's face.

'Get down!'

Ethan shoved Lopez toward the ground as he leapt up, dropping his pistol and magazine and dodging the bayonet as he drove his shoulder into the charging man's chest. The attacker's impetus smashed Ethan backward down the hillside, crashing through bushes and scrub in a cloud of dust and sand. The soldier landed on top of Ethan, his heavy musket pinned between them as they rolled over each other. Ethan slid to a halt with the soldier kneeling on top of him with one hand on his musket across Ethan's chest. As the man raised a fist to punch him, Ethan saw that his kepi hat had fallen off to expose a scalp half decayed, chucks of matted hair spilling out across his shoulders, strips of desiccated skin hanging from the bone.

Ethan shot one hand out as the bony fist flashed down toward him, catching the soldier's hand and twisting it hard. The soldier cried out as his wrist was wrenched to breaking point, and Ethan smashed his knee up into the man's back and then hit him hard enough to send him sprawling across the dusty ground. Ethan leapt up, looking desperately for his pistol. The soldier struggled to his feet and whirled to face Ethan, the musket and its wicked bayonet pointing at him once again. Ethan lunged forward to grab the weapon, but as he did so the soldier twirled it over, the bayonet vanishing as the butt whipped up and smacked Ethan under the jaw with a crack that sent sparks of light flashing across his eyes. Ethan staggered backward and collapsed onto the dusty earth as a voice called down the hillside from the darkness.

'Copthorne? You got 'im yet?'

The bearded soldier grinned down at Ethan with a smile full of gaps, the bayonet hovering above his chest.

'He ain't nothin' but a new piece o' history, Ellison!'

The man glared down at Ethan and smiled. 'Time you took a taste of my Arkansas toothpick, boy!'

The soldier took a deep breath and then lifted the bayonet to plunge it into Ethan's body.

A gunshot shattered the night, louder than all the muskets and pistols, and Ethan saw the soldier above him cry out and leap for cover into the bushes. Another shot followed, gouging a plume of dust up under the soldier's feet. He leapt up, fleeing down the hillside. There was another gunshot from below and Ethan stayed flat on his back as round after round blasted across the hillside, rattling the bushes further up where the voices had come from. Ethan heard a scattering of panicked cries, and then the sound of boots pounding soft earth receding down the hillside into the distance.

Slowly, Ethan clambered up onto one knee and peered into the darkness.

'Who's there? Identify yourself.'

Lopez rushed up alongside Ethan, the pistol now loaded and aiming into the darkness.

A figure stood upright from the bushes, not more than ten yards from Ethan, and in the starlight he could just make out the figure's long, thick blonde hair and a shotgun.

'We meet again, hero,' came Saffron Oppenheimer's voice as she strode toward them. She looked at Lopez and the pistol in her hands. 'I'd put that down if I were you.'

Lopez didn't move. Saffron grinned and clicked the fingers of one hand. From around them in the bushes half a dozen people rose up, each holding a gun of some kind.

'You're the ones who were sky-lining yourselves, not the soldiers,' Ethan said.

Saffron nodded once as Lopez, hopelessly outgunned, lowered the pistol. Saffron walked forward and took it from her before looking at Ethan.

'A lot's happened since we last met,' she said simply. 'We need to talk.'

46

Saffron Oppenheimer led Ethan and Lopez down to the valley floor. On Ethan's advice, she sent her colleagues moving along the top of the valley, deliberately making themselves visible to deter any further attacks from the soldiers he knew must be somewhere ahead of them. After a mile Saffron changed direction and moved down a different canyon. Within ten minutes Ethan spotted the glow of camp fires nestled in the canyon's depths. Above them the sky was ablaze with trillions of distant stars glowing amid the sweeping veil of the Milky Way.

The last time he had really looked at such a panorama had been deep in another desert landscape, searching desperately for Joanna Defoe among the warrens of Gaza City. Ethan watched Saffron Oppenheimer as she led them toward the camp fires ahead, and was struck by the similarities between the eco-warrior and Joanna; the same determination and drive, the same disregard for danger, and an almost identical passion for justice. It was that passion that had almost gotten Joanna killed in

Bogotá, Colombia, long before she finally vanished from the streets of Gaza City. Ethan felt a sudden surge of compassion for Saffron as he realized that her unwavering determination could also only lead to tragedy.

'Is this where your band of merry men hide out?' he asked her as they walked.

'We move around,' Saffron explained, 'never the same place twice and always concealed. The rangers spot us occasionally but they don't bother us to speak of. We don't cause any trouble.'

'Except when you're shooting at people,' Lopez pointed out.

'Saved your ass, didn't it?' Saffron lobbed back and stopped on the track. 'And you speak when I tell you to, not before.'

Ethan stared in surprise at Saffron. He was aware of her dislike of Lopez, but her reaction was excessive.'You nearly killed that man,' Ethan said, impressed and yet appalled at the same time. 'You didn't hesitate.'

Saffron sighed as they walked.

'That wasn't a man,' she said with what sounded to Ethan like pure contempt. 'Leastways not as far as I'm concerned. They've lived out here for a long time and they've chased us out of camps more than once and stolen our supplies. They're usually armed and they're as cunning as wolves, but we've generally avoided each other.'

'You're armed too,' Ethan said. 'Sooner or later someone's going to get hurt.'

'Have they killed any of your people?' Lopez asked.

'No,' Saffron replied coldly, not looking at Lopez,

'but they've shot at us often enough. My people aren't armed as a rule, I just brought them along because I wanted those guys to think they were outnumbered *and* outgunned.'

'You said it wasn't a man,' Ethan pointed out. 'What do you mean?'

'I'll tell you later.'

The camp was small, with two fires and Saffron's questionable comrades arranged in a figure of eight around them, variously cooking, smoking and drinking beer. They looked up and watched silently as Saffron led Ethan and Lopez through the camp and beyond, to a small outcrop of rock overlooking the valley some thirty feet above the camp. She sat down cross-legged and wrapped a shawl around her shoulders.

Lopez sat down as far from Saffron as she could get. Ethan gestured to the camp.

'You don't want to sit down there by the fire?'

'I don't want them to hear this conversation,' she replied. 'They don't really know what's going on.'

Ethan sat down beside her.

'And what is going on, exactly?'

'Do you know where Tyler Willis is?' Saffron asked him, not looking him in the eye but staring down toward the flickering camp fires below.

'He's dead,' Ethan said, seeing no sense in skirting the issue. 'He was found yesterday.'

Even in the faint glow from the fires, Ethan thought he could see Saffron's features turn pale. He heard her take a deep breath, then let it slowly out before speaking.

'And Lee Carson?'

Ethan felt a jolt at the mention of Carson's name and stared at Saffron for a long moment.

'You knew him?'

Saffron's eyes closed and her head sagged, and Ethan realized he'd spoken about Carson in the past tense.

'What happened?' Saffron asked, finally looking at Ethan. 'I heard rumors that something bad went down in Socorro. I went to the town and friends filled me in on what little they knew. That's why I came looking for you out here. What happened to Lee?'

'He was shot and killed, probably by one of his own,' Ethan said. 'Saffron, I need to know what's going on here. Things are already out of hand, people are dying and we can't solve this until somebody starts talking.'

Saffron nodded, swatting a tear from her eye with her sleeve. Her breathing was ragged, but she seemed to Ethan to be holding herself together.

'There's something about the men who live out here,' Saffron said finally, 'something that my grandfather wants to use. He's willing to do anything to get hold of them, including kill.'

'How do you know all this?' Lopez asked as Ethan saw her hand move inside her pocket, keying a button on a recording device.

'Lee Carson,' Saffron said to Ethan, ignoring her. 'He and I . . . we were friends.'

'For a long time?' Ethan asked.

'A few months,' Saffron said. 'It wasn't serious, and I figured out long ago that Lee wasn't the kind to settle down or anything. We had fun, but he kept disappearing for days on end, no contact. In the end, I decided to follow him and find out what was going on.'

Saffron hugged her legs, pulling her knees up under her chin against the chill night air as she went on.

'He came out this way, right out into the deserts to a place called Golden. You ever heard of it?' When Ethan and Lopez shook their heads, Saffron went on. 'It's a ghost town, one that's stood empty for decades. Lee went there and met with other men who seemed to be his friends. But there was a shouting match, a lot of pushing and shoving, and eventually Lee took off with some other guy, an old man with a gray beard.'

'Hiram Conley,' Lopez guessed. 'He's also dead, and his body was taken from a morgue in Santa Fe along with the medical examiner working on him.'

Ethan reached into his jacket pocket and produced the photograph of the old soldiers around the wagon. He held it out to Saffron, who pulled out her cell phone and illuminated the photograph with the screen. Ethan saw her eyes widen at the image as she recognized faces, and then she saw the dates.

'It's got to be some kind of fake,' she said.

'It's not,' Ethan said. 'I checked through the public records and found the original image, correctly dated. This is a copy, but of a genuine 1862 photograph.'

Saffron stared at the image for a moment longer, and then out into the darkness where small free-tailed bats were just visible fluttering across the star fields.

'You're saying Lee Carson was about a hundred fifty years old?'

'Give or take,' Lopez said. 'And so are all the others.'

'How is that possible?' Saffron asked.

'According to Tyler Willis,' Ethan said, 'it's something bacterial that must have evolved to reside within humans. These men must have at some point been exposed to that bacteria and ingested it in some way.'

Saffron thought for a moment.

'So that's what Jeb's been after,' she realized. 'Something like this would be worth more money than exists in the whole world. He'd do anything to get his hands on it.'

'It's worse than that,' Ethan said. 'Jeb's plan isn't just to provide the elite with biological immortality. He wants to make sure that the rest of the world is effectively bred out of existence by the fortunate few. He's a eugenicist, determined that only the best and brightest human beings should have the right to breed.'

Saffron looked as though she were about to throw up.

'And I've been helping him,' she gasped in horror.

'Why though?' Lopez asked. 'Why did you attack the Aspen Center? Why not attack SkinGen instead and do us all a favor?'

Saffron looked away from them. 'It's complicated,' she said.

'I don't think it is,' Ethan said. 'You're working for Jeb Oppenheimer.'

'My job is to steal data from rival companies working in the same fields as SkinGen,' Saffron said. 'I then destroy the existing records, effectively rendering the company useless, and deliver the stolen data to Jeb who uses it to advance his own clinical studies. It helps him get the jump on the competition.'

Ethan nodded slowly as he finally got it.

'Jeb's got something on you and he's using it to black-mail you into making these attacks,' he said. 'It can't be your inheritance because you've said you don't want it, so my guess is that it's something to do with the death of one of your colleagues in an attack several years ago: you must have been involved, and Jeb knows it.'

47

DEFENSE INTELLIGENCE AGENCY ANALYSIS CENTER BOLLING AIR FORCE BASE WASHINGTON DC

10.56 p.m.

Doug Jarvis hurried toward Director Abraham Mitchell's office, weaving between the oncoming personnel bustling through the corridors. He had not heard from either Ethan Warner or Nicola Lopez for twenty-four hours now. While Ethan had gone dark for long periods of time in the past, this time Jarvis had a suspicion that it was not a voluntary act. If his instincts were right about USAMRIID and Donald Wolfe, Ethan could potentially have an army in pursuit of him. The last time that had happened, Doug Jarvis had almost lost both his daughter Rachel and granddaughter Lucy Morgan – only Ethan's tenacity had saved their lives.

Abraham Mitchell was sitting at his desk behind a mountain of paperwork as Jarvis walked in.

'I hope this is important,' Mitchell rumbled.

'That depends on how concerned you are about missing agents,' Jarvis replied crisply, shutting the office door.

Mitchell looked up. 'Who?'

'Warner and Lopez,' Jarvis said. 'They've been off the grid for twenty-four hours.'

Mitchell looked back down at his paperwork. 'They're not agents.'

Jarvis formed a tight smile that made his jaw ache.

'They're working for us, which puts them on the right side of things. I told you that without back-up they risked being compromised.'

'Everybody who works for United States Intelligence risks being compromised,' Mitchell said without looking up. 'They know that.'

'So, we just abandon them then.'

Mitchell sighed and finally looked up at Jarvis.

'Doug, we've got people scattered over half the globe tracking everything from drug lords to terrorists to suspected Russian sleeper agents. Some of our people are involved in investigations so serious and so dangerous that even I don't know the full implications of their activities. I would imagine that by comparison your two rogues are having a riot down in New Mexico. Probably living *la vida loca*.'

Jarvis shook his head.

'There's something more to this than just a vanished medical examiner. Donald Wolfe is hiding something, and it's got to do with SkinGen and its CEO Jeb Oppenheimer. We've had three dead bodies turn up, two of which are now in the hands of departments to which we have no access, based on claims of infectious outbreaks for which there is no evidence. This whole thing stinks!'

Abraham Mitchell put his pen down, sighed and rubbed his temples.

'Doug, I really admire what you're doing here, okay?' he said. 'I know what you sacrificed to get this little experimental unit of yours up and running.'

'I didn't want to be sitting in your chair,' Jarvis said without melodrama, gesturing to Mitchell's seat. 'This was more important, an entirely deniable, civilian contracted investigative unit to work on cases that the Pentagon dismisses as anomalous. It was what the DIA needed – it was the right thing to do.'

'Right for who?' Mitchell challenged him. 'You've put all your eggs in one basket. Having a dedicated but unofficial investigative force is all well and good, and I'm sure the Republicans amongst the hierarchy here think it's a great idea to remove government control and sub-contract our work force out to private investigators. But that means that you relinquish that same control, and the people you've hired can be unpredictable.'

'Ethan Warner is as reliable an investigator as I've—'

'He's a wild card!' Mitchell cut across him. 'The man's a walking war zone. Since he got down to Santa Fe, he's been involved in several shootings, an exploding apartment block and was last seen riding a goddamned horse down the I-25!'

Jarvis managed to keep a straight face. 'He's resourceful and self-reliant.'

'He's reckless!' Mitchell brought his wrath under control. 'What do you want, anyway?'

'I think that we should organize some kind of search of SkinGen, if we can get the warrants.'

'Sublime.' Mitchell smiled in disbelief. 'You want people to go in there and raid one of the most powerful pharmaceutical firms in the world on the basis of a hunch. I can't wait to see what Congress makes of that during the inquests that will doubtless follow.'

'Ethan Warner was certain that Tyler Willis was being held under duress in the building before he was found dead a few hours later. It was Wolfe's men who prevented Ethan from accessing the room in which Willis was being detained.'

Mitchell's expression became somber.

'It's not enough for us to gain access to SkinGen,' he said. 'We'd never get the warrants, and nor would state police under the same circumstances. The state attorney would throw the request out at first glance without probable cause. Not to mention the fact that even if you are right, Donald Wolfe works for USAMRIID. Wild accusations aren't enough for me to go crap on their doorstep.'

Jarvis handed Mitchell a piece of paper that he'd printed out minutes before.

'How about this then?' he asked. 'Donald Wolfe travels down to New Mexico for a meeting with Jeb Oppenheimer. He stays overnight and then flies here to meet with you yesterday. Check the flight times.'

Mitchell scanned the sheet of paper and looked up at Jarvis.

'It's eight hours out.'

'Eight hours and fourteen minutes to be precise,' Jarvis agreed. 'He didn't stay overnight in New Mexico. I managed to pull the flight plans but they don't add up either, so I got on the phone and contacted air-traffic controllers in several states, managed to track the aircraft north to Alaska.'

'Alaska?' Mitchell rumbled.

'I got in touch with the National Security Agency over in Maryland and pulled a few strings. They sent me tracking data from one of their KH-11 keyhole satellites that passed over the Bering Sea and Alaska at the time the SkinGen jet would have been in the area.' Jarvis handed Mitchell another piece of paper, this one bearing a photograph. 'This shows the aircraft at Bethel Airport.'

'What the hell would he be doing up there?' Mitchell asked.

'It wouldn't have raised a question if he hadn't tried to cover his tracks,' Jarvis pointed out. 'There's more. Wolfe got into a private aircraft, hired not by USAMRIID but by SkinGen, and flew north to a remote outpost called Brevig Mission.'

'To do what?' Mitchell asked.

'I don't know,' Jarvis admitted. 'But I'd sure like to find out.'

Mitchell looked at the image for a long moment, and then nodded.

'Okay, fine. Send a team from the nearest FBI field office in Alaska to find out what he was doing there. Tell them we need something solid within twenty-four hours.'

'What about my people?' Jarvis asked. 'I need just a small unit to go in and find Warner and Lopez. For all we know they could be rotting in the desert somewhere while we sit here twiddling our thumbs waiting for a phone call.'

'We're looking at a time discrepancy here, Doug,' Mitchell said, 'not a homicide.'

'You really want to take a risk like that?' Jarvis prodded him. 'If they're onto something big and we hang them out to dry . . .'

Mitchell's eyes scanned the paperwork for a long moment as he digested the meaning behind Jarvis's words before he spoke.

'There's a Marine-recon unit conducting training operations out of Holloman Air Force Base, New Mexico. If you haven't heard from your little John Wayne by the time the FBI report back to us, you can re-task them to infiltrate the area. But I don't want to hear that you've gone in heavy unless there's concrete proof, understood?'

Jarvis nodded and turned to leave the office.

'Doug.'

He turned at the door to see Mitchell regarding him seriously.

'This experimental unit of yours is becoming more and more difficult to keep under wraps. If your boy Warner can't do his work without incinerating city blocks, it will get shut down before year's end and everything you'll have done will be for nothing.'

Jarvis held onto the door handle for a long beat, and then left the office. As he walked down the corridor he realized there was no longer anything he could do cooped up in DC. He pulled out his cell phone and punched in a number. His secretary answered on the second ring.

'Karen, get me on the first available military transport out of Joint Base Andrews Naval Air Facility to Holloman Air Force Base, New Mexico. And get me the number of the USAMRIID unit chief operating in Santa Fe. I'll be needing a quiet word with him.'

48

NEAR GLENCOE

Saffron Oppenheimer didn't say anything for a long moment as Lopez picked up the threads. 'The activist that died,' she recalled. 'You were there and the police suspected that you were involved, but there was a lack of evidence. But if Jeb withheld that evidence from them as leverage against you . . .'

'CCTV footage,' Saffron said finally to Ethan. 'He had it digitally stored and then had the cameras erased before the police could confiscate them as evidence.'

'What happened?' Ethan asked. 'Why were you there?'

'To make a statement,' Saffron said, 'to expose what people like my grandfather were doing to animals all in the name of cosmetics. We managed to get into the SkinGen compound and began attacking the building with stones and rocks. We were there to make a fuss, but not to hurt anybody.' She shook her head. 'One of the protesters got out of line, began assaulting staff as they tried to leave the building.'

'And you got involved,' Lopez guessed.

Saffron nodded.

'There was a fight, between protesters, staff, everyone. It got real hectic. The guy that died was hitting one of the SkinGen scientists, and I was behind him trying to pull him off. He turned and hit me instead, and I just snapped. There were rocks lying everywhere from when we'd been pelting the windows with them. When he came forward to hit me again, I picked one up and let him have it.'

Saffron fell silent, staring at her boots.

'Unlucky hit,' Ethan surmised.

'Blood clot on the brain,' she replied bitterly. 'I must have caught him at a million-to-one angle. He died two days later in hospital. The confusion of the fight meant that nobody knew who did it other than my grandfather, who'd had the cameras erased to prevent any lawsuits against his own staff. He watched the digital copies, saw what had happened, and has used it against me ever since.'

Ethan sighed, looking out over the darkened wilderness for a moment.

'You need to come clean about this.'

'I tried!' Saffron retaliated. 'I whacked Colin Manx in the hopes that he'd spill everything to the police. I was waiting for them to pursue us out here, where I'd conveniently lead them to all the data Jeb's been blackmailing me to steal from other companies and tell them how it's all happened.'

'You copied everything you stole,' Lopez guessed. 'But Jeb could still worm his way out of it.'

'I recorded the conversations I had with him

whenever I delivered data.' Saffron nodded. 'There's almost an hour of it. My plan wasn't foolproof but I'm tired of running. It was working out until you two showed up and got in the way of the police.'

'It has to stop,' Ethan said finally. 'If you don't come forward with this information Jeb's got you over a barrel until the day he dies – if he ever does – and I'd put money on it that he'll find a way to control you from beyond the frickin' grave.'

'The guy's a creep,' Lopez added. 'He'll pay someone to keep you under control. He knows you're in line to inherit the entire company and he'll want to make sure you don't just sell it off for nothing as revenge.'

'He's my grandfather,' Saffron snarled at her. 'It's called *loyalty*.' Saffron coiled the last word up and spat it into Lopez's face. Ethan looked at both of them curiously, but didn't dare push Saffron too hard while she was still talking.

'Why did he agree to leave the entire company to you when he died, if you're so opposed to him?'

Saffron's lips curled into a bitter smile.

'He didn't. His wife, my grandmother, Eloise Oppenheimer, suggested that he should from her death-bed after my parents died in a car crash – the same one that eventually killed her. She was the polar opposite to Jeb: kind, caring, compassionate. Even Jeb was still pass-ably human back then, but when Eloise died it's like he turned into a monster.'

'One who will kill to get whatever he wants. Jeb Oppenheimer killed Tyler Willis, probably to find out what Tyler knew of Hiram Conley. It's possible that

Hiram was trying to find a cure for their condition and Lee Carson was helping him. The remaining old soldiers figured it out and came after Carson while Oppenheimer was chasing Hiram Conley's body after he was shot and killed.'

Saffron frowned.

'Tyler Willis was probably trying to isolate whatever was in Hiram Conley's blood, to figure out why he hadn't aged,' she said. 'I doubt he would have been able to resist trying to patent what he found. If some kind of anti-aging drug could be made from whatever bacteria were within Hiram Conley's body, it would have made Willis a multi-billionaire.'

'True,' Lopez said, 'but at least he wasn't slicing people up to achieve it. Hiram probably realized that Tyler was in danger of selling out and they argued about it up at Glorietta Pass.'

'When Conley finally shot Willis and tried to flee,' Ethan said. He thought for a moment, and then looked at Saffron. 'There's another hostage in all of this.'

'Who?' Saffron asked.

'Lillian Cruz,' Lopez explained. 'She's the medical examiner who disappeared, and the main reason we're down here is because we're searching for her. Hiram Conley's remains were stolen at the same time and we're pretty sure it's Jeb Oppenheimer who's behind it all.'

Saffron nodded.

'He'll be trying to extract useful biological remains from Lee Carson's corpse now that he's got it.'

'And using Lillian Cruz to do the work for him,' Ethan said. 'Your grandfather was willing to torture and then kill Tyler Willis to get what he wanted. Now he's got Lee Carson's remains too. Lillian Cruz may yet be alive and she's an innocent caught up in all of this. We couldn't save Tyler but we might be able to help Lillian if we can get into SkinGen's premises.'

Saffron looked at them for a moment and then closed her eyes before she spoke.

'Probable cause,' she said, almost a whisper. 'The police would need a good reason to obtain a search warrant.'

'You're that reason,' Ethan said. 'Give yourself up to state police, tell them everything you've just told us and we'll have Jeb Oppenheimer by the balls.'

Saffron shook her head.

'I can't do that,' she said.

'Can't?' Lopez echoed. 'Or won't?'

'It's not that straightforward,' Saffron shot at her, before turning to Ethan. 'I killed another human being. Do you have any idea what the media will do with that? The estranged anti-vivisectionist daughter of a billion-aire vivisectionist is arrested, not for killing animals but one of her own activists? I can see the goddamned head-lines already: Saffron Oppenheimer opposes the killing of animals but is happy to murder her friends. The pros-ecution will smash any defense I might have. I'll be up for second degree murder at the least, no parole. My life will be over. I'll become the world's only multibillionaire heiress who can't spend a single dime of her fortune!'

Ethan kept his voice calm.

'People are dying,' he said. 'If Jeb Oppenheimer gets his way a lot more will follow, starting with Lillian Cruz. You're the only person who can stop this.'

Saffron ran a hand through her long blonde hair, her skin tight across her knuckles. Ethan was suddenly struck by how vulnerable she seemed at that moment, still just a young girl struggling to find her way in life and dealing with far more than she should be at her age.

'It's not just that,' she said finally. 'If I give myself up and send the police in, Jeb will be arrested. He's too old for prison, he'll never survive.'

Lopez said out of the darkness, 'The old man's a tyrannosaur who's just about universally hated by the entire population of this planet. Who gives a damn?'

'I give a damn!' Saffron wailed, and Ethan saw her hand move to the handle of a Bowie knife lodged in her pants.

'Nicola,' he said, sensing that whatever was between the two of them was about to explode into violence, 'why not head down to the camp. See what you can find out about where those soldiers might have been headed?'

Lopez shot him a severe look, but she got up and walked off into the night down toward the camp below. Ethan turned back to Saffron.

'Why defend him?' he asked gently. 'He may have killed people.'

'So have I,' Saffron replied.

'Not for financial gain. It was an accident – Jeb Oppenheimer killed for information.'

Saffron sighed.

'He's all the family I've got left,' she said. 'Even if he is twisted and bitter, it's not him. He was never the same after my grandmother died, because he couldn't save her. That's what's driven him to become so completely focused on wealth and power: he really believes that if you have enough influence you can control anything.'

Ethan inclined his head in understanding. He had once traveled dangerous streets, scoured a land by day and night for years in search of Joanna Defoe, yet despite all his painstaking efforts he had never heard from her again. If he knew one thing for sure, it was that when you loved somebody you really would travel to the ends of the earth and sacrifice everything, even your own life, in order to protect them.

'But you never can, no matter how wealthy you become,' he said.

'He'll destroy himself,' Saffron said. 'And most likely take me with him just for the sake of it. We're doomed one way or the other, but I can't bring myself to betray him. I did it once before when I attacked his buildings and started this whole goddamned charade. I won't do it again.'

'Even though he blackmails you into those attacks?'

'I'd have done them anyway, most likely,' Saffron said, and then looked at him. 'You got family?'

Ethan nodded. 'Parents back in Illinois, a sister too.'

Saffron smiled.

'You're lucky to have them,' she said. 'Do you speak to them often?'

'I call my sister now and again,' he replied.

'And your folks?'

Ethan considered lying, but he instantly decided that Saffron Oppenheimer had most likely inherited her family's bullshit detector. He shook his head.

'Why not?' Saffron pressed him.

'Because I left the Marine Corps,' Ethan breathed finally. 'My dad's a Vietnam veteran and wanted me to reach higher in the ranks than he did. I served my commission in Afghanistan and Iraq but decided to do other things with my life after.' He shrugged. 'Guess he couldn't understand why.'

Saffron moved closer to Ethan, and he felt a small but strong hand grip his forearm.

'Call him,' she said seriously. 'Don't leave it another day, you understand? Crap like this separates families all the time and then when someone dies all they can say is pathetic crap like: I wish I could have said goodbye. Get on the phone and do something about it, okay?'

'He wouldn't answer the phone,' Ethan said, then realized almost immediately how thin the excuse sounded.

'Like hell,' Saffron shot him down. 'Tell him you're from the corps, organizing a veteran's dinner or something. You've been there, you know how to pull it off. Who cares if it's crap? Just talk to him.'

'For what?' Ethan asked gently. 'We don't get along, always at each other's throats. I doubt it would do any good: it would probably make things worse between us.'

'They can't get any worse than when you're not speaking,' Saffron pointed out. 'I've been trying to change Jeb's ways for years. It probably won't work, but I daren't give up in case I lose him and then spend the rest of my life wondering "what if?"'

'I don't think my old man's going anywhere fast yet,' Ethan pointed out.

'Maybe not,' Saffron conceded. 'But you're sitting in the middle of one of the most dangerous deserts on earth and being shot at on a regular basis. You want him to suffer if it's you who goes first?'

Ethan had a momentary vision of Joanna, and of how he had suffered when she had vanished without trace from his life. Suddenly, making a phone call seemed trivial in comparison.

He nodded.

'I'll do it, but only if you'll turn yourself in and provide evidence against Jeb Oppenheimer.'

Saffron was about to say something when Ethan heard Lopez calling up to him from below.

'Ethan, get down here! Now!'

49

SKINGEN CORP
SANTA FE

11.17 p.m.

Lillian Cruz looked down at the operating table before her, breathing slowly as she observed Lee Carson's naked body.

In life, Lee Carson had been an impressive figure, that much she could tell from the corpse. The broad plain of his chest met wide shoulders, and his flanks reached a narrow waist that led down to long, muscular legs. He had the chiseled features of a matinee idol, thick and wavy black hair that fell to his shoulders and piercing blue eyes.

Although those features still shone through, what remained was a rapidly decaying carcass of graying flesh that even now was beginning to fall in clumps from Carson's arms and sagged from his ribcage in drooping folds. Despite being on ice for several hours, Lee Carson's remains were aging at a terrific rate, internally as well as externally. The large 'Y'-shaped incision across his chest and down through his sternum to his pubic bone, where Lillian had opened him up, revealed his internal organs crumbling within. His kidneys and liver were shriveled, his intestines and stomach reduced to leathery rags coiled like the discarded skins of desert snakes. Lillian pushed the dried sacks of Carson's once vibrant lungs up into his chest cavity to cover his heart.

'Well?'

Lillian had almost forgotten about the man standing watch over her, his every breath rasping as though he were Darth Vader without the black outfit. Jeb Oppenheimer leaned on his cane, his face glaring at her like a wrinkled prune.

'The decay is irreversible,' Lillian said, more sickened by the presence of the live man in the room than the dead one. But she was also intrigued by her findings, even in her current predicament unable to quell her fascination with the bizarre human biology she was witnessing before her. 'It doesn't make any sense. You say that this body was frozen within twenty minutes of death?'

Oppenheimer nodded.

'Give or take a minute or two. USAMRIID was on the scene within fifteen minutes of the shooting. I put them on standby myself, in case any of these men used the re-enactment in Socorro as cover to move freely.'

Lillian shook her head.

'Then any bacterial activity, whether beneficial or detrimental, should have ceased once the body had cooled. That's the very reason why biological remains are chilled to preserve them, to reduce bacterial activity. But this body is still decaying regardless.'

Oppenheimer moved closer, looking at Carson's remains.

'How could that be?'

Lillian shook her head.

'I've never seen anything like this before. This is an entirely new kind of biology, something that hasn't yet been described by science. It could take weeks or even months to understand what's happening here at a cellular level, but this corpse will be nothing but dust by lunchtime tomorrow.' She turned to look at Oppenheimer. 'What's left of Hiram Conley?'

Oppenheimer gripped the top of his cane more tightly.

'Not enough to fill a bag,' he rattled. 'I need results from this body.'

Lillian raised her hands helplessly.

'Results of what?' she demanded. 'Even if I took tissue samples they'd crumble before I could do anything with them. This decay is not the action of bacteria eating the flesh, or even of biodegradation. This is a human body decaying at a cellular level: complete and utter disintegration. Even the bones are starting to crumble.'

Lillian turned, and with a blunt instrument tapped Lee Carson's forearm sharply. The pallid flesh sagged beneath the blow and the bone within splintered with a dull crack.

'What do you need?' Oppenheimer asked.

Lillian put the instrument down and folded her arms. She knew there was only one way in which she could identify what had happened to Hiram Conley and Lee Carson. If she could understand that, then she had a possible ticket out of Jeb Oppenheimer's hands.

'It doesn't matter what you do, to me or to anyone

else,' she replied. 'What you need is a live specimen, nothing less. You won't need to carve them up or torture them. You'll just need to sit them down, run some blood through a bypass machine so that it doesn't decay when it's outside their body, and study it. Whatever is inside these men, it is as reliant upon them as they are upon it. Apart, they are nothing.'

Oppenheimer glared at Lillian angrily for a long moment, and then turned.

'Keep working while there's still something left,' he ordered, and left the theater, slamming the door after him.

Lillian waited for a moment until she was sure that he had gone, and then turned her attention back to Lee Carson's remains. She stretched over his chest and peered down into the depths of his ribcage, deliberately keeping her own body between Carson and the cameras she knew were watching her from the corner of the room. She pushed aside the brittle tissue of Carson's lungs with her gloved hands until she saw what she'd been looking at for the past half-hour, before Oppenheimer had stalked into the theater.

Buried deep within Lee Carson's heart, at the end of a ragged passage where it had torn through the tissue, was a single musket ball, the dull metal gleaming at her from within the left clavicle of the heart. Lillian felt her own heart skip a beat. The ball was gleaming because the tissue around it was still moist, as live and fresh and healthy as it had been for over a hundred fifty years. Whatever had kept Lee Carson young for over a century and a half had relied upon the one thing that his body could supply, and when death had finally come, whatever wonders it had achieved were lost with it. Only the musket ball, buried within his heart, had provided it with the fuel it required to stay alive in that tiny vicinity. Tyler Willis had been right.

Iron.

Oppenheimer took the elevator from the operating theater to the first floor of the SkinGen building, then turned right and walked through a warehouse packed with boxes of pharmaceutical tools and chemicals. His cane clicked through the open spaces until he reached a loading bay where ten men were waiting for him. All were dressed in black jump-suits, their bodies festooned with weaponry. He knew that they represented the command element of a combined force of some one hundred men, who were already waiting at a pre-arranged location out in the deserts of New Mexico.

Be ever prepared, his father had once told him, and be not beleaguered by the unexpected.

Oppenheimer disliked mercenaries. Hired guns were unpredictable and liable to self-preservation rather than loyalty, and the fact that Wolfe had sent them instead of trained troops bothered him immensely. Sure, their presence and service would be entirely deniable to either USAMRIID or SkinGen, but mercenaries could just as easily abandon the chase or even turn against him - or indeed Donald Wolfe if the going got too tough. He knew well enough the art of betrayal. A line from recent memory infiltrated his thoughts: 'In the end, only one remained, the strongest of them all. But as that individual was now entirely alone they were worth nothing, and collapsed and died, having eradicated themselves from existence.'

He extinguished Saffron's words from his mind as the leader of the hired men, a man named Red Hoffman, stepped forward. He was tall and bulky, with a flat-topped buzz cut of ginger hair and a pallid face pock-marked with what had likely been childhood acne.

'We're ready to go, sir,' he said. 'What's our target?'

'How many of your men have served in the military?' Oppenheimer asked, gesturing to the men behind Hoffman.

'All of them, sir,' Hoffman replied, raising his chin. 'Every single man I've hired has served at least one tour of duty in—'

Oppenheimer walked past Hoffman. The man disgusted him already, acting as though he were commanding a Delta Force legion when his pasty skin and sagging guts suggested otherwise. Oppenheimer selected a scrawny-looking man with receding hair and bloodshot eyes, whose face bore crooked scars that ran from the corners of his mouth up his cheeks in a permanent macabre grin.

'You. When and where did you serve?'

'The '80s, sir, US Army, First Infantry Division.'

Oppenheimer took in the man's slumped shoulders and skinny hands. 'Where were your headquarters?'

'Fort Hood, Texas, sir,' the man replied with a slight quiver.

Oppenheimer turned to look at Hoffman.

'The First Infantry are based at Fort Riley, Kansas,' he said quietly. 'First Cavalry are at Fort Hood.'

Hoffman's proud demeanor slumped.

'A genuine mistake, sir,' he muttered. 'Been a while since our service years for most of us.'

Oppenheimer stepped up to glare into Hoffman's eyes and spoke loudly enough for the men behind them to hear.

'I dislike liars,' he rattled. 'You're being paid good money to go out there and track down several men, but judging by your fat gut and your double chin the closest you've gotten to the army is playing with toy soldiers in your grandma's fucking garden.'

Hoffman's pocked skin flushed pink as he stared over Oppenheimer's head into the distance. Oppenheimer turned and paced up and down as he addressed the men as one.

'The man you are looking for is Ethan Warner. He is a former United States Marine with combat experience who is likely more capable than every man standing here combined. I suggest that you lose your fantasies of being elite soldiers and concentrate on your strengths.' He looked at each and every one of them with revulsion. 'Your only strength being numbers.' He turned to Hoffman. 'Get these assholes off my property and out into the desert. Ethan Warner is searching for a small group of men who must not be harmed. As for Warner, the first person to shoot him dead and bring his head back here will receive enough money to buy a small island in the Bahamas, is that clear?'

The men bellowed a cry of 'hoo-rarr' and began jogging out of the warehouse and down to the loading area outside, where two coaches were waiting for them.

Oppenheimer reached into his pocket and retrieved his small GPS locator, checking its screen. There, in the middle of a map of the New Mexico desert, a signal beeped and flashed once every second.

Oppenheimer smiled.

'There you are, Ms Lopez,' he said. 'Everybody can be bought.'

He turned to Hoffman, who was shouting orders as his men loaded heavy cases into the coaches.

'Hoffman! Get Lillian Cruz up here! We'll need her on the scene if we capture our targets.'

Hoffman selected two of his men and stormed off toward the theater. Oppenheimer watched them go and then checked his GPS tracker one last time before walking toward the coaches, determined that he would witness his finest hour with his own eyes.

50

NEAR GLENCOE

'What is it?'

Ethan hurried down into the flickering light of the camp fires to see Lopez gesturing for him to follow her, pointing toward a young girl who sat quietly amongst a small knot of Saffron's followers.

'This girl,' Lopez said. 'Her name's Ruby Lily, or so she says. She's seen the soldiers out here before, says she knows where they hide out.'

Ethan followed her to where the young girl sat alongside a fidgety teenage boy who stared at Ethan with wide eyes, as though he were afraid of his own shadow. Ethan sat down on an old rug that had been spread on the desert floor, amazed once again at how Lopez was so easily able to win people into her confidence. He figured it was something to do with her diminutive frame and her exotic looks – attributes which on occasion had seen bail runners hand themselves over without a struggle when Lopez had flashed them an easy-going smile and promised a lenient report upon their return to jail.

'Ruby,' Lopez said to the young girl. 'Tell my partner here, Ethan, what you told me.'

The girl looked at Ethan and began to speak, glancing occasionally at the bats flickering past in the night sky above them, their wings visible as they flashed over the flames of the fire. 'I've only seen them now and again,' she said shyly, 'most times out in Otero County, west of Carlsbad.'

'You sure we're seeing the same people,' Ethan asked. 'The same ones who were attacking Lopez and me tonight?'

'Yeah,' Ruby said, 'no doubt about it. They're the only people I've ever heard talking so funny. Y'know, like real old people.'

'Where can we find them, Ruby?' he asked. 'This is very important; we need to find them.'

Ruby smiled in the firelight as the logs crackled and spat, the sparks reflected in her dark eyes.

'They don't wanna be found, that much I know for sure,' she said. 'They always turn away from us if we see them and disappear as fast as they can. We figured they're scared of us.'

Ethan saw Lopez smile at the little girl's audacity, and for a brief moment Ethan felt his breath catch in his throat as he saw Lopez's face glowing golden in the fire-light, her smile bright and her eyes sparkling. He thought again of how easily people trusted her, and of how with such a small act she could capture his attention so completely. The fact that she could also break the law with almost casual abandon struck him forcibly a moment later, and he wondered if he really knew her at all, or whether somehow she was deceiving him too. He blinked his gaze away and focused on Ruby Lily.

'Anything you can tell us might help save a life, Ruby. Somebody has been abducted and we believe the person who has taken them may kill them soon. We're running out of time and these people you see in the desert might be able to help us.'

Ruby Lily looked at him for a long moment, and then at Lopez, before speaking.

'I like you both,' she said. 'I can tell about people by their aura. You both shine brightly, and you obviously care for each other a great deal even if you don't trust each other right now.'

Lopez's eyes widened. 'What?'

'You work together,' Ruby Lily said clairvoyantly, 'yet you live different lives and hide things from each other. You both have a sadness about you that you can't leave behind.'

Ethan glanced at Lopez, and saw her look away from him sharply. Ruby Lily glanced at her companions as though she had revealed unto them great knowledge, and then looked again at Ethan. 'You gotta pen?'

Lopez pulled out a small notebook and pen and handed them to Ethan. Ruby Lily spoke softly.

'We always see them near ghost towns, abandoned mining outposts and such like out in the desert. They headed south from here, so most likely the place they'll be headed is Brice. Find a place called Oro Grande, and follow the old railroad bed until you reach the town. There's not much there, just some buildings, a graveyard and a few mines. If you don't find them there, at the end of the railroad bed there's another ghost town called Zora that just has a few old mines.'

'You think that they hole up in these sort of places?' Lopez asked her.

Ruby Lily shrugged.

'Seems that way. Maybe they store stuff there, or shelter in the caves. Indians used to mine places like Brice hundreds of years ago for turquoise, gold, copper, iron. The school house basement still remains, the Nannie Baird mine office, a powder magazine, railroad loading ramps and old cisterns.' Ruby smiled. 'Some people say you can still hear the sounds of the old town on the wind when you walk through.'

Ethan frowned.

'Why would they run so far south, so far away from their supply line in Santa Fe?' he wondered out loud. 'Seems like a hell of a risk with their health problems.'

Ruby Lily answered for Lopez.

'We reckon they're headed for Lechuguilla.'

Ethan felt a tingle down his spine.

'Lechuguilla? Where's that?' he asked.

'Carlsbad Caverns someplace,' Ruby said. 'Everyone's heard of it but nobody's allowed anywhere near the caves because they're protected by the state as an environmental treasure, in pristine condition. Nobody knows where the entrance to Lechuguilla is.'

Ethan thought hard for a long moment, and Lopez frowned at him.

'What's up?'

'Lee Carson,' Ethan said. 'Before he died he said "Saffron, let you kill her". I didn't know what he meant, but now it makes sense – he was trying to say *Lechuguilla*. He must have seen Saffron out here and knew they had some idea of where the soldiers were hiding out.'

A voice spoke from behind Ethan, Saffron's tones somber and weary.

'He told me they went there from time to time,' she said. 'When things got rough, to lie low until everything quietened down. Nobody goes into Lechuguilla, but they had access to a place called Misery Hole. The caves run for miles beneath the ground, and not every entrance is located close to Carlsbad. Some are way out in the desert.'

'You think that they can get deep enough to hide out there?' Ethan asked her.

'It's not just that,' Saffron said. 'If what you're saying about these men is true, then they may have another motive. I've heard about Lechuguilla Cave, some of the scientific studies done there in the past. Rare, chemo-lithotrophic bacteria are believed to occur in the cave. They feed on the sulfur, iron, and manganese minerals and studies indicate that some microbes may have medicinal qualities that are beneficial to humans.'

Lopez looked at Ethan.

'Maybe they think they can cure themselves by going there? That's why they're running so far south.'

A sudden urgency raced through Ethan.

'We have to get there before they do, or they'll disappear. They've had decades to map those caves.'

'You have no choice now,' Saffron agreed, gesturing out into the night. 'They know you're following them. They'll keep moving through the night, and they won't leave a trail. Only way to catch them up will be to beat them down there and cut them off.'

Ethan got up, searching his pockets for his cell phone.

'We're going to need back-up,' he said, looking at Lopez. 'These guys will start shooting the moment they spot us. See what else you can find out from Ruby here.'

Ethan stepped away from the firelight, jogging up the nearby hillside for a clear signal before dialing Doug Jarvis's number. The line picked up on the second tone.

'Jesus, Ethan, where are you?'

'We're out in the desert, west–northwest of Artesia. We need a ride.'

'That could prove a problem,' Doug replied. 'DIA has suspended all support operations for you out there until USAMRIID has confirmed its findings in Santa Fe.'

'They're working with Jeb Oppenheimer at SkinGen,' Ethan said quickly. 'Oppenheimer's got somebody at USAMRIID in his pocket and he's trying to hold us up or get rid of us altogether.'

'I think I may know who,' Jarvis replied. 'Donald Wolfe. But there's not much we can do about it this end unless we can prove Wolfe is setting you up out there. The word here is that USAMRIID suspect that you and Lopez have had something to do with the murder of Tyler Willis, and since you've now disappeared into the deserts . . .'

'They're onto us.' Ethan finished the sentence, cursing under his breath. 'Has all support been pulled?'

'You've got a special-ops team at Holloman standing-by, but I can't give them the green light until I've got proof that Donald Wolfe is setting this all up on Oppenheimer's behalf.'

'Fine,' Ethan said, reverting to soldier mode – accept the problem and deal with it. 'We're heading for Carlsbad Caverns, specifically a site called Lechuguilla Cave. As soon as you can, send them in to support us.'

'I'm on my way to Holloman right now and I'll do what I can, but you should operate as though you're alone.'

'We're getting used to it.'

Ethan shut the phone off and hurried back toward the camp.

51

Lopez finished up talking to Ruby Lily, pocketed her notebook and stood up. The crackling fire was dying, and the rest of Saffron Oppenheimer's followers had drifted away to their tents. Lopez was about to go looking for Ethan when Saffron appeared beside her.

'So what's the deal between you and Ethan?' Saffron asked.

'What do you mean?'

Saffron folded her arms and smiled brightly.

'You know what I mean. I've seen the way you two look at each other, there's obviously something going on.'

Lopez struggled to keep the smile off her face and felt her skin flush hot as she turned and walked away from the fire.

'There's nothing going on between us.'

'Really? Is that why you got in a car with Jeb Oppenheimer?'

Lopez froze mid-pace, then turned slowly. The thought

crossed her mind to deny everything, but Saffron's smile had vanished quicker than a desert mirage and her eyes were as hard as stones.

'Oppenheimer pulled up alongside me,' Lopez admitted. 'The creep wanted to talk, as he put it.'

'Bet you had a nice chat,' Saffron said, her arms falling loosely to her sides as she strolled toward Lopez. 'See, I've got a problem here. You guys think Jeb has abducted and killed anyone who stands in his way. Yet you get into his car, have a nice cozy chat and then you get out and just walk away. You know what that says to me?'

Lopez raised a questioning eyebrow as Saffron stopped barely inches from her.

'That you sold out, and you're going to betray Ethan. You took Jeb's money because whatever you promised is of value to him and that's the only reason he let you go.'

'Funny,' Lopez smirked, 'that every time Ethan's spoken to you we've later ended up being chased by the police or nearly blown sky-high. Trustworthiness doesn't exactly shine out of your ass, Saffron.'

'That's rich,' Saffron shot back. 'Thinking of taking your little bounty and hiking over the border?'

Lopez let a cold grin flicker across her features.

'Sounds like you're as paranoid as your dear old grandpa, little girl. I don't need a lecture from a murderer who hasn't got the guts to stand up to a ninety-year-old.'

Lopez saw Saffron's Bowie knife flash in the firelight as she swung it toward her face, but Lopez was already moving, stepping outside the arc of the blade and using her right hand to bat it past her face with an inch to spare.

Lopez darted in and closed her right hand round Saffron's knife wrist as she shoved her left hand up inside her elbow, folding the arm on itself and pointing the blade back at Saffron's face. Saffron, startled by Lopez's speed, wedged a foot behind her ankle and leaned in, trying to throw her off balance. Lopez went with the movement, but spun on her heel and threw Saffron down into the dust. Saffron leapt to her feet with the Bowie knife still in her hand, circling like a wounded leopard.

'What's up, little girl?' Lopez taunted her, realizing Saffron's martial-arts skills were not quite up to Lopez's street-fighting instinct. 'Not used to playing with the big girls?'

Lopez saw Saffron dart in toward her again, dodging into a quick left feint before stabbing out with a straight right, the blade flashing toward Lopez's sternum. Lopez twisted aside from the weapon, catching Saffron's wrist again and this time jabbing her free elbow straight into Saffron's face with a sharp crack. Saffron yanked her head away as Lopez twisted her blade arm viciously round on itself at the wrist. Saffron spun around and cried out as the blade fell from her grasp, her arm cranked up high at an awkward angle in Lopez's grasp.

Lopez leaned in behind her and whispered into her ear.

'I don't want you here anymore,' she hissed. 'Take off, or I'll finish you for good.'

Lopez lifted her boot and shoved it into Saffron's ass. Saffron stumbled forward and crashed onto the ground, her arm smashing through the glowing embers of the fire. Lopez winced as Saffron's shriek of pain wailed out across the desert night like the cry of an injured bird of prey, a shower of embers drifting down around her as she clambered to her feet. Cradling her scorched arm, Saffron ran out into the darkness with a wounded, desperate gait and vanished into the night.

Ethan rushed into view at the edge of the firelight and stared at Lopez in alarm.

'What the hell's going on?'

Lopez gestured out into the night.

'Saffron and I had a difference of opinion,' she replied. 'Mine was stronger.'

Ethan looked out into the darkness and Lopez felt an unexpected dismay as she noticed a disappointment in his expression.

'Damn it, Nicola, we needed her help.'

'She's a liability,' Lopez shot back. 'We can't trust her. For all we know she's reporting everything that we do back to dear old Grandpa.'

Ethan sighed and rested his hands on his hips for a moment before speaking.

'We need to get out of here and down to Carlsbad by dawn,' he said. 'DIA can't help us right now, until Doug's done some digging on who's helping Oppenheimer at USAMRIID.'

'Can we make it that far by dawn on foot?' Lopez asked.

'It's a fair way,' Ethan admitted, 'but we don't have much choice.'

At that moment Ruby Lily appeared, her wide, dark eyes looking at Ethan as she held something out to him. Lopez watched as Ethan took a set of keys from her.

'The van,' Ruby said. 'It's an ancient beat-up old GMC Suburban, but it'll get you there a lot quicker than walking.'

Lopez looked at her. 'Must be the van they switched to after the attack on the Aspen Center. I thought the van was Saffron's?'

'It was,' Ruby said softly, 'but I don't think she's coming back after what Lopez did.'

Lopez caught Ethan's questioning gaze.

'We had a fight,' she said. 'She fell and grazed her arm in the fire, then took off. Wasn't my fault. She'll be okay. My guess is she'll head for a hospital, at which point the police will get involved and she'll be forced to 'fess up.'

She saw Ethan almost laugh. 'You serious?'

'She'll tell them where we are and where we're going,' Lopez said. 'She'll want revenge, on me. That way we get some support instead of USAMRIID on our ass, but we'll have to move fast. If they get to us before we reach the caverns it's all over.'

Lopez watched Ethan weigh up the situation in his mind for a moment.

'I hope to hell you're right. Come on, let's go.'

52

BRICE
NEW MEXICO

11.48 p.m.

Ellison Thorne stood beside the crumbling walls of an old powder magazine and scanned the darkness with his eyes and his ears for the sounds of his compatriots. Despite the scratches of nesting animals in the rafters of ancient buildings, the whisper of the wind and the distant sounds of the desert beyond, a dozen decades of living out in the wilderness had tuned his ear sufficiently to be able to pick out the sound of a human footstep from a hundred yards.

Which was just as well, because he was no longer in any condition to run far, should he be surprised by an enemy action. He yearned for the comfort of his pipe but refrained from lighting it until the others arrived. The smell of burning tobacco would be detectable from a hundred yards, the light from the pipe twice that far.

He shifted his weight onto his other foot and felt a brief respite from the weariness aching through his bones. He was dying, of that he felt certain. Whatever blessing, or curse, God had bestowed upon him was fading and his time was coming to an end. Not before time, some might say, but then . . .

'Who goes there?'

Ellison aimed his rifle into the darkness. The sound was small, a shifting of weight on loose soil, but to Ellison's ears it may as well have been a herd of cattle moving through the ghostly silent town.

'Copthorne, standing to!'

'Come for'ard,' Ellison called back, 'make yourself known.'

From the night came Edward Copthorne, limping from a leg injury he'd sustained in 1936 when one of the newfangled automobiles had almost run him off the road near Mescalero. He would have heard it coming, as the earliest vehicles clattered along like runaway horses, but he'd lost the use of one ear after a mortar had exploded alongside him in 1861. As Copthorne approached, he called out.

'Company, stand for'ard!'

From the darkness appeared three more men whom Ellison recognized from their shape and gait alone: Kip Wren, a forty-two-year-old sergeant during the conflict; John Cochrane, late thirties and a corporal; and Nathaniel McQuire, a private aged twenty-nine. Each carried a long-barreled Springfield rifle at port-arms. Ellison himself had been a sergeant promoted to first lieutenant, and commander of the small unit trapped into a fateful flight south after the Battle of Glorietta Pass in 1862.

'I see you,' Ellison called as the four men made their weary way up the steps of the powder magazine and stood in the darkness. 'Anybody snoutin' your trail?'

'Not a soul out there,' Copthorne said. 'We diverged thrice south of the mountains since our encounter with the out of towners. We're alone.'

Ellison nodded, and gestured to the men.

'Stand down.'

They gratefully turned their rifles around and slung them over their shoulders before Ellison led them across the street to where the dilapidated remains of the Nannie Baird mine office crouched against the darkness. He led the way in through the open doorway, the aged timbers creaking beneath their boots as they sought the relative concealment within the building.

Ellison sat on an old upturned barrel and lit his pipe, most of the others following suit or pulling tumblers of liquor from jacket pockets.

'You got any spare Lucifers?' Copthorne asked him, and Ellison tossed him his box of matches.

Kip Wren drew deeply on a cheroot, the glowing tip briefly lighting his rugged features and tight gray beard. He exhaled a cloud of smoke and coughed before speaking.

'I take it we're all still sufferin' the same affliction?'

A murmur of agreement drifted through a darkness punctuated by brief flares of light from the pipes and cigars, ghoulishly illuminated spectral faces watching each other.

'We were always on borrowed time,' Ellison said. 'We knew that to a man.'

'But *this* way?' Nathaniel McQuire, the youngest of their number, said in horror. 'It ain't natural. I don't bear to think what might'n happen to us next.'

John Cochrane, his drooping moustache framing his pipe, pointed at Ellison Thorne.

'It weren't right to shoot poor Carson neither. He was one of us, no regard to what you thought he might be doing in Santa Fe.'

'Carson was likely to endanger us all,' Ellison growled. 'It wasn't my desire to take his life but he left me no choice. You all saw who he was talkin' with, the police and those hired hands from out of town.'

'He was as likely lookin' for help as trouble,' Copthorne pointed out reasonably.

'So was poor old Hiram,' Ellison replied, 'and look what happened to him.'

'He was the first with symptoms,' Cochrane said. 'Ain't no surprise he was panicked. God knows, I'd have done the same if'n it were me.'

'Which raises the point,' Nathaniel said, 'as to what the hell we're going to do. We can't keep runnin', not like this. Every time I move I'm compelled to look behind me in case somethin's fallen off.'

A ripple of grim chuckles fluttered through the darkness, but Nathaniel shook his head.

'I'm done jestin'. We need to do something.'

In the silence that followed the soldiers looked at Ellison Thorne, who drew thoughtfully on his pipe before speaking.

'We do the only thing we know,' he said finally. 'We go back, and see if'n we can't make it happen again.'

There was a long silence before Kip Wren spoke.

'Ain't no guarantee of that.'

'Even if Lechuguilla's still there,' Nathaniel said, 'Misery

Hole could have been sealed off by now. Its location's been protected by the government for years.'

'It's well concealed,' Ellison agreed. 'The scientists that found it in 1986 are long gone. Nobody got no business snoutin' around it.'

'Nobody got no business hunting us down either,' John Cochrane said, 'but it's happenin'. And what do we do now without our supplies? We can't last more than a day or two out here before this affliction takes a turn for th'worse.'

'Not to mention those damned flying machines,' Kip Wren said. 'It's getting' harder to stay hidden out here, Ellison.'

Ellison nodded slowly. In the decades that had passed, they had seen remote frontier outposts become thriving towns and cities, empty wilderness skies filled with contrail streams from flying coaches that seemed as big as entire cattle ranches, and all manner of computerized gadgets that seemed able to find a man in even the most remote corners of the desert. He himself had seen some such devices: keypads attached to boxes of strange lights on the counters of stores in Santa Fe, and moving pictures on panels in shop windows that showed distant lands so realistic it seemed he could reach out and touch them with his hand.

'We stick together,' he said finally.

The men nodded to themselves in the brief glows from their pipes, eyes fixed expectantly on his. It didn't matter that the army was long gone, or that the war was long over. Maintaining their discipline as a unit had kept them alive and their secret safe for well over a century, and Ellison had led them both by rank and by merit these long decades past. Only Hiram Conley's fear, his panic, had broken their seal of silence and started them on the path to destruction.

'We're on our own now, boys, just like before,' Ellison added.

'We're even following the same trail,' Cochrane noted. 'That there's irony for ya.'

Ellison stood up from the barrel, breathing deeply on the night air as he tapped the remaining embers from his clay pipe and slipped it into his jacket pocket. There was no other way, and nowhere else to run.

'Let's move out.'

'Hold on a second,' Nathaniel said. 'What about those two out of towners who followed us? They might'n be allies, not foes. They din' shoot until we did.'

'We don't know who they are,' Ellison said, 'and they ain't our concern.'

'One of them moved like he was a soldier,' Copthorne said, standing to join Ellison but his tone conceding Nathaniel's point. 'He kept our heads down with his pistol but he din' shoot to kill. The other one din' shoot at all. It was only that damned fool girl who let fly with her shotgun, damned near blew my ass off.'

'Yeah,' Nathaniel said, 'and did you see him out of Sedillo Park, ridin' that goddamned horse like a bat outta hell? He almost had us but he never shot no gun. I don't reckon he was bearing arms at all.'

Ellison shook his head, picking up his rifle from where it was propped.

'It's too risky to talk to them.'

'My guess, for what it's worth,' Cochrane said, 'is that they'll keep coming. Whoever they are, they were willing to trek out through the Pecos after us and that ain't something a tenderfoot does lightly.'

Ellison turned to face his men four-square, and his tone brooked no argument.

'Either we reach the caves and are saved, or we reach the caves and we disappear. Whatever happens, as long as I've a breath left in my body I ain't letting Jeb Oppenheimer or anybody else touch my bones.' He checked his weapon and gestured to the door. 'An' if anyone else comes after us, I'll give 'em the good news from the end o' my rifle.'

53

HOLLOMAN AIR FORCE BASE, NEW MEXICO

17 May, 3.10 a.m.

Doug Jarvis stepped off the boarding ramp of a gigantic C-5 Galaxy transport aircraft onto the floodlit service ramp, listening to the huge aircraft's engines whine down as he sniffed the mixture of aviation fuel and desert air. The vapors reminded him of a dozen other similar airbases across the Middle East he had seen when serving with the Marines.

'Mister Jarvis?'

A tall, robustly built man extended a hand to Jarvis.

'Butch Cutler,' the man said as they shook. 'Can I ask why I'm here, sir?'

Jarvis gestured to a waiting USAF bus.

'Best we get ourselves inside first,' he said cryptically, refusing to be drawn.

Cutler asked no further questions and led Jarvis to the bus that drove them across the vast servicing pan past ranks of razor-sharp F-22 Raptors, the latest air-dominance fighter to join the United States Air Force. It pulled up alongside a row of administrative offices, where a young subaltern met them and led them to a small room where a table, two chairs and two Styrofoam cups filled with steaming coffee awaited. Jarvis thanked the subaltern and closed the door behind them, then joined Cutler at the table.

'You have powerful friends, whoever you are, Mister Jarvis,' Cutler said. 'It's been a long time since someone's been able to drag me out of my bed at three in the morning.'

'Bad habit of mine,' Jarvis said, feigning humor in order to draw Cutler in. 'Never was able to sleep more than four hours at a time since leaving the corps.'

Cutler raised an eyebrow. 'Marines?'

'Fourth Marines,' Jarvis confirmed. '15th Expeditionary.'

'Not another one,' Cutler said. 'Is there a corps retirement home down here or something? I've been chasing another ex-Marine all over the state, someone named Warner.'

'Ethan,' Jarvis confirmed. 'He works for me.'

Cutler's casual manner seized as he looked at Jarvis.

'Well, your man is a world-class pain in the ass. Wherever he is people die, vehicles crash and things blow up. If he shows up in Santa Fe county again while I'm still there I'll have him in irons.'

'He's not in Santa Fe,' Jarvis said. 'In fact, that's why I'm here. He's heading south toward the border with Texas, and he's acting alone. Ethan's got a troubling habit of putting himself in danger to achieve his objectives and he may be biting off more than he can chew.'

'What the hell's that got to do with dragging me here?' Cutler asked.

'I needed you somewhere we could talk freely,' Jarvis replied. 'Put plainly, there's something going on behind the scenes at USAMRIID and I suspect you could be compromised.'

'Like hell,' Cutler shot back as he slammed his cup down, spilling coffee across the table. 'My unit's tight.'

'I didn't say your *unit* was compromised,' Jarvis pointed out.

'What then?'

'You called USAMRIID headquarters a few hours ago, trying to reach Colonel Donald Wolfe.'

'How the hell would you know about—'

'We work with the National Security Agency,' Jarvis explained.

'You've been watching me?' Cutler shouted, standing up.

'We've been watching USAMRIID as a whole,' Jarvis said, raising a placating hand. 'We know that you were approached by Jeb Oppenheimer, who has offered a bribe for you to obtain materials on his behalf.'

Cutler slowly sat down, his gaze fixed on Jarvis's.

'He came to my hotel room with four of his heavies,' Cutler said. 'I reported it in as soon as they left.'

'An act I admire immensely,' Jarvis said. 'There aren't many people I know who'd turn down half a million bucks for such a minor indiscretion.'

'I serve my country,' Cutler replied with a sigh and a shrug of his heavy shoulders. 'Doesn't mean I enjoyed turning down enough money to retire on.'

'How often do you speak to Colonel Donald Wolfe?'

'Most days.' Cutler frowned. 'He's my boss. Why?'

'I need you to tell me how it was that your unit was called down here to New Mexico, specifically to Santa Fe.'

Cutler glanced upward in thought for a moment.

'The call came in from Donald Wolfe himself, I guess maybe three days ago at USAMRIID. They had some concern that there was a danger of unspecified bacterial agents being released from a site in or near Santa Fe. We were asked to secure the relevant areas and provide support to the engineering and clean-up teams.'

'They didn't tell you what the supposed agents were?' Jarvis asked.

'We often don't know what we're looking for,' Cutler explained. 'Most times we're searching domestic premises being used by enemies of the United States to produce toxic chemicals or so-called dirty bombs. Our engineers go in fully protected against any airborne pathogens like anthrax, and then identify the agent at work.'

Jarvis took a sip of his coffee and eyed Cutler with interest.

'So you're brought down here, and you head for where?'

'An apartment block, downtown Santa Fe. The only lead we had was that of a man named Tyler Willis, some kind of big-shot brain out of Los Alamos.'

'Why was he mentioned as a target?' Jarvis asked.

'It was pretty vague,' Cutler admitted. 'Something to do with experiments outside his remit or something, general suspicion but no probable cause. We'd been told it would be a discreet operation, but your man Warner rolled up and then the apartment was blown sky-high just before we got there.'

'And what was it that you were looking for, specifically?' Jarvis asked. 'They must have had some idea in order to send you in there in the first place. Was it a vial of something, or maybe vats of chemicals?'

Cutler shook his head.

'No, mostly just a directive to be prepared to encounter toxic substances. Wolfe did mention that I should keep an eye open for any blood I might find.'

Jarvis raised an eyebrow.

'Blood?'

'Yeah,' Cutler said. 'He briefed me verbally that Willis might have been tinkering around with a pathogen that infected people through the mixing of bodily fluids, specifically blood. He said that if I was to find any, I should have it sealed and sent directly to his office in Maryland.'

Jarvis leaned back in his chair and looked out the window between the gaps in the blinds at the rows of aircraft parked beneath the twinkling lights.

'And did you find any?' he asked.

'No,' Cutler said. 'Anything left in that apartment was completely incinerated. If there was blood there its presence might be traceable but that's all. There won't be any means of identifying who it belonged to.'

Jarvis drained his coffee and crushed the cup in his hand before looking at Cutler.

'Tyler Willis was working on a project regarding a particular type of bacteria that can infect and live in the human body. The blood he took was from a man named Hiram Conley, who was subsequently killed in a fracas with state troopers outside Santa Fe. My problem is that Tyler Willis told only two people about the blood he took: Ethan Warner and Nicola Lopez. So, how could Donald Wolfe have known about that blood and sent your team down here, if he hadn't himself been told by someone else where that blood was?'

Butch Cutler opened his mouth to reply, then hesitated.

'He must have been tipped off,' he said finally. 'Maybe by a concerned citizen?'

'Not likely,' Jarvis said. 'Tyler Willis was conducting his work under the utmost secrecy – he hadn't even told his own secretary what he was doing. Ethan Warner talks to him, the labs come under attack and then Tyler Willis goes missing. Warner searches for Willis and the chase leads to SkinGen, where's he's convinced Tyler is being held against his will. You guys then get another mysterious "tip-off" from Donald Wolfe and Willis later turns up dead.'

Cutler frowned as he thought.

'Oppenheimer?'

'The only way Donald Wolfe could have known about that blood is if either Tyler Willis or his abductor told him about it. Colonel Wolfe is involved in the homicide of Tyler Willis, either willfully or inadvertently.'

Cutler slowly raised his hands to his face and drew them down his cheeks as Jarvis watched a terrible realization set in.

'I called the bribe in to Wolfe,' he said, and then a

new horror blanched his face. 'And I pulled Warner out of SkinGen. Tyler Willis might have been just a few yards away.'

'You weren't to know,' Jarvis said, convinced that whatever Donald Wolfe was up to, Cutler almost certainly had nothing to do with it. 'We need to get Wolfe in custody and out of the loop before he can cause any more damage.'

'What do you mean? What's he been doing?'

Jarvis tossed the photographs of the SkinGen jet at Bethal airfield in Alaska, and explained the colonel's missing flight hours.

'He visited a place called Brevig Mission, right out on Alaska's west coast, before flying from there direct to New York City. You got any idea why he might do that?'

Cutler shook his head.

'None whatsoever,' he said. 'There's nothing up there that I'm aware of that would hold any interest for USAMRIID. Nothing that's not already frozen under the permafrost anyway.'

'So there may be something?' Jarvis pressed.

Cutler rolled his big shoulders in a shrug.

'Most departments have at one time or another traveled to habitats bordering the Arctic Circle, mainly to study the victims of novel diseases. Their bodies are preserved by the cold when they're interred, sealing in whatever killed them for future study.'

Jarvis felt something cold slither through his veins as he considered what Cutler had said.

'Like infectious diseases,' he suggested. 'The plague, for instance.'

'Sure,' Cutler nodded, 'a whole bunch of viruses and bacterial infections.'

Jarvis's mind began racing as he plotted Colonel Wolfe's movements in his mind.

'Why is Donald Wolfe in New York City?' he asked.

'He's there to present a key-note speech on population before the United Nation's General Assembly. What he says will probably shape global pandemic policy for decades to come.'

A vision of the United Nations building, set in the heart of one of the most populous cities on earth, flashed dark and foreboding through Jarvis's mind.

'How many nations will be attending?' he asked.

Again, Cutler shrugged. 'All of 'em, I think. A hundred ninety-two.'

Jarvis nodded slowly. It was a little-known fact that although Western nations generally guided UN policy, the United Nations was mostly representative of developing nations who outnumbered their developed brethren by two to one. Gripped by a sense of impending disaster, Jarvis leaned forward on the table.

'Whatever Wolfe is planning, it's not pretty,' he said finally. 'I'm going to need your help to stop him.'

Cutler gathered himself together and looked at Jarvis with a steady eye.

'What do you need me to do?'

54

BREVIG MISSION
ALASKA

17 May

A brutally cold wind swept in off the peninsula, chased by the feeble light of the midnight sun just below the horizon as FBI Special Agent Pete Devereux led three men across the tundra. The small town of Brevig Mission with its spindly church shrank behind them in the strange blue shadows cast across the snow fields. Devereux was following an Inuit guide who was almost entirely concealed by thick coats and a fur-lined hood.

Devereux's voice seemed weak as it was snapped away by the wind.

'You sure they were out here?' he asked, shouting to be heard.

The Inuit nodded, gesturing ahead of them.

'They were here. Two men. They did not ask the elders to dig here, and refused to talk to us.'

Devereux looked out across the frozen wastes to where magnificent mountains crouched against the cold vista. He was about to say there was nothing to see when he spotted a series of geometric shapes huddled in a small knot amidst rippling clumps of hardy grass. A different kind of chill enveloped him as he realized what they were.

Gravestones.

The Inuit led the FBI team to the edge of the stones, and pointed to a spot on the ground some ten feet away.

'This is where the man was working. He had tents and a vehicle. He stayed for a few days, and then he must have died here because another man came and took the tents away.'

Devereux looked at the ground. Half hidden by snow and ice he could just see where tent posts had been driven into the permafrost. Trampled, muddled snow and ice betrayed the presence of men in the last few days. His eye traced the ghostly outline of the tent, and he realized it had surrounded a single grave. Treading carefully, Devereux stepped across the snow and looked down at the grave. He lifted one foot and placed it on the earth in front of the gravestone, and instantly felt it give slightly beneath him.

Devereux turned to his companions.

'Unpack the shovels.'

The Inuit tracker looked at him, his tiny eyes squinting against the bitter wind and little specks of ice encrusting his eyelashes.

'This is not proper,' he said. 'You disrespect our people by digging here.'

Devereux shook his head as one of the agents began handing out shovels.

'It's not our choice,' he said. 'Your people have already been disrespected, we're just trying to put it right. We've been ordered to do this for public safety.

Whatever the people here were doing, it may not have been safe.'

The Inuit frowned.

'I'd have thought that was obvious.'

Devereux stared at the Inuit as the agents behind him began driving their shovels into the icy earth. He was about to join them when, over the shoulder of the Inuit, he saw the town of Brevig Mission in the distance. The church spire of the Lutheran Memorial Church caught his attention. With a sudden jolt of memory, he recalled seeing an entire graveyard behind the church as they'd passed by.

Devereux whirled around to look at the gravestones behind him. His eyes flicked across them one by one, and the dates leapt out at him. 1918. 1918. 1918. 1918. 1918. They stretched away until they were too far to be read.

Beside him, another FBI agent drove his shovel into the snow. Devereux grabbed his arm and held it fast. The agent looked at him quizzically.

'C'mon, Pete, let's get this over with. It's goddamn freezing out here.'

Devereux turned to the Inuit guide.

'These people, they all died at the same time?'

The Inuit nodded. 'They all got sick.'

'How many?' Devereux asked.

'Half of the town died. It killed them very quickly, just a few days.'

Devereux turned to the agents behind him.

'Get the bio-suits out and have this area cordoned off right away.'

As the agents hurried to carry out his orders, Devereux turned to the Inuit.

'What killed these people?' he asked.

'The great sickness,' he replied. 'You call it the Spanish Flu.'

Devereux stood rooted to the spot as the man's words echoed through his skull, provoking memories of long forgotten stories learned at high school and from television documentaries. The 1918 Spanish Flu had been an extremely severe influenza pandemic that spread across the entire globe during the aftermath of World War One. Most victims had been healthy young adults, in contrast to most influenza outbreaks which predominantly affected juveniles or the elderly. Lasting three years, the pandemic killed between fifty and one hundred million people, making it one of the deadliest natural disasters in history. At least five hundred million people had been infected. Although little was known about the geographical origin of the disease, it had been concluded that it killed via what was known as a cytokine storm, a massively excessive response of the human body's immune system. The influenza's modus operandi explained its severe nature and the age of its victims. The strong immune systems of young adults ravaged the body, whereas the weaker immune systems of children, middle-aged and elderly adults resulted in fewer deaths.

'It killed half of the town?' he asked the Inuit.

'More than that. This town was known as Teller Mission at the time. It lost eighty-five percent of its population in less than a week.'

Devereux turned and watched as his agents, now

dressed in bio-suits, began digging down into the hard soil, making far greater progress than could be expected through permafrost; evidently the soil had already been turned over recently.

'You think the man died here because he dug up the body?' the Inuit asked.

Devereux nodded but did not reply as he slipped on his own bio-hazard suit. Another, more insidious suspicion had already crept into his mind as he watched his men digging deeper and deeper into the frozen soil until suddenly one of the shovels hit something. Devereux waved the Inuit back from the grave.

'Stay upwind of us,' he said, acutely aware of the possibility of airborne infection.

Devereux approached the grave, coming to stand on the edge. He looked down into the depths of the freezing earth and felt a primal fear creeping through his veins. The muddied corpse of a woman who had clearly been dead for at least a century stared up at him, gruesomely preserved by the rock-hard permafrost in which she had been interred. Devereux's men backed nervously away from the body, covering their noses and coughing as a pungent waft of putrefaction spilled onto the cold air.

'Looks normal enough to me,' one of the agents said, 'for somebody who's been dead a hundred years.'

Devereux nodded thoughtfully, and was about to turn away when a sudden thought occurred to him.

'A hundred years,' he echoed. 'If she's been here that long, then why is she stinking like she died yesterday?'

A silence enveloped the men for a moment, and then

Devereux grabbed a shovel and stepped back to the edge of the grave. He plunged the shovel down into the earth alongside the body of the woman, and then hauled back on the handle, prizing her rigid body free of the earth and tipping it up against the side of the grave before driving the shovel into the earth behind her to pin her in place.

'Give me another shovel here!' he said urgently.

An agent passed him a shovel, and Devereux scraped away at the loose soil beneath where the woman's corpse had lain. As the soil fell away, the stench became over-powering and a patch of flesh appeared. Devereux scraped furiously until half of another body was revealed encased in soil.

The face of a man stared back up at him. One eye was open, the eyeball rolled up and the white exposed. Soil smudged his face and filled his slackly hanging mouth, and through the dirt Devereux could see blood staining his shirt. What bothered him more was that the man was wearing a modern fleece, thick boots and a digital watch on his left wrist.

'Er, boss,' said one of the agents beside Devereux, 'that ain't no 1918 corpse.'

Devereux nodded, his voice a ghostly whisper above the buffeting winds.

'That's not what bothers me,' he replied. 'What I want to know is: what the hell were they doing with that original, infected corpse?'

Beside them, the Inuit pointed toward the distant airstrip and made a sweeping gesture with his hands up into the sky.

'The other man who came here, he fly away with bits of the body.'

Devereux pulled a photograph from his pocket, one sent to him by the DIA, and showed it to the Inuit. The native nodded vigorously and pointed at the image. Devereux pulled out a satellite phone from his jacket and punched in a number as he wondered what kind of unimaginable shit-storm was going to go down at the Pentagon when they found out that Colonel Donald Wolfe had apparently turned into an international terrorist.

55

MUDGETTS WILDERNESS STUDY AREA, NEW MEXICO

5.12 a.m.

'Pull off the main road here.'

Lopez pointed out a dust track illuminated by the weak beams of the GMC's headlights and Ethan turned off the highway and onto the track, the vehicle bucking and loud knocking sounds emanating from the suspension. Lopez put the map she had been consulting into her pocket.

'This is about as far as we can go in the truck,' she said.

Ethan slowed down as the vehicle struggled through ruts in the sand, then killed the headlights and turned off the engine.

'Where are we?'

'A few miles north of the main entrance to Carlsbad Caverns,' Lopez said, 'just on the edge of the park. This is the area where Ruby Lily said the soldiers have been seen in the past.'

Ethan climbed out of the truck and peered out into the darkness. The whisper of bat's wings fluttered through the night sky above.

'We need high ground and we need some light, or we'll miss them when they come through.'

Lopez scanned her map again and orientated herself to their position.

'Out that way,' she said, pointing into the night, 'there's an old river course that's carved a valley. We can climb to the top of the ridge and hopefully spot them as they come in.'

Ethan grabbed his Bergen from the back of the truck and checked his pistol before setting off. Lopez followed behind, whispering urgently.

'There's hundreds of square miles of desert to cover,' she said. 'And we don't even know which cave they're heading for.'

Ethan spoke between breaths as they hiked up the steep hillside.

'They'll most likely pick the route of least resistance, following key features like dry river beds. As for the cave, we'll just have to make sure we don't expose ourselves until they find it.'

'That could be harder than you think,' Lopez pointed out. 'They're experts at living out here and can probably move undetected far better than we can. Following them unobserved will be tricky at best, impossible at worst.'

Ethan shrugged, striding toward the top of the ridge.

'Maybe, but at least there's no chance of them knowing we're here ahead of them. The greatest weapon we have right now is surprise. As long as we've got that, there's no chance of them finding us first.'

Ethan climbed the last few steps and reached the top of the hill to come face to face with a bayonet pointed unwaveringly at his face. Ethan looked past the bayonet and the gaping muzzle of the long-barreled rifle and straight into the eyes of the big man he'd last seen at Sedillo Park, fleeing the scene of Lee Carson's murder. Ellison Thorne.

Lopez walked straight into his back as he froze, the steel of the bayonet scant inches from his face. For a brief moment he thought that Ellison might simply pull the trigger, but then his gravelly voice growled in the darkness.

'Sound travels a ways at night, specially when you're jawing like old women.'

Before Ethan could react, four more men appeared from where they were crouching amongst the scrub, their weapons trained on Ethan and Lopez. He could see that they were carrying pouches of ammunition, water bottles and leather sacks filled with what looked like sticks of dynamite.

'You'll be droppin' your weapons now,' Thorne said.

Ethan didn't move.

'We're not carrying,' he lied smoothly. 'How did you get here so fast?'

Soft chuckles of disdain rippled through the men as they looked at Ethan. Ellison Thorne smiled coldly.

'You've never heard of horses then?' he asked rhetorically. 'Plenty for the takin' if'n you know where to look. Much better than that noisy old bucket you came clattering out here in.'

'We're not here to hurt you,' Ethan said quickly. 'We already know who you are.'

'That so?'

'Your name is Ellison Thorne,' Ethan said. 'Your companions here are Nathanial McQuire, Kip Wren, Edward Copthorne and John Cochrane. Every last one of you was alive in 1862.'

There was a silence on the hillside as the men stared at Ethan. One of them, a young man whom Ethan assumed was McQuire, spoke up.

'How'd you know that?'

'Tyler Willis,' Ethan answered. 'Hiram Conley went to him for help when something began happening to him, when he began aging. Lee Carson wanted to do the same, didn't he, but you wouldn't let him because you know that Jeb Oppenheimer at SkinGen is hunting you. The man's insane, wants to patent the bacteria that caused this and sell it to the wealthy elite while the rest of the world is forced to cease reproducing.'

John Cochrane spoke over the barrel of his rifle.

'You sayin' this is bacteria we've got?'

'You don't know about that?' Ethan inquired.

'Doesn't matter what we don't know,' Ellison Thorne cut across them. 'What we do know is that we need to get back to where this all started, and you're in our way.'

'Doing that doesn't make any sense,' Ethan protested. 'If you don't know what's happened to you in the first place, then running back to those caves might not do anything for you at all.'

'It'll do a damned sight more than standing here listenin' to your balderdash, boy!' Ellison boomed, losing patience and turning to Copthorne. 'Bind them up good, Corporal, then we move out!'

Ethan saw Copthorne hesitating, as though he wasn't

sure that by following Ellison's order he could be sending himself to his doom.

'I don't know, Ellison,' Copthorne said. 'What if there's a bit of truth in all he's sayin'?'

Ethan didn't wait for Ellison to answer.

'There's more to this than just all of you,' he said urgently. 'Jeb Oppenheimer is an old man himself. It's not going to be enough for him to just arrest his aging. He'll be like all of you, frozen in time as you were back in 1862.' Ethan looked at Copthorne, guessing his age. 'I'd bet that being stuck aged sixty or so for a century and a half isn't all it's cracked up to be, is it?'

Copthorne raised an eyebrow. 'You wouldn't believe the goddamned arthritis, and—'

'Better alive than dead,' Ellison Thorne cut his corporal off with a sharp glance. 'We don't have time for this. Sooner or later we'll be tracked down, and out here we're sitting ducks. Either you're in or you're out.'

'It's not as simple as that,' Lopez said. 'There's a bigger problem. Jeb Oppenheimer's plan is to genetically modify the bacteria that you carry, so that it can rejuvenate the carrier instead of just delaying their aging.'

A moment of silence fell over the soldiers as they digested this new piece of information.

'Is that true?' Kip Wren asked.

'As far as we can tell.' Ethan nodded. 'A drug that inhibits aging would be valuable enough, but Oppenheimer's not doing this out of the kindness of his heart. He wants to be young again and will stop at nothing to achieve it. His plan is to stop his own aging in its tracks, before working out how to reverse it. If he succeeds . . .'

Nathaniel McQuire figured it out quickly enough. 'He'll make sure that only people like him, the rich and the powerful, will have the drug.'

'And everyone else will grow old and die,' Copthorne said. 'I'll be damned.'

Ethan took a pace closer to Ellison and looked up at the man who towered over him.

'You've got a chance to do something more, something better with your lives than just exist. If this bacteria gets into Oppenheimer's hands we're all dead regardless. But if we can shut the caves down, hide them from existence, then Oppenheimer won't be able to finish his crazed little scheme, and from what I've seen he'll be dead before the end of next year. Problem solved.'

Ellison Thorne glared down at him.

'And when you shut those caves down, what happens to us?'

Ethan held his gaze for a moment before speaking.

'You die,' he said finally, looking at the other soldiers, 'and countless millions of others live. You've already lived the lives of three men each, and whatever bacteria is in your bodies or whatever Jeb Oppenheimer might achieve, it's too late for you to reverse what's begun. Hiram Conley was mummified overnight after he died. None of you can survive much longer. It's your choice: save yourselves and maybe risk Jeb Oppenheimer locating you and sacrificing the lives of millions of people, or sacrifice yourselves for the chance to stop him.'

Lopez moved to stand beside Ethan. Ellison Thorne

was now silhouetted against a horizon glowing with the first light of dawn.

'This is your chance to stop running,' Ethan said, 'and start fighting back. This is your chance to do the right thing, Ellison.'

The soldiers looked at each other for a long moment, before looking at Ellison Thorne. Slowly, the big man lowered his rifle.

56

SANTA FE POLICE
DEPARTMENT
CAMINO ENTRADA

6.35 a.m.

'Hands up! Stay still!'

The desk sergeant reacted instantaneously, a heavy-looking pistol whipping from its holster to point directly at Saffron Oppenheimer as she strode through the doors of the station as though it belonged to her. She raised her hands above her head as through a door poured a frenzied mass of officers. Before she knew it she was face down on the cold tiles, a thick forearm pinning her neck and chest to the ground as cuffs were snapped around her wrists. Pain bolted through her shoulders as she was yanked to her feet and hustled past the front desk and into the depths of the police department, surrounded by the black-shirted bodies of the police officers.

'I want to see Lieutenant Zamora,' she said as she was shoved along.

One of the officers grunted a reply. Moments later she was propelled into an interview room and searched, a USB hard drive lodged in her pocket was taken from her before she was dumped down into a chair behind a bare desk that was bolted to the floor. The cuffs were looped through a steel chain welded to the legs of the desk, and locked in place.

'Coffee?' asked a female officer.

Saffron shook her head, watching as the woman left and shut the door behind her. Ten long, slow minutes passed as she sat alone in the room, barely able to hear the sounds of officers passing by outside the door. Then, finally, a man walked in. He had the deep tan and grizzled gray hair of the seasoned New Mexico trooper, and for some reason she was relieved when he closed the interview room door and sat down opposite her.

'My name is Lieutenant Enrico Zamora,' he said. 'You asked to see me?'

Saffron nodded.

'You've seen the hard drive?'

'My colleagues are examining the contents as we speak,' Zamora said. 'Right now, I'm trying to understand what it all means.'

'Have you seen the CCTV imagery, taken from the Aspen Center's data banks when I raided their laboratory?'

'Yes,' Zamora said. 'You'd placed it first on the list of files. It shows a man named Tyler Willis being dragged from the Bio-Science Division building by four men.'

'Who had removed their disguises, so it should be easy to identify them,' Saffron said. 'They were working for Jeb Oppenheimer of SkinGen. Jeb, my grandfather, was responsible for the abduction and murder of Tyler Willis, and the abduction of a woman named Lillian Cruz. He is still holding her against her will.'

Lieutenant Zamora scribbled in his notebook as he spoke.

'And you're telling us all of this now. Why?'

Saffron quickly explained to Zamora the evidence that Jeb Oppenheimer held, of her role in the death of an activist years before, and how he had used it in order to force her into attacking rival companies and obtaining data that had put SkinGen years ahead of the competition. Zamora listened to every word of it before speaking.

'And you're coming clean now in order to bring him down?'

Saffron shook her head.

'Jeb is hunting people out in the desert near Carlsbad,' she said. 'One of them is a friend of yours, Ethan Warner.'

Zamora's eyes locked onto Saffron's. 'Ethan's out near Carlsbad?'

'Listen to me. Ethan Warner's partner, Nicola Lopez, she's being paid by Jeb Oppenheimer to betray Ethan. I saw them meet, and when I confronted her about it she freaked.'

'You expect me to believe that?' Zamora asked her.

Saffron raised her left arm slightly and ducked her head, biting the fabric of her sleeve and yanking it up her arm. The sleeve was stained with blood and clogged with fragments of scorched skin. The underside of her arm was a ragged, bloody mess of welts and blisters where the fire had burned her.

'This is what she did to me. I barely got out of there alive,' Saffron said, her voice taut against the pain.

Zamora stared at the hideous wounds and then got up

from the desk, opened the door and shouted down the corridor outside.

'We need a medic down here, right now!'

He walked back to the desk, leaving the door open.

'I need you to tell me exactly what they're up to out there,' he said. 'Does it have anything to do with a man named Hiram Conley?'

Saffron sighed as she realized that Zamora knew more than she had suspected.

'There are a group of men who live out in the Pecos and they've been there for a very long time. For some reason, these guys don't age. They're the same age now as they were when serving in the Civil War. Jeb Oppenheimer wants to experiment on them to produce a drug that prevents aging in human beings, and sell it to the rich and powerful while withholding it from the poor. His plan is to breed people that he considers underachievers out of the population.'

Zamora nodded.

'That's what Ethan believed,' he said. 'But without proof, I can't go in there and arrest Jeb Oppenheimer or search for evidence that he's involved in anything.'

'You've got video of Jeb's men abducting Tyler Willis!' Saffron snapped in disbelief. 'What more do you want, a gilt-edged invitation?'

'The law doesn't work like that,' Zamora shot back. 'Just because you say those men are working for Jeb Oppenheimer doesn't mean that we can prove it is so. The video footage is evidence enough to apprehend the men, if we can find them, but it's not enough to issue a warrant for Jeb Oppenheimer's arrest.'

'Jesus.' Saffron shook her head. 'Doesn't it mean anything to you that right now, Jeb Oppenheimer could be torturing people to get what he wants. I heard what happened to Tyler Willis. Are you going to stand by and let the same happen to that medical examiner?'

Zamora shook his head.

'Not for a moment, but we have to take this one step at a time. Where exactly were Warner and Lopez heading?'

'You'll never find them without me there,' Saffron replied quickly. 'It's too remote, and the place they're searching for too small to find.'

Zamora leaned on the desk, glaring down at her.

'We have patrol teams and we can call in helicopters,' he growled. 'You give me a twenty-square-mile radius and we'll have Oppenheimer's men in custody within the hour. You hold out on me, and I'll make damned sure you spend the next twenty years looking at the walls of rooms just like this one.'

Saffron bolted out of her chair, the chains around her wrists yanking painfully.

'I'm already going to be doing that!' she shouted. 'This isn't about me!'

'How can I be sure of that, after the stunts you've pulled over the years?'

She glared at him.

'For a moment there I thought you were probably smarter than the rest of your team,' she snarled. 'Your patrol cars and goddamn helicopters will be useless in finding those men out there, and most likely Ethan and Lopez.'

'How's that?'

'Because they'll be underground.'

Zamora was about to ask how she knew this when the desk sergeant hurried into the room with a phone in his hand.

'Enrico, there's a guy from the DIA on the phone. You need to listen to this, believe me.'

Zamora frowned as he took the phone.

'Who is this?'

'Douglas Jarvis, DIA, Washington DC. I'm calling regarding an urgent matter involving a man named Jeb Oppenheimer of SkinGen Corp out of Santa Fe. Are you familiar with the man?'

'I've heard of him,' Zamora said carefully as he glanced at Saffron. 'What can I help you with?'

'Sir, our agency has evidence from Butch Cutler at USAMRIID suggesting that SkinGen may have in its possession a Level-Four bio-hazard material obtained illegally from a cemetery in Alaska. We also believe that it is the intention of Jeb Oppenheimer to genetically modify this material to create a pandemic specifically designed to target the populations of developing nations and reduce, or eradicate, their populations. We need your men to obtain a warrant immediately for the arrest of Jeb Oppenheimer and a search of all SkinGen premises.'

Lieutenant Zamora stood for a long moment in the center of the room and tried to digest the magnitude of what he had just heard.

'You're sure?' he asked, and felt stupid for having done so.

'Believe me,' came the reply, 'I wouldn't be making

these claims if I wasn't positive. I'm on my way to the United Nations building as we speak, and I'm awaiting a call from the FBI agents on site in Alaska to confirm the exact nature of the hazardous materials.'

'I have Saffron Oppenheimer in custody,' Zamora said. 'You may want to speak to her.'

Zamora handed Saffron the phone, and watched and listened as Doug Jarvis filled her in on her grandfather's activities. Slowly the color drained from Saffron's face, tears welling in her eyes. She let the phone fall from her ear to clatter onto the table and looked up at Zamora in disbelief.

'We must hurry.'

57

MUDGETTS WILDERNESS STUDY AREA, NEW MEXICO

7.07 a.m.

'Great work, genius.'

Lopez's voice sounded tiny in the dawn as the rising sun illuminated the endless plains and steeply rolling hills of the New Mexico wilderness. Ethan winced, shuffling about on the hard desert floor as the bark of the tree to which he was bound dug into the skin of his back.

'I tried to reason with them,' he shot back, looking over his shoulder to where Lopez was bound on the other side of the trunk. 'It's not like we're their enemy. But they're facing death whichever way they go and I guess Ellison Thorne doesn't like outsiders.'

'Thanks, Sherlock,' Lopez muttered, struggling to escape from the thick ropes that bound her wrists and ankles and wrapped around them both to secure them to the tree. 'We're pretty useless without your pistol and cell phone too.'

Ethan squinted out to the east, seeing the glow of the sun nestling just below the rugged horizon. Bats fluttered across the dawn sky above him as he struggled to escape from his bonds and figure out just how long it had been since Ellison Thorne and his men had tied them to the tree. Thirty minutes? Maybe forty, no more. Forty minutes on foot, on this kind of terrain, would take them maybe two miles, three if they were pushing it. From what he'd seen, most of the soldiers were suffering from some kind of debilitating illness that prevented them from pushing their bodies too hard. Two miles then, a fifteen-minute run in this kind of terrain if he could only get free from the ropes.

Ethan froze as a noise from somewhere further down the hill caught his attention, a rustle of some kind that seemed immediately out of place in the silence of the dawn. He recalled seeing a number of small caves down on the hillside from when they'd ascended, the caves probably amplifying the sounds of movement.

'Stay still,' he whispered to Lopez.

Lopez fell silent as Ethan listened to the breeze in the leaves above them. Something else, the soft but unmistakable crunch of a footfall, carefully made but audible in the otherwise quiet morning air. Ethan moved only his eyes, keeping his head still as he searched for the source of the movement.

He wasn't expecting the voice that broke the morning stillness with a cackle of delight.

'Now, *this* is a sight to behold.'

Ethan saw a craggy head appear over the brow of the hill to his right, as Butch Cutler puffed his way up to the tree and squatted down alongside them, wiping sweat from his brow.

'Fine mornin', Mister Warner,' he said cheerfully. 'I

see you're in control of things as ever, keeping momentum in your investigation, so to speak.'

'I'd have been happy to see just about any other face but yours, Cutler,' Ethan said. 'How about you stop showboating and cut these ropes?'

'Seems a shame to,' Cutler said, 'without first recording the event for posterity.'

Cutler stood and pulled a digital camera from the rucksack on his back, snapping a shot of Ethan and Lopez scowling before exchanging the camera for a large knife. He knelt down alongside Ethan and held the blade to his face.

'You're lucky I don't take bribes from men like Jeb Oppenheimer,' he said quietly. 'Right now, I could have earned me a dime or two.'

Ethan glanced at the blade flashing in the sunlight, and then Cutler whipped the weapon in a vicious downward stroke, the ropes wrapped around the tree parting as he sawed through them. A minute or two of frenzied hacking and Ethan and Lopez were free.

'That's one you owe me,' Cutler said as he slipped the knife into its sheath at his belt.

'How did you find us?' Ethan asked, looking around for Cutler's men as he stood and rubbed his wrists where the ropes had bitten into his skin.

'I was a ranger, remember?' Cutler replied, somewhat annoyed. 'I found that little camp of hippies easily enough and they told me what happened. I drove down this way, the GMC you'd taken was parked down the road from here and you left a trail like a herd of bison through a wheat field. A blind four-year-old could have tracked you down.'

'I meant who did you speak to?' Ethan said. 'Saffron Oppenheimer?'

'No, your buddy from the DIA. You've got some powerful friends in the capital.'

'Doug's here?' Lopez asked in surprise.

'He's on his way to New York, so he said.'

'Which is why you're here on your own,' Lopez surmised.

'Sure is,' Cutler replied. 'Doug filled me in on everything, asked me to come out here and make sure his little golden boy wasn't being bullied by the natives.'

Ethan thought for a moment.

'What did you mean about bribes from Oppenheimer?' he asked.

Cutler smiled a cold grin.

'The devious old bastard approached me in Santa Fe,' he said. 'Got his heavies to come up to my hotel room and organize a little chat. I went along with it of course, but not with any intention of following through. He wanted me to turn on my own boss, and forward anything I found directly to him instead.'

Ethan blinked. 'Are you the only one he's approached?'

'Nope,' Cutler said. 'Either he or his men have approached mine on a few occasions. Like I said, I run a tight team. They all reported back to me.'

Ethan looked at Lopez.

'Oppenheimer could have turned anyone,' he said. 'Hell, for all we know he could have bribed Ellison Thorne. He's got enough money to buy half the population of the state.'

Lopez remained silent. Ethan looked at the rising sun

now blazing across the horizon as Cutler shifted the rucksack on his back.

'So, where to now, cowboy?'

Ethan surveyed the wilderness.

'They can't have gotten more than a couple of miles from here, but they're experts at camouflage and conceal-ment. They won't have left an easily identifiable trail, if they've left one at all.'

'Well, we ain't got time to stand here talking about it,' Cutler said. 'Carlsbad Caverns are that way.' He pointed out to the southeast. 'Faster we move, quicker we get there.'

'I just saw you get to the top of this little hill,' Ethan said. 'You were almost having a coronary, and we need to cover a couple of miles real fast in order to have any chance of catching them up.'

Butch Cutler frowned at Ethan.

'You sayin' I ain't man enough for this? I'll wind your goddamned neck in and—'

Lopez moved between the two of them.

'All right, children,' she said. 'Cutler, get to your vehicle and get back-up. You know where we're going to within a reasonable area, so get Doug Jarvis to send in the cavalry. They'll find us quickly enough.'

'What about the guys you're chasing?' Cutler protested.

'They're going underground,' Lopez replied. 'If we send in a helicopter now they'll hear it coming and we'll never find them. We've got to catch them unawares before they descend into the caves and follow them in, or this is all for nothing.'

Cutler laughed, his breath condensing in billowing clouds on the morning air as he looked at Ethan.

'Oh yeah? And how are you going to do that then? They've got a two-mile head start, leave no trail and the last time you tracked them Boy Scout here got himself disarmed and tied to a tree by a bunch of geriatrics.'

Lopez glanced at Ethan, who looked away and sought desperately for something clever to say. He was coming up short when he saw something flutter past across the orb of the sun. His mind went momentarily blank as a sudden revelation dawned within.

'What's up, Buffalo Bill?' Cutler chortled, drunk on his own mirth. 'Lost for words?'

Ethan smiled in the sunlight. 'Give me your gun,' he said.

'What the hell for?'

'I can find them,' Ethan replied. 'I know *exactly* where they are.'

58

RATTLESNAKE CANYON
NEW MEXICO

Jeb Oppenheimer felt like a twenty-five-year-old, mostly because he intended to be one again soon.

Two anonymous coaches containing his men had pulled up some two miles away from the main entrance to the caverns. The heavily armed men under his command disembarked before the vehicles pulled away to park unobtrusively in a lot nearby. With his troops organized into two files, he had walked at the head of the little army alongside Hoffman as they marched out into the desert under cover of night. Ahead, somewhere in the murky darkness, lay his prize.

It had gone by many names over the centuries: the Philosopher's Stone; the Fountain of Youth; the Elixir. In centuries gone by, alchemists had spent their entire careers attempting to forge this most precious of potions from chemical elements, all the while unaware that somewhere in nature it existed already. Driven by archaic fantasies such as astrology and religion, the fools had sought to conjure gold from lead, diamonds from charcoal and life from piles of seeds. He recalled the medieval belief that living things appeared spontaneously from inanimate foods, based upon the fact that baby mice were often seen to scurry from grain mountains. It beggared belief that people could have believed such things. Yet now, those who had doubted, shunned and mocked Jeb Oppenheimer for his beliefs would be silenced at last in this, his greatest moment of triumph.

'You'll never find them.'

The voice was quiet but insistent. Oppenheimer looked at Lillian Cruz beside him. She was staring ahead as they moved across the desolate desert, the rising sun beaming shafts of golden light like the fingers of God across the landscape.

Oppenheimer grinned, not letting her spoil his buoyant mood.

'I already know where they are,' he said. 'You'd be surprised how easily loyalty can be bought, how quickly people can be turned when money is waved in front of their greedy faces.'

Lillian remained impassive. 'Money isn't everything.'

'Isn't it?' Oppenheimer asked. 'Where would we be without it? What would life be without it? Our societies would not function, our lives would crumble and fail. What would be the point of working, of striving to be a success?'

'Life,' Lillian said, 'is not dependent on dollars.'

'Only if you like spending it cowering in a cave foraging for grubs or growing rice in fucking paddy fields,' he spat back. 'Money moves us forward, and without it we'd slip backwards into the Dark Ages. You know who did all the building in the Dark Ages, all the study and learning? It was the Vatican, because they hijacked Rome and stole all the money! Everybody else was reduced to living in mud huts and eating leaves for the next thousand years.'

'Something you'd like to see repeated, Jeb?' Lillian suggested. 'You and your grubby little elite sitting in palatial mansions while the rest of us grovel in the dirt?'

Oppenheimer cackled and almost doubled over as the cackle turned to a hacking cough. He hawked something up in his throat with a growl and spat a drooping globule of mucus out on the dust at his feet.

'The unwashed masses have *always* groveled in the dirt,' he muttered, wiping the corner of his mouth with a white handkerchief. 'Think about all the people out there, in their hundreds of millions, slaving away every day in their jobs to pay their mortgages and send their kids to school, to eat and pay for their homes. It's no different to slavery, except with better holidays. All the while the elite, as you call us, make billions of dollars and live on luxury yachts. When the world economies crash, as they must every few decades to allow continued growth, we disappear with our profits and leave governments to tax the masses to buy their way out of the debt.'

Lillian Cruz ground her teeth in her jaw as she replied.

'We know what you people do,' she muttered with undisguised contempt.

'And yet you do nothing about it,' Oppenheimer pointed out. 'Look at Egypt, at Libya, at Tunisia. Their people didn't have two sticks to rub together. Their leaders were worth billions of dollars. Their people had no democracy, were under the control of ruthless thugs and secret police, and yet they rose up and overthrew their dictators. I have the greatest respect for them, and nothing but contempt for whingeing cretins like you who complain but do nothing to change the status quo.'

'You're saying that you think we should overthrow the government and people like you?'

Oppenheimer smiled as he struggled across the stony ground.

'Democracy is not the rule of the people,' he said simply. 'It is people voting for leaders, who then go ahead and do what they want anyway, regardless of the wishes of their countrymen. May as well be a dictatorship. *Isocracy* is the real rule of the people, the original desire of ancient Greeks for the people to control the destiny of their nations as one voice, and from where our modern *democracy* derives. But if left to the people our countries would collapse into anarchy, because most people are too damned stupid to understand the subtleties of government. They simply soak up the crap they're fed by a free media and spout it in their bars and homes, tangible fallacies like religion and global warming and homeopathy, all the while oblivious to real life passing them by.'

Lillian shook her head slowly.

'I think that you underestimate people,' she said softly, 'like all dictators who are suddenly overthrown and don't even understand why.'

'Poetic,' Oppenheimer conceded as he used his cane to lever himself up the hill they were climbing, 'but also tragically doomed. Don't you see? There are just too many of us now gorging on what's left of our planet's resources, changing our environment beyond repair. Do you know what happens when populations of any species become so bloated in a confined environment? Novel disease appears and eradicates the excess, its ability to spread, mutate and become lethal exacerbated by the density of the population, its food source. It's time to excise the demon, to lance the cyst and return to a simpler, less populated world where we can govern our resources with greater ease.'

Cruz scowled at him, deliberately taking a route up the hill that made Oppenheimer's progress as difficult as possible.

'You're a damned fool, Oppenheimer. Most people living in the developing world consume a glass of water and a plate of rice a day. They barely dent the world's resources despite their numbers. Did you know that fifty percent of the world's population has never made or received a telephone call?'

'Probably just as well!' Oppenheimer shot back.

'You don't know how lucky you are,' she replied. 'Most people in the West don't. A quarter of the world's population don't even have access to electricity. In contrast, New York City's twenty million people consume as much electricity annually as the entire population of Sub-Saharan Africa, all eight hundred million of them.'

'And what happens now that all of those people wish to live as we do?' Oppenheimer asked. 'How can they? Tell me how twelve billion people can live as Americans do, when the world is clearly struggling to support seven billion, of whom two-thirds live in mud huts in damp forests eating their own dung?'

Lillian skirted a large boulder, blocking Oppenheimer's path.

'If we consumed less, allowing them to consume more, there would be no issue.'

'Pah!' Oppenheimer jabbed his cane at her. 'The United Nation's Food and Agriculture Organization has warned that we'll need seventy percent more food to supply the two and a half billion extra people living on earth by 2050. There'll be the equivalent populations of Europe, Russia and North America added to our planet by then. If I don't do this, it'll all be over for all of us.'

Lillian was about to answer when ahead Hoffman raised his hand above his head and clenched it into a fist. Instantly, the mercenaries stopped moving and sank down into the grasses and thorn scrub.

Oppenheimer crouched down, wincing as his joints ached and creaked beneath him. He edged forward to come alongside Hoffman.

'What is it?' he asked. Hoffman made a show of sniffing the air and squinted thoughtfully at the hills surrounding them. Oppenheimer swiped at him with his cane. 'You're not Crocodile fucking Dundee, Hoffman, so cut the crap.'

Hoffman gestured down the valley ahead.

'If we troop further down this valley, the noise could alert them to our presence.'

'Shall we *levitate* down instead?'

Hoffman shook his head, too caught up in the throes of his hunter's prowess to notice Oppenheimer's jibe.

'The marker cairns we've been following end here at the floor of the valley where it crosses the canyon wash. We've descended about six hundred feet and must climb up the mesa opposite. We need to know where they are before we can attack or we'll be skylined and they'll see us coming.'

Oppenheimer reached down into his pocket and pulled out the GPS tracker. The screen lit up as he touched the display, and instantly he saw the tiny orange flashing light. He turned the compass to match the direction he was facing, and compared the topography on the screen with the view down the valley. He smiled.

'You have them?' Hoffman asked.

Oppenheimer lowered the tracker and pointed ahead.

'They're less than a hundred yards away,' he said. 'We go now!'

Hoffman turned, shouting over his shoulder. 'Lock and load, we're moving in!'

With that, the sound of clicking rifle mechanisms clattered like an army of giant ants rattling through the dawn as the mercenaries got to their feet and began quick-marching toward the hills ahead. Hoffman led them at a swift jog as Oppenheimer struggled along on the rough terrain behind them.

All at once he saw a cave ahead, and then the mercenaries charged as one with their rifles pointed in front of them with a volley of shouts and war cries as they swarmed into the entrance of the cave and were swallowed by the shadows.

Oppenheimer limped along behind them, reaching the cave just as it fell silent and the cries faded. He came to a halt at the entrance to the cave and stood there for a long moment until he saw Hoffman walk out into the sunlight and scowl at him.

'What the hell do you call this?'

Hoffman tossed a small black device to Oppenheimer, who caught it in one hand. The old man looked down at it and felt rage sear through his veins. The GPS transmitter he'd given to Lopez glinted in the early morning sunlight.

'The bitch!' he shouted, and slammed the end of his cane against a nearby rock. 'She lied! The bitch lied to me!'

From behind him, Lillian Cruz's voice reached him softly.

'Money isn't everything, Jeb.'

Hoffman looked at the tracking device that Oppenheimer slipped into his pocket, then at the nearby cave.

'Maybe she didn't lie,' he suggested. 'We've been following their trail for hours. She wouldn't have held onto the tracker all this time only to drop it at the last moment. If she'd wanted to lead us away, she could have tied it to a goddamn coyote or something. Maybe she had no choice?'

A mercenary jogged down from a nearby hill top, where stood a lonely-looking tree.

'I found these up on the hill,' he said, showing Hoffman a pile of severed ropes. 'There's tracks too, fresh. Less than an hour.'

'They may have been captured and then somehow got free,' Hoffman speculated. 'Might be why she tossed the tracker.'

Oppenheimer scowled but said nothing.

Hoffman whirled and snarled at his men as they spilled out from the empty cave.

'Get up to that tree and get on their trail! Whatever she's up to, they can't be far away!'

59

EAST 46TH STREET, MANHATTAN NEW YORK CITY

Doug Jarvis made his way to the corner of 46th Street, on the intersection with First Avenue and close to the United Nations Headquarters complex. The Secretariat Building towered over the East River, a 550-foot-tall wall of aluminum, glass and marble, the south facades of the building faced with countless tons of Vermont marble. Jarvis turned aside to an identification office that supplied grounds passes to officials pre-cleared to enter the United Nations. He hurried inside, his path cleared after a swift call to General Mitchell at the DIA. A pass and an identification tag were waiting for him at the main desk, and he was already out of the door when his cell phone rang. Jarvis took the call, straining to hear the voice on the other end of the line.

'Special Agent Devereux, FBI.'

'Jarvis. What have you got for me?'

The reply, when it came, was distorted by both digital encryption and distance. Jarvis could hear the snap and thump of frigid winds in the background.

'We've finished excavating the target site,' came the reply. 'We think we know what they were up here for.'

'Go ahead.'

'There's the body here of a researcher of some kind who was working out here. He was shot in the chest, and buried in a cemetery of Spanish Flu victims who died in 1918.'

Jarvis stopped walking.

'Do we know who the victim is?'

'Not yet,' Devereux replied. 'It could take weeks. He doesn't have any identification on him, nothing to say who he was working for or if he has any family.'

Jarvis thought for a moment.

'Start by working through current and former employees of USAMRIID, out of Maryland,' he replied. 'My money's on there being a link between Donald Wolfe, SkinGen and this victim of yours in Alaska. We need ballistics from the bullet as soon as possible.'

Devereux spoke again, clearly struggling to make his voice heard above the howling winds sweeping across Brevig Mission.

'The body that originally occupied the grave is missing some tissue from the chest cavity, almost certainly taken from the lungs.'

Jarvis felt his heart miss a beat as he digested Devereux's revelation.

'Are you sure?'

'Positive, sir,' Devereux replied. 'What the hell would Donald Wolfe want with a hundred-year-old flu victim's tissues?'

'USAMRIID often works with lethal biogens,' Jarvis

mused out loud, 'and I've been told that researchers occasionally dig up victims of disease to study tissues and such like, but nothing like this. Spanish Flu killed eighty-five percent of Brevig Mission's inhabitants in 1918. Whatever strain it belongs to, it's damned near lethal.'

Jarvis stood on the sidewalk and watching the passing traffic and the flowing waters of the East River beyond as he spoke.

Devereux's voice was laden with apprehension as he replied.

'Whatever the reason, it's important enough for him to have snuck up here to the ass of the world, kill a man and steal infected tissues. I don't want to know what he might have in mind. About the only consolation is that he's got no way of infecting people worldwide, if that's his plan. I mean, how could he be able to infect people in so many countries all at the same time? It would be impossible to cause a pandemic that way.'

Jarvis nodded, turning slowly as he did so, and then his eyes settled on the United Nations Headquarters Building, the flags of its one hundred ninety-two member states arranged in alphabetical order in front of the building, fluttering on their high poles.

And a sudden, terrible realization shot through him.

'I've got to go.'

Jarvis clicked off the phone as he struck out across 46th Street toward the UN Building, glancing at his watch and hoping against hope that he was wrong. He dialed another number, this time getting Butch Cutler on the other end, sounding as though he was traveling in a vehicle.

'Doug? What's the story?'

'Get the New Mexico sheriff's office and get them into the SkinGen building as fast as you can. We've got the evidence you need, but there's no time to collate it all and present it to the attorneys. Just go in and find out what the hell they've been up to in there.'

'Any idea what they'll be looking for?' Cutler asked.

'Tissues belonging to a victim of the 1918 Spanish Flu pandemic,' Jarvis said as he jogged down the street. 'I think Donald Wolfe's planning to infect the United Nations General Assembly during his speech there. I need to know how he might do that.'

Butch Cutler didn't reply for what felt like a long time as Jarvis jogged toward the vast edifice of the United Nations General Assembly, wishing with every step that he exercised more regularly.

When the reply came, it was tinged with horror.

'There's only two ways he could do it,' Cutler replied. 'It's either going to be in the air, or it's going to be in the water. My guess is he'll infect the water that they're drinking, either through the water supply or directly into their glasses somehow. Viruses don't survive long in the open air.'

'Got it.'

Jarvis shut off his phone and broke into a run toward the north entrance of the complex that opened onto a landscaped plaza, where the curved façade of the General Assembly Building and its rows of international flags loomed. Translucent glass panels set into marble piers gave the public lobby a subdued glow as Jarvis burst through the doors and found himself surrounded by memorials to men who had worked, or even sacrificed their lives, for world peace.

He headed for the stairs that led to the second-floor ceremonial entrance to the General Assembly Hall, passing a huge stained-glass panel, symbolic of man's struggle for peace and dedicated to the memory of Secretary-General Dag Hammarskjöld and others who died with him in a plane crash in 1961. Adjacent to the panel were four bronze plaques commemorating members of the Secretariat who had died in the line of duty while serving the United Nations. Nearby, a facsimile of the United Nations Charter stood proudly, and Jarvis felt a nausea descending on him as he realized that such a building was about to become the latest stage for an act of international terrorism.

He rushed up the stairs, praying his heart wouldn't give out as he passed a Foucault pendulum, a gift of the Netherlands Government, offering visual proof of the rotation of the earth, suspended from the ceiling above the stair landing connecting the lobby with the second floor.

He had almost reached the entrance to the Assembly Hall when two uniformed security guards stepped out and caught him between them in mid-stride.

'I'm sorry, sir, but you can't enter the hall right now.'

Jarvis gasped for breath as he wheezed a response.

'You don't let me in there, right now, half of the world's leaders will be dead within a week.'

'Of course they will, sir.' One of the guards smiled

and rolled his eyes at his colleague. 'The assembly is in a closed session, and you'll have to wait until it's finished before you can save the world.'

Jarvis gathered his breath and slipped his identification card from out of his jacket pocket.

'Doug Jarvis, Defense Intelligence Agency,' he rasped. 'You don't help me, I'll have you both reassigned to a radar station in goddamned Labrador within twenty-four hours!'

The security team looked at him curiously.

'Where's your evidence?' the taller of the two demanded.

'It's being collated,' Jarvis replied. 'There's no time for this. We need to—'

'The hell we need to do anything,' the guard replied. 'We have our own security force, and this building is secure. You got a problem with that take it to my boss, but there's no way in hell I'm letting you in there without a damned good reason.'

Jarvis stared at the guards in despair for a long beat, then turned away and dashed toward the adjoining Conference Building.

60

UNITED NATIONS
GENERAL ASSEMBLY
NEW YORK CITY

Colonel Donald Wolfe stood in full military uniform amidst almost a thousand dignitaries milling about near the entrance to the General Assembly Hall as he glanced at his watch for the fifth time in ten minutes. World leaders surrounded him, talking through translators and to a small number of television crews allowed access to the United Nations complex. He stood for another five minutes, fielding questions from the British Prime Minister, before he finally slipped away into an annex and pulled a cell phone from his pocket that he'd bought for cash two days previously. He would dispose of it as soon as he'd finished.

He punched in a number from memory and listened to the ring tone warbling in his ear for several long seconds before finally a man's voice answered.

'Donald?'

Wolfe spoke slowly and clearly, aware that the line was most likely protected by levels of encryption far more advanced that even his own at Fort Detrick:

Bilderberg's most powerful attendees took no chances with their anonymity.

'It is time,' he said. 'Oppenheimer is in position and ready to strike, as are my men. I only need you to give me the go-ahead and assurance of my security.'

The voice replied, calm and in control. 'Everything is in place, Donald. As soon as you order your men in, your role in this will be unidentifiable. We will contact you directly at the next Bilderberg meeting once everything has been achieved and the dust has settled. By then, everyone will have forgotten about Jeb Oppenheimer and his crusade.'

The line went dead in Wolfe's ear. He immediately punched in a second number and waited for the line to pick up.

'Hoffman.'

Red Hoffman was breathing heavily, as though he were slogging his way up a hill.

'What's your status?' Wolfe asked without preamble.

'We're within two miles of them,' Hoffman said under his breath. Wolfe could hear other footfalls around him, the sound of troops marching. 'We'll have everything under control within the hour.'

Wolfe breathed a sigh of relief.

'As soon as you do,' he said with finality, 'obtain a live subject and leave the area. There must be absolutely no witnesses. Do you understand?'

Hoffman's reply was brisk and uncompromising.

'Understood, sir.'

'Bring the subject back to me as soon as you have them, in person.'

'Will do. Hoffman out.'

The line went dead. Wolfe shut the phone off, unclipped its rear panel and slipped the SIM card out from within. He tossed it onto the floor and smashed one heel down on the delicate card. Then, he slipped the untraceable cell phone into his pocket and turned, striding across the chamber toward the exit.

He was almost there when he saw two security guards flanking the doors, talking to an old man in a smart blue suit. Wolfe froze on the spot as he recognized Douglas Jarvis, gasping for breath, his face flushed with urgency, gesturing wildly at the two guards.

Wolfe turned and hurried away to take a different exit from the hall, walking across the connection between the General Assembly Hall and the Conference Building, cantilevered over Franklin D. Roosevelt Drive. He then took an elevator to the fourth floor. He weaved his way to the Delegates' Dining Room and just beyond it, to a kitchen that served VIPs in the dining room and was often used as a short cut by delegates between the Conference Building's dining rooms and the General Assembly Hall. Wolfe strode into the kitchens, one hand in his pocket as several members of staff within glanced at him.

'Can I help you, sir?'

Wolfe smiled at the head chef, gesturing to the kitchens beyond.

'Just a routine search of the premises before the assembly convenes,' he said, flashing his USAMRIID identity card. 'Ask your staff to give me the room, if you will. I'll walk through here, then exit the same way I came in and report to you there. Is there anything out of order today in here that I need to know about?'

'No, sir.' The man shook his head and headed for the kitchen door, instantly recognizing Wolfe's identity and rank. 'All's running smoothly.'

Donald Wolfe waited until the staff had all left the kitchen, keeping his head up and his eyes alert as he turned to stride between the endless worktops, steel vats, pans and ovens. As he walked he saw two rows of approximately fifty large glass jugs filled with water. Each would be taken down to the Assembly Hall and used to fill the glasses of hundreds of world leaders as they sat listening to the lectures and speeches that were part of the General Assembly's convention.

Wolfe lifted his hand from his pocket, a large plastic syringe concealed beneath his sleeve. As he walked casually past the huge jugs, he lifted his hand and squirted brief jets of clear fluid, one for each jug, one after another. He then turned at the end of the row and repeated the action down the second row on the other side, dumping jets of infected water into the jugs until his syringe was empty. Wolfe slipped the syringe back into his pocket and walked toward the exit, leaving the kitchens and nodding to the chef by the door as he departed.

By his best estimate, given the travels of world leaders, the handshakes, the hordes of staff, the telephones and faxes and interviews, cars, aircraft and beds, from the United Nation's General Assembly Building to a world pandemic would take less than two weeks.

And the best of it was, nobody would show symptoms

for at least four days after infection. Within ten, they would be dead.

Doug Jarvis ran across the connection between the General Assembly Hall and the Conference Building, staggering into the elevator and punching the button for the fourth floor. He sucked in air with ragged gasps as he leaned on the aluminum walls and watched the digital floor counter change agonizingly slowly. The elevator alarm pinged, and the doors slid open.

Jarvis took a step out, and stared straight into the eyes of Donald Wolfe.

The colonel filled the corridor before him, resplendent in his uniform. Before Jarvis could react, Wolfe rushed forward and slammed his shoulder into Jarvis's chest, plunging them both back into the elevator with a crash of bodies against metal. Wolfe thumped down on top of Jarvis and the impact forced the air from the older man's lungs. Jarvis saw him punch a fist out at the buttons beside them and the elevator doors closed behind them before he reached down and drew a small ceremonial silver pistol from a holster at his waist.

Jarvis struggled against Wolfe's iron grip, but the younger man was too strong for him.

'You're finished, Colonel,' Jarvis growled up at him. 'Doesn't matter what happens here now. We know everything: Brevig Mission, the flu corpse, SkinGen's involvement. It's over.'

Wolfe nodded, jabbing the pistol against Jarvis's cheek.

'Yes, it is indeed over. Or at least it is for the majority of the world's population. It doesn't matter what happens to me now, Mister Jarvis. This is more important than my survival, or yours. This is about the survival of our species. One way or another, by the end of today one hundred ninety-two world leaders and their staff will walk out of the United Nations plaza carrying the most virulent influenza virus ever to have existed. They will contaminate each other, pass the infection on at a trimetric rate throughout the global population. Hundreds of millions will meet an early grave, for the benefit of those remaining.' Wolfe grinned a hawkish smile. 'Cruel to be kind, as they say.'

Jarvis shook his head.

'You'll never get that far,' he said. 'SkinGen's already being raided as we speak, and Jeb Oppenheimer's little experiments in New Mexico have unraveled already. The police will be here any moment.'

Wolfe chuckled as he glared down at Jarvis with his piercing gray eyes.

'Not soon enough,' Wolfe said. 'I'm due on stage in ten minutes. This will all be over by then, if not before. As for you, your time's already done.'

Wolfe raised the pistol above his head and brought it crashing down on Jarvis's temple with a sickening crack. Jarvis felt an instant of skull-piercing pain, and then everything turned black.

61

MISERY HOLE
NEW MEXICO

7.48 a.m.

Ethan jogged forward in a low crouch, dodging left and right between bushes of thorn scrub as he tracked north along a dry riverbed weaving through a rugged valley. The tops of the hills were now bathed in brilliant sunlight that flared brightly off the rocks. The flutter of bat's wings whispered through the air above him as the tiny mammals raced away from the spreading dawn. Behind him Lopez followed his every footstep, whispering as she did so.

'You sure you know where you're going?'

Ethan, his pistol held before him in both hands, nodded.

'Damn straight I do. Be quiet, we're nearly there.'

Ethan saw that the valley ahead became steeper, and to his right a narrow track heavily lined with trees and scrub climbed the side of the hills before vanishing entirely on a ridge above them. Somewhere within, he now knew, was an entrance to the caverns concealed from humanity by Ellison Thorne and his men over one hundred fifty years before.

Ethan crept up to the ridge and looked over the edge as Lopez joined him.

Below them, the angular, stacked rocks of the hillside vanished into a yawning chasm perhaps thirty feet across, surrounded by trees and the lechuguilla bushes that had given the mysterious cave somewhere within its name.

'Misery Hole,' Lopez said. 'Looks deep.'

Ethan peered over the edge into the depths and felt his guts convulse as vertigo scrambled his senses.

'Maybe a hundred feet,' he whispered, sweating from more now than just the heat. 'I can't see the bottom, too dark.'

'We've got to get down there,' Lopez said. 'Fast.'

Ethan nodded as he stepped back from the edge and took a deep breath, staring into the distance. Lopez looked at him for a moment and then chuckled.

'Oh, you're kidding me,' she said in delight. 'The rough and tough Marine's scared of heights?'

'Why do you think I joined the Marines and not an airborne unit?' Ethan muttered.

'Oh come on.' Lopez punched his shoulder. 'Surely you must have jumped out of airplanes or something?'

'Sure we did.' Ethan nodded. 'Never had a problem with that, due to having a goddamned parachute on my back. But this . . .' He gestured to Misery Hole. 'This is different.'

Ethan spotted a thick rope ladder bound to some trees fifty yards away. He reluctantly pointed to it. 'They're already here.'

Lopez followed him around the ragged rocks and through thick scrub until they reached the ladder. Ethan glanced at her.

'You want me to go first?' Lopez offered in an ingratiating motherly voice.

'Like hell.'

Ethan took hold of the ladder, easing himself onto it and descending out over the edge. Don't look down. Just face the rocks. *Semper fi.*

The ladder hung vertically over the abyss, vanishing into the plunging depths below as he clambered one careful step after another. The shadows of the cave engulfed him as he descended, the ladder swinging and twisting precariously as Lopez swayed on the rungs above him.

'Jesus! You wanna keep still?' he snapped, looking up at her and wincing as the whirling vertigo spun his senses again.

'Sorry, honey,' Lopez called back with a smile. 'Baby steps now, okay?'

A strange odor assaulted Ethan's senses as they clambered down, a damp and almost metallic reek of ancient soil that offered a welcome diversion of his attention. A breeze drifted up past them, cool and moist compared to the swiftly warming desert air above. Rock walls engulfed them as they climbed down, and the pure blue sky above them grew smaller. As his eyes adjusted to the gloom, Ethan was relieved to glimpse below him a dimly illuminated floor strewn with the detritus of rock falls and the desiccated timbers of long-fallen trees, a maze of obstacles criss-crossing the sandy floor.

He climbed down the last few feet of the ladder and dropped onto the dust with a heavy sigh of relief near the entrance to Lechuguilla Cave, a broad and forbidding maw hewn into the side of the rock walls that exhaled the metallic air of the earth itself. He had the brief impression of being in a giant dirty fishbowl, the light streaming down from above in shimmering shafts and the earth littered with debris as though a tornado had blown through.

Lopez dropped down alongside him and looked into the depths of the cave.

'Now what?' she asked.

Ethan was about to reply when the mouth of the cave spoke for him.

'Satan's teeth, you just don't know when to quit, do you, boy?'

From the inky blackness within Lechuguilla Cave, five bayonets glinted in the light beaming down from above. Ethan watched as Ellison Thorne led his companions out into the light, their rifles pointed unwaveringly at him.

Ethan raised his hands, his pistol still in his jeans.

'We're not here to fight.'

'How the hell did you find us?' Ellison Thorne growled at him down the barrel of the rifle.

Ethan walked forward to stand within a few yards of Thorne and his men, keeping his hands raised as he spoke.

'We followed the trail,' he said.

'We didn't leave a trail,' Copthorne shot back.

'I didn't say we followed *your* trail,' Ethan replied, and pointed up to the entrance high above. 'We followed theirs.'

He glanced up into the distant disc of blue sky far

above. The four soldiers followed his gaze to see small bats fluttering past against the heavens, some of them diving down toward Lechuguilla and flashing past them into the darkness beyond. Ellison Thorne looked at Ethan, his eyes narrowing.

'Those critters roost in any one o' a thousand caves around these parts,' he said.

Ethan slowly lowered his hands, letting his arms hang loosely by his sides as he explained.

'We had a rough idea of where you'd be,' he said. 'Saffron Oppenheimer's friends have seen you out this way before now. You said you don't know what's happened to you, that Hiram Conley shouldn't have gone to Tyler Willis for help when he started becoming sick. Well, if he hadn't, I wouldn't have been able to find you now. You need to listen to what I have to say.'

Copthorne, McQuire, Wren and Cochrane all looked at Ellison Thorne.

'We ain't got nothing to lose,' Kip Wren said. 'Let 'im say his piece, then we'll be gone.'

Ellison Thorne sighed and lowered his rifle.

'Speak your mind, boy,' he rumbled, 'but be quick about it.'

Ethan nodded.

'Tyler Willis told us that Hiram Conley wasn't blessed with some kind of miracle gene that stopped him from aging. He told us that he was infected with bacteria that must have somehow been able to reside in his body, and in doing so been able to repair cell damage and therefore prevent aging.'

Lopez lowered her hands as she spoke.

'The reason Conley became sick is that for some reason the population of bacteria in his body slowly decreased with time as they died off, and he began to age rapidly.'

'You sayin' there's something living inside of us?' Nathaniel asked in horror.

'Everything that's alive has bacteria inside,' Ethan explained quickly, 'that's just normal. What's unusual is that the bacteria inside your bodies keep you from aging, and for that to happen they must have evolved over extremely long periods of time to be able to exist symbiotically with human beings.'

'Symbi-whatally?' Copthorne muttered in confusion.

'Symbiotically,' Lopez said. 'It means that you need them to be alive, but they also need *you*. All the bacteria in our bodies are as dependent upon us for survival as we are upon them.'

Ethan gestured up to the bats fluttering through the dawn sky above them.

'The only mammalian species that lives in these caves is the Mexican free-tailed bat,' he said. 'They've lived here for millennia, and over that time the bacteria that also live in the caves must have somehow evolved to exist symbiotically with the bats, which are known to have extremely long lifespans for their size.'

Thorne frowned in confusion.

'But we didn't eat any bats when we came here.'

'You didn't have to,' Ethan said. 'The bacteria would have found a way inside you somewhere in these caves, maybe through cuts or in the water that you drank here. Humans are mammals, just like bats, and the bacteria would have been able to survive inside of you in the same way. Once inside, the bacteria would have multiplied, requiring some form of energy from your bodies in return for their existing and altering your cells to prevent aging.'

'Iron', Ellison Thorne said. 'We needed extra iron in our diets, else we became anemic. These bacteria must have used it as a fuel.'

'And many mammals have been known to get minerals from the walls of caves,' Lopez said, 'which would replace the bat's own iron deficiencies after infection.'

'All this is fascinating,' Ellison Thorne said, 'but right now all I give a damn about is whether or not we have ourselves a cure here.'

'That I can't tell you,' Ethan said. 'The only thing we can do is get you all out of here and somewhere safe before Jeb Oppenheimer and his crew arrive.'

'There isn't anywhere safe for us but Misery Hole,' Ellison Thorne snapped. 'We're not going anywhere with you or anyone else, y'hear?'

'We don't have much time,' Lopez said urgently. 'Oppenheimer's men could be here any minute.'

'We'll take our chances,' Ellison replied.

Ethan was about to speak when a gunshot shattered the silence and Kip Wren let out a cry of agony as his right leg buckled and his rifle spun from his grasp.

Ethan hurled himself to his right as the old soldiers scattered for cover. As he rolled through the dust and pulled his pistol from his jeans, he saw dozens of figures dressed in black lining the edge of Misery Hole far above them. A hail of tracer fire zipped down into the darkness amid the clatter of automatic weapons.

'Oppenheimer!' he shouted. 'How the hell did he find us so quickly?'

Lopez, crouched low behind a scattering of rocks, shouted back.

'I don't know! We need cover right now!'

Ethan looked at the swarms of mercenaries now running toward the ladder, and knew that there was only one direction left for them to take.

'Fall back!' he shouted. 'Into the cave!'

62

Ethan ducked down low and dashed toward the dark maw of the cave behind them as bullets whipped the dust at his feet and sprayed wood chips from fallen branches around him. He followed Ellison Thorne as the big man hefted Kip Wren onto his shoulder and loped into the darkness of Lechuguilla Cave. Almost immediately they were engulfed in a billowing cloud of cordite smoke as Copthorne, McQuire and Cochrane opened fire with their Springfield rifles straight up at the ladder above. As Ethan crouched he saw the shots hit their marks to the sound of dull thumps, the leaden Minie balls slamming mercilessly through clothes and flesh. Three of the attackers screamed and fell from the ladder to plunge with their limbs clawing the air.

Ethan and Lopez leapt aside as the bodies thumped down onto the floor of the cave in puffs of dust and the crackle of splintering bones. Ethan aimed his pistol at one of them as he lay screaming in agony and fired a rapid double-tap. The first round hit the man in his belly, the second high on his temple, silencing him instantly.

'Keep them off that ladder!' Ethan shouted.

Realizing that their quarry was armed and now veiled in wreaths of thick white smoke, the attackers suddenly scattered for cover, throwing themselves down behind rocks on the lip of Misery Hole seventy feet above them.

'Three down!' Cochrane shouted. 'I'm reckonin' about ninety-six to go!'

Ethan flinched as wild shots smacked into the solid bedrock nearby, stone chips and a fine powder of shocked rock spilling onto the air around them. Lopez crawled to Ethan's side.

'We're outnumbered here,' she shouted above the crackle of gunfire. 'There's no way out but up.'

Edward Copthorne reloaded his rifle and glanced across at her.

'There's no way to us but down!' he pointed out. 'We've got thousands of passages behind us. We go inside, they'll never find us.'

'We'll stand a better chance against those guys inside the caves,' Ethan agreed. 'Out here, they could rush us at once and it'll all be over and we can't hold them off that ladder forever. Besides, they look like amateurs, missing more than they hit.'

Lopez didn't reply, but she got to her feet and dashed off into the darkness behind them. Ethan looked at the old soldiers alongside him, and gestured with his pistol.

'Let another volley off, then go. I'll cover you with the pistol.'

Copthorne nodded, and along with the others he aimed his rifle straight up at the lip of Misery Hole.

'Fire!'

A blast of gunfire smacked Ethan's eardrums as thick smoke drifted across his field of view, stinging his eyes and burning in his throat. Copthorne, McQuire and Cochrane leapt to their feet and dashed for the cave entrance, using the drifting smoke to conceal their flight. Ethan aimed at several black shapes moving amongst the bushes and rocks high above, firing at them randomly. He was about to turn and flee when a flash of white caught his eye, a man moving from left to right. Ethan squinted through the smoke, and saw the man's awkward gait as he struggled from cover to cover, dragging someone else along behind him. Ethan recognized Jeb Oppenheimer immediately. At that moment, four small, round objects thumped down to land on the cavern floor around him. Ethan only needed one glance to see what they were.

'Grenades!' he shouted.

He fired off another two rounds and then fled into the darkness of the cave. He hurled himself down behind some rocks as four deafening blasts rocked the cavern behind him.

'Y' git any of 'em?' Copthorne asked from somewhere in the darkness.

'Just the one,' Ethan said, and reminded himself that he'd fired seven shots, which left eight in the pistol. 'Mostly just kept their heads down. How's Kip?'

Ellison Thorne's voice reached them from somewhere deeper in the cave.

'He ain't right. Bullet's in his leg and it ain't goin' nowhere.'

Damn. Right now they needed all the firepower and hands they could muster while they tried to figure out a way of escaping the assault. Ethan looked at the entrance to the cave, the low crevice appearing brightly lit now compared to the depths in which they huddled. The cave behind descended gently, ragged walls and a low ceiling vanishing into impenetrable blackness from which drifted a gentle breeze, as though the earth itself were breathing. There were potentially hundreds of miles of unexplored caverns within, plunging to depths of more than two thousand feet below ground, some flooded, others prone to collapse. Ethan was suddenly acutely aware that they lacked even the most basic expeditionary gear required for a descent into such a complex underground maze. Thousands of people over the years had ventured into such places never to return, hopelessly lost and doomed to starvation and a cold, lonely death far below ground in absolute blackness.

'Heads up!'

John Cochrane's voice startled Ethan as it echoed through the cavern, and he turned to see the shapes of men drop into view from the ladder and rush toward the cave entrance. Instantly, three Springfield rifles blasted out a volley of shots that cut down three of the men. Ethan fired on a fourth, another double-tap that sliced through the attacker with a fine spray of blood that spilled onto rocks at the cave entrance. The man fell to his knees before toppling over sideways.

'They're trying to overwhelm us!' McQuire shouted

as he struggled to reload his weapon in the eerie half-light.

John Cochrane and McQuire fired at the same time, dropping two more men who materialized at the entrance to the cave, firing their weapons as they searched for cover from which to continue their assault. The Minie balls slammed into them as they ran and the two men cartwheeled into the dust.

Ethan's ears began aching and ringing from the infernal blasts of the rifles, the terrible noise amplified in the narrow confines of the cave as several more mercenaries tumbled into view. From behind Ethan, Ellison Thorne loomed, a pistol in each hand that spurted smoke and flame as he fired both weapons at once, cutting an attacker down in mid-stride to fall face first onto the rocks.

'Stand tall, lads!' Ellison bellowed, his huge chest and the narrow cave amplifying his voice to thunder out above the gunfire. 'Up an' at 'em!'

With a sudden and unexpected war cry, Ellison led his men at a run toward the cave entrance, their bayonets and knives flashing, and for an instant Ethan's vision blurred as he no longer saw the mercenaries plunging toward them, or the antiquated rifles or the pistol in his hand. A flash-vision of other caves from years before filled his mind, the bitter peaks of Afghanistan's Hindu Kush mountains, the screams of the Taliban and United States Marines locked in hand-to-hand combat in the deadly warrens of the Tora Bora cave complex. Young men, far from home, flashing long-knives and bayonets, the primeval grunts and cries of mortal combat as crazed terrorists with no fear of death fought idealistic soldiers struggling to preserve their way of life.

Semper fi.

Ethan leapt up on impulse and rushed forward as Ellison's men collided with six soldiers who had managed to breach the entrance to the cave. He saw Ellison Thorne grab the barrel of one man's M-16 and twist it aside before stepping in and head-butting him with a sickening crunch, the mercenary's legs crumpling as he sagged onto the floor of the cave. Screams soared through the darkness as bayonets plunged deep into unexpecting flesh, stubby machine guns batted aside by the long-barreled Springfields before they could be brought to bear.

Ethan charged at the nearest attacker, glimpsing a wiry-looking man with scars that spread from the corners of his mouth and back toward his ears, the victim of a mugging or maybe some kind of gang ritual. Either way he didn't look like a soldier, more like one of the heartless bastards Ethan had fought in those terrible caves in Afghanistan, the kind of men who stoned women to death, the kind of men who might have abducted his fiancée, Joanna, in Gaza City. The ugly barrel of the soldier's M-16 swiveled toward Ethan, who rushed in with almost suicidal rage and grabbed the gun's stock and smashed it aside before driving his thumb in behind the trigger. A jab of pain lanced his thumb as the man squeezed the trigger desperately, only for nothing to happen. In the light of the cave entrance Ethan saw the soldier's features dissolve into panic, just as Ethan hopped violently and drove his right knee up into the man's groin with as much force as he could muster.

The mercenary gagged, his tongue quivering in his gaping mouth and his eyes wide and sightless as exquisite pain wracked his body. Ethan yanked the M-16 from his grasp and stepped one pace back, spinning the weapon into his grip and then whipping the butt up to crack the man under his jaw. The mercenary's teeth cracked together and crunched through his tongue, the useless muscle spilling sideways out of his mouth in a torrent of thick blood as he collapsed to his knees in agony. Ethan aimed at the kneeling man's head and fired a single shot. The round hit the man square in his right temple and neatly blew off the left side of his face in a spray of blood and bone chips. Ethan blinked as the body wavered for a moment and then seemed to collapse in slow motion onto its side.

A deep silence filled the cave, Ethan's world suddenly filled with a ringing in his ears and the deep, rapid rhythm of his own breathing. His heart thundered in his chest and his eyelids fluttered erratically as adrenaline surged through his synapses.

'Sweet mother of Jesus,' McQuire's voice uttered in the humming silence as he looked at Ethan's victim. 'You sure know how to pain a man.'

Ethan blinked as his hearing returned and he saw half a dozen bodies lying in the entrance to the cave, some groaning, some weeping and clasping gunshot wounds and savagely mauled stomachs, others staring sightlessly at the ceiling of the cave. He looked down at the ruined body of the man he had slain and felt a sudden chill of shame.

'This ain't over,' Ellison Thorne said, wiping the

bloodied blade of his knife on his pants. 'Let's fall back afore they try again.'

Ethan was about to follow him when from somewhere outside a voice shouted down to them.

'Give up the cave, or this woman dies!'

Ethan edged forward and squinted up into the bright light to see two men standing either side of Jeb Oppenheimer far above, whose hands were cupped around his mouth.

Kneeling beside them was Lillian Cruz. As he watched, Oppenheimer's mercenaries began descending the rope ladder, prodding and pushing Lillian before them as a human shield.

63

UNITED NATIONS GENERAL
ASSEMBLY HALL
NEW YORK CITY

Donald Wolfe stood to one side of the speakers' podium and stared out across the huge blue, green and gold General Assembly Hall beneath the towering, domed, seventy-five-foot ceiling. Representatives of member states sat behind tables that faced the raised speaker's rostrum. At the podium sat the president of the General Assembly, with the secretary-general of the United Nations to his right and the under-secretary-general for General Assembly Affairs and Conference Services to his left.

The secretary-general moved to the rostrum as he addressed the leaders of the majority of the world's nations arrayed before him in the enormous amphitheater. Behind him, two massive screens flanked an eight-foot-diameter United Nations emblem, each screen showing his face as he spoke. Heads of state and their translators occupied hundreds of chairs rising up and away before him, listening intently to the man often considered to be the true leader of the free world.

'Our purpose, today, is to deal with the debate on our population: its growth, health and future over the next fifty to one hundred years. There have been a number of studies conducted by official bodies both within and outside of government, each attempting to provide a solution to the growing problem of supply and demand, in real terms, across the globe and, now, the situation is reaching crisis point.'

Donald Wolfe sat amongst the audience, trying to ignore the prickly heat irritating the collar of his shirt. He was nervous, he realized, more so than he had expected to be as he listened to the secretary-general.

'Ladies and gentlemen, to lead the discussion on this most serious of topics and the implications for the spread of infectious disease, please welcome Colonel Donald Wolfe of the United States Army Medical Research Institute for Infectious Diseases.'

There was a polite ripple of applause as Wolfe got to his feet and walked across to the dais, shaking the secretary-general's hand before clearing his throat and looking up at the massed ranks of world leaders.

'Ladies and gentlemen, let me begin by warning you that what I have to say to you today will not be palatable. It will not be considered politically correct, perhaps not even morally correct, but in the light of the threat we face from an unspoken truth that is becoming more dangerous to human survival than climate change and nuclear proliferation I believe that somebody must speak out, and I take this opportunity to do so.'

Three hundred faces were fixed upon his, an absolute silence as every man and woman listened to the sound of his voice. Perhaps for the first time in his life, Wolfe realized why people fought their way to the top of the political sphere: for the power. The knowledge that what you were saying could change the lives of millions, perhaps even billions, was intoxicating. He took a breath before continuing.

'Today, the population of our planet stands at approximately seven billion. Of those, just over one billion live in the developed Western world. We are the consumers, the guzzlers of gas. But daily we are being joined by millions more from the developing world, as emerging powerhouse economies like China, India and a resurgent Russia seek to emulate our success, our prowess, our prodigious consumption of energy and resources.' Wolfe paused for a moment, before hitting them with a big one. 'It has been estimated that by 2006, we were consuming resources forty percent faster than the earth could replace them. When those resources are gone, we will see the utter collapse of modern society into something approximating medieval Europe.'

A ripple of whispers fluttered through the audience, and Wolfe capitalized on the energy among them as he continued.

'It has been calculated by scientists that due to technologies improving such things as farming, humans are now ten thousand times more populous on our planet than nature would normally allow any predator to be. Your own United Nations Environment Program, involving fourteen hundred scientists over five years, concluded that human consumption now far outstrips available resources.' Wolfe smiled, and gestured outside.

'New York City consumes as much electricity in one day as the island of Crete consumes in one year.'

Wolfe scanned his audience with eagle eyes, saw that they were waiting for his next revelation.

'Our planet has what's known as a carrying capacity: an ability to support a finite volume of flora and fauna. Since the middle of the last century, our bloated consumption of the most crucial substance to the survival of life – fresh water – has caused a chain reaction that now threatens to be the catalyst for the fall of mankind. Without sufficient water, agriculture, the very thing that has allowed our species to spread across the globe, is being undermined. A global decline in world agricultural capacity began in the 1990s and continues to this day, growing exponentially. Groundwater aquifers around the world are failing, producing a grain deficit. Despite all of our efforts and all of our charities, the number of people malnourished in the world has grown by one hundred million per decade, not because we haven't exported grain to those countries who need it, but because their populations have swollen to such gargantuan proportions as to be unsustainable even with our agricultural technology.'

Wolfe looked around at the various individual countries' heads of state.

'Algeria, Egypt, Iran, Mexico and Pakistan are all importing grain due to internal deficits or are on the verge of doing so. Northern China's food production is forecast to decline by almost forty percent by the end of this century. Here in America, the Los Angeles basin, an area reckoned to be naturally able to support a maximum of one million people, is home to a mega-city of thirty million people, and our population is the only one in the developed world still growing, predicted to rise to four hundred thirty million by the year 2030. By that time, we may no longer have enough resources to export the grain that keeps so many other countries from starving, because we'll barely have enough water to produce enough grain to feed ourselves.'

Wolfe subtly changed his tone to a more hopeful oratory.

'We have talked, endlessly, of reducing our carbon footprints, of recycling and carbon capture, of alternative energy sources and radical economic strategies to reduce our consumption of both the electrical energy and resources available to us on our planet. We have passed laws to drill into pristine environments in the pursuit of oil, gone as far as the Antarctic to assuage our thirst for energy, and yet all of this time we have ignored the fact that as fast as we seek solutions to our crises, they are made irrelevant by the increased demands of our growing population. It is estimated that global human population could exceed twelve billion people in the next fifty years.' Wolfe paused. 'Just think about that number for a moment. Twelve billion people, almost twice as many as are alive today.'

Wolfe shook his head.

'We are fighting a losing battle, when within our reach all along has been the solution to our problem. Population itself. It has been estimated by the United States National Research Institute on Food and Nutrition that world population needs to be reduced by two-thirds in order to achieve a sustainable use of natural resources.' Wolfe let the weight of his words sink in. 'If all nations were to follow this advice, resources would no longer be an issue for humanity, nor would pollution or the specter of anthropogenic climate change.'

Wolfe looked about at the hundreds of faces watching him.

'It is time to act before the escalation of resource wastage becomes irreversible and our security upon this planet unsupportable. If we are not willing to do it for ourselves then at least we should consider doing it for our children, for it is they who will shoulder the burden of our inaction. But it will not be conflict through inadequate resources that will bring about their down-fall. There is a far greater disaster awaiting them if we do not act.'

Silence reigned throughout the chamber as they listened.

'Forty-five percent of humanity live in cities, often in conditions of squalor and disease. It is only a matter of time before a major pandemic, one that festers and flour-ishes in these hotbeds of sickness and is able to spread rapidly, begins the next major disaster in human history. We think of pandemics as explosions of some new and exotic disease that appear without warning, but in fact they fester for years, decades even, before becoming established. The HIV-1 virus entered the United States many times before taking hold in 1969, over a decade before it was identified. Modern flu viruses like HN-51 appear and disappear, struggling to take a permanent hold in human populations. Soon they too will emerge as true killers, and they will decimate the populations they infect.'

Wolfe looked around the amphitheater at the people of power arrayed before him.

'I have provided you with press packs that cover these facts in more detail. Pass them on,' Wolfe said, 'to your staff, to your ministers, to anyone with the will and the means to influence what we do next on the global stage to prevent the eradication of our species by disease. We have a choice, ladies and gentlemen: either we control population for ourselves, without unnecessary loss of life, or I predict that within the next five decades nature will control population for us, and millions, perhaps billions, will pay the price. Our sons and daughters will be among them.'

Donald Wolfe reached into his pocket and produced a bottle of water that he had purchased a week before – one of several thousand he now stored in his home to guard against the coming apocalypse, and lifted it to show the entire audience before him.

'Water. Something so simple that we take it for granted – we even bottle and sell it when we can so easily access it from our taps. Yet one billion people worldwide cannot perform this simple act, of accessing clean water. Ladies and gentlemen, I'd like you to raise your glasses and show your support for action against the destruction of our world, of our species, which has begun already in the draining of the world's fresh water supply. We must act now, before it's too late to act at all.' Wolfe paused. 'Is there anyone in the hall who is not willing to act?'

Wolfe watched as every single man and woman sitting before him lifted their glasses.

'To humanity,' Wolfe toasted. 'And our role in saving it.'

64

UNITED NATIONS
GENERAL ASSEMBLY
NEW YORK CITY

Doug Jarvis awoke as pain ripped across his skull. Bright light seared his eyeballs as a voice spoke in his ear.

'Just lie still, sir, you're going to be fine.'

Jarvis struggled to focus against the pain, and saw a man leaning over him, smiling encouragingly.

'Where am I?' Jarvis rasped.

'You're going to be fine, just relax. You've had quite a bash.'

Jarvis saw that he was in a small room, a first-aid box hanging from the wall nearby. A sudden flurry of memories bolted through his brain and he fought to sit upright. The sound of metal on metal clanked in his ears, and he realized that he was cuffed to a gurney.

'What the hell?'

'Please stay still, sir,' the man beside him said.

'Why the hell am I cuffed? Where's Donald Wolfe? He's trying to poison the General Assembly and—'

'There's no need to worry about that,' said the doctor softly.

Jarvis peered at him and saw the kindly smile on his face, the look of a man tending to a child.

'Have you got my identification?' Jarvis demanded.

'You didn't have any,' the doctor said, dabbing gently with a crimson-stained cloth at Jarvis's head. 'You were found slumped in an elevator. You must have taken quite a fall. It's a wonder how you got into the Conference Building at all.'

Jarvis felt a sudden impending doom descend upon him as he looked up at the doctor.

'Sir, I've been stripped of my identification by Colonel Donald Wolfe. The man is armed. He intends to infect the water within the General Assembly Hall with a strain of Spanish Flu that is highly lethal. You know what Spanish Flu is, I take it?'

The doctor looked down at Jarvis.

'Yes, I do. But I can assure you that there is no danger. Colonel Wolfe was the man who found you and called the medical team. He seemed quite concerned.'

'He was the one who hit me!' Jarvis shouted, pain barraging his weary brain with salvos of agony. 'Get on the phone to the Defense Intelligence Agency, Lieutenant-General Abraham Mitchell. He'll confirm who I am!'

'I'm sure he will,' the doctor nodded patronizingly, and continued to dab at the head wound.

Jarvis mustered every last ounce of his patience.

'Doctor, if you don't make that call and get me out of this goddamned gurney, a lot of people are going to die. Do you understand? If I'm lying, you'll have wasted two minutes on a call. If I'm not, you'll have wasted millions of lives. What's it going to be? A hundred second phone call or a hundred million lives?' He leveled the doctor with a steady gaze. 'Your call.'

LAKEWOOD

New Mexico

'All vehicles: suspects armed and considered dangerous, proceed with caution.'

Lieutenant Zamora keyed off his microphone and glanced in his rear-view mirror at the line of four patrol cars following him in convoy down the I-285, their lights flashing.

Alongside him sat Butch Cutler, while in the rear seat of his car, cuffed and silent, sat Saffron Oppenheimer.

'I'm taking a hell of a goddamned risk bringing you out here,' he said, keeping one eye on the road ahead. 'You try to make a break for it, I'll hand your case over to US Marshalls and have them hunt you down day and night.'

'Story of my life,' Saffron replied without concern. 'How much further?'

'We're ten minutes away from the caverns.'

'Stay north of the hills,' Saffron said. 'I've never seen those old men head south of them.'

Lieutenant Zamora shook his head in confusion.

'What the hell is it with those people? If they even exist, why the hell would they stay in the state at all? If

SkinGen and people like Jeb Oppenheimer are hunting for them, surely they'd be better hidden in rural Wyoming or something?'

'I don't know,' Saffron replied. 'Maybe they have people here in New Mexico who help them, keep them supplied with food and water and such like. Whatever the reason, it's enough to keep them here. We wouldn't have seen them in the deserts as much as we did if they were roaming the entire continent.'

Cutler stared thoughtfully at the road ahead for a moment before speaking. 'What makes you so sure that Nicola Lopez will betray Ethan Warner? Near as I could see, they're pretty tight together.'

'I know what I saw,' Saffron insisted. 'Lopez met with my grandfather and there's only one reason that he would do that – to buy her off. Did you get the warrant to access her bank accounts?'

Cutler looked at Zamora, who said nothing. Saffron smiled coldly.

'So you did get them,' she purred. 'Incriminating, were they?'

'Money is money,' Zamora said. 'There was an anomalous sum deposited in one of her accounts yesterday, yes, but we haven't traced its source yet. It could be anything.'

'Yeah,' Saffron uttered, 'course it could.'

65

UNITED NATIONS GENERAL ASSEMBLY HALL NEW YORK CITY

Donald Wolfe lifted his bottle of water, watching as the hundred-strong audience did the same. Just as the liquid touched his lips, the ceremonial entrance smashed open with a crack that echoed through the hall as hundreds of presidents, prime ministers and their staff turned away from their glasses at the noise.

Doug Jarvis burst into the hall, shrieking at the top of his lungs. 'Don't drink the water!'

Donald Wolfe stared wide-eyed at Jarvis, who staggered unsteadily into the chamber, his head wrapped in a bloodied bandage and two security guards flanking him.

'What the hell is this?' he uttered, the microphone amplifying his voice.

Jarvis shouted as loud as he could in the hall.

'The water is infected!'

A rush of horrified gasps echoed through the hall as dignitaries put the glasses down as though they were filled with venom. Jarvis pointed up at Donald Wolfe.

'He's organized a pandemic, starting from this hall!'

Wolfe stammered his response even as hundreds of heads turned to look at him.

'That's ridiculous!'

'He's armed!' Jarvis shouted, and the two security guards flanking him placed their hands on their weapons. 'We know everything,' Jarvis said. 'It's time to come clean about New Mexico and Alaska, Donald.'

Wolfe felt a tingling sensation creep uncomfortably down his spine as he felt the eyes of the entire amphitheater watching him.

'What in the name of God are you talking about?'

'The death of Tyler Willis,' Jarvis replied with an impassive expression. 'The abduction of Lillian Cruz. The men you have dispatched to New Mexico to assist Jeb Oppenheimer of SkinGen Corp in abducting men for biological experiments into longevity, and the murder of a scientist in Brevig Mission, Alaska.'

Wolfe opened his mouth to reply but Jarvis cut across him, turning to look up at the surrounding world leaders.

'Whatever you do, do not drink the water in your glasses. It's infected with a strain of 1918 Spanish Flu, obtained by Donald Wolfe from a mass grave in Alaska and brought here to New York.'

A rush of gasps crashed across the delegation.

'That's preposterous!' Wolfe snapped in alarm. 'Why on earth would I do something like that?'

'In the next half-hour, more people could die,' Jarvis shot back at him. 'We have tracked your movements ever since you left SkinGen in Santa Fe two days ago, and the FBI are already at Fort Detrick and searching your office.'

Wolfe flustered behind the dais, looking this way and that for an escape.

'SkinGen is a private corporation! I have no connection with them and the FBI can't just walk in and—'

'Yes they can,' Jarvis replied. 'Jeb Oppenheimer is on the run, Donald. It's over. Your little scheme to reduce the world's population through disease is finished, and your partner in crime is wanted for the murder of Tyler Willis. This is your chance to ensure that more innocent people don't die. Tell us exactly where your men are and what they're doing, before this becomes a multiple homicide investigation.'

Wolfe gaped at Jarvis and tried to force his brain to feed words to his unwilling vocal cords. 'I really don't know what you're talking about. I'm in the middle of an address and you're—'

'The hell with your address,' Jarvis shot back. 'I've had men watching you for forty-eight hours. You dispatched over one hundred mercenaries into New Mexico yesterday under cover of a training mission to kill American citizens!'

More gasps filled the auditorium as Wolfe felt dread plunge through him. His throat dried out as he struggled to speak.

'This is preposterous!' he shouted, and turned to the secretary-general. 'I demand that this man be removed from the chamber!'

The secretary-general glanced at Jarvis and then at Wolfe.

'Denied. Explain yourself.'

Wolfe was about to speak but Jarvis cut across him again.

'You sent biological clean-up teams into Santa Fe to investigate claims that you made of infected blood or agents being spilled in precise locations within the city,' he said. 'We have this on record as your own agenda for sending the teams in the first place. However, we also know that only two people knew that there was infected blood in those locations, and both of them are involved in the murders. My problem, Mister Wolfe, is that unless you'd been informed by those individuals of the presence of infected blood, you could not have known that it was present at the scene.'

A silence descended over the auditorium. Wolfe felt the weight of the world's political machine bearing down upon him. Jarvis took another step closer to the dais.

'In addition, you flew from Santa Fe to New York City yesterday, to attend a function last night and this United Nations meeting. However, your flight took some eight hours longer than it should have done. I have proof that you traveled to Brevig Mission in Alaska, and that since your arrival there a scientist working on the glacier has been found buried in the grave of a victim of Spanish Flu.' A flurry of horrified whispers filled the hall as Jarvis went on. 'Tissue samples from the infected corpse were found in the laboratories of SkinGen Corp just moments ago, sir. Can you explain how you came to acquire them while in Alaska, or how they ended up in the hands of Jeb Oppenheimer?'

Donald Wolfe tried to answer but his jaw ached as he gaped and he couldn't think of a single thing to say. Jarvis gave him no quarter, speaking before he could muster a reply.

'You're not here to convince the nations of this world to reduce their populations. You're here to spread a lethal virus across the globe while trying to ensure the longevity of select groups of businessmen. You're a eugenicist, using disease and genetics to shape the human population just how you think it should be, trying to remove those you deem to somehow be less worthy of life.' Jarvis tapped his own forehead. 'If I'm lying, hand your gun to these police officers and let them run tests on the blood residue that I know is on the handle. It will match mine!'

Wolfe stared with wild eyes into the middle distance, as though aware of his exposure and yet unable to bring himself to focus upon his inevitable demise. Jarvis took another couple of paces toward the dais, his voice carrying across the entire amphitheater.

'Sir, I do not care if you are innocent, framed, incompetent or just plain guilty. Right now, all that concerns me is that if you do not inform us of where those men are, right now, several citizens of this country that you *swore* to protect will die. Do you understand?'

Wolfe swallowed thickly and then nodded once. As he did so, he saw one of the dignitaries watching the exchange discreetly reach into his pocket and retrieve a cell phone upon which he began typing.

'Where are they?' Jarvis repeated, getting Wolfe's attention once again. 'Where is Jeb Oppenheimer and the soldiers you sent into the desert?'

The words fell from Wolfe's mouth as if of their own accord.

'Near Rattlesnake Canyon, Carlsbad,' he uttered. 'East of the Guadalupe Mountains.'

A deep silence filled the hall as Wolfe's guilt lay bare for all to see.

Jarvis turned and called out to the police behind him, who immediately began running for the exits with radios to their mouths. Wolfe glanced up at the dignitary with the phone, a Bilderberg member, who was looking down at him with a disapproving gaze. Wolfe realized in that moment that it was all over for him.

Jarvis turned toward him.

'Sir, if you would accompany the police to . . .'

Wolfe stepped down off the dais in one fluid motion and reached down, slipping the ceremonial pistol from its holster. He barely heard the cries of alarm from the chamber around him as he cocked the weapon, scarcely saw the security guards draw their own weapons with amazing speed to point at him. Wolfe turned to face the secretary-general, saluted once with his free hand, and then put the pistol's barrel to his head.

He saw Doug Jarvis rush toward him, his mouth open and his eyes wide.

'Donald, no!'

A deafening blast filled the hall and Wolfe's world vanished into blackness.

66

LECHUGUILLA CAVE
NEW MEXICO

Ellison Thorne peered up from the shelter of the cave, and Ethan watched as his craggy face screwed up in fury, his big hands clenching and unclenching around the handles of his pistols as he bellowed back in reply.

'You're sure one cowardly tyke, Mister Oppenheimer.'

A distant laugh rippled down toward them from far above, the old man obscured now by the mercenaries working their way down the ladder.

'A determined one,' Oppenheimer replied. 'You're the ones cowering in a cave.'

'Why don't you come down here and join us?' Ellison Thorne thundered back. 'If'n you're hankerin' so bad to be here?'

No reply came, and Ethan turned to Ellison Thorne.

'He's already murdered one man,' he said. 'He'll have no problem killing Lillian Cruz.'

Ellison squinted up at their attackers for a long moment, and then made a decision.

'We don't take orders from you, Jeb!' he boomed.

'We'll decide how this goes down!'

Oppenheimer's voice echoed down at them in reply.

'You've got five minutes before we finish this for good!'

Ethan and the rest of the soldiers withdrew into the cave to see Lopez hurrying to join them.

'Kip's not good,' she said. 'He's bleeding out and there's nothing I can do about it.'

Copthorne, McQuire and Cochrane all looked to Ellison Thorne, who in turn looked at Ethan.

'If'n that man gets hold of what's in these caves, you say he'll destroy the human race?'

Ethan nodded.

'He'll only let a certain few people have access to the drugs he's going to develop using the bacteria in your bodies. Those people will become biologically immortal, just as you are, while the rest of the world will be prevented from raising families. Oppenheimer, and people like him, will rule without end over the population.'

'But we're dying,' McQuire said. 'Whatever this thing is, it doesn't last forever.'

'It will, once Oppenheimer's had his chance to genetically mess with it,' Lopez said. 'Imagine a man like Oppenheimer being able to rejuvenate himself: young, fit, immortal and in control of a drug that every human being on the planet would kill to acquire. The world will be ruled by a dictator class with him at its head.'

Ellison Thorne turned away and rubbed his temples.

'If'n we get deep enough into the caves they won't be able to follow,' he said quickly. 'We can get ourselves sorted and come back out fighting.'

'You'll never be able to do it quickly enough to prevent Jeb from killing Lillian Cruz,' Ethan said. 'She's innocent in all of this.'

'So are we!' Ellison shouted. 'We didn't ask for this, but how can we now surrender it just because of one man's greed?!'

Ethan spoke quietly.

'Because this isn't about just you, or us, or Lillian Cruz. The simple truth is that people like Jeb Oppenheimer think they can control everything and they can't. Sooner or later, the science of this bacterium will be lost, or stolen, or leaked. No matter how hard they try they won't be able to prevent it from reaching the public domain, through a disgruntled employee or maybe one of those heroic whistle-blowers who leaks these things to the public for no financial gain, or maybe even through a population-wide revolution. It happened in the Middle East, the people toppling their dictators one after the other.'

Lopez stepped forward.

'When that happens,' she said, 'and it will, then we'll have an entire population of people who will never die. Can you imagine what will happen when the population rises so fast that the resources dry up, when there's no more water, no more food, no more fuel? When people will kill each other for a morsel of food or a sip of water? One day, this will not result in a human population that lives forever. It will end our species, completely. We will all die.'

Ellison Thorne stared at Ethan and Lopez for a long moment, and then looked at the other soldiers.

'What the hell do you think?'

McQuire, Copthorne and Cochrane exchanged glances, and then they nodded slowly. As they did, a voice came from behind them.

'I agree too.'

Ethan turned in surprise as Kip Wren limped toward them, using his rifle as a cane. His right thigh was bandaged with a makeshift tourniquet.

'You're in no condition to be standin',' Ellison said.

'Well I am standin',' Kip Wren replied. 'But I'm all played out, and I don't intend to spend my last sweet seconds sitting on my ass back there. You ever remember that old sayin' we used to live by during the war when we din' know if we'd ever see our homes and families agin?'

When none of the soldiers replied, Kip Wren spoke for them.

'The greatest act of courage a man can make is the surrenderin' of his own life for others, when nobody will ever know of his sacrifice.'

Ethan felt a rush of emotion as he heard the words, thought of countless comrades in the Marines and in other units who had served and died to protect democracy and the way of life that he and so many millions of others cherished. Through the world wars and countless other conflicts, souls far too young to die had sacrificed themselves upon the altar of freedom for the benefit of generations they would never meet. Ethan wondered briefly just how many heroes had anonymously given their lives throughout the history of mankind, their courage lost in time.

A sound from Misery Hole caught his attention, and he saw dozens of black-suited soldiers drop into the floor of the chasm and dash for cover behind rocks and fallen branches around the mouth of Lechuguilla Cave. Ethan and his companions crouched down behind cover as they watched Lillian Cruz being manhandled by the soldiers nearby, and the white-suited Jeb Oppenheimer appear at the bottom of the ladder, protected by an honor guard of his men. Ellison Thorne watched the gathering troops for a long moment, struggling between the desire to live and the altruism that Ethan suspected ran strongly through his veins. The big man finally sighed and looked at Kip Wren.

'What d'you propose?' he asked. 'That we bring the whole damned cavern down on top of ourselves?'

Kip Wren grinned against the pain wracking his body, and from his pocket produced a stick of dynamite that looked almost as old as he did.

'I've got me an idea, and I think you'll like it.'

67

'We want to make an exchange!'

Jeb Oppenheimer heard the sound of Ellison Thorne's voice boom out of Lechuguilla Cave as though a god of the underworld were addressing him. He peered down at the darkened, ragged cavern entrance, unable to see where the big man was hiding. The entrance was littered with the bodies of eleven men, some writhing in delirium or agony, others motionless.

'Of what?' Oppenheimer called.

'One of my men for your hostage!'

Oppenheimer looked at Hoffman, who frowned.

'One of them was injured,' he said. 'I'm damned sure I got him in the leg before they ran into that cave.'

Oppenheimer cleared his throat and shouted his reply. 'I don't want tainted goods!'

Ellison Thorne's reply thundered back from within the cave.

'Your men can't shoot for shit, Oppenheimer! He's got a minor wound to his leg, nothing more, but he needs attention. We'll send him up to you for treatment, you send us the woman. Everybody wins.'

Oppenheimer heard Hoffman speaking from behind him.

'Can't hurt, and it gets us what we want real easy.'

Oppenheimer peered at Hoffman.

'If something looks too good to be true,' he growled, 'then it probably is. Their man is most likely mortally wounded and they're looking to buy us off long enough to escape.'

Hoffman appeared to consider this for a moment and then chuckled.

'Well, we can't storm their little hidey-hole there without incurring too many casualties, so I say we let them send their man up. We send this woman of yours down, and then besiege them just the same. We win, both ways.'

Oppenheimer nodded.

'For once, I'm in complete agreement with you,' he said, looking back at Lillian Cruz where she knelt just out of sight behind them. 'Bind and gag her so she can't warn them, then arrange the exchange. We'll fetch her back as soon as we're ready.'

'Looks like they're goin' forrit,' Nathaniel McQuire said.

Ellison Thorne snorted in the half darkness.

'The hell they are,' he rumbled. 'That Oppenheimer's as slippery as a rattlesnake and no less deadly. He'll mean to kill us all, one way or another.'

Ethan watched as Kip Wren concealed his dynamite stick up his sleeve and took a cigarette lighter from Nathaniel McQuire.

'You sure about this?' he asked the soldier, whose breath was labored and his brow sprinkled with sweat.

'I am,' Kip replied, 'I can't lose: either I die here or I die up there. But be quick about it. I ain't certain how long I'll be able to stand.'

Ellison Thorne looked down at Kip.

'Once you're up there, light it fast and get a hold of Oppenheimer just as tight as you can,' he advised him. 'This thing'll smoke like all hell once it's lit, and they'll try to get it off you.'

Lopez frowned.

'What if they shoot him before it goes off?' she asked.

'Then Oppenheimer will definitely die,' Ethan said. 'Kip's body will seize and they'll never get him off the old bastard in time.'

Kip nodded, his teeth gritted in an awkward smile.

'Damn straight,' he said. 'Then this will all be over.'

A voice drifted down to them from beyond the cave entrance.

'We're ready, bring him out!'

Ethan watched as, with surprising care, Ellison Thorne mopped the sweat from Kip Wren's face and brow. Kip drank from Copthorne's water bottle before turning to Ellison. The two men stared at each other for a long beat, and Ethan realized that they were parting company for the first time in a hundred forty years.

Kip Wren, leaning on his rifle, held out his hand to Ellison. The big man took it, and then stepped in and briefly embraced his old comrade for a few moments before releasing him.

'As you were, Corporal,' he said finally, his gravelly voice taut.

Kip Wren saluted once, and then began limping away toward the light.

Ethan and Lopez followed, seeing Oppenheimer's soldiers arranged behind rocks near the entrance, their rifles aimed at the old soldier limping toward them. Kip Wren, mastering his pain, strode out into the cavern.

Ethan watched as Lillian Cruz, bound and gagged, was prodded toward the cave by two men carrying assault rifles. Carefully she descended toward them, her eyes fixed on the cave ahead and the old man making his way up toward her. The two glanced at each other as they passed, before Lillian reached the mouth of the cave, hesitated and looked back over her shoulder. Kip Wren strode toward their enemy, visibly favoring his left leg but valiantly reaching the spot where Oppenheimer crouched.

'Do it,' Copthorne whispered from behind gritted teeth, 'do it now, Kip.'

Ethan shifted his position and edged forward as Lillian Cruz stepped cautiously into the depths of the cavern.

'I've waited a very long time for this,' Oppenheimer said, looking at Kip Wren as though he were studying a work of art.

'Not as long as I have,' Wren replied, one hand closed around his cigarette lighter, the other holding the dynamite stick out of sight up his sleeve. Shafts of light shimmered down through the veils of cordite smoke swirling above their heads, the smell of blood and of scorched flesh staining the air.

'I assure you that you will not be harmed,' Oppenheimer promised. 'I've already realized that you're no good to me dead.'

Kip Wren peered at Oppenheimer.

'What are your intentions?'

'To study you,' Oppenheimer said. 'To discover what makes you biologically immortal, and use it to enhance the quality of the human race, the better for all mankind.'

'The better for you and your ilk, Oppenheimer,' Kip corrected him. 'You're in this for yourself, not for anybody else, and always have been.'

Oppenheimer gave a brief shrug.

'The world's full of winners and losers, the haves and the have-nots,' he replied with a cold smile. 'I'm just going to ensure that the losers are bred out of existence, leaving only the haves and the have-mores.'

Kip Wren felt a surge of hatred mix violently with the pain seething through his body, and with a cry of vengeance that echoed through the chamber he lunged forward and grabbed Oppenheimer with both arms, whirling him around as he pulled the old man against his chest. His hands met across Oppenheimer's waist, the dynamite stick and the cigarette lighter clear for the mercenaries to see.

'Stand down!' Kip Wren shouted. 'Or I'll blow this bastard sky-high!'

Oppenheimer squirmed in panic as he struggled to free himself from Kip Wren's grip, his rheumy eyes fixed on the explosive held against his belly. Five soldiers rushed in to try and prize him off even as Oppenheimer shouted at them.

'Get back!'

Hoffman waved frantically at his soldiers.

'Don't shoot! We need him alive!'

Kip watched as the mercenaries fell back, then turned to look over his shoulder. Lillian Cruz was already in the shadows of Lechuguilla Cave, almost out of sight.

'Come on out, Ellison!' Kip yelled with a maniacal chuckle. 'I got 'em surrounded!'

He was about to manhandle Jeb Oppenheimer toward the ladder when a voice yelled out at him.

'No!'

68

Saffron Oppenheimer leapt out of Lieutenant Zamora's patrol car before it had even stopped rolling, sprinting away up the hillside track toward Misery Hole at a terrific pace. Butch Cutler and Enrico Zamora labored after her in pursuit, but she gave them no quarter as she raced ever upward and then came to a sliding halt at the dizzying edge of Misery Hole.

She spotted the rope-ladders hastily rigged at the edge of the shaft nearby, and rushed around the edge before clambering onto the nearest one and hurriedly climbing down into the shadows. From her vantage point high above the floor of Misery Hole, she could see what was happening. Some kind of gunfight had filled the floor of the cavern with thick smoke that boiled up around her, stinging her eyes and choking her throat, but it also concealed her presence as she slid the last few feet to the ground behind the massed ranks of Oppenheimer's mercenaries, all aiming assault weapons at a low cave slicing across one wall of Misery Hole.

Saffron didn't wait for Lieutenant Zamora or Butch Cutler to reach her. Instead she charged at full sprint past the crouching ranks of soldiers toward where her grandfather writhed and twisted in the hands of an old man with a thick moustache, a stick of dynamite grasped in one bony-looking hand.

'No!' Saffron shouted, her arms outstretched as she ran. 'Don't kill him! There has to be a better way!'

Jeb Oppenheimer's crinkled jaw fell open as he stared in amazement at Saffron.

Kip Wren yelled, 'Stay aback, ma'am! I ain't bluffin'!'

'What the hell are you doing down here?' Oppenheimer said. 'This isn't your business, Saffy, get out of the way.'

'It's my goddamned business now, Grandpa,' Saffron shot back, 'ever since I went to the police. They know everything.'

Oppenheimer stared at her for a moment longer.

'You wouldn't.' He smirked. 'You wouldn't risk the jail time.'

The voice that answered came from behind them all.'Yes she would.'

Oppenheimer, Hoffman and the mercenaries turned to see Zamora standing behind them in full uniform, his pistol aimed at Oppenheimer. 'It's over, Jeb, no matter what happens. The entire New Mexico Police Department is on its way here right now.'

Butch Cutler stood alongside Zamora, clearly not intimidated by the mercenaries as he aimed a large Colt revolver at them.

'So is USAMRIID,' he reported. 'This whole thing's been blown sky-high.'

Oppenheimer appeared completely overwhelmed, unable to speak. Saffron stared at him in horror.

'How could you do it?' she asked. 'All those millions of people? You're planning to kill them all.'

Oppenheimer's features hardened again as he took his eyes off the dynamite at his belly.

'It will happen sooner or later all on its own,' he spat back at her. 'I'm just controlling the situation.'

'You can't control nature!' Saffron wailed. 'It's not possible!'

'Either way,' Butch Cutler said, 'it's not going to happen. No pandemic, no population control, no nothing. It's over. The police will be here any moment.'

Hoffman peered suspiciously at Cutler.

'If so,' he asked, 'then where the hell are they?'

Neither Cutler nor Zamora replied.

Saffron looked at the old soldier holding her grandfather hostage. His face was twisted in upon itself in agony, sweat thick on his brow and his legs trembling with the effort of staying upright. She took a careful pace forward.

'I can help you,' she said. 'Let him go and we can get you to a hospital.'

Kip Wren glared at her, but his strength was failing and she saw in his expression the realization that he was out of time. He smiled at her, almost regretfully.

'Apologies, ma'am,' he said through gritted teeth, 'but I can't do that.'

The old soldier's hands twisted, and she saw him light the dynamite stick's fuse in a flash of sparks and smoke.

Saffron hurled herself at Kip Wren and threw a fast right jab that drove her fingers into Wren's eyes. The old soldier shrieked and jerked backwards, and as he did so Saffron smashed her hands down across the smoldering dynamite stick and yanked it from Kip Wren's hands. Instantly, half a dozen soldiers plunged down onto Kip in a frenzied tangle of limbs and shouts, binding his arms and legs.

Saffron hurled the hissing dynamite stick into the depths of Lechuguilla Cave and whirled toward her grandfather.

'Get down!'

To her surprise, the mercenaries and Jeb Oppenheimer ignored her and fled away from the entrance to Lechuguilla Cave in a chaotic tumble. Confused, Saffron turned and saw the dynamite stick come whirling back out of the darkness to land at her feet.

'Oh shit.'

Saffron turned and ran hard, hurling herself flat to the ground behind scattered rocks as the dynamite exploded with a deafening boom and hurled the severed body parts of dead mercenaries in all directions to land with soggy thumps around her. She staggered to her feet, her ears ringing and pink blood spots staining her white T-shirt. She heard a laugh echo around the chamber as Jeb Oppenheimer struggled to his feet from behind a boulder and slapped his spindly thigh with one hand as he looked down at the cave entrance.

'We've got our man!' he shouted, and turned to Hoffman. 'Kill them all.'

Hoffman, his M-16 rifle once again cradled in his grip,

grinned and strode toward Jeb Oppenheimer. One huge hand reached out and gripped the old man by the throat with enough force to bulge his eyes. Oppenheimer gagged in shock as he was lifted onto his toes, his cane still dangling from his wrist.

'Your time, old man,' Hoffman hissed, 'is over.'

With a heave of effort, Hoffman turned and hurled Oppenheimer toward Lechuguilla Cave, the old man's limbs flailing as he tumbled through the desert dust to land in a heap near the entrance. A ripple of grim laughs from Hoffman's men followed him.

Saffron stared in disbelief at Hoffman. 'What the hell are you doing?'

Hoffman ignored her as he turned to Cutler and Zamora.

'Drop your weapons and get in that cave or we'll blow you away right here and now.'

Half of the mercenaries whirled and trained their assault rifles on Cutler and Zamora. Cutler looked at them and then glanced across at Zamora.

'Fancy going down in a blaze of glory?'

'Not so much.'

Cutler slowly lowered his revolver as he called out to Hoffman.

'Whatever Wolfe is paying you, it won't be nearly enough to get you out of this.'

Hoffman appeared unimpressed. 'I don't really care,' he said with a grim smile that conveyed an utter ruthlessness. 'Because neither of you will be around to report anything, and we'll be gone within minutes.'

Hoffman gestured to his men, and they disarmed

Cutler and Zamora and shoved them down toward the depths of the cave. They stumbled in the darkness as they struggled to see their way. Saffron hurried down with them and took her grandfather's arm. Oppenheimer struggled to his feet, steadied himself with his cane and turned to glare up at Hoffman.

'I'll pay you double,' he shouted, 'triple, whatever you want!'

Hoffman shook his head.

'You're a damned fool, old man,' he shouted. 'You think that you're powerful because you're rich, but you're a small fish in a very big pond and I work for the sharks. You're nothing, Oppenheimer, a nobody compared to who I work for!'

Hoffman turned away, and looked at one of the soldiers next to him.

'Don't shoot any of them. We need this to look like an accident. Get the explosives out and blow the cave. It'll hide any evidence that they were here at all, and if we need anything in the future we can come back when they've all rotted to hell.'

69

Ethan, along with Lopez, Ellison Thorne and the remaining soldiers had watched the entire exchange in amazement, from Saffron's unexpected wrecking of their plan to Oppenheimer being hurled toward them to land at the mouth of the cave.

'What the hell?' McQuire uttered in disbelief.

Ethan replied grimly, 'Looks like Oppenheimer's finally getting what he deserves.'

Beside them, Lillian Cruz scowled at the mercenaries.

'They've got one of your men now,' she said. 'He's still alive. Whatever you all planned hasn't worked.'

Ethan looked across at Ellison Thorne. 'You sure Kip's not going to make it?'

Ellison Thorne shook his head.

'Can't see how, even with all of those clever sawbones and new-fangled contraptions they've got today in hospitals. He'll have mustered out by noon.'

'None of it matters a damn,' Saffron snapped, and pointed at Lopez. 'You were all doomed when she cut herself a deal with my grandfather.'

A silence descended within the cave, even the breeze from the depths seeming to hang listless as Ethan stared at Saffron for a long and disbelieving moment before he turned to look at Lopez. Everyone in the cave was staring at her, and Ethan watched her glaring back at them defiantly like a cornered wildcat.

'What the hell, Nicola?' Ethan asked, staring at her.

Lopez glared back at Saffron.

'And we had a ticket out of here until you dropped in and screwed everything up saving that worthless old bastard,' she shot back, pointing at Jeb. 'Nice work.'

Ellison Thorne glowered at Lopez from the shadows.

'What trickery has she gone an' done on us?' he growled. 'We wondered how the old man found us so swiftly.'

'She betrayed all of you,' Saffron said, and looked at Jeb Oppenheimer. 'How much did it cost you, Grandpa, for another traitor to join your ranks?'

Oppenheimer was not looking at them, staring instead with interest into the dark depths of the cave, but he answered her question.

'A quarter million bucks,' he muttered as he hobbled off into the darkness of the caves behind them. 'Cheap at twice the price.'

Ethan stared at Lopez in horror. To his surprise, Lopez smirked as she leveled Saffron with a cold gaze.

'Predictable, to the last,' she said coldly. 'You're damned right I took his bribe, and you're damned right he paid me to guide his mercenaries to this cave. Gave me a GPS tracker to reveal the location of Lechuguilla

Cave. If you'd thought about it, you'd have also guessed that I'd tossed the GPS tracker long before we got here.'

'Not long enough to avoid a bloodbath!' Saffron shouted. 'People are dying because of what you did!'

Nathaniel McQuire turned his rifle to point at Lopez. 'Well if that don't beat the Dutch! You sold out on us!'

Ethan leapt forward between Lopez and the weapon. He looked at her and saw a glimmer of shame in her dark eyes.

'Why?' he finally managed to ask.

'We needed a way to get support here quickly,' she snapped back at him. 'I figured if I dropped the tracker somewhere close by, Jarvis would be able to locate it if he had the IP address of the device.'

Ethan eyed her uncertainly.

'That's a hell of a risk, Nicola,' he said. 'It could have backfired on us.'

'You're goddamned right there!' Saffron hissed, reaching out for Lopez.

'Cut it out!' Ethan snapped, blocking Saffron's way. 'We can sort this another time, right now we need to get the hell out of here.'

'There ain't no way out,' Ellison Thorne said. 'We searched plenty.'

Ethan turned to Butch Cutler and Zamora.

'Some rescue you've pulled off here. Any other great ideas?'

'We were too late,' Cutler said, 'couldn't get in front of them in time.'

'Where's the cavalry?' Lopez asked them.

McQuire laughed at her. 'You can't get horses down here, ma'am.'

Cutler looked at McQuire oddly before replying to Lopez.

'They can't move unless your man, Jarvis, can prove Donald Wolfe's involved. I haven't heard from him and our damned cell phones won't work down here, so now all we've got is the tracker you've supposedly dumped somewhere in the deserts.'

Lopez smiled coldly.

'They got here real fast, so they almost certainly found it,' she said. 'Which means that Oppenheimer most likely picked it up, being the scrooge that he is.' Lopez looked across at the old man. 'He won't have left it behind.'

Oppenheimer stared at Lopez in horror and then reached into his jacket pocket. He pulled out a small black device that lay in the palm of his hand, his face twisted with rage at Lopez's betrayal. The old man hurled the device into the darkness and turned away, hobbling deeper into the cave.

Ellison Thorne looked at Lopez for a long moment as he realized what she had done.

'I'll be damned,' he murmured, his eyes twinkling with suppressed admiration.

Saffron shook her head.

'You've risked all of our lives on a gamble, and made a profit to boot!'

Ethan was about to reply when he saw movement at the mouth of the caves. Mercenaries were sneaking forward carrying boxes of what looked suspiciously like explosives, and were mounting them near the cave mouth.

'Damn,' he said. 'They've got Kip Wren, so now they're going to blow the cave mouth in and seal it.'

Ellison Thorne nodded.

'That's what we did, more than a hundred years ago now,' he said. 'Blew the entrance so that nobody would find it. Was a bunch of goddamned scientists that decided to dig through the rubble and found these caves back in 1986.'

Ethan turned as he heard Oppenheimer arguing with Saffron as they backed into the cave. The old man hurried away from her with his awkward gait, his cane clicking in the darkness until they could no longer hear it.

'Now where the hell is he goin'?' asked John Cochrane.

'He still wants the bacteria,' Ethan said. 'Even now it's all that he's interested in.'

'To hell with him,' John Cochrane said.

'I can still change him,' Saffron protested. 'He's not completely destroyed yet.'

'Leave him,' Ethan said to her, grabbing her arm. 'He doesn't care about you or anybody else. All he gives a damn about is his own immortality.'

Saffron shook her head as she leapt to her feet. 'I can't leave him down here!'

Ethan watched her dash away before he turned to Ellison Thorne. The big man sighed heavily.

'We don't have time for this.' He looked around the cave at them all, and then his features creased with concern. 'Where's Lillian?'

Ethan scanned around them, but could see no sign of the medical examiner.

'Oh you're kidding,' Lopez uttered, looking behind her into the depths of the cave.

'She's going after the bacteria too?' McGuire said in disbelief.

Ellison loaded his rifle as he gestured to the cave entrance and looked at Ethan.

'*You've* got to get out of here,' he said. 'And you need to take Saffron and Lillian with you. We'll hold out until your reinforcements arrive, if they ever do. We can blow this cave in from the inside once you're clear, which will prevent Oppenheimer's men from getting to us. We've got enough dynamite left to do it, and Kip won't survive beyond noon. We win.'

Ethan glanced at the mercenaries outside the cave, and saw in the background two of them trying to stabilize Kip Wren, an intravenous line now in his arm.

'Don't worry,' he replied, 'Doug won't let us down. Shall we do this the old way, as one?'

Ellison Thorne nodded, and as he did so he and his comrades began loading their rifles once more. Behind him, Lopez picked up Kip Wren's rifle and began stuffing a Minie ball down the muzzle, following it with wadding. Ethan checked his pistol – six shots remaining, and he had a spare magazine. Twenty-one shots in total, plus five rifles: twenty-six shots, against maybe seventy or eighty heavily armed men.

'It's suicidal,' Lopez pointed out. 'Even if we do get clear, we'll still be outnumbered and we can't climb back up and out of Misery Hole without getting shot.'

'Ain't got no choice,' John Cochrane said. 'I'd liked

to have had all eight of us here and an army behind us, but those days are long past.'

Ethan stared at Cochrane, and then suddenly something smashed through his thoughts like a freight train as he squatted in the half darkness, watching Ellison and his men loading up.

'Eight of you?' Ethan said.

Ellison Thorne glanced at him but said nothing as he finished loading his rifle and aimed it at the cave entrance. Ethan slapped his head in disbelief.

'My God, I've been such an idiot!'

Lopez smiled in the darkness.

'Nothing new,' she chortled, and looked at Ellison Thorne. 'Something you need to tell us?'

Ellison shook his head, but Ethan spoke for him.

'The supplies,' he said, 'the medicines and clothes and everything that you would have needed to survive this long. Paperwork, documents, evidence that you weren't a hundred fifty years old. Damn it, you *do* have someone protecting you.'

'That ain't no concern of yours,' Ellison warned him with a pointed finger.

Ethan wasn't about to be intimidated, and on an impulse he fished the old photograph from his pocket and looked at it.

'You all said the same thing,' he pointed out. 'This photograph was taken after the Battle of Glorietta Pass, 1862. I didn't realize it until we got here this morning, but now I get it. This photograph was taken *after* you'd escaped from the Confederate retreat into Texas. It was taken *after* you'd sheltered in these caves.'

Lopez frowned curiously.

'So what? There's seven of them in the picture,' she said.

'Sure there are,' Ethan nodded. 'But who was holding the camera?'

Lopez stared at him for a moment as she realized his point. Ellison Thorne was about to answer when Edward Copthorne shouted out a warning.

'Enemy to the front!'

Ethan whirled to see four mercenaries plunge into the entrance and open fire randomly into the darkness, the staccato clatter of their assault rifles deafening in the confines of the cave. Behind them, Ethan glimpsed a half-dozen more men carrying what might have been plastic explosives, hugging the walls of the cave as they prepared to blow the entrance.

'Take out the shooters first!' Ethan hollered as Ellison's men took aim.

Ethan ducked his head away from the noise and the smoke as all five rifles fired at once, the barrel of Lopez's weapon barely a foot from his head as she blasted one of the attackers deep in the belly, the soldier folding over the round and tumbling to his knees.

Ethan aimed at one of the men carrying the explosives and fired, catching him cleanly in the chest. The soldier crumpled and dropped his explosives as Ethan leapt up from behind cover and charged forward through the thick veils of smoke, aware of the bayonets glinting alongside him as Ellison, Copthorne, McQuire and Cochrane all dashed out toward the entrance with a volley of war cries.

As they crashed into another wave of attackers rushing down toward them, Ellison Thorne shouted to Ethan above the din.

'Find Lillian and Saffron! I don't want any o' these bastards slipping past and killing them, and you'll need to get them out before we can blow the entrance!'

Ethan whirled to see Lopez ramming the wicked bayonet of her rifle straight into the chest of a screaming soldier. He shouted her name and tossed his pistol in a graceful arc toward her. Lopez whirled and caught the pistol before diving for cover behind scattered rocks and opening fire on their attackers.

Ethan dashed back into the cave, struggling to see as he plunged into the darkness.

70

Jeb Oppenheimer cackled to himself as he clambered awkwardly over endless jagged rocks in the darkness, his way lit only by the solid-gold lighter he held like a lantern in front of him, a white handkerchief wrapped around it to protect his fingers from the heat. The interior of the cave was low, forcing him to stoop in order to move forward. But he could smell a breeze that drifted into his face from somewhere ahead in the impenetrable black-ness, cool air touched with the scent of damp but also of something else, an almost clinical smell that he could not identify but which seemed somehow familiar.

The noise of fighting behind him had faded, the complex turns and twists in the cave deadening all sound. Drops of water plopped in fat drips into puddles on the ground, seeping through the bedrock from hilltops hundreds of feet above his head. The thought of millions of tons of solid rock bearing down upon the chamber from above sent a wriggle of fear twisting through his gullet but he pushed on, driven by the knowledge of what resided somewhere deep within these prehistoric caves.

Ahead, the weakly flickering flame of his lighter reflected off something embedded in the rocks that glittered like pearls. Oppenheimer slowed as the low ceiling of the tunnel rose and he squeezed through a narrow vertical cleft in the rocks into a chamber filled with a shimmering pool of crystalline water so clear that the light of his flame illuminated the floor perhaps twenty feet beneath the surface.

But that was not what drew his eyes and caught the breath in his throat.

Above his head, immense crystals like giant geometric tree trunks were lodged at angles to span the width of the chamber above the shimmering water. Like giant causeways made of translucent glass, they criss-crossed above the water and sparkled in the weak light of the flame as though encrusted with jewels.

'Gypsum,' Oppenheimer gasped, recognizing the immaculate nature of what was otherwise a nondescript mineral.

But here it possessed a purity the likes of which he'd never seen. He began easing his way into the cave, staring in awe at the crystals and the flickering water. The strange scent he'd detected earlier tainted the air around him, and he recognized it as ammonia. A flickering motion on the cavernous ceiling caught his eye, and he looked up to see bats roosting in their thousands above him, their wings fluttering as they clung to their rocky domain. As they did so, he saw an occasional droplet of fluid fall from the heights, dropping into the water with a tiny splash and ripple, the cause of the endless shimmering of the surface.

Slowly, placing his feet near the edge of the pool, Oppenheimer peered over the edge. There, deep below the surface, he watched the tiny droplets fall through the beautifully clear water to join a bizarrely colored deposit deep beneath the surface, a kaleidoscopic multitude of fungi and mosses. Oppenheimer guessed that the droppings in the water must clear overnight when the bats were out hunting, settling on the bottom of the pool. In the reflection from the surface of the water that illuminated his wrinkled face, Oppenheimer saw his own smile beaming back at him like a shimmering ghost as a disembodied voice echoed through the cave around him.

'It's guano.'

He whirled to see Lillian Cruz watching him from the entrance to the chamber. Oppenheimer regarded her for a moment and then decided that she was no threat to him as he turned back to the water.

'The guano has ammonia in it,' he said, almost to himself.

Lillian stepped into the chamber, gesturing to the water. 'It also has high levels of phosphorus and nitrogen,' she said. 'Along with ammonia it contains uric, oxalic, phosphoric and carbonic acids, various earth salts and nitrates.'

Jeb Oppenheimer's mind was working overtime as he nodded to himself, gesturing to the giant gypsum crystals soaring above the chamber.

'The gypsum and sulfur crystals mean speleogenesis: cave forming by sulfuric acid dissolution,' Oppenheimer said. 'The limestone cavern would have formed from the bottom up, in contrast to the normal top-down carbonic acid dissolution mechanism of cave formation. Sulfuric acid, derived from hydrogen sulfide, would have migrated from nearby oil deposits.'

'The cave then floods over time with water draining through fissures from the ground above, creating these pools,' Lillian added.

Oppenheimer nodded eagerly, gesturing up at the crystals with his cane. 'The water falls,' he said, 'hitting the crystals and sometimes taking with it bacteria that were encased within the crystals when they formed millions of years ago, bacteria like *Bacillus permians*.'

Lillian nodded.

'The bacteria fall into the water and mix with the guano at the bottom. Phosphorus in guano is an essential plant macronutrient,' she said, 'that's why it's used so heavily in fertilizers. The guano, laden with the bacteria, are kept in solution by the water in the pool. The bacteria, provided with a nutrient source by the guano, are reanimated and come into contact with all manner of mosses, fungi and bottom-feeding invertebrates.'

Oppenheimer's laugh rattled out in the chamber, echoing back and forth around them as he spoke.

'Some insect and invertebrate species are semi-aquatic, and others live on the surface. They consume the bacteria-laden guano, and are likewise consumed by the bats that hunt them!' Slowly he turned to face Lillian, his wrinkled features alive now as finally, after so many years, he realized that he had found something that had existed in folklore for millennia. 'The bats carry the bacteria, giving them their unusually long lifespans. They also process the bacteria through their gut and excrete many of them back into the water, or spill blood through injury into the pool.'

Lillian nodded, and despite the fact that he knew she hated him, she smiled.

'Which over time ladens the water with the very fluids the bats have ingested, alive with a form of *Bacillus permians* that has evolved within these caves to live symbiotically within mammals.'

'But what was the fuel?' Oppenheimer struggled to understand. 'What metabolism was required to sustain them for such long periods inside human beings?'

Lillian no longer held the truth back from Oppenheimer. In fact, she appeared to enjoy revealing to him what she had learned. 'Iron, from the hemoglobin in blood,' she replied. 'Anyone who carries the infection will suffer from anemia if iron supplements are not provided in their diet.'

Oppenheimer looked at her pleadingly, like a child who has misbehaved yet yearns desperately for one last chance.

'But how could it have made the transition to humans through a single encounter?'

Lillian regarded the old man for a long moment before replying.

'Cross-species communication is possible in bacteria through something known as quorom sensing. The bacteria use it to coordinate gene expression via the density of their population. If there's enough of them present in a biological species, the genes are activated and any infection shows symptoms.'

'My God,' Oppenheimer exclaimed. 'Like the bioluminescent luciferase in fish that glow underwater, produced by *Virbio fischeri*. The gene cannot be expressed by a single cell, only when the population is large enough does the production of luciferase begin.'

'The bacteria's ability to express the gene is only activated when enough are consumed by the host species,' Lillian confirmed.

Oppenheimer gasped, touching his head with one hand.

'The only people who have ever been down here long enough to consume enough of the bacteria to activate them were those Civil War soldiers. Which means that they must have got their infection from . . .'

Oppenheimer stared at the beautiful waters at his feet as Lillian took a few paces forward to join him. Her voice, soft as it was, carried throughout the cavern and into Oppenheimer's ears with the words he had once believed he would never hear.

'This is the water,' she said quietly. 'This is the elixir, the *real* fountain of youth. Ellison Thorne and his men drank the water here while they waited for the Confederate army to pass them by in 1862. They did not age from that day onward.'

Oppenheimer, his eyes alight with joy, let his cane fall onto the rocks beside him as he got down on his knees, tears dripping from his face to ripple into the water.

'And this is our ticket out of here,' he whispered to his own reflection. 'They dare not shoot us, if we're uninjured and already carrying the infection.'

Slowly, he lowered his lips and they finally touched

the surface. It was icy cold, clear, finer than the most expensive wine he had ever tasted. It surged through him as though he were forcing ice cubes down his throat, filled him with a tingling sensation as though his very nerve endings were sparking electricity onto the charged air in the chamber.

Finally, Oppenheimer stopped drinking and turned as he knelt beside the water, looking up at Lillian Cruz. He smiled broadly, just in time to see Lillian's features melt into an expression of pure hatred as she lunged down and grabbed the back of his head and plunged it beneath the surface. As the freezing water swallowed his head, Oppenheimer heard Lillian's voice shouting at him above the bubbles and splashes as he fought for his life.

'You wanted to be here so much? Now you can damned well stay here!'

Oppenheimer's ruined lungs ached, his aged heart thumped in his emaciated chest and his eyes bulged as he fought the urge to breathe. The clear view of the bottom of the pool swirled and starred as his vision faded. He was losing consciousness when he saw Lillian's hand plunge into the water beside his head, holding a small plastic container that held what looked like a ball of iron surrounded by flesh. Water from the pool filled the container, and then it vanished again as a black cloud descended over his vision. He heard a faint voice from somewhere on the periphery of his consciousness.

'Get off of him!'

Suddenly the immovable weight of Lillian's body vanished, and Oppenheimer lurched upright and out of the water. He sucked a huge volume of air into his lungs. His vision returned as he sagged backwards onto the damp rocks just in time to see Saffron hurl Lillian Cruz to one side.

Ethan burst into the chamber just in time to see Lillian Cruz staggering to her feet, water pouring from her arms. Oppenheimer sat in a drenched huddle beside the pool, Saffron standing protectively over him.

'We've got to get out of here!' Ethan yelled, grabbing Lillian and propelling her out of the chamber. 'Get to the surface!!'

Lillian glared at Jeb Oppenheimer and Saffron, but she obeyed and dashed out of the chamber. Ethan turned to Saffron.

'It's time to go,' he said.

'I'm not leaving him here,' Saffron shot back.

'Fine!' Ethan shouted, losing patience. 'Let's just get out of here!'

Jeb Oppenheimer struggled to his feet.

'I'm not leaving without samples,' he insisted, gesturing at the huge crystals with his cane. 'Help me get them before we leave.'

Ethan almost laughed.

'Like hell,' he said, and grabbed Saffron's arm. 'Come on, let's go.'

Ethan had almost turned his back when he heard the sound of a gun's mechanism being cocked. He turned to see the old man holding a small, snub-nosed pistol in his right hand. Ethan froze as Oppenheimer smiled grimly.

'I never leave home without one,' he said. 'Now, get

up there and get me some of those crystals or I'll put a bullet in you.'

Ethan stared in disbelief as Oppenheimer walked away from the pool and positioned himself between the chamber exit and Ethan and Saffron.

'Are you really that insane?' Ethan demanded. 'We could be buried alive in here at any moment.'

'Best hurry then!' Oppenheimer cackled, gesturing with the pistol. 'Move!'

Ethan shook his head.

'No. You'll never be able to climb up there on your own, so without me you're screwed.'

Oppenheimer's face wrinkled up on itself in furious defiance.

'Not quite.'

Oppenheimer shifted his aim and before Ethan could even register what he was about to do, he fired a single shot that rang out deafeningly loud in the chamber. Saffron cried out as the bullet thumped into her belly and out through her side, ricocheting off nearby rocks and zipping away into the chamber.

71

Ethan lunged forwards and caught Saffron as she toppled sideways from the impact, her eyes wide with shock and disbelief and her face suddenly pale. He lowered her down as gently as he could, pushing fist-sized rocks out of her way before setting her down. He let his hand fall on one of the rocks as he spoke to her.

'Don't panic,' he said desperately. 'Keep your heart-beat as slow as you can, so you don't bleed too quickly.'

'It's a stomach wound,' Oppenheimer cackled, moving closer. 'She'll leak the contents of her gut into her blood-stream and die from blood poisoning. You've got about five minutes before it'll be too late to save her.'

Ethan let go of Saffron's body and turned to glare at Oppenheimer. For a moment he considered simply doing what the old man said, but suddenly he was over-come with an intense desire to deny the old bastard what he wanted once and for all.

'Go to hell,' he uttered. 'I'd sooner die.'

Oppenheimer glared at Ethan.

'Get up there and collect those crystals or I swear I'll shoot you where you stand.'

'Do it,' Ethan said. 'You'll never get them, not from me and not from Saffron. You're finished, Jeb, totally finished. At least let Saffron live even if you kill me.'

Oppenheimer turned slightly and pointed the pistol at Saffron again.

'Do it, you cretin, or I'll shave another few minutes off her life.'

Ethan looked down at Saffron, who stared up at him through her pain and shook her head vigorously. Ethan looked back up at the crystals and then turned, swinging his arm to hurl the rock in his hand up into the cavernous vault of the chamber. The rock smashed into the ceiling above and instantaneously the giant flock of bats screeched in unison, spilling from the chamber's roof in a screaming black avalanche of wings and teeth. Ethan ducked down as the bats raced past in a thick black fog and blasted into Jeb Oppenheimer as they raced for the cavern exit. Ethan heard the old man curse and drop his cane as the bats slammed into him, the pistol firing a wild shot in Ethan's direction.

Ethan launched himself forward and crashed into Oppenheimer, pinning the pistol between them as they smashed into the rocks. Oppenheimer gagged in agony as sharp stones stabbed through his dirtied suit and punctured his skin, flecks of saliva and mucus spilling from his mouth as he cursed and scratched at Ethan's face with his nails. Ethan pulled away from the attack, keeping hold of Oppenheimer's gun and twisting it from his grasp. The old man cried out in fury, reaching down to one foot with his free hand. Ethan glimpsed a small knife that Oppenheimer grabbed from a sheath at his ankle and whipped around toward Ethan's flank. Ethan reached out for the blade but he couldn't move quickly enough to block the blow. Something grated against his ribs and vibrated through his flesh as the blade plunged hilt deep into his side with a dull thud. He jerked away from the blade and rolled off the old man as he grabbed the blade's handle. Oppenheimer scrambled to his feet, the pistol still in his grasp as he aimed it between Ethan's eyes and glowered down at him as his chest heaved for breath.

'Nice knowing you,' Oppenheimer cackled, and squeezed the trigger.

'Grandpa!'

Ethan glanced behind Oppenheimer, to see Saffron on her feet and looming behind Jeb. The old man whirled in surprise, just in time for Saffron to catch his gun wrist in her left hand and twist it violently upon itself. Saffron's shrill scream of anguish echoed through the chamber as she yanked Oppenheimer's arm down and brought her knee up into his elbow. A crack like the snapping of a twig echoed through the cavern as Oppenheimer's arm broke mid-joint, the pistol clattering to the rocks at his feet.

Ethan, pain searing his body, watched as Saffron glared down at her grandfather as she held him by his broken arm.

'My grandmother would have hated what you've become,' she hissed at him.

Oppenheimer, his voice tight with agony and fear, pleaded with her.

'This is worth it, Saffy,' he croaked. 'Every step of this journey, it's worth it.'

Saffron twisted his arm harder, provoking a squeal of pain.

'Not for me.'

Saffron drove her knee into Oppenheimer's gut. The old man's eyes bulged as a blast of foul air spilled from his lips. Saffron spun on her heel and pulled hard, hauling his wiry body over her shoulder. Jeb Oppenheimer screamed in pain as he was flipped over her body and plunged backwards into the pool, Saffron's weakened legs buckling as she fell on top of him and clasped her hands around his throat.

Ethan dragged himself up onto his elbow to see the old man thrashing hopelessly in the water, his white suit weighing him down and his broken arm useless by his side as he sank below the surface in Saffron's furious grasp. Above the thrashing water of her grandfather's desperate death throes he could hear Saffron crying, and then the water fell still beneath her, expanding ripples drifting out toward the distant reaches of the chamber. Saffron stared down at the roiling surface of the water and cradled her bleeding stomach. Ethan struggled over the pain in his side, and clambered up the rock face beside him to regain his feet and limp across to her. He looked down into the pool, where Jeb Oppenheimer sank slowly away to sprawl motionless on the bottom, staring up with wide, lifeless eyes.

'I'd say this pool's been contaminated,' he said.

Saffron nodded and then fell sideways. Ethan managed to catch her in one arm, his other hand still on the handle of the knife wedged in his side.

'We need to get out of here,' he said quickly, and turned them both toward the cavern exit.

Saffron was breathing heavily as she struggled to keep moving through the low, awkward passage, and Ethan could feel thick blood flowing warmly from around the knife still wedged in his side. He tried not to think about what damage the steel blade might be causing inside him, forcing himself onward one step at a time toward the dim light ahead from the cave entrance.

Another blast of noise from explosives thundered down the passage, a shock wave hitting Ethan and a fine mist of particles stinging his face. The cavern ahead was filled with thick smoke, and he could hear the occasional crack of a rifle as he staggered toward the light.

He instantly saw John Cochrane lying halfway between the cave entrance and the last line of defense, sprawled on his back and staring wide-eyed at the ceiling. Half of his forehead was missing, his ear hanging from his scalp in a web of tattered fronds of skin and bone. The cave entrance was littered with bodies and fallen chunks of rock.

Lopez saw him coming over her shoulder as she lay with her pistol propped up on the rocks.

'We're pinned down!' she shouted. Then she saw their wounds. 'Are you okay?'

Ethan nodded and managed to struggle up alongside her before both he and Saffron collapsed, breathless and sweating, in the darkness. Lillian Cruz dashed across to them, her eyes wide as she took in their injuries. Lopez saw the knife in Ethan's side, and her skin turned pale as she looked at him.

'Jesus, Ethan, we need to get you to a hospital.'

'We need to get out of here first,' Ethan said, his own voice a raspy whisper in his ears.

'They're still trying to blow the entrance to the caves,' Lillian shouted above the crackle of gunfire. 'We can't hold them off much longer.'

Ethan looked across at Ellison Thorne. His shoulder was stained with crimson blood where a bullet had hit him, his features tight with terminal defiance. Nathaniel McQuire appeared uninjured but he was clearly exhausted, his face smeared with soot and scratches from the blasts of the explosives. Edward Copthorne was lying unconscious alongside them, several patches of blood on his clothes betraying multiple bullet wounds.

'He ain't stayin' with us much longer,' Ellison said, and gestured to the cave entrance. 'It's time we end this, for once and for all.'

Ethan nodded, one hand clutching the blade impaled in his side as he looked at the cave entrance. There, he could see sticks of dynamite piled loosely around the sides of the cavern, connected by a fuse wire that ran to a simple detonator lying beside Edward Copthorne's inert body.

Ethan crawled to his knees and picked up his pistol from where it lay beside Lopez.

'We're ready,' he said.

Lillian Cruz helped Saffron to her feet and Lopez stood up with her rifle held at port-arms, bayonet fixed and ready. Ethan looked down at Ellison Thorne one last time as the big man picked up a handful of dynamite sticks and cradled them in his arms, a cigarette lighter in his big fist.

'Who was holding the camera, Ellison?' he asked. 'They'll still be in danger, they'll need help.'

Ellison Thorne smiled. 'Not now they won't,' he said.

Before Ethan could challenge him again, Ellison lit the dynamite in his grasp in a fizzing cloud of sparks and blue smoke. Lillian prodded them all toward the edge of the cave entrance as Ellison staggered to his feet, holding his lethally blazing explosives and nodding once at Ethan. Ethan turned and hurried toward the light, squinting through the smoke and aiming his pistol ahead as they burst out into the vertical shafts of sunlight beaming down to the bottom of Misery Hole.

A single soldier was squatting amid boulders right in front of Ethan, fiddling with a pack of C4. Ethan aimed and fired a single shot, the round snapping the man's head sideways as though he'd been clubbed with a base-ball bat. He saw Lopez fire a round at a man further up the slope, hitting him squarely in the chest and taking him clean off his feet to land with a thud on his back.

Ethan split to the right of the cave entrance with Saffron and Cutler as Lillian and Zamora hurled them-selves in the opposite direction.

Ethan shouted out as he crouched down with one arm across Saffron's shoulders and Cutler shielding the pair of them with his body. 'Get down, now!'

Ethan glimpsed dozens of mercenaries all aiming assault rifles at them, when the cave entrance exploded as Ellison Thorne's dynamite ignited.

72

A superheated blast wave of shattered rocks and flame roared from the mouth of the cave, spitting a cloud of supersonic debris that radiated out across Misery Hole. The mercenaries besieging the cave hurled themselves aside as they were hammered by the deadly shrapnel, shielding their faces as they hit the ground. The infernal blast rolled and echoed through the cavern as a tumbling shower of dust, stone chips and shattered vegetation fell from around them. Ethan took his hands from over his head, wiping dust from his eyes as he looked back to see the mouth of Lechuguilla Cave now obscured by a mountain of shattered rocks still tumbling down to thump onto the ground nearby.

Lopez and Lillian Cruz lifted their faces from the dust, but Saffron remained motionless. Ethan struggled across to her side and gently rolled her over. Her face was pale and her eyes rolled up in their sockets, but she was conscious, groaning with the pain that was now beginning to seep like acid through her body as the contents of her stomach leaked into her bloodstream.

'She needs a hospital, now,' Cutler said, 'or she won't make it.'

Ethan was about to reply when some of the mercenaries began to recover themselves and leapt from cover, M-16s at the ready as they surrounded them, a tall man with pallid, pock-marked skin at their head. His red hair glistened in the sunlight above his paunchy face as he looked down at them.

'At last,' he said, lifting his rifle to point at Ethan, 'it's time to bring this to a close.'

Zamora, on his knees and with a rifle pointing at him, shook his head.

'Don't do this.'

The man ignored him and aimed his assault rifle, the ugly black barrel pointing straight between Ethan's eyes, and then a deafening gunshot burst the air around Ethan's head. He heard himself cry out and grab his face in shock, only to see the assault rifle aimed at him spin wildly away through the air. The pale-skinned man doubled over in shock as he stared at the ragged, bloody hole torn through his hand.

A barrage of voices shouted out, laden with fearsome rage as they raced closer, and as Ethan looked up through the shimmering beams of light sweeping down through the clouds of dust and smoke, he saw dozens of figures rappeling down toward him.

'Put your weapons down! *Down down down!*'

Ethan, his eyes itching with grit, watched as United States Marines plunged into the cavern around them.

Snipers enshrouded in bush camouflage popped up
from the edge of the ridge a hundred feet above, weapons pointed unwaveringly at Hoffman and his men. The
sudden sound of distant thunder became a deafening,
hammering chorus as a pair of Bell-Boeing V22 Osprey
aircraft roared past against the disc of blue sky above,
escorted by two Apache Ah-64 gunships, the sound of
their amassed rotors thundering down through the
cavern like the footfalls of a charging army of giants.

'That'll be the cavalry,' Lopez said as she lowered her
pistol and spat dust from her mouth. She crawled to
Ethan's side and gently pressed her hand around the
blade lodged in his side, trying to stem the bleeding.

Ethan saw Hoffman being forced to his knees by a
Marine, blubbering like a child as he was cuffed and
forced flat onto his stomach. Other Marines thundered
down to surround them as Lopez called out.

'Medic!'

Within moments a pair of medics were alongside
them, dropping their Bergens and fishing out IV lines
and saline bags with practiced efficiency. Ethan lay back,
ignoring the line being inserted into his arm and watching as the other medic worked on Saffron Oppenheimer
nearby. The man turned his head, holding a small microphone attached to his helmet as he spoke into it.

'Delta-Four, CASEVAC, repeat, casualty evacuation
immediate, stand-by.'

Ethan heard a warbled response through the medic's
earpiece, and then the noise from the approaching
Ospreys became overpowering.

Cutler and Zamora appeared beside him, concerned

looks on their faces, and then were pushed aside by four marines who surrounded him.

He lay back and looked up past the towering rocky walls of Misery Hole, saw swathes of golden desert dust sweeping across the sky as the two huge aircraft landed somewhere nearby. The four Marines lifted him onto a makeshift field stretcher, the medic carrying his saline bag as he was lofted upon their shoulders and attached to a winch lowered hastily by troops far above.

Ethan saw Lopez watching him with a furtive expression, her long black hair caked with dust, and then he was hoisted up and away from the floor of the cavern, spiraling slowly as he was pulled all the way to the lip of Misery Hole and then lifted clear of the chasm.

One of the Ospreys had landed 'hot' on a plateau a hundred yards away, the huge pivoting engines directing their immense thrust downward for vertical landing. The blades were kicking up a fearsome dust storm around the aircraft, but the medic carrying the saline bag shielded Ethan's face with one hand as he was rushed aboard the aircraft. The Marines laid him down on a canvas bed that had been folded down from one side of the fuselage wall.

Ethan lay back, watching as Saffron was lifted aboard moments later and carried with reverential care by the battle-hardened Marines to lie nearby on another fold-down bed. The Marines rushed off the Osprey and moments later Ethan felt his stomach plunge as the aircraft's engines roared even louder and it lifted off and accelerated into forward flight.

Medics fussed over Saffron's inert form nearby, and

Ethan watched with concern until a soldier carrying what looked like a laptop computer squatted beside him and rested the computer on his chest. A flickering image of Doug Jarvis offered him a brief smile from beneath a hastily bandaged and bloodied forehead.

'Good morning.'

Ethan closed his eyes briefly before replying.

'I wouldn't call it good,' he said, glancing again at Saffron. 'Saffron's been hit bad.'

Jarvis nodded.

'Don't worry, she's in good hands now and will be in the best of care once you get back to Holloman. I've alerted their best people to take care of her once you arrive. I take it your meager flesh wounds won't prevent you from attending a detailed debrief once we're there?'

Ethan sighed.

'Sure. What's a few inches of Toledo steel between friends? Where the hell are you? And what happened to your face?'

Jarvis grimaced.

'New York, and if you think I look bad, you should see Donald Wolfe. Get some down time, Ethan. I've already got the DIA on the case.'

'How did you know where to find us?' he asked.

'Lopez sent me a text,' Jarvis said. 'An IP address for a GPS tracker. I'd only just got out of the UN building, but we managed to figure out what she'd done. I dispatched the Marines right after.'

'She lied to me, Doug,' Ethan said with a sigh.

'She got the job done,' Jarvis countered. 'Anyway,

don't worry about the details – my teams are already on their way to clear up, and by lunchtime none of this will ever have happened.'

Ethan rested his head against his pillow, staring up at the ceiling of the Osprey.

'I doubt that,' he said quietly.

'Why?' Jarvis asked. 'Jeb Oppenheimer suffered a tragic accident this morning and will be buried in a private ceremony – he didn't have any friends to speak of so no need for a public funeral. His mercenaries will be tried by military court and convicted of conspiracy to murder DIA agents. Donald Wolfe effectively confessed to conspiracy to murder Tyler Willis and for the homicide of an unknown male in Alaska in front of the entire United Nations before he shot himself. I take it that Lillian Cruz has been liberated and will no doubt testify as and when required regarding her abduction. And as for the soldiers you located out here . . .'

Ethan nodded slowly.

'They're all dead,' he guessed. 'Have been for decades.'

'Longer,' Jarvis said, and his voice became somber. 'The Marines found one of them in the hands of Oppenheimer's mercenaries. He wasn't alive.'

'Kip Wren,' Ethan identified him. 'A very brave man. They all were.'

Jarvis nodded.

'Their remains will be allowed to decay as appears to be the norm and then be retrieved from the caves for further study. Butch Cutler and Lieutenant Zamora will be signing non-disclosure forms within the hour. The chamber within Lechuguilla Cave will be sealed and its location removed from any public forum. Best that we keep whatever's in there under lock and key, for obvious reasons.'

'What about Saffron?' Ethan asked.

'Tricky,' Jarvis said. 'For whatever reason, she developed a conscience and handed herself in to state police, told them everything. I'd have sent people in to retrieve the incriminating evidence on her behalf, but the police are already there and apparently have recovered video tapes that implicate her in an unsolved homicide some four years ago.'

Ethan sighed heavily.

'The circumstances were different to how they appear on the images, apparently,' Ethan said. 'After all this, they'll use everything they can to send her down for life. You need to do something to help her, Doug, she doesn't deserve this.'

Jarvis shrugged on the screen.

'What can I do? This case is resolved and everything the DIA needs is now in their hands, including Kip Wren's body and the site itself. They're not going to let me interfere in a civil case.'

Ethan looked at him seriously.

'They might have to,' he said. 'Because it's not over.'

'What do you mean?' Jarvis asked. 'There's nobody left.'

'Yes, there is,' Ethan explained. 'There were eight of them, not seven, because someone was holding the camera when that photograph was taken in 1862.'

Jarvis's features creased as a realization dawned in his eyes.

'The subject is still alive?' he asked.

'Very much so,' Ethan said. 'Protect Saffron and I'll help figure out who it is. Let her go down, and the DIA can go to hell for its information.'

73

CHRISTUS ST VINCENT MEDICAL CENTER SANTA FE

19 May, 3.47 p.m.

Ethan packed the handful of dust-covered clothes that he'd worn in Misery Hole, pausing to glance at the thick bloodstains on his shirt before stuffing it into a bag and dropping it into the waste bin in his hospital room. The movement caused a painful twinge low on his flank where Oppenheimer's blade had sunk into his flesh, the scar tissue only half healed beneath the surgical dressing wrapped around his waist. He slipped into the fresh clothes sent to him by Doug Jarvis, and turned his back on the room, walking down the corridor outside to where he knew Saffron Oppenheimer was staying, easily identifiable by the two state troopers guarding the door. Ethan introduced himself to them, and they stood aside to let him in.

The room was pleasantly spacious, and Saffron lay with her eyes closed at a comfortable angle on her bed with only a saline drip to show any evidence of her trauma. Ethan slipped quietly into the room and closed the door behind him.

'About time you showed up, tough guy,' Saffron said, opening one eye to peer at him. 'Last I heard you were at death's door with a little splinter in your side.'

Ethan grinned.

'Go to hell,' he said, crossing the room to her bedside. 'The doctors have told me I'm not to exert myself for five days. It could lead to complications.'

'Sure,' Saffron said, but her eyes were dancing with humor.

'How're you doing?' he asked.

'I'll be fine,' she said, shifting her position slightly and propping herself more upright on her pillows, 'now that I don't have my breakfast running through my blood-stream. Took a while for them to stitch me up but I'll make it.'

'You did good,' Ethan said. 'If you hadn't walked into that police station, Lopez and I would have ended up beneath a few tons of New Mexico rubble and Jeb Oppenheimer would have been planning who lived and who died in his new world order.'

Saffron smiled faintly.

'Didn't do me much good though,' she said. 'Guards at my hospital door and a lengthy prison sentence to look forward to. You should have left me in that cavern with Jeb.'

Ethan sighed and sat on the edge of the bed.

'I'm doing what I can,' he said. 'I've got the DIA over a barrel about what happened in Lechuguilla Cave, both last week and in 1862. They're looking at options for you.'

'Why doesn't that phrase fill me with confidence?'

'It's not easy,' Ethan admitted. 'You've become a

high-profile victim of these events, but it's still going to be hard to keep you out of jail.'

Saffron became melancholy, staring at her bed sheets.

'I killed him,' she said finally. 'I killed my own grandfather.'

'You defended yourself,' Ethan replied. 'He shot you first, remember?'

Saffron didn't appear to hear his last words as she reached out and gripped his hand.

'Promise me, you'll call your parents,' she said.

'Why?'

'Because you still can,' Saffron replied. 'Don't leave it another day, okay? Just do it, before you wake up one morning and realize you no longer can.'

Ethan held her gaze for a long moment and saw the determination in Saffron's eyes. He nodded and flipped her a mock salute.

'Okay, I'll do it. I promise. Scout's honor. But you've got to do something for me.'

Saffron raised a questioning eyebrow as Ethan gestured out of the window.

'You're the heir to SkinGen Corp,' he said.

'I don't want any of it,' she said. 'The whole goddamned company can go to hell and—'

'That's what I mean,' Ethan cut across her. 'You want to change things for the better? Selling the company off for nothing will achieve exactly that: nothing. Take the helm, organize something, even if it's just distributing drugs to countries and people who can't afford them. SkinGen is not a legacy to be avoided, it's an opportunity. Use it.'

Saffron leaned back against her pillows with a sigh and released his hand.

'I wouldn't know where to start,' she said.

'Anywhere will do,' Ethan said. 'Just start. Jeb Oppenheimer was a monster but much of what he believed made sense, especially to ordinary people. Find those things, act on them. Don't leave SkinGen tainted with the memory of Jeb: reinvent it in the image of Saffron.'

Saffron laughed briefly, but she saw Ethan's expression and the laugh faded.

'You think it's worth it?'

'It's a no-brainer,' Ethan replied.

'Fine, I'll do it,' Saffron said. 'Now get out of here, I've got a genuine injury to recover from.'

Ethan grinned and walked to the door. He was about to open it when she called over to him.

'I won't be seeing you again, will I?'

Ethan hesitated at the door.

'If the DIA gets you out of this, you'll be hidden away for quite a while.'

'Maybe I'd have looked you up.'

'Maybe you still should.'

Saffron shook her head and smiled. 'I don't have a chance while your Mexican spitfire's watching your back.'

'Lopez?' Ethan said. 'We're just partners and—'

'Like hell,' Saffron cut across him. 'She likes you, I can tell it from a mile away. You just watch your step with her though.'

Ethan sighed softly.

'You mean because she sold out to Jeb Oppenheimer? You know she tossed the tracking device before we found the caves, right after she'd sent the DIA the IP address? She had a plan.'

'She looks out for you alright, but she's a firecracker, hard to handle.'

Ethan wasn't sure how to react. 'What do you mean?'

'Put it this way,' Saffron said, 'if you're walking about with a grenade in your pocket, you step lightly because it could kill you just as sure as it could save your life. She's a wild card, Ethan, nobody knows what she might do next.'

Ethan opened the door, thoughts of Lopez clouding his mind.

'I'll bear that in mind.'

74

The New Mexico sun blazed brightly in a flawless blue sky as Ethan stepped out of the hospital foyer, shielding his eyes. Across the street stood Nicola Lopez, leaning against the trunk of a Ford Taurus and jangling the keys in her hand. Ethan stepped across to her, the hot wind rippling his shirt and lifting one corner to reveal the thick dressings. He touched them self-consciously as he walked.

'You're not going to start showing that thing off to people, are you?' Lopez asked.

'Looks good, doesn't it?' he said. 'Another war wound to add to the collection.'

Lopez smiled and shook her head.

'People will just assume you've had your appendix out or something. Jesus, you were in hospital for two whole days. Anyone would think you got your head blown off.'

Ethan, affronted, covered the wound back up.

'C'mon, I suffered for this one. Doctor said a half-inch higher or lower and I'd have been in real trouble.'

'Yeah,' Lopez agreed. 'My point exactly.'

Ethan shook his head in dismay.

'Just because you can walk out of a gunfight looking like you've been modeling swimwear doesn't mean everyone can,' he mumbled.

Lopez looked at him as a smile blossomed on her face.

'You really think that?'

Ethan sought to backtrack.

'Sometimes,' he admitted. 'But don't get used to compliments, I'm not paid to blow sunshine at you.'

Lopez smiled again, but the moment passed. Ethan watched her for an instant, and then gestured to the car.

'We need to talk.'

Lopez climbed into the car with Ethan and drove out of the hospital grounds, heading toward the I-85. Ethan let the cool breeze funnel in through the open window onto his face as they drove.

'What's the news on Saffron?' Lopez asked.

'She's recovering well,' Ethan replied, 'but she'll be going to trial in Santa Fe as soon as she's well enough to stand.'

'Doug's working on it,' Lopez said. 'They've been going insane trying to figure out who the eighth person is, but I don't think it's getting them anywhere. I'm surprised they haven't tried blackmailing us yet.'

'With what?' Ethan smiled smugly, settling back into his seat. 'They can hardly fire us as we don't work for them directly. Either they work it out for themselves or they uphold their end of the deal.'

'Do you know who it is?' Lopez asked.

'I'm working on it.'

'Are you tryin' to tease me?'

'Are you enjoying it?'

'You're an asshole, Warner.'

'I'm not the one who sold out,' Ethan replied.

Lopez kept her eyes on the road ahead for a long moment before she replied. 'I took an educated gamble,' she said finally. 'It made sense at the time, okay? Everybody came out the other side of it.'

'By the skin of our goddamned teeth, Nicola!' Ethan shot back, dragging a hand across his face. 'Jesus, we're going up against some pretty unsavory people here and I don't know if I can trust you from one day to the next.'

'You can trust me,' Lopez said instantly, locking her dark eyes onto his.

'How can I when I don't know what you're doing behind my back?' Ethan replied. 'That little scheme of yours could have cost us all our lives, and for what? A quarter million bucks? Is that what I'm worth to you?'

'That's not how it went down!' Lopez protested. 'I didn't do anything behind your back. Jesus, we're not married, you know.'

'Yes we are,' Ethan insisted, 'ever since we went into business together.'

'Hey, I'm not just the dutiful wife in this arrangement, cowboy,' she shot back, the wind rippling her hair in a dark halo. 'I'm not just a passenger here, your damsel in distress, okay? I can make my own calls, and I'll goddamned follow my own leads with or without you.'

Ethan chuckled bitterly and shook his head.

'You didn't do this for your equality,' he muttered. 'You did it to make hard cash, and you risked my life along with everybody else's to pull it off. Where will it stop, Nicola? Breaking into jeeps is one thing: this is something else entirely. What will you do next?'

'There is no *next*,' Lopez said, more reasonably. 'I did what I set out to do, and now it's over.'

'Is it?' Ethan asked. 'I thought it was over when Doug Jarvis pulled us over two days ago. You said it was.'

Lopez stared ahead as she drove, and sighed heavily.

'It's over,' she repeated, and then looked at him. 'I won't let you down, okay? Let's just drop it for now.'

Ethan turned away from her to look out across the blistering deserts passing by.

75

SANTA FE POLICE
DEPARTMENT
CAMINO ENTRADA

Claire Montgomery sat in the police department's interview room with Lieutenant Enrico Zamora facing her across a desk. Two Styrofoam cups sat between them and the unblinking black eye of a closed-circuit camera watched them from one corner of the room.

'He made you do that?' Zamora asked. 'Every day?'

'Most days,' Claire replied. 'Jeb Oppenheimer liked his assistants to provide him with all and any services. He called them our "targets". Trouble for him, and fortunate for us, was that most days the old bastard couldn't get it up.'

Zamora stifled a grin, nodding as he looked down at his notes.

'Okay, so you're sure that Tyler Willis was being held within the SkinGen building when he died.'

'Definitely.' Claire nodded. 'I heard him on the intercom shouting something, but I had no idea what was happening down there in that theater. Christ, it just doesn't cross your mind that someone could be so evil. I mean, maybe Nazis or something, but not your boss.'

Zamora nodded.

'Okay, well that's all we really needed to know, Miss Montgomery. We were pretty sure that Tyler Willis died at the hands of Jeb Oppenheimer, and the only other witness we have other than Lillian Cruz was one of Oppenheimer's bodyguards, who died out in New Mexico last week and . . .' Zamora paused as he noticed Claire's confused expression. 'What?'

'You said Tyler Willis died at the hands of Jeb Oppenheimer?'

'Yes.'

'That's not possible,' Claire said. 'He was alive when Oppenheimer left the building. Willis died hours later.'

Zamora was about to reply when an urgent knock sounded at the door of the interview room, and a sergeant stepped quickly in with a sheet of paper in his hand.

'Results of the autopsy on Tyler Willis,' he said to Zamora. 'You need to see this.'

Zamora took the piece of paper and scanned it, his eyes widening with each line. He stood up out of his chair.

'You're sure? Absolutely sure?'

The sergeant nodded.

'And that's not all,' he said. 'There's been another abduction.'

76

SANTA FE

4.38 p.m.

Ethan sat on the edge of his bed in the hotel room and stared at the face of his cell phone, the Illinois number waiting there to be dialed taunting him in silence. The absurdity of his own reluctance, nervousness even, to just call the damned number wasn't lost on him. But through Ethan's moral compass he owed Saffron a promise, and despite himself he jabbed the dial button and listened to the phone ringing in his ear. To his surprise, it picked up on the second tone.

'Ethan.'

There was no detectable tone in the voice to suggest surprise, concern or awareness that his father hadn't received a call from him for two years. Ethan found himself suddenly unable to think of anything to say.

'Hi, Dad, how's things?'

Lame. The towering rock that was Henry Warner would probably laugh in his face and cut the line off with a shake of his craggy head and . . .

'Not so bad, son. Haven't heard from you for a while,

thought you'd forgotten what goddamned phones were for.'

'I've been busy,' Ethan replied, strangely feeling a little bit more relaxed. 'I've started a new business.'

'Doing what?'

'I work for the government, investigations and such like. It's going good.'

'Where are you right now?'

'Santa Fe.'

'Good for you. To what do I owe the honor of this unexpected communiqué?'

Ethan took a breath.

'I just thought I should call. We haven't spoken in a long time and I didn't want to leave it any longer.'

'You didn't have to leave it at all, Ethan. Your mother's found this all very difficult, you know.'

'So have I.'

A long silence enveloped the line as Ethan struggled to find something useful to say. Nothing came. He considered hanging up, but his hand refused to obey. Henry Warner's voice suddenly sounded down the line, startling him.

'I take it you've gotten over what happened in Palestine, Ethan, Joanna's disappearance and your . . . difficulties afterward.'

'Diplomatic as always, Dad,' Ethan responded.

'No sense in treading on eggshells,' his father replied. 'Ever since you resigned your commission your life hasn't followed a steady track.'

'There's no such thing as a steady goddamned track, Dad. Life doesn't work like that.'

'Your mother and I have done okay by living how I—'

'Mom just does as she's told because it's easier than having to negotiate with *you*!' Ethan shot back, unable to contain himself any further. 'People are not machines, Dad! Families are not the Marine Corps, and home is not a barracks! When are you going to learn that?'

A long silence filled the line. Ethan realized that he was now holding his breath.

'The Corps did you proud, son, you should remember that. There was a time when you were afraid to climb up that tiny tree in our garden, let alone go to war for your country.'

'People change as they grow up,' Ethan said through gritted teeth. 'You should try it someday. Is mom there?'

'She's out visiting,' came the response, then a long pause. 'Has there been any word, about Joanna?'

Images of his long-vanished fiancée flickered through Ethan's mind. It had been so long now since she had disappeared from Gaza City that he had begun to associate her memory with the four years he had spent searching for her, instead of the good times they had shared. Now, he tried not to think about her at all.

'Nothing,' Ethan said in a whisper. 'Four years now. Whatever happened to Joanna, I don't think she'll be coming back.'

'Then perhaps you can finally move on.'

'Sure,' Ethan muttered. 'Sounds easy if you say it quickly enough.'

He heard a heavy sigh in response, as though his father was already tiring of the conversation.

'I didn't mean it like that, Ethan, and you know it. Why don't you come by when you're back in the state, come and visit? Natalie's here too, on sabbatical.'

Ethan was surprised to become aware of the broad smile breaking across his face. He hadn't seen his sister in two years. Last he'd heard, she was studying politics at college. He took a breath.

'Sure. I'll hopefully have some time off when we get back to Illinois.'

'We?'

'My partner and I,' Ethan replied. 'That is, my *business* partner and I, at least for the moment.'

'Well, you're welcome to bring her too. Just make sure you bring yourself, okay? It's been too long, son, you know that, don't you?'

Ethan avoided answering the question directly.

'Sounds great, Dad, I'll be there within a few days.'

'Good. We'll all be glad to see you, Ethan, after all that's happened and despite our . . . differences. If there's one thing that's more important than anything else it's family.'

Ethan smiled again, and was about to reply when a sudden realization slammed into his field of awareness like a bullet through glass. Ethan's smile vanished as he stared blankly into nowhere and his jaw fell open as he heard his father's words echoing around in his mind. *If there's one thing that's more important than anything else it's family.*

'Ethan?'

'Dad, I've got to go, something just turned up.'

Ethan leapt up from the bed and dashed from the

room, sprinting down the corridor outside and down a stairwell three at a time. He burst into the hotel foyer, where Lopez was casually leafing through a magazine.

'They've got away!' Ethan shouted.

Lopez dropped the magazine, leapt to her feet and stared at him.

'Who's got away?'

'I can't believe I've been so stupid,' Ethan said, holding his head in his hands.

'What the hell's going on?'

'Get the car,' Ethan said. 'We've got to go, right now.'

MEDICAL INVESTIGATOR FACILITY, ALBUQUERQUE

Ethan opened the car door and stepped out even before Lopez had fully braked to a stop, the outside of the facility swarming with police cars. Ethan hurried to the police cordon and asked for Lieutenant Zamora, who emerged from the facility a minute or two later and waved Ethan and Lopez forward.

'I can't believe it,' Zamora said.

Ethan looked at him.

'There's been another abduction, right?'

Lieutenant Zamora nodded, running a hand through his hair.

'We put a guard on the house just in case and extra security here, but it's like they just vanished into thin air. I can't understand how it happened.'

Ethan closed his eyes. 'I can.'

Lopez grabbed Ethan's shoulder and squeezed it hard.

'Will you tell me what the hell is going on?!'

77

HOTEL DE BILDERBERG
OOSTERBEEK, HOLLAND

8.12 a.m. (European Time)

Gregory Hampton III sat in the plush surroundings of his penthouse suite and looked out of the window at the sumptuous grounds of Veluwe Park. A fine early morning mist had enveloped the park, street lights glowing like candle flames amongst the trees, and at this early hour there were no pedestrians. He stood and walked to the door of the suite, opening it at 8.10 am (European Time) and moving into the corridor outside.

Hampton was not a man who was used to being recognized, but he saw clear recognition in the smartly dressed person striding confidently toward him, precisely on time.

Gregory Hampton had been born in Hampshire, England, in 1936, just before the world collapsed into the chaos and destruction of World War Two. Sent away from his family to live in the West Country away from the Blitzkrieg blasting England's major cities, he returned home an orphan and determined that he would never be subject to the whims of others again. Within fifteen years he was a millionaire magnate presiding over a booming property portfolio in London, profiting from a rebuilding frenzy in the aftermath of the war's destruction. Twenty years later, he was a billionaire. Another decade after that, he stopped even trying to count his fortune. He owned islands in the Pacific, a significant proportion of Dubai and Manhattan and several cruise liners, but prided himself on the fact that nobody would have known him if they passed him on the street.

The person who recognized him stopped at the entrance to his suite, their dark gray suit immaculate, shoes highly polished, hand extended.

'Thank you for agreeing to see me.'

Hampton shook the proffered hand.

'I must ask: how did you know where to find me?'

His visitor smiled.

'I've watched you for many years, Mister Hampton, long before you chose to recede into anonymity. I suspected that if it was not you that I needed to see, then you would at least know where to send me.'

Hampton's eyes narrowed.

'And you are approaching me now, after all that has happened to you. Why?'

Again, the calm smile.

'Can we speak inside?'

Hampton nodded and gestured into the suite, following his guest in and closing the door. Inside the suite, four more men waited patiently, each wearing suits that cost as much as some cars and cautious expressions as they surveyed their visitor.

'I hope,' one of them said to Hampton, 'that this is

worthwhile. We're taking an awful risk here.'

'As am I,' the visitor said, 'after what happened to Donald Wolfe.'

Gregory Hampton gestured to their guest.

'Gentlemen, please do me the courtesy of listening to what our new associate has to say. I feel certain that you will appreciate it.'

'Who are you?' one of the men asked the guest.

The guest sat down, crossing one long leg over the other.

'My name is Lillian Cruz,' she said, 'and I was born in Montrose, Colorado, in the year 1824.'

A silence descended upon the men in the suite as they looked at her.

'Go on,' Gregory Hampton prompted her. 'My associates here are familiar with the basic potential of human longevity.'

Lillian Cruz regarded the men for a long moment before speaking.

'I am the last survivor of eight soldiers of the Union army who took sanctuary in a place called Misery Hole in New Mexico in 1862, just after the Battle of Glorietta Pass.'

'What on earth were you doing in an army?' one of the younger men asked.

'I was one of many women who served alongside their countrymen in the Civil War,' Lillian said hotly. 'In my case, I met my husband within the ranks, an officer named Ellison Thorne. He died recently after being pursued for years by a man named Jeb Oppenheimer, so that I might still live today.'

Lillian took a moment before continuing.

'I have been alive for a hundred eighty-seven years, and in that time I have seen this country, and this planet, gradually destroyed by the parasite that we call humanity. We are the only species that consumes without replenishing, that takes more than our fair share without giving anything back. For over one hundred forty years, five of the seven men who had sheltered with me in Misery Hole lived in a small area of the New Mexico desert with barely anybody knowing they were even there. They took only what they needed, and in doing so were a part of their environment, not a predator upon it.'

Lillian reached into the pocket of her jacket and produced a small vial filled with a clear liquid that caught the light streaming in through the suite's broad windows. She held it up to the men demonstratively.

'I have tested this serum,' she said, 'because we were dying of old age. The bacteria that infected us when we were in the caves began dying because they were unable to sustain themselves indefinitely on the iron we consumed in our food, perhaps because of our physical size compared to other, smaller mammals such as bats who I believe may have originally harbored them. I myself have not yet suffered any symptoms, possibly because females tend to live longer than males in many mammalian species. This serum has corrected the deficiency in the bacteria *Bacillus permians*, allowing them to sustain cellular senescence indefinitely within the bodies of large mammals such as ourselves.'

'How?' one of the younger men demanded. 'How can you be sure that the bacteria will work this time?'

'The degradation of our bodies was being caused by a

hemoglobin deficiency,' Lillian said, 'itself caused by the bacteria's demands for iron, effectively making us permanently anemic. Hemoglobin deficiency decreases blood-oxygen carrying capacity, causing loss of blood, nutritional deficiencies, bone-marrow problems and kidney failure - the red blood cells in iron deficiency anemia become hypochromic and microcytic. Hemolysis, the accelerated breakdown of red blood cells, follows and jaundice is caused by the hemoglobin metabolite bilirubin, which can cause renal failure. The increased levels of bilirubin improperly degraded the hemoglobin and clogged small blood vessels, especially in the kidneys, causing kidney damage and muscular breakdown. We were essentially falling apart. The same quorom sensing that caused the infection to extend telomere life in us eventually also caused us to become anemic and then began to break down our bodies at the cellular level. The reason for all of this was that our immune systems were finally overpowering the bacteria as they gradually died off over the years due to lack of iron. The bacterial population reduced sufficiently that quorom sensing ceased, and we aged rapidly. The bacteria within us simply had not evolved enough to exist in symbiotic harmony with human beings.'

'I take it,' one of the men asked, 'that you have overcome this unfortunate flaw?'

She shook the vial in her hand.

'This serum is the result of my work since: it is still not perfect, but it's already more effective than the naturally occurring bacteria. It no longer causes anemia and, as you know, lasts for at least a hundred fifty years. By that time, we'll have worked out how to make it last a lot longer, producing a bacterium that exists in perfect harmony with our own bodies.'

Gregory Hampton looked at her for a long moment.

'Your colleagues died to protect that,' he said. 'Why would you now betray their memory?'

Lillian sighed.

'Because they had not really lived in the modern world,' she said. 'They hadn't seen what it has become. And because you are all already wealthy beyond avarice and I suspect your interest in this is not financial. I take it that you wish for there to be a world for humans to live in in a hundred years' time, a thousand?'

The men regarded her with respect for the first time. Hampton spoke softly for them.

'The Bilderberg Group has a greater cause than merely acting as an annual reservoir for political discourse,' he said solemnly. 'Unless there are major technological breakthroughs in the fields of energy generation, farming and pharmaceuticals in the next ten years, it is highly likely that civilization as we know it will collapse, the burden of our population too great for even human ingenuity to support it. It has already begun, as fossil fuels are now running out and fresh water is becoming increasingly scarce. We exist as a think tank dedicated to preserving human endeavor after the coming apocalypse, and rebuilding it in the future.'

Lillian nodded in understanding.

'Then this serum could help extend your leadership, should the need arise.'

'How much do you want for it?' one of them asked.

Lillian shook her head.

'I don't want money,' she said. 'What I want is to be protected, so that I don't have to spend my life hiding from people like Jeb Oppenheimer. I want this serum to be used only by those who *earn* it, and I want the reduction of the population of this planet to be achieved humanely over time. If there's one thing that we absolutely agree on, it's that if either our population or our rate of consumption is not reduced then humanity is ultimately doomed. Any species that becomes too numerous eventually suffers a collapse, and I fear that ours is well and truly overdue. In that, at least, Jeb Oppenheimer was right.'

Hampton looked at his accomplices, and they all nodded together.

'Security is the one thing that we absolutely can guarantee,' he said to her finally. 'You will be safe amongst us, I can assure you.'

Lillian stood and handed the vial to Hampton. She fixed her gaze onto his.

'This serum can be cultured and grown. As a bacterium, it will by its very nature divide and propagate without limitation. You have in your hands the fountain of youth,' she said, 'the elixir. Use it wisely.'

78

SANTA FE
NEW MEXICO

'Lillian Cruz is the eighth soldier?' Lopez said in disbelief.

Ethan nodded as he leaned against a squad car.

'It was staring us in the face all along and I never realized it,' he said. 'I even read about women serving as soldiers during the Civil War in the records office, but didn't make the connection.'

'When did you figure it out?' Zamora asked.

Ethan shrugged.

'Too late. We were all pretty sure that Ellison and his men needed someone on the inside to handle things, but we assumed it would be somebody they had befriended. It only crossed my mind when I thought about Hiram Conley. He had accrued injuries throughout his life, some of them serious enough to have required hospitalization, maybe even surgery. I'd wondered how his great age could have been covered up if he'd died in some other way, in an operating theater surrounded by surgeons and nurses or similar. There had to be a plan in place to cover that eventuality.'

Lopez caught on quickly.

'Like a coroner,' she said. 'Damn, somebody even mentioned that Lillian Cruz had worked there for longer than they could remember.'

'Lillian could get them in and out of a laboratory without attracting attention,' Ethan said. 'She could administer medicines to them, possibly even perform surgery. Hard to make friends like that over decades as the faces would keep changing, and the secret would be too hard to keep. But if Lillian took on a medical role, an official position, then they'd be in good stead to survive just about anything. All she'd have to do is move occasionally, or change her name and such like, to avoid exposing herself.'

'So she was the one who took the photograph?' Zamora asked.

'She must have fought alongside the men during the Civil War,' Ethan said, 'maybe been married to one of them. Lillian could have taken her maiden name when she took up residence in Albaquerque, to hide their connection. Lillian came back to work very soon after the gunfight at the caves, didn't she?'

'Yeah, within an hour or two,' Zamora said. 'That's why we put a guard on her, just in case. How'd you know about that? You were in hospital.'

'Because she would have needed to use her laboratory to check that the bacterial samples she'd gotten from Lechuguilla Cave were alive,' Ethan said. 'She went after Jeb Oppenheimer when we were trapped underground, and when I caught up with her she'd tried to drown him in the water. She was drenched herself, and only Saffron

Oppenheimer's arrival just before me had stopped her from killing him. But she didn't care whether Jeb Oppenheimer lived or died, she just needed a sample of the fluids in that pool.'

Lopez frowned.

'But I thought that wasn't enough, that the infection doesn't last forever in the body?'

'No,' Ethan agreed, 'but by having a sample that she could test, and samples of the remains of both Hiram Conley and Lee Carson, she could experiment. Lillian must have known that it was something to do with iron. When Doug Jarvis's team went into the SkinGen labs they found Conley's and Carson's remains, but in both cases tissue had been removed from the area surrounding the bullets that killed them.'

Enrico Zamora thought for a moment.

'The iron kept the tissues alive?' he asked.

'It stopped the tissue samples from decaying,' Ethan said. 'So by comparing the bacteria in the living tissue and the raw bacteria from the cave, Lillian may have been able to understand how to develop a method to genetically modify the bacteria to survive indefinitely within a human body. The perfect elixir.'

Ethan had finally realized what had been happening all along, perhaps even before he and Lopez had arrived in New Mexico the previous week.

'Lillian hasn't been abducted – there's just no need for her to hang around anymore. She's taken everything she's got now that Ellison and his men are dead, and has probably sold it off to the highest bidder.'

Lopez shook her head thoughtfully.

'No way,' she said. 'Lillian may have taken off with whatever she's gotten from that cave, but I don't believe she would have done that, not after Ellison gave his life so we could escape from the caves.'

'I wouldn't be so sure of that,' Enrico Zamora said. 'We got the autopsy reports back this morning for Tyler Willis. It turns out that he died not from a beating or at the hands of Jeb Oppenheimer. He died from blood loss caused by the severing of an artery in his left thigh, a tiny cut that was almost missed by the coroner.'

'Oppenheimer had him killed though,' Lopez said. 'He was holding Willis hostage.'

'Yes,' Zamora agreed, 'but Willis died when Oppenheimer was nowhere near him. Claire Montgomery, his assistant, confirmed that for us, and despite her earlier indiscretions she has no reason to lie now that Oppenheimer's dead. The only person in the room with Willis with the skill and knowledge to make an incision like that was Lillian Cruz, and Willis would never have known as she'd just hit him with shots of morphine after Oppenheimer had finished torturing him.'

'Let me guess,' Lopez said. 'The morphine shot went into his leg.'

'He bled out right there and then,' Zamora nodded. 'Never knew a thing about it.'

'As don't you,' Ethan said. 'You stick to the non-disclosure policy from this point on, okay? I don't want the DIA hounding you out of a job down here or something.'

'I ain't got nothing to say,' Zamora replied. 'Been a pleasure, in a weird kind of way.'

Ethan shook Zamora's hand, and Lopez gave the cop a hug before he turned and walked back into the facility.

Ethan turned for their car, knowing deep inside that wherever Lillian had gone it was highly unlikely they would ever see her again.

'Well, whatever happens, I hope she knows what she's doing. It's likely the last time that anyone will ever hold the fountain of youth in their hands again.'

Ethan climbed into the car, Lopez joining him in the passenger seat. They sat for a long moment in silence before he looked across at her.

'You ready to go home?'

Lopez stared into the middle distance for a long moment before replying.

'I'm not sure where home is right now.'

Ethan glanced south toward the Pecos and the endless deserts beyond that led to the border with Mexico and her distant hometown, Guanajuato.

'Can I ask you something?' Ethan said finally.

'Shoot.'

'Do you trust me?'

Lopez looked at him but did not respond immediately, and Ethan realized that she was thinking seriously about it.

'Yeah, I do,' she said finally.

'Then why not confide in me?'

Lopez held his gaze for a long beat before turning away again. One hand played idly with her long black hair.

'Because I don't want to go through what happened to my last partner again,' she said finally. 'Ever.'

'Lucas Tyrell,' Ethan said, recalling Lopez's detective partner from Washington DC who had died the previous year.

'He was a good man,' Lopez said, 'who didn't deserve to die the way he did.'

Ethan leaned back in his seat. Fact was, he also had avoided close relationships since losing Joanna. The fear they both carried, veiled just beneath a thin veneer of normality, was that anybody could lose anyone at any time and never see them again. Be it by a bullet, or accident, or just plain stupidity, people died all the time. Only those left behind grieved for their loss, and all too often were unable to let go.

'I take it you got all of the money that you swindled out of Jeb Oppenheimer,' Ethan said. 'And that now he's dead, there'll be no comeback.'

'No sense in crying over spilt milk,' she said with a brief smile.

'Doug and the DIA won't have missed something like that,' Ethan warned. 'They'll know what you've pulled.'

'Let them,' Lopez said. 'Every last dime's been taxed. There's nothing they can do about it. You're welcome to half, seeing as we're partners.'

Ethan shook his head. He couldn't resist a wry sense of admiration for Lopez's sheer audacity, but it was that same recklessness that had almost gotten them both killed.

'I can't do this, Nicola,' he said, 'unless I know for sure that you've got my back.'

Lopez nodded.

'I know.'

'Then make your call. Are you in, or are you out?' he asked.

'Of what?'

'Of this, of Warner/ Lopez Incorporated, bail bonds and investigations. Where's home, Nicola? It's your call, you can do anything you want. Do you want to head north back to Chicago with me, or south for Mexico?'

'What would you do if I went back over the border?' she asked.

'I'd carry on,' he replied without hesitation. 'Probably get more work done without you in the way, and Warner Inc. rolls off the tongue nicely anyway.'

Lopez smiled faintly.

'I just need time to figure everything out,' she said. 'It's only been a year since I left the police and we started this little venture. You lost Joanna four years ago, and you're still not quite who you were before, are you?'

Ethan couldn't bring himself to meet her gaze, but he shook his head briefly.

'Then let's just take this one step at a time, okay?' she suggested.

Ethan sighed again, knowing he could hardly pressure Lopez when he was barely over Joanna himself. Lopez and Tyrell hadn't, as far as he knew, been an item, but they'd been partners and sometimes that bond could be just as strong. Ethan had experienced just such camaraderie in the Marine Corps: men who had faced death together tended to face life together as well, a brotherhood forged in shared hardship that felt as though it could last for an eternity.

'Okay,' he agreed finally. 'I just don't want to be wearing dentures before I know I can rely on you.'

Lopez smiled brightly.

'Maybe we should have saved some of that elixir for your wrinkled old ass.'

'Like hell,' Ethan shot back as he started the car's engine. 'Every crease has been earned.'

He sat for a moment, thinking about Saffron Oppenheimer, and then looked across at Lopez again.

Lopez stared out to the south, toward the shimmering mountains and the hard blue skies, and then back at Ethan.

'I want to go home,' she said. 'North.'

ACKNOWLEDGEMENTS

Once again I owe an enormous debt of gratitude to my brilliant literary agent Luigi Bonomi, who upon our first ever meeting suggested that I should pen a story based upon the search for immortality. He felt that nobody had ever attempted to concoct a potentially viable method by which eternal youth could be achieved. If he's still representing authors in the year 2176 we'll know he had an ulterior motive. My heartfelt thanks go to my editors Maxine Hitchcock, Emma Lowth and the team at Simon & Schuster, who never fail to impress me and whom I count myself lucky to work with, and to everyone at LBA. I'd also like to thank so many of my friends who have been incredibly supportive and enthusiastic since the launch of my debut novel Covenant – you all know who you are. Finally, as ever I owe my parents Terry and Carolyn everything, for without them I would not have such a love of the written word nor such an example in life to live up to.

Dean Crawford
COVENANT

Some things man was never meant to know . . .

Humanity has always believed it is the only intelligent species
of life in the universe. But while excavating in Israel, an
archaeologist unearths a tomb that has remained hidden for
7,000 years. Inside lies a secret of such magnitude that the story
of mankind is instantly rewritten - and its future thrown into
terrible danger.

Only one man can piece history back together again. Only one
man will risk everything to prevent a catastrophe that could
tear the world apart.

That man is Ethan Warner.

ISBN 978-0-85720-469-1

Dean Crawford's novels are available from your local bookshop or can be ordered direct from the publisher.

978-0-85720-469-1   Covenant   £6.99